Penny Benjamin was born and raised in central Alberta. Surviving a serious car accident when hit by a drunk driver, she came out of the coma to find herself on her own at the age of sixteen, until meeting her partner at eighteen. Together, they rebuilt their lives. Eventually, Penny balanced a successful career in real estate with a loving relationship and family, which included their two sons and numerous animal rescues. Throughout it all, Penny found peace in writing and an escape in dreams.

I would like to dedicate this book to my mother who always encouraged me to be creative, and my partner and our kids, who gave me the courage to follow my dreams.

Penny Benjamin

A Widow's Kiss

Austin Macauley Publishers™

LONDON * CAMBRIDGE * NEW YORK * SHARJAH

Ordering Information
Quantity sales: Special discounts are available on quantity purchases by corporations, associations, and others. For details, contact the publisher at the address below.

Publisher's Cataloging-in-Publication data
Benjamin, Penny
A Widow's Kiss

ISBN 9781638294221 (Paperback)
ISBN 9781638294238 (ePub e-book)

Library of Congress Control Number: 2022923277

www.austinmacauley.com/us

First Published 2023
Austin Macauley Publishers LLC
40 Wall Street, 33rd Floor, Suite 3302
New York, NY 10005
USA

mail-usa@austinmacauley.com
+1 (646) 5125767

I would like to thank everyone at Austin Macauley Publishers for their faith in me and their guidance and expertise in getting *A Widow's Kiss* published.

Prologue

London, England

May 1812

Henry Gomersal slanted his aging body, elbows at rest comfortably on the age-worn oak writing desk, his plump double chin propped in his hands.

Outlandish.

Bloody odd. To receive a letter of this nature now that his days of practicing law were long since over. If only Thomas had come to him in person.

Perhaps, Thomas had selected him because he was no longer active.

Whatever the motive, he could not begrudge his final request. Henry tapped a finger to the underside of his nose. Damned anomalous to receive the missive not forty-eight hours following his death; sighing, Henry picked up the copy of yesterday's *Times*, which had thankfully been saved from the hearth. Flipping it open, the page he sought stared boldly back at him.

Henry re-read the commentary pertaining to his friend's demise.

Well written.

Informative.

A footpad.

The article would have been believable for anyone not connected to Thomas; the damned thing was, Henry was connected. Sighing, he fumbled with his gold-rimmed spectacles before picking up the letter and examining it anew:

30 March 1812

Sal,

It is imperative that upon my departure from this world, word be sent to Roland Acworth, the Duke of Fairhaven, as he is to be the sole custodian of my beloved family. I fear I have left him with a monstrous undertaking of righting my injustices.

It will not be easy. For, to protect those I loved all fatherly ties had to be severed.

I can detect the uncertainties shadowing your eyes, Henry. I'm afraid, my friend, the story is a long and complicated one. And the least you know of it, the healthier you'll remain.

Fairhaven will untangle the web of deception. A man of many talents, I trained him and trust him implicitly. He will come up to scratch. He must.

Contact him by way of his superior, the Earl of Beaumont, when the need arises. I ask that you not reveal his name to my children. Should Caralyn ask, simply tell her a guardian has been contacted. See to it that Caralyn is made privy to only the stipulated parts of my will. I pray she will not be too hard on your old friend.

My daughter is a smart young woman. She'll find a way to care for the family until such time as Fairhaven returns to London. Do whatever you must to ensure she has use of her dowry, I fear they will need it. The Danforth funds must remain hidden until Fairhaven is here to protect them.

All else within these pages is for Fairhaven's eyes only. It is to be concealed from the eyes and ears of my children until their guardian deems it fit to tell them.

The sealed letter and packet accompanying these wishes may not be opened by anyone, including you, my friend until Fairhaven has a chance to view the contents firsthand.

I realize that as my friend and heretofore a retired solicitor, you may find this all a trifle odd. All I can say, and I cannot stress this enough, is that it is a matter of grave importance, life and death, in fact, that you abide by my wishes.

Yours,
Thomas Rexley Danforth II

Chapter One

The Gables, Devonshire, England
June 1812

Damn Papa! Damn him to the fiery infernos of hell!

She hurt. Never would she have dreamed he could hurt her more than he already had.

Cara stood gazing out the extended picture window in what, up until a month ago, had been her father's study. He had not been in residence enough to use it.

She tried to reconcile her feelings regarding her father's untimely death. Teetering on a precipice of dread, she stared into a constant abyss of bewilderment. And it would only get worse.

Pushing the unpleasant thoughts away, she focused on three identical children as they frolicked on the lawn below. Not a care in the world. Grieving…perhaps? Then, it was hard to miss what one had done without for so long. Was that right? An absentee father who had barely taken time—over the past three years—to acknowledge Cara or her siblings; should he be missed still? Did they really understand he would never return?

Had he grown to resent them? Their presence, their appearance, and their very existence is an ever-present reminder of all he had lost. Had he blamed them?

It wasn't their fault Mother died giving birth. One baby could be a hazard, twins even more of a risk, but triplets? Giving life to three healthy babes proved to be more than Mother could bear.

Memories flickered. At one time she believed her mother ailing, barely recalling an occasion when confinement was not the daily routine. She inquired, why were there no siblings closer to her age? Such questions were taboo and therefore went unanswered.

An ocean of physicians came and went like the tides, checking on her mama. For the longest time, nightmares of her mother gravely ill, dying, just as Grandpapa had, consumed her. The wasting disease: a shiver coursed through Cara as she remembered the final visions of her grandfather.

When she was older; she realized the regal Lady Danforth had suffered from miscarriages. Thus, personally consigned herself abed, out of stubbornness and conceivably love to give her beloved spouse an heir. Father accused, more than once, that she was as headstrong and obstinate as her mother. Mayhap she was the reason her father left.

Each day she endeavored to be optimistic. Not allowing her anger—her hurt—to show for the benefit of those younger. Satisfying their questions concerning a transient father they scarcely knew, and a mother they had never known.

Cara pressed her forehead against the cool pane, sighed, and rubbed her temples. Such a muddle! There had to be a way out. There just *had* to be.

If it was only her, she'd take off for ports unknown; explore the many places she read about while blissfully bidding adieu to England with its hypocritical elite prone to gaming and debauchery. But it wasn't just her. There was Becky, Robby, and Rex. And Mrs. Brown. What would become of her?

Lord knows she could not leave their future in the hands of an unknown benefactor who deemed to make himself as scarce as her elusive father. Most like they were cut from the same cloth. Careless ne'er-do-well…

No. They'd never be able to count on him. How she needed a knight in shining armor. Had her father gone mad, it would have been easier. Psychosis would explain why he was there loving and attentive one day, then gone the next with barely a word and never a goodbye. An occasional brief visit, nothing more.

Deluding oneself… never good, Caralyn, she admonished. One relied on facts and oftentimes facts stated a cruel reality. Father no longer wanted them. Rex, Becky, and Robby appeared not to suffer as Cara did. She missed the man who had bounced her on his knee when she was younger. Talked to, comforted, and loved her as she grew older. She had been sixteen then. Mature enough to remember better times and she missed what she remembered, dearly.

Sunshine glinted off Rex's ebony tresses, shaggily blown this way and that, sweaty and undoubtedly dirty, not at all the prim-proper appearance of Baron

Thomas Rexley Danforth III. Master of *The Gables*, or *Wonderland*, as her father affectionately dubbed it.

Ah, Wonderland. A whimsical name to be sure, not as historical as Eden, the ultimate paradise, but the feelings the small estate evoked, at least before Papa left, were wonderful indeed.

She tried to maintain it, keep it strong, something Rex could always be proud of. With its gently rolling grass-covered hills, and pastoral landscape, truly a simple breath of fresh air after a summer downpour.

A cobbled circular drive led to Wonderland's forecourt, at the center was a fountain, Cupid shooting his arrow into the heart of a fair maiden as she filled her urn with the waters from the stream cascaded into the basin. Yews and beech trees lined either side of the drive circling the hall in a giant horseshoe. Within the shoe, beautiful gardens burst with color emitting every scent imaginable. Ivies crept up the east wall, almost covering the brick exterior, supplementing the mansion's character, a mixture of age and untamed magnificence. The three-story, age-worn, whitewashed manor, Danforth Hall, was the place of dreams…Danforth dreams.

Cara loved it. And she vowed come hell or high water, entailed or no, she would do everything in her power to keep it.

It would be years before Rex could provide for Wonderland, his family, and all that went with it. She didn't have that kind of time. Waiting stagnantly for an eleven-year-old 'to right the wrongs of thy father' wasn't an option.

Wonderland would be lost; Rex would be shunned and all because of a man he never really knew. None of them really knew. Especially her; for the love of saints, *she* should have known!

She couldn't let everything go. Would not! For Rex's sake and for the girls, she'd hedge through the thickets, suffer the thorns and provide for them. The question was how?

Becky looked up at the window, waving, a glorious smile pasted on her angelic face. Knowingly Cara nodded and left the chamber. Her head would clear with a bit of fresh air. Wearing a smile that didn't quite reach her eyes, she headed out to spend time with the children. She was their constant, a lifeboat, in troubled waters. Somehow, with a little luck, she would keep them afloat.

"Good afternoon, imps, and what troubles hath thou wrought today?"

Cara was met with a chorus of giggles.

Rex admonished in a grown-up tone. Cara paused wondering if mayhap he was maturing more rapidly than anticipated.

Crossing her arms over her chest, cocking her head in quiet contemplation, she raised a brow and silently tapped her slippered foot on the overgrown lawn beneath. Rex folded his arms, raised his brow, and tapped his foot. Again, the girls giggled. Cara found it challenging to suppress a smile. When she could contain it no longer, she dropped unladylike to her knees. Arms sprung wide. The girls came like a colossal wave while Rex lingered like a receding flood, not wanting to appear overeager.

"I sure could use a hug; I have been told yours can be exceedingly superb."

No one remarked on Cara's usage of similar lines once more breaching Rex's emotional barriers. He came forth with slow noble grace, totally at odds with his tattered appearance, to kneel beside Cara on the lush grass; chivalrously he drew her into his embrace. Cara completed the façade by resting her head on his small shoulder.

She tried her best to be a stable parental figure to these children, even though she was their sister. She endeavored to show them love and acceptance, right from wrong; even when she had nothing to work with except rapidly fading memories…

Sitting, listening to the children's chatter, Cara questioned how she could have been as naive as to not have seen the signs of a rapidly depleting fortune sooner. They were there she just rejected them.

The earliest sign would have been when she reached fifteen. Her father dismissed their governess. Stating in a superior manner that she could instruct the family. Now that she thought back, it was so unlike the man she knew him to be. Astonished by his unexpected lack of consideration; she gave in to his demands. Yet *why*, had always baffled her.

Away much of the time, even so, whenever he was at home, there was nothing he would not do for his children. She depleted every waking moment with him; seeing his handsome face transform into a tired, troubled countenance until only an empty shell remained.

Now she wasn't so sure that *not* needing a governess was behind her father's decision. Looking back his complete mindset drastically changed within months of that incident.

Now after reviewing the ledgers and talking to her father's solicitor, Mr. Gomersal, a chill settled deep inside her bones. Aside from the signing over her dowry, five hundred pounds, there were no monies. Mr. Wiggs, Gables' so-called estate manager, demanded payment of past wages in full. She had two weeks. Sixty pounds! It was a drop in the bucket, considering the other bills she had, yet should she use her dowry there would soon be nothing left.

Then there was his generous offer. Hah! Just the thought of being married to that roach made her skin crawl. She shuddered, scrunching up her nose. No. Absolutely not, she would find another way to repay him…without the use of her body *or* her dowry. Then she'd gladly send the lowly insect on his way. If he were any good at his job in the first place, harvests would be flourishing not deteriorating.

Since her father hadn't been around to oversee his work, Mr. Wiggs neglected his duties tenfold. She broached the matter countless times fruitlessly. He wasn't about to take instructions from a mere female and a young one at that. Moreover, he'd stand there, long untended brows resembling insect antennae, furrowed; his bald head with tuffs of fuzz on the sides, looking down his long-pointed nose at her, a feat to be sure since Cara, as short as she was, stood at least a hand taller.

She could do better. How?

The dowry would guarantee them sustenance in the coming months. They would have to let go of the London staff, possibly the house too but overall, it alone would not be enough to maintain them through the coming years.

There ought to be a way to generate more funds.

Fourteen days. Not a great deal, nonetheless it was all she had. Then Mr. Wiggs would make good on his threats to either spread rumors throughout the Ton or force her to wed him. *The Gables had run aground,* or *the Danforth wealth was non-existent.* Phantom gossip taunted her. It would signify disaster for the Danforth name, for her brother and sisters after the rumor mill was finished; even the fact that The Gables wasn't entailed wouldn't help them. They would never obtain a fair price; still selling it wasn't an option she wanted to consider.

Excusing herself, Cara walked back into the house.

She'd go through the library. Perchance there were volumes she could sell to Mr. Jones at Travel's Tome Emporium.

Having numerous dealings with Mr. Jones in the past, Cara had no doubts concerning a fair price or suspicious inappropriate cross-examinations. A benevolent elderly, white-haired, bespectacled-faced, studious gentleman as owlish in nature as in stature he was well matched to his trade.

Cara's optimism quickly diminished; standing, lips pursed, brows creased, facing hundreds of tomes. Countless generations heralded a limitless number of books. Useless!

Most, if not all, were worthless to anybody save for her and her ancestors. Literary interests in her family were evidently set apart from the norm.

With her initial plan puffing up in little white wisps of smoke, Cara's head resumed throbbing. If she thought for one moment, she'd be able to stomach the weakling in her; she'd give in to the megrims, swallow down a little of that vile willow bark tea Mrs. Brown was always ranting about and allow herself to hide abed until the nightmare passed.

Instead, grabbing a book off the shelf, she settled comfortably on the settee; the woes of others might cure her headache or at the very least cast her own troubles in a better light. Tucking her feet under her, enveloped in the embrace of squishy age-worn velvet, she opened the small leather-bound tome.

"Cara! Cara, *do* wake up; it's time for supper." Opening her eyes, she found Rex washed and standing over her. *Lord of the manor.*

She'd fallen asleep. She had so little, since… Well, it didn't matter anymore. Sleep proved therapeutic. She had a plan. Glancing at the book, now on the floor where it fell; Athene had had the right of it, 'But grim vengeance upon him. Ere long the Goddess wreaked, repaying insult with mortal sufferance. Yea, she would not look upon the infamy, but clad herself with shame and wrath as with a cloak'.

The quote played over and over in her mind. If Athene wreaked havoc and vengeance of such magnitude, to even the score for wrongs against her… Surely Cara could pull the wool over the eyes of a few egotistical members of high society, to save the coffers. Repay insult.

Yes. Sleep proved to be medicine for the mind, well, that and an old copy of *The Fall of Troy.*

Cara stood taking Rex's extended arm so he could guide her to the dining room.

An idea! One that was sure to work. Now some carefully laid out stratagems and they would have money in the bank. *Literally!*

Foremost was to go through her father's post; staff at Danforth House thankfully sent all her father's correspondence here. No inkling why? Most likely for the elusive guardian to take care of. She snorted.

Evidently, she couldn't wait for him.

The initial steps of her plan were falling swiftly into place, like tumblers on a well-picked lock. Yes, a well-picked lock indeed. Cara grinned wickedly as she felt the weight of the world ease off her shoulders. For the first time in more days than she could call to mind, she breathed a contented sigh of relief.

***

Goodnights from the children weighed heavy on Cara's heart, for tonight she didn't stay reading them a story after tucking them in. They were after all eleven years old, aside from which, hitherto, the stories seemed a way of compensating for what they were missing out on. Nevertheless, she needed this time to gather information and then formulate the remaining details of her masquerade. It was for the greater good, she told herself. If…no, when she pulled this off, their worries would be over.

There would have to be little sacrifices from all in the coming weeks.

At the desk she pulled a sheet of vellum from the drawer, and inking the point of the quill, she scribbled hastily. Once finished, she tilted the page toward the candle and scanned the list. After a satisfied smirk, she set it aside to open her father's personal ledger, pondering the puzzling last sixteen entries.

Among them were eleven names, with enormous dollar amounts recorded in the column on the right. The notation, which appeared after each name, stated simply; 'PAID'. All payments were within the month of April, one month before he died.

For what purpose? Exorbitant amounts marked paid but nothing to show for it? Other entries were much of the same, though the amounts were minuscule in comparison and accompanied by detailed descriptions of merchandise received.

Gaming?

Blackmail?

Gaming wasn't only legal but also a common pastime for men of her father's ilk. No recourse there at all. Blackmail, though illegal, would be difficult to prove. She tapped her finger on the notation and sighed—most likely, there would be little or no recourse through the courts.

It was up to her, one way or another she would recoup their father's losses, she must. *It was the principle of the thing.* Reaching for the letters, forwarded from Danforth House, Cara began sifting through them. Creditor statements… Invitations… Correspondence… Several invoices… Most she set aside for closer inspection after the current crisis ended.

The sun raised with vengeance the next morn pouring in through the naked windows. Her fault for not closing the drapes the night before; being up until the wee hours reviewing Papa's papers, resulted in little sleep. One letter tugged at reins on her carefully harnessed temper, she struggled to put it down. Each time it was placed in the pile for later consideration, her eyes were pulled toward the elegantly masculine bold strokes. Even as her heart and her head screamed no, her hand reached for it. Again and again, she'd read the words substantiating her worst suspicions, their benefactor was a no-good, low-down, dirty rotter who didn't give two shillings about them!

It hurt. More than she cared to admit.

For until she'd seen the words, she wanted, yearned, to believe that perhaps a knight in shining armor would swoop in and save the day. Save her. Cara let loose an unladylike harumph at the errant declaration.

Written over two years ago…

Why then, had her father kept it? The only unsealed letter from London. As her father had obviously read the letter, why had he not changed his will? Reflect a new guardian, a caring guardian? Why leave it stipulating someone who didn't fancy them? Fancy them? She snorted aloud.

Even cursing in an unladylike manner didn't dissipate her outrage as it usually did in similar circumstances beyond her control. Cara really hoped Mr. Roland Acworth remained in his precious colonies. She feared if he dared to show his face at Wonderland, she'd be imprisoned for far more than debt, far more than theft.

Unless of course, they decided to hang her for his murder in which case they'd be in an even bigger pickle than they already were. "Keep holding onto that thought, missy! You kill him, others will suffer," she stated to the empty room. She would do it for them. After all, it wasn't a surprise; she already guessed the sort of man her custodian was.

"God help you, Acworth if you set foot on my property!" Cara shook her fist in the direction of the window, punctuating the vow.

She may not be able to kill him, but there were things much worse than death. The snake! With that she flung back her covers, stomping over the faded burgundy and gold Axminster carpet to the washbasin, a lethal grin on her face. "Too young and too busy to look after four hapless children", Mr. Acworth, what an ass you must be! No mind, we will survive without your interference quite nicely, I think! Babes in short pants," she gave an un-lady-like snort, "the bloody arse doesn't even know us!" *Babes in short pants indeed*, she grumbled.

The dratted man had even robbed her of her sleep. Curse him. She doused cold water on her face hoping to dispel the images of the nightmare.

***

"Cara! Cara, where are you!"

Cara's attention turned to Rebecca's voice shouting from the top of the third-floor stairs.

"I'm in the attic. What is it, Becky? I'm busy!" Cara listened to the hammering of Becky's feet as she sprinted up the stairs.

She cringed; an effort toward teaching proper deportment to young ladies would have to be made. The instant they were out of this tangle, she decided as Becky rounded the corner off the landing and came to a screeching halt. Cara winced. It wouldn't do to have the girl running willy-nilly down the stairs at her come out.

Not the way to catch a husband! A husband! Good Lord, what was she thinking?

She was just a little girl. There was time to be a little girl? Wasn't there? Cara sighed; these were the kinds of things she wished she knew more about. Eleven; at nineteen, she could care less about catching a husband and wouldn't know the first thing about how. Surely, she couldn't expect Becky and Robby to be in training just yet. Perhaps her rush was a sign plans were going magnificently. It was simply planning, she reasoned.

In no way whatsoever did it have anything to do with the fact that she was haunted all night with nightmares of a 'young' faceless virile guardian, whisking her in his strong arms, kissing her, carrying her away. *No.* Shaking off the unwanted images of the night before, she looked at her bedraggled sister.

"Wut ye doin' up 'ere?"

Cara's lips twitched at the girl's poor choice of grammar.

"It's *what are you doing? And what I am doing* is going through old trunks."

Becky turned up her nose at the amount of dust flying through the air. Waving a tiny hand back and forth, she grabbed for her small twitching nose. She missed. Her ferocious a-a-a-c-h-o-o sent more unsettled dust soaring about the room.

"Bless you," Cara said, holding back the giggle threatening to burst forth. "If you find it so difficult to breathe, mayhap you should go back down and finish your studies?"

"I'm all done," Becky said sweetly smearing dust into her sleeve.

"You are? *Everything*?" Cara's brows rose.

"Well, mayhap *not everything* but most certainly all I could do without your assistance," Becky reassured, her head bobbing up and down.

"I see." There was a long silence, in which both girls eyed each other. One all feigned innocence and one very much knowing it for the façade that it was.

Finally, Cara nodded, standing, flicking the grime off her hem she followed her sister to the nursery, to *assist* her with her studies.

It wasn't assistance as much as companionship they craved; this ever-growing constant need of her must be caused by their father's untimely death, perhaps the situation affected them more than she cared to realize. She had so many other things to cope with.

The nursery was a large carpetless common room used for studies and indoor playing. When the children were younger, they would eat meals with their governess at the table in the corner. At one end of the room, to the left was a door leading into Rex's bedchamber. To the right, a room was reserved for a governess, at the opposite end, were two more doors. One used to be Cara's and the other Becky and Robbie's. Then two years ago shortly before turning seventeen, she moved into her mother's apartments giving the girls their own room.

She sat in silent contemplation. Waiting for the time the children would go outside and play, then Cara could make her way back to the attic.

***

Striding by the trunk she had previously searched an hour before, she knelt beside another filthy, black metal chest. Lifting the latch, she raised the lid. Reaching in Cara removed each piece of her mother's clothing holding it toward the light. She required disguises, something sensuous. Mature. Alluring.

Cara recalled when her mother wore gowns of black and gray, on the few occasions she rose from the bed. Matching headpieces boasted falling veils of lace, which covered her mother's delicate features. Mourning attire, for Cara's grandfather. There should be enough costumes to do what must be done. Currently, she had found only two outfits.

As the sun altered, and the light in the loft dimmed, she bundled up her finds glorying in the fact that she had found most if not all, she had been looking for. At her bedroom, she balanced gowns, veils, stockings, and garters between knee and door so she could give the handle a twist.

Dropping the bundle on the bed for later consideration she opted to ready herself for dinner. Nancy, a niece to their housekeeper Mrs. Brown, performed mending for them in the past. Moreover, she was a complete genius with needle and thread. Her son, Jonas, helped out at the stables and around the yard whenever Nancy's husband, Wyatt, could spare him from their farm. What would she have done without Mrs. Brown and her family?

Mrs. Brown, a portly little dragon of a woman whom Cara and the children loved dearly was their only source of parental guidance. And the only real remaining staff member at Danforth Hall since the others moved on, their families in tow. Some were lucky and obtained land locally coming by to lend a hand when they could, for the sake of her and the children.

Cara dipped a cloth into the washbasin, shivering when the chilly water touched her skin. Scrubbing, she looked upon the mirror, satisfied, that she'd managed to clean away most of the filth, she smoothed her gown as best as she could and ventured down to the dining room.

During the simple fair of leek consommé and venison sandwiches—compliments of Wyatt's last hunt—Cara enlightened everyone about the upcoming excursion to London. Mrs. Brown harumphed she walked about the table making sure all was in order but said not a word.

Ecstatically, the girls nattered and tittered throughout dinner; Rex's intently clever gaze never left Cara's face. Trying to determine the real reason behind going to a city she never had any interest in seeing when their father was alive. Cara felt akin to a bug under a microscope. She didn't like it.

Later in the drawing room, while Becky and Robby practiced pianoforte, Rex sat beside Cara grimacing when, more often than not, a note they played was less than perfect.

"Give them time, Rex, they are but little girls, they will have it well enough in hand I should think by the time it really matters."

"So, you say. I only pray we will not be deaf and unable to hear their accomplishments." Rex drawled a disbelieving mischievous twinkle in his eyes.

"I do say."

Rex's twinkle left and once more he studied her.

"Oh, do quit looking at me like that? You have been doing it all evening! It's… It's unnerving," Cara hissed.

"Like what?" The feigned nonchalant response came naturally as he pointedly examined his fingernail.

"You know like what!" Cara spat quietly. "Like I'm some newly discovered species of insect, for heaven's sakes. I am only doing what must be done! Surely, you're smart enough to perceive that?"

Rex dropped his nail; his gaze once again bore into that of his sister. A mixture of anger, hurt and confusion warred behind the deep blue depths.

"For whom, Cara; you hate the city. Now you want to pack us up on the spur of the moment? Like this? It is not right, I tell you! What are you really doing, Cara? Don't expect me to believe the same story you gave Rebecca and Roberta because I won't buy it! I may be the same age, but I am no longer a child! Do you hear me? I am the Lord of this manor. I am… Thomas…Rexley…Danforth…The III. I have a right to know!"

Rex's voice steadily climbed. Before long he would attract the attention of the girls. That, she must not let happen. They should not know the kind of mess their father left them all in. Even Rex should be allowed some sense of goodness attached to the memories of their father, no matter how few. Thinking quickly, Cara waved a hand to silence her brother.

"Do hush up. All right! I'll tell you. No, let me speak. And in the future, lower your voice before the girls think something is wrong."

Straightening his spine, Rex looked every bit the gentleman he was to become. Arranging his faded dinner jacket, he leaned back into the settee, bringing up his leg and casually hooking it over his other. When comfortable, he looked toward Cara, twirling his index finger and giving a nod spurring her to continue.

"I must go to London to find a husband. There, now you know. It is for neither learning nor shopping expedition and no, I do not have to check on things at Danforth House." Mixing a monstrous lie with bits of the truth, she still barely avoided choking on it.

"Before you say anything, I know. I am only nineteen. " Cara ticked off each point on her fingers. "True. I have never expressed a wish to marry, also true." Cara went from co0unting to playing with the folds in her skirt eyes downcast lest he read the lie hidden in the gray pools. Hurriedly, she sustained, "Except that I no longer have the luxury of putting off what must be done."

"Most women are already married by my age or at the very least betrothed. I have a small dowry that Grandpapa left me and before that is gone, I must secure a husband. That is why we go to London. Understand?" She met his gaze, the plea clearly detectable.

Rex didn't look very understanding; his stillness, and set of his jaw, told her he was willing to accept her reasons, for now. Cara knew he wouldn't let the matter drop not entirely. Quite the opposite, she would have to be careful around her quick-witted little brother or he'd unknowingly bring the walls down upon them all.

"It is getting late. If we are to pack and be on the road in the morning, I think it is past time we were all in bed." Cara watched the realization of what she said to spread across her sisters' faces. She searched the elated expressions; there was no sign indicating they had overheard the previous conversation. Their mirror images showed nothing save joy.

Raven black hair neatly plaited swung to and fro as they skipped away. Bidding their goodnights, with a kiss on the cheek, they turned to go, chatting wildly, and disappeared.

They were beauties. As the years went by, they would become more so. If Cara's plan worked, she could hold on to what they had, put a little away for each of the girls, then one day they were sure to make excellent matches for themselves. Cara heaved a sigh. They deserved to be duchesses, and could do it too, if only they were given the chance. It was Cara's place as the eldest to see that they did.

Her gaze swung back to her brother. The same ebony hair glistened in the firelight, though wavy and slightly longer than acceptable he already held a rakish appeal. The hearts of girls across the land would be set a flutter with one look from those intense blue eyes. Brooding intelligence flickered through them a hint of knowledge the girls didn't carry.

He should be getting ready for Eton suffering the next passages of Greek translations or algebraic equations; instead, he was here. Assessing her; no doubt trying to find the real reason behind their quick departure. With luck, he'd never find out. It would sour the likeness of the gentleman he could become. A likeness Cara painted with her own brush nevertheless a portrait she would not taint.

No. He must never find out they were near destitute.

Smiling, Cara extended her hand a silent plea for Rex's assistance, forestalling further examination. The ploy worked. Her brother reached for her hand. Cara stood, placing her hand upon the crook of his arm. Together, they walked out of the salon—a picture of sophisticated elegance.

***

Cara tried on every dress.

Luck was on her side. There would be no waiting for alterations, each fit like a glove.

A rather tight glove, Cara decided as she assessed her image in the full-length cheval glass, especially in the vicinity of her chest. She must be greater endowed than her mother. No matter. Tilting her head back and forth, she watched the exposed creamy flesh rise and fall above the extremely low neckline. The silk moved with her. The black and dark gray hues against her alabaster skin did something for her. Though she could not rightly determine what, she felt every man would seek purchase to the area exposed above.

It worked in her favor.

Cara groaned as she removed the last gown. Would she boast the necessary thespian personality for this play? *Well, you can't back out now.* Picking up the gowns she skimmed her hands over the smooth satiny fabric as she hung them, fifteen in all, in the clothes press.

24

If her plans were successful but unfulfilled before each of them was worn, she'd commission more. It would not do to be out in London society wearing the very same gowns day after day. The missions she was about to embark on were already scandalous enough without adding clothing infractions. Even if most of them, God willing, would never discern who she was.

Clutching the last veil Cara couldn't resist placing it on her head. Just like the others, the wide-brimmed-low-crowned hat rested delicately on her head, casting shadows over her face from forehead to mouth. Venetian lace draped beautifully down the front stopping above her lips then rounding to the sides draping just below her ears. Aiding further by shutting out the contours of her face. Darkness would be a problem, for although she could see her vision was nevertheless impaired.

Spinning, the lace flowed moving with her. Rose-colored lips were accentuated as the lace fluttered. Mysterious. And perhaps… almost…beautiful, yes beautiful, a word she did not normally associate with herself. It would be perfect, just perfect!

***

In the library, a lone candle gripped high with one hand, Cara's fingers crept over the spines of each book, searching for ones she needed to take.

At fourteen, her interests encompassed herbal remedies; she procured numerous books on the subject from Mr. Jones. At the time he jested she was becoming too fond of potions, lest she is careful else others may think her a witch. He said it with a knowing amused twinkle in his eyes, Cara replied, anyone accusing her of such a craft might well heed her knowledge of potions lest they become somewhat toad-faced in appearance. They both laughed.

She wasn't laughing any longer.

Taking down each book, she counted. Five. Not all would contain the information she sought nevertheless, it would be dreadful to get to London and find the information she required was in one she left behind. Best take them all.

Extinguishing the candle, Cara picked up the books and made her way to the study. From the desk drawer, she removed the list and a bundle of invitations. Her eyes scanned the room. Coming to rest several times on the decanter of brandy stationed at the sideboard. She had never so much as taken a sip. She had, on occasion, tasted wine, but to do what she must, she supposed it was time she tried the amber-colored spirit.

Pouring a small amount into a glass, she sniffed. It didn't smell at all bad. She held the glass to the candle; the color sparkled like gems and appeared as smooth as satin. How could anything so pretty be that bad?

Again, she swirled the glass beneath her nose, it smelled, almost…sweet. Shrugging, she brought the glass to her lips and gulped.

Fire gripped her throat, her eyes watered, her lungs closed, and she gasped for air. A burning sensation ran down her insides straight to her stomach. Cara grabbed the sideboard. Her vision blurred the room spun. Heaven help her, it was too old. Or poisoned.

Don't be foolish, her mind argued, liquor does not spoil, and who would poison the brandy? Standing massaging her flaming throat, Cara's mind finally convinced her nothing was amiss. Nothing that a little practice wouldn't cure.

She glared at the vile liquid. How could she possibly… No. Straightening her shoulders and lifting her chin, she raised the glass to her lips. She would stay right here, in this room until she could either, sip the vile stuff without making a face or it killed her, the former she feared impossible, the latter she feared all too much a reality.

Taking her newfound enemy, she sat quietly in front of the dying fire, sipping, albeit gingerly. She would get used to it. Eventually.

Chapter Two

London

June 1812

"Oh Cara, it is so much bigger than I imagined!" Robby said leaning out the carriage window. Cara smiled indulgently through the pounding headache she had since waking that morning. Her throat was raw, who would have thought just three glasses of brandy would see her sipping with the casual ease of a master. But oh, how she paid upon waking.

The girls chatted about the sights as they passed. Though Cara had never been to London before she had no misconceptions about the place, its size, or its people. She knew or at least assumed through reading her father's correspondence, that much of the ton was of his sort. Careless wastrels concerned about proprieties except behind their respectable facades were gamblers and carefree rogues with arrogant mannerisms toward women. And *that*, Cara would use in her favor; with each passing hour, she felt more and more confident.

The carriage came to a halt outside a lovely three-story whitewashed brick and limestone townhouse on Brook Street. Not the poshest of neighborhoods by London standards; nonetheless, Danforth House made a statement of wealth, and privilege.

Within walking distance from Hyde Park, the fashionable shops on Bond Street, and The Strand; it was surrounded by no less than thirty identical townhouses. Large white pillars from the landing to the gabled roof accentuated white double doors and brass knockers; a neighborhood, which declared prosperity.

How had her father afforded such a place?

Cara awaited the footman, listening while the children, babbling wildly across from her, kept trying to emerge from the carriage before the door even opened. "Girls! Enough! Are we country bumpkins with no sense of what is right? Enough now, you must behave," Cara admonished softly, her head wishing for peace.

"It is important that while we are here, we behave in a manner fitting our station. I know you are excited; you may continue once we have been shown our rooms. Ah. Here is the footman now. Quick now, tidy yourselves at once."

"My Lord, sir, I am Daniels, welcome," the footman said as he opened the door. Rex, as was his right, descended the stairs before Cara. Turning, he raised his hand to her. Daniels was noticeably attired in the deep burgundy of Danforth livery, a reminder of wildflowers of the same hue blossoming each year in the gardens surrounding Danforth Manor, offered an arm first to Becky who giggled, then to Robby who followed suit. To his favor, he showed not a sign of shock at aiding two identical little girls. Together, the entourage ascended the six white stairs to the front of the townhouse.

As their feet hit the landing, the doors swung open; a starched-looking man, in black and white dress, opened the door.

Tibs. His graying hair slicked back on the sides, his back-rim rod straight and his face showed no outward signs at all. Cara remembered Tibs. She did know for certain until she saw the flicker of something, recognition most like, reached his eyes, he remembered her.

"Thank you Tibs," Cara acknowledged as they made their way into the foyer.

Richly appointed, Cara made a mental note to examine further the paintings that dressed the walls and the art that adorned the hall; perchance she could sell one or two pieces without comment or notice.

"Tibs, let me introduce you to the rest of the family. I am certain you remember them, although it was so long ago, I am positive they have no idea as to who you are."

If Tibs noticed the coldness with which Cara pronounced each word, he didn't show it; his face remained sternly arrogant, impassive, a practiced statement that Cara felt sure, took him many years to master.

Cara knew it was her father's fault that Tibs was removed from Wonderland all those years ago; however, the slight hardly detectable lines of disapproval about his eyes irritated her temper like sand scraping against one's skin.

Finding him, the rest of the staff, some new some old, here, and the house in such a state of grandeur compared to Wonderland, Cara couldn't help being infuriated. Cara followed through with the introductions. Mrs. Leeks, the housekeeper, entered the foyer and Cara commenced with yet another round of introductions.

"Your chambers have been prepared, Miss Caralyn. I will have Lucy show you the way."

Chambers prepared? How did he know they were coming? No note was sent. Determined not to let her confusion show, Cara thanked him.

Tibs rang; the maid appeared in short order, she was a small girl a little younger than herself appeared. Overall neat and tidy, her hair was stuffed under a mobcap, with a few tendrils escaping at the back. Cara noticed it was red. With a smile and a bob, she whisked the children to their prospective chambers. Excitedly, they followed Lucy.

Thankfully, they went with elegant albeit elated steps up the long stairway. Cara smiled. The girls would enjoy it here. Rex would too if he would simply let down his guard and enjoy being a kid. It hurt that he didn't have enough faith to trust her at her word. Even if she was lying through her pearly white teeth, he didn't know that.

"Was there something else, Miss Caralyn?" Tibs asked when Cara didn't follow along obediently with the others.

Cara waited to respond as the ruckus of footmen coming in the back door, presumably with their trunks, clomping up the servants' staircase somewhere at the back of the house, would have forced her to raise her voice.

She would have to reacquaint herself with the staff, learn their names and positions of the new ones. Exploring the rest of the townhouse that would have to wait. It was high time the long-time servants, such as Tibs, realized she was no longer a little girl, and that she meant to take charge of the household as well as the family.

Cara looked at Tibs. "Show me to the office, there are some matters I would like to address." Tibs nodded, leading Cara down the hall to a door at the far end.

"Will that be all, Miss?" he said as he opened the door.

Cara managed, just barely, to control her astonishment at the richly adorned room; she nodded toward Tibs. "That will be all, please tell Mrs. Leeks we are on country hours, we should like to dine early. I think a good night's rest is in order after such a journey."

Tibs acknowledged with a brief nod before retreating.

Astonished, Cara slowly walked toward the desk, very large, and very masculine. Running her fingertips over the smooth surface, she rounded and sat mechanically in an equally expensive high-backed leather chair.

Everything was new.

Not just here in *his* domain, but everything. Nothing was worn or color-faded from years of use, Cara sat letting anger cement her resolve.

"I will succeed, Papa! Do you hear me? I will succeed, you bastard! No longer will this family know failures such as you have shown me. Never again!" Cara brought her fist down on the desk. Tears pooled in her big steel-gray eyes, the only thing other than her hair that set her apart from her siblings, the only things she got from the man she called Father. She wondered if ever there might come a time when she could look at herself in the mirror and not see his eyes on her face, his hair color upon her head, and not detest herself for his failings.

***

"But Cara, we want to go too!" the girls protested in unison.

"Not today. Tomorrow. There are items I wish to obtain for all of you; however, you must let me research. I'll search out the shops, so as not to embarrass the Danforth clan by appearing in a shop that is not of our station. Please let me do this. Okay, princesses, I promise tomorrow will be for all." Cara's comments seemed to mollify the girls although Rex wasn't so easily satisfied.

Figures, she thought peevishly, though it couldn't be helped. She couldn't possibly take them with her while she was shopping for the finishing touches to her disguises. Cara looked at Rex; he followed her out of the Blue Room, named for the deep rich royal blues, which accented each nook and cranny, "Don't start, Rex. I am doing what I must."

Rex nodded, saying not a word his teeth gnashed so tightly together she feared his jaw would break; turning on his heel, he headed in the direction of his room. Cara hated having to be so abrupt with him; he was growing up, in some ways much too fast, in others not nearly fast enough.

Cara fastened the hook on her faded light blue summer wrapper and then stepped outside into the bright sunshine. "Good morning, Daniels. Where's Farley?"

"Good morning, Miss Caralyn. Farley gives his apologies, it appears he had to hie himself back to the country, something of a family matter as I understand."

"Oh yes, I should have realized, Mistress Wells is about to give birth I believe, how very inconsiderate of me to have overlooked that. I hope all is okay," she said more to herself than to Daniels. "I shall send a letter off to The Gables and ensure he made it back safely."

"I'm sure he'd like that. Farley will be fine, Miss, he left with the country coach this morning. Where are we off to today?"

Cara looked toward the brightly shined black town coach, the Danforth crest embossed in gold leaf shone like a beacon.

"I am sure you are right. I do hope you do not mind being coachman, at least until I am able to refill the position. I must see a reputable apothecary, please take me where you think is best. As I am new to London, I trust your judgment is a far sight better than mine."

"An apothecary, Miss? Everyone is healthy, I trust? I could fetch a doctor if you prefer?" Daniels said, clearly uncomfortable with the idea of escorting a lady to the areas of London where an apothecary shop would be found.

"Everyone is fine. There is no need for a doctor. Now, please, let us be away at once."

Noting the subject closed, Daniels opted for lighter more acceptable talk as he handed Cara into the coach.

"Really, I do not mind driving for as long as you need. I rather enjoy the ribbons. Drove for your father, I did. Only stepped out 'cause there really wasn't much call for a coachman with him gone. Tibs figured I'd be of more use around the house."

Once the door closed; light danced between the dim shadows in tune with Cara's thoughts. She moved the thick burgundy velvet curtain aside allowing additional light into the darkened interior. Daniels settled himself in the driver's box, clucking to the horses, a matched pair of chestnuts that were sure to have cost a pretty penny, while silent deliberations continued, the carriage jerked and clattered as the horses clopped down the drive.

As Cara leaned back, the plush burgundy velvet seats enveloped her. The plan was going famously, she purchased ample opiate to prepare enough of the sleeping potion to last a couple of weeks, and the herbalist didn't question why a gently bred woman would purchase such an amount. Thankfully, like so many other shops along Durbin Lane, money bought silence along with wares. The crone seemed more than willing to confirm the amounts. The last thing Cara wanted was to murder someone. Accidentally—of course…

There would be no more need for sneaking about. That was a great relief. Rex was sure to interrogate her upon her return. If she remained lucky, she would be able to safely stash her wares before the inevitable confrontation.

"Well?" Rex stood in the doorway of Cara's bedroom, arms crossed over his chest. It would have happened eventually; Cara counted her lucky stars that she'd gotten this far before he'd come fishing for answers.

"Well, what, Rex? It would help if you were just a tad more specific in your demands, young man."

"Balderdash Cara! Don't do that, it won't work." Rex came through the door; pulling out the elegant chair at Cara's escritoire, he straddled it, his gaze locked with hers.

Cara smiled. She couldn't help it; he looked like a miniature rake. An upset miniature to be sure… His brow arched. "All right, come clean. Where did you go?" He paused long enough to run his fingers through his hair, causing bits at the front to stand on end. As Cara looked on trying not to laugh, he mistook her silence entirely.

"Why won't you be honest with me? I can take it. Did father leave us destitute because you have been acting peculiar for a while now?"

Cara managed to keep a straight face, how, she didn't know. She knew there was more to Rex than met the eye however, she had had no idea he would decipher the problem so quickly.

"Don't be daft, Rex," she said with a calm she didn't feel, "I told you I come in search of a husband. That is all there is to it. For God's sake, I'm nineteen!" She threw up her hand in emphasis. "All but on the shelf. Do you want me to be a spinster?"

Rex could do naught but stare. Cara was hiding something. He knew his sister well enough to know it would take Wellington and all his armies to drag it out of her. Never before did he wish to be older. Noting Rex's expression, Cara realized mayhap she had been a little too harsh. She must get better at this, or she would turn Rex into the very man she was fighting to avoid.

"Rex, I'm sorry. I'm nervous; tonight, is my first ball, might you help me choose something? I realize a question of this nature is not normally put to a man, yet, as it is a man that I am trying to catch mayhap you will be kind enough to lend your expertise." Cara bit her lip, hoping he'd take the bait.

Rex chuckled. "Come on Cara, my expertise?"

Cara's lips twitched, rarely hearing Rex laugh; oh, the glorious sound! "Well, okay, mayhap not expertise, nevertheless, you are a man, more so every day, you know what looks nice, do you not? If that isn't enough, my dear brother, there is still the fact that you are the only man I currently know. Fair enough?"

Cara was awarded another smile and her heart warmed. Even as he shook his head, he walked to the bureau. Throwing open the doors, Rex peered inside.

"Odd's Blood! What's this?" he challenged.

Too late, Cara remembered exactly what type of gowns the closet held.

"Whatever do you mean, Rex dear?" she asked innocently.

"Cara, these are all the most uninteresting colors, I fear they will make you look like a wishy-washy dowager. No, I correct myself; at least a dowager would be colorful. Oh, Cara. How on earth are you planning to snag a husband, not that I believe that by-the-by, when you are wearing nothing save for outdated widows' weeds?"

"They are not widows' weeds!"

Rex raised a brow, oh my, he was getting far too good at that, Cara thought briefly.

"Rex, Darling, don't you see I have to wear mourning, society would shun me should I dare show my face in anything else with Father not yet cold in his grave."

"Cara, you cannot possibly grieve for that man! I know you have never said anything against him nonetheless, I've seen the look in your eyes every time Mrs. Brown mentioned his name, I am not a fool!"

"That is neither here nor there, he was our father, and as such, I am required a minimum of one-year mourning. It would not do to flout convention surely you must see that?" She had him there.

"I gather you are correct sister dear. Barring that, how will you explain being out at all? It has been little over a month since Father was installed in the Wonderland crypts."

"That is easy enough to explain, Rex, do not worry."

Rex looked as skeptical as Cara felt; both lapsed into silence while Rex selected a gown of the nicest cut. Black satin. Very fitting.

33

Rex vacated the room, allowing Cara time to dress. Lucy would arrive soon to help her. Cara checked her reticule for the two vials of elixir. Satisfied, she closed the latch just as a tap sounded at the door.

"Enter."

The door opened, and Lucy walked through, closing the door behind her. "Ready Miss?"

"Yes Lucy, let's be about it. It would not do to arrive too late."

"No Miss. It would not. Not at all."

A short while later, Cara descended the stairs, Lucy had done her hair wonderfully for a girl of her age, far too much fuss considering it would be covered, but Cara could hardly tell the girl that.

Tibs looked up from his post. "The carriage awaits, Miss."

"Thank you, Tibs. I shan't be late."

Cara handed Tibs her reticule while she secured her wrapper. Daniels was waiting atop the carriage, Johnny, a footman in training, assisted her up. Cara looked back at Tibs standing between the open double doors, looking none-too-pleased. *Old Coot!* She harrumphed, once safely inside, he was concerned with propriety, yet Cara didn't have a choice.

No money to waste on a companion, and without that damnable benefactor here to aid, she had to take matters into her own hands. Not that she would want him here, interfering and infuriating her most likely. As far as anyone at Danforth House knew, she was in search of a husband, there were certain dictates that must be met. She would meet all that she could and bugger the rest.

Smiling, she placed her hat upon her head, taking a few pins from her reticule she stabbed them in. From under her black summer pelisse, she pulled the high-necked fichu out of her gown, stuffing it into the carriage seat. A short while later, Daniels pulled the carriage into the drive halting in front of Huntington Place. Cara peeked behind the curtain; the mansion made her father's townhouse seem minuscule. A footman opened the door, offering his hand to help Cara descend. Taking it, Cara hoped he could not feel it tremble in his own.

"Thank you," she murmured; grateful her voice was steady.

Cara walked up the stairs, her hands sweating in her gloves, she hoped the receiving line would be disbanded, not that she wanted to sneak in, but it would be in her best interests to keep her acquaintances to a minimum.

As the footman was about to open the door, Cara remembered her veil. Would it look conspicuous to don it now? Would it be better to get inside mayhap find a retiring room? How many people would see her face before she lowered the veil? Would the footman make note of her features, remembering her should any part of this venture come to light? There was no help for it; her choices were slim…one man or many. Cara gently squeezed the footman's arm, stalling him from opening the door.

"I must lower my veil."

The footman nodded as Cara slipped her hand into the brim of her hat. Removing the black lace, she pulled the lace down, effectively covering her face.

"Thank you, it was so dark tonight I feared I would trip, injuring myself greatly."

"Understandable Madam. Shall we?"

Cara nodded; the footman opened the door. Escorting her inside, he let go of her arm. A butler came forth immediately requesting her cloak. He waited patiently for her to retrieve from her reticule the elegantly penned invitation, her calling card adorned only with her name and a single black rose.

"Madam Black?" he said, glancing at the card.

Cara gave a slight nod; mayhap handing him her calling card wasn't the thing to do although she wasn't about to answer his questioning look. She walked with a slow elegance up the rounded glistening marble staircase, her gloved hand brushing the top of the dark twisted iron railings.

Taking in all the paintings that adorned the walls as she passed by. It was like a fairytale. Never had Cara seen such wealth. She'd read about it to be sure. But then, she read about a lot of things. That proved to be her only saving grace in this whole matter. Finally, her bluestocking ways were going to pay off. Literally.

Things she didn't know, proper decorum, for dancing or eating at a fine table, would not matter. In mourning she would not be looked upon to dance—as to supper, it was anyone's guess. Cara hoped to be on her way from the Huntington's residence before the supper bell rang. Just like Cinderella, she would be gone by midnight…

Music wafted through the doors at the top of the winding staircase. Cara rounded the corner through the grand double doors only to be taken aback by the total ambiance of the scene before her. *It was beautiful!* And packed. There were so many people. How was one to go about finding the host or hostess? Would they come to her? Cara stood in the doorway surveying the crush. There were so many people. She hadn't accounted for this.

She took an unsure step forward as a lady descended upon her. Cara stopped.

"Madam?"

"Lady Huntington?"

"Yes. Whom might you be, my dear?"

"I am Mrs. Black. Your butler took my invitation. I hope that is all right. I am afraid I have been in the country for far too long."

Lady Huntington was a gorgeous woman. Her beauty went beyond skin deep. She took in the sight of what appeared to be a young woman in mourning then drew her own conclusions.

"Come, child. Mrs. Black. All will be well. Let me show you around. How long have you been in the country?" Her motherly manner had Cara feeling at ease in no time as Lady Huntington ushered her about the room.

She apologized for the lack of people; all Cara could think of was if this was a *lack*, what was a lot? It was supposed to be the off-season, most of the elite spent their time in Brighton or Bath enjoying the healing waters, still, there were to two hundred people in attendance.

She liked Lady Huntington. One thing she hadn't counted on. Names on paper could not reach in and twist one's heartstrings as this woman did in person. It would have been easier if the woman were a barracuda like her husband. At least, she assumed Huntington was a barracuda; he was a friend of her father's, after all.

Hopefully, Lady Huntington would suffer no ill effects from what she must do. As she listened, Lady Huntington named many people. Cara tried to match faces to some of the names on her list. It would be easier in the future to know just what her mark looked like.

Before long, they orbited the gigantic ball, room coming to an area set aside for dowagers, and their companions, a couple of lounges set aside, so the ladies could converse while the younger generation mingled and danced. Cara stayed close to Lady Huntington; she'd yet to meet her Lord. Confidently, she stayed close to his wife waiting for him to come to them.

An hour later, Cara was ready to give up. Try again later. More than a few people were by to pay respect to the dowagers; in turn introductions to the mysterious Mrs. Rose Black were made. Cara smiled though being out had created far more of a stir than she ever intended. Cara's thoughts were interrupted, when a portly, elderly gentleman pushed his way through the crowd before her. She ignored his presence as he turned to the other side of the chaise.

"Huntington!"

Cara's head snapped to attention as Lady Huntington addressed her husband.

"Hello, My Lady, you have outdone yourself this evening. Even the card room is a veritable crush, I had to escape. Very good indeed for summer entertainment."

Lady Huntington preened in the praise of her husband. Cara could not believe the difference between the two.

Lady Huntington was lovely even in her advanced years; her black hair streaked with strands of gray that shone silver in the candlelight. Her eyes shimmered like a green lake dancing under a hot sun and her face remained, for the most part, creamy smooth. Whereby her husband was, well, Cara could not think of exactly how to describe the short round, egg-shaped gentleman.

Something seemed amiss. Lady Huntington was clearly in love with her husband. She must, how else would she be able to overlook such obvious faults? Cara fretted her plan might very well go up in smoke if Lord Huntington was also equally infatuated with his wife.

"Ah and who might you be, my dear?"

Immediately, her confidence reinstated itself, as Lord Huntington's gaze never left her bosom as he conversed with her. What could she have been thinking? Of course, he was just like any other man. Only interested in one thing. Cara felt like telling him her eyes were slightly higher than his gaze but raised her hand instead. Taking it to his lips he brushed a kiss as his wife introduced her. Fighting the curdling of her insides as his fleshy mouth descended upon her upraised hand. *Thank Gawd for the gloves.*

"Lord Huntington. The pleasure is mine. Your wife's a jewel for taking me under her wing."

"Yes, yes, quite right, my dear. I see you are in mourning; a dance then would be inappropriate, however, let us see if we cannot introduce you to more of the younger set. A lady such as yourself should not be sequestered back here with the dowagers, isn't that right, My Ladies? Ah. I see Alberon, Redding,

Stimes; there is sure to be more of your age group there, my dear, let me escort you."

Cara briefly looked at Lady Huntington who seemed to notice nothing amiss with her husband escorting another about the ballroom. Sure, the lady wasn't to be offended, Cara placed her hand on Lord Huntington's arm. "Thank you, Your Grace, please lead on." Inclining her head toward the dowagers, Cara and Lord Huntington set out.

Lord Huntington placed his beefy hand atop Cara's in a possessive manner as he led her through the throng. Cara wasn't surprised when he didn't head in the direction of his aforementioned friends but veered in a different direction altogether Cara let him lead, without protest, through the balcony doors.

"A spot of fresh air, Mrs. Black?"

"Rose. Please. And I would sooner fortification, Your Grace."

"Fortification?"

"Why yes, I fear I am not used to such parties, a smidgen of something stronger than champagne would not be amiss."

"Ah! I am afraid, my dear Mrs. Black, the cognac is in my study. Wouldn't do to serve hard liquor with women present don't you know."

"I am sorry I meant no offense; I fear being raised and stationed in the country…"

Cara let the sentence drop hoping it wouldn't be long before either Lord Huntington's intellect would kick in, registering what she was saying or his libido would take over, do the job for him. Perhaps she'd best rely on his basic animalistic instincts he seemed a little short in the smart's category. She took a deep breath knowing the effect it would have.

His eyes darted to the creamy flesh. "Let us repair to my study?"

Huntington pressed close to Cara; she could smell the sweat mixed with the terrible odor of the insidious man even beneath the tons of perfume he used. Cara pulled back slightly, hoping to spear the man into action and stop her churning stomach. The ruse worked; he gave her breasts a longing glance, smacked his lips, and turned on his heel.

He poured equal amounts of cognac from the Tantalus into two crystal glasses while Cara looked about. Designed to comfort men retiring, smoking cigars, and drinking brandy, it was done in butter-soft Italian leather. Great wealth spoke volumes.

Cara wasn't naïve enough to think that this man could have decorated a room in fashion, with such terribly horrid taste. The brightly colored green breeches he wore were only outdone by the canary yellow evening jacket and underlying pink waistcoat. His valet must be very incompetent indeed not to mention the poor Duchess; she must fear blindness whenever in his presence.

"Ah my dear, dear Rose," Huntington said, coming up behind her. Placing the shot tumblers on the table, he spun her around with surprising quickness for a man of his stature, anchoring his arms about her waist. Cara could almost look straight into his bulging brown eyes until he bent his head and placed his slimy lips upon the curve of her breast. The shudder that racked Cara's body was thankfully mistaken for something other than repulsion.

"Ah, Rose. You like that, do you, my love?"

Cara lowered her voice in what she hoped was a seductive murmur. "Oh, yes, Your Grace, I do. Though I fear I am not ready for such strong passions yet. May sit a minute? I assure you; you will not be disappointed."

"Yes, yes quite right, my dear, so sorry to press. I was overcome by your beauty you see."

Beauty, huh more overcome by my breasts most likely; you're a slimy little embryo.

"Understandable, Your Grace, such as I was overcome by your masculinity as well, we still have time, do we not? The night is young?"

Huntington relinquished the hold upon her waist, with another quick kiss to her left breast, and retreated offering her access to her drink.

Chapter Three

"I hear tell; your family is quite famous. Was it not a descendant of yours that battled for the renowned Joyas Españolas?"

"Yes, quite right, Mrs. Black. My great-great-grandfather Osamus fought for possession. It was a bloodthirsty battle from what I am told. Osamus lost an arm. He returned with a trunk load of jewels to help finance the King's war."

"Very interesting indeed, 'Your Grace'. So, the jewels are all gone then?" Cara said, all innocence, regret, and intrigue.

"No. Osamus was very crafty and made sure quite a few gems were inset. Necklaces. Bracelets. 'The Huntington Family Jewels', a rare mixture of rubies, sapphires, emeralds, and diamonds."

"Together? An odd mix, is it not, Your Grace?"

"Yes, exceedingly rare indeed though I do favor such a mix. I realize being reared in the country, you haven't seen Duchess Huntington display their ornamentation; I assure you they are quite remarkable. Still to this day they are mentioned."

"Mentioned, not seen? Does the Duchess not wear them about town?"

"No, I am afraid the current Duchess wants nothing to do with them. Wouldn't even wear them for our wedding. She feels they are, how to put this delicately, 'cursed'."

"Cursed?"

"The previous Duchess who wore them died at young ages; suffice as to say she doesn't so much as look at them."

More the reality of walking about town looking like a French version of Turkish Delight, just what someone of the Duchess' ilk would like to be remembered as…a jellybean, Cara thought with a shudder.

"That is too bad. I know that if I were she, not only would I be honored to wear a thing of such beauty, but I would also definitely be extremely rewarding to the gentleman who offered such a gift."

Huntington's eyes flew to Cara's breasts; a strange glint seemed to take over his eyes, and Cara hoped it was desire, although she wasn't too sure. The way he licked his chops when he looked at her bosom, like they were a couple of lemon tarts, was decidedly uncomfortable.

Uncomfortable… but necessary…. If she kept telling herself that, she would make it through tonight.

"I know it is highly unusual, sir, you might very well think me forward, barring that I should like to witness the jewels. If only so that I may return to the country with pleasant memories to reflect upon." Running a fingertip down his thigh, Cara murmured, "I would be very grateful, Your Grace."

Huntington's eyes left her breasts for a moment; he looked at her veil-covered face. Cara could see the contemplation in his eyes. His eyes dropped to her lips, the only part of her face which wasn't obscured by the veil.

"I could be persuaded, my dear."

Oh Drat! Cara was afraid this would happen. Leaning forward, she pressed her breasts into his chest. He groaned sounding like an animal in pain; Cara licked her lips and brought her mouth closer to his.

"You could, Your Grace?" she whispered.

His hand came up to cup the back of her head as he crushed her mouth to his. It was gross! It was disgusting! Worse than she anticipated as his tongue saturated, and his teeth mashed. Cara could not help the gag that escaped her; fortunately, Huntington seemed to think it a sound of mounting passion. After a horrible minute that seemed a lifetime, Huntington broke the kiss allowing Cara a chance to right her stomach.

"Very impressive, my dear, yes very impressive indeed. I cannot wait to see what you have planned for the finale; let me open the safe."

Cara watched, inconspicuously scrubbing her mouth as he sauntered to the enormous self-portrait behind his desk. She quickly reached inside her reticule, withdrawing a tiny vial; her drink in hand so as not to get them confused, she broke the wax seal, emptying the potion into the other. Giving it a swirl, she dropped the vial back in her bag and turned around to await His Lordship.

Leaving the door to the safe open, Huntington glided toward her with an intricately carved mahogany chest an exact replica, of a treasure chest, only smaller. Placing it on the table he positioned his signet ring, the key, into the latch. A push then a turn to the right and the lid slowly lifted of its own accord. He turned the chest toward Cara.

"They are magnificent! Never have I seen the like!"

Cara slowly took a bracelet out, appeared to admire it in the candlelight. Huntington drank, imagining the look of awe on a face he could not see. Damn, he wished she would remove that hideous veil. Mayhap when she was finished, she would reward him with a look of her face, the pouty lips that uttered a smattering of French here and there fed his imagination as to what the rest of her looked like.

It mattered not, if she refused to take it off. He would have her anyway. With a body such as she possessed, he cared little about what her face looked like. Keeping her veil on would only add a certain mysterious quality to their sexual encounter. A woman with no face… Yes. Yes. Let her keep the damn thing on. The more he thought about it the more his loins tightened and the more his loins tightened the more he drank.

Cara was still looking over the jewels when Huntington got up to pour himself a third glass. She knew she would not be able to stall him much longer, why wasn't the cursed sleeping draught working? Mayhap it wasn't enough. Panic started to grip at her. Her hands were sweating worse than before beneath the covering of her gloves. She felt the perspiration bead on her brow. She was tense. Even holding jewels, worth more than she'd seen in her life, mayhap more than she ever would, though the cold smooth feel of the gems, could not calm her frenzied nerves.

He was back. Cara could feel his hot breath on the nape of her neck.

"Rose."

"Your Grace," she whispered softly. Cara patted the settee beside her. Anything to get his lips off her neck. "Come, Your Grace, let me thank you for your generosity."

Huntington waddled around to the front lifting the tails of his evening jacket, he lowered his considerable weight beside her. Cara looked at him, his eyes appeared heavy; surely, she would not have to entertain him long before the drug kicked in. She placed her gloved palm aside of his face in a gentle caress. It was something she used to do for her brother and sisters if they could not sleep, the gentle motion while she talked usually soothed them quickly, she was hoping Huntington was far enough gone that the deception would work.

42

"You are so very kind, Your Grace," she murmured as she kissed his brow, "to indulge this country bumpkin. You have given me a glimpse at something here in this great city that I shall treasure in my dreams."

Cara spoke slow and sultry, kissing now and then. Better her lips on his brow, than his on her mouth. Soon his eyes began to flutter. She forged on. Singing his praises until his breath slowed. She tried to rise, but slowly, Huntington's arms reached out, seizing her, and pulling her back down. *Don't panic. Don't panic.* Over and over, she told herself as he leaned in, and his great weight pushed her backwards pinning her beneath him. His mouth crashed down on hers, hands roamed freely over her breasts down her sides to the juncture of her legs, back up again.

"I'sh do believe it's time for the Rose to unfurl her petals. I'sh so ready to taste yer sweet nectar," he slurred.

Cara worried mayhap she hadn't given him enough; he was obviously inebriated, yet he showed no signs of passing out.

"Open up, Rosy," he sniggered.

Oh cute!

His hand came up to remove the veil. Cara panicked, bucked beneath him. It only served to excite him more. His head came up, chanting choruses of yeses and excited moans. She looked around for something to hit him over the head with; sadly, there was nothing within her reach. When suddenly, he let out an animalistic roar then quickly subsided into silence.

Cara didn't wait to see if he was truly out. She pushed, wiggling until she dislodged herself from beneath his mammoth weight. *Bloody Hell! This is harder than I thought!* Cara hit the floor with a resounding thump. Picking her now tender backside off the Aubusson rug, she quickly listened to see if anyone heard. Hearing nothing, she stood and walked toward the safe.

Quickly, she came back to where Huntington was passed out on the sofa. Reaching beneath the folds of his many chins, she worked the knot of his cravat free. *How could she have been so simple-minded as to forget something to carry her spoils home in?* Placing the cravat flat on the desk, Cara took the candle using it to peer into the deep cavern of the safe. As quickly as possible, she searched for the deed to Wonderland.

It was dark inside the safe. Cara took several things out at once to search properly. Placing the bank notes, gold and silver into the center of the cravat, Cara opened scroll after scroll searching for the deed. When at last she came to the deed, a small piece of paper fell from its center. Cara picked it up, read it, there were a jumble of terms and figures, nothing that made sense at first glance, clearly signed with her father's autograph, and the Danforth seal was imprinted at the bottom. Cara didn't take the time to speculate further, she promptly placed it on top of the cash and the deed to Wonderland. She would contemplate everything when she returned home; overall, for her first job, it would be a good haul.

Taking up the corners of the cravat, she brought them together then tied a secure knot. Raising her skirts, they were wet on top, how… no matter. She secured the precious bundle to the ties on her stays. There was a little lump showing at the front, with a little luck, no one would notice.

She shut the jewel chest, raising Huntington's heavy hand she pressed the ring back into the lock and gave it a twist. Then placed it back in the safe. She returned her glass to the sideboard.

Securing the safe, she moved the picture in front to conceal its location and quietly slipped out of the study. Taking her wrap from a bored-looking footman, she walked outside. Waiting patiently at the top of the stairs for another footman to inform Daniels of her impending departure.

Cara didn't realize she'd been holding her breath until she spied Daniels pulling the carriage in front of the steps, taking in a great gulp caused her to cough. Grasping the veil, she tucked it into the band on her bonnet before Daniels could see.

A concerned Daniels sped up the stairs taking her arm before the footman could assist her to the carriage. It dawned on Cara once the carriage was moving that Daniels' odd behavior attributed to the fact that he heard her coughing and assumed she was under the weather.

She had left rather early, all things considered. She hadn't even paid respects to her hostess. Somehow it didn't seem right. Patting the front of her gown, she felt for the makeshift pouch. Feeling it, she relaxed allowing the tension to subside as she listened to the hypnotic echo of each hoof beat on the cobblestones.

***

"Odds Blood, Beaumont, I was just getting settled into the last assignment! What is so bloody important you dragged me back here?"

"In case the matter eludes you, my dear friend, the reason you were called back is because there is a matter of far greater importance here that requires your attention. Secrets vital to this country's survival could very well be at stake! Why worry about the Colonies, the Cavalry can deal with them. Something bigger is brewing right here on our own soil."

"Fine! I understood from your letter that something was afoot here, but bloody friggin' hell, Beaumont. How am I to ever regain the trust of the Colonials? It took me three years to get on the inside. All of it gone, gone because I stole away like some bloody thief in the night!"

"We will find someone else should the need arise. Though I doubt from reports it will, I hear the Americans are ready to launch a full-scale war. That is a matter for the army and navy. Not the agency. The French are much closer to home, my friend. They, for now, are the greater threat.

"I realize the Americans have asked favors of Napoleon, still it will take him time to maneuver his troops. While he is aiding the Colonials, he will not be at our backs. That should buy us some time.

"Will it? I can't take that chance. Besides, with Danforth's untimely demise, you would have been needed here anyway. Good thing I contacted you when I did, or you would still be another two months in coming. If not more; then what would those children do?

"Nothing has changed really. I still believe Danforth was involved in trade secrets; however, he was terminated before we had a chance to send an agent in to cipher out the situation. Namely… you. According to our sources, a full list divulging the whereabouts of foreign agents in Home Office is still missing. There is every chance Danforth had it amongst his possessions at the time of his demise. No, not bodily possessions, but somewhere.

"We know his correspondence was forwarded to his countryseat. The Gables, I believe it is called, in Devonshire, of which, by the way, you are benefactor. Lord knows what has been done with the missing information. I want you to find it as quickly as possible." Beaumont pointed a look at Acworth that brooked no refusal. Still Acworth didn't heed it. *Typical.*

"Yes, I understand the urgency, never doubt that. Frankly, I cannot believe Thomas engaged in treason. While I am here, I will find your bloody list, but don't think for one moment that I'll not to try my damnedest to clear Thomas' name in the process—before word of his alleged treachery can be leaked. It is the least I can do to try and repay all he has done for me."

Roland eyed Beaumont, challenging him to state otherwise. Beaumont looked as though there was more; if so, he wasn't saying. Damn, how he hated this secrecy. The not knowing; Roland cleared his throat, "There's something else. You're jumpier than a newly saddled colt. What is it?"

Beaumont paced the floor of the dingy little back room at The Cock & Crow. His overheated complexion showed his agitation more than his pacing ever could. Acworth leaned the chair back on its hind legs, rocking, somewhat contented after his outburst. Finally, Beaumont stopped in front of him. He tapped the side of his noble hawk-like nose.

"Something smells."

Acworth knew Beaumont wasn't referring to the general surroundings, so he waited while his long-time friend gathered his thoughts.

"Lately, mind you. Not that I have proof you understand regardless of how I feel the matter the Danforth problem is of the upper most importance right now, yet I cannot help being concerned, you see."

No, Acworth didn't see, something was making Beaumont even more complicated than customary. Knowing an interruption would likely stall the matter further, Acworth sat back, nodding appropriately, waiting for the older man to voice something that made a modicum of sense.

"There have been three to date, you see. Just three. Still…I somehow have a bad feeling; I cannot quite escape. Yes, this could be bad. Very bad… Though then again…"

"Damnation Beaumont! Get to the bloody point. I do not want to be in this hellhole one moment longer than I have to!" Acworth spat, temper rising, patience at an end. It had been a long journey, filled with many quiet moments of contemplation, the assignment, his responsibilities; he was twenty-eight for Christ's sake, now in the span of what seemed like two fortnights, Danforth, his teacher, had died. His death turning his world upside down and leaving him guardian of Danforth lands and four small children. To compound the matter, he seemed to have gotten himself in hot water with the Organization, for which it was up to Acworth to set to rights. Acworth hadn't even the time to contemplate the vast attention he needed to pay to his own long neglected estates.

"Yes. Quite right, old chap. You see there have been some mysterious thefts of late. Three thus far. Started within the last week or so as far as I can tell. Mind you, I haven't delved deeper into the issue therefore it could be longer, though I think not."

"Thefts are a matter for Bow Street, old friend, leave the matter with them. It is not like you to get so agitated over something so totally out of our authority."

"Normally, I would agree. But you see. Out of the three thefts I have learned about, none have been reported to Bow Street. On each occasion no jewels were taken; only, if I am to understand this correctly, available cash and what could possibly be mistaken as vowels. The victims are unsure of what transpired, they can remember little or nothing of what happened before or after. The only thing linking these three cases, and I am sure this is the reason the dolts found their safes burglarized in the first place, was the removal of their neckties and a single black rose found lying in the safe."

Acworth came down hard on the front legs of the chair. This was odd, very odd; still, it was theft. Pure and simple.

"Beaumont, this is all very intriguing I must say. Plenty thespian too, black rose and all, but it is still a simple case of burglary."

"Again, I would normally agree, except, insofar as all have been members of the Organization."

"Bloody Hell, you mean they are agents?"

"No, not agents per se, more like former members of the Home Office, retired from active duty; nevertheless, helpful in certain circumstances."

"Bloody Hell!"

"Oh, by the by, the deed to The Gables seems to be one of the things stolen. Most likely, the only reason Huntington came forth. You know how he can be, always thinking he is better than the rest of us. A missing deed I'm afraid would not be so easy to hide."

"Bloody Hell! The Gables. As in Thomas' countryseat, what would anyone want with that?"

"I am not worried about the deed. Most like whoever broke into Huntington's safe knew our Thomas was dead and could not protest the fact that the familial seat ended up in someone else's hands. It wasn't entailed, you know. For that matter, Huntington never should have had access to it in the first place, yet he did. That, too, bothers me."

"Bloody hell, Beaumont, this is giving us more questions than answers. The agency—"

"Quite right Acworth. You begin to see, as I do, the big picture."

"And none remember if they had anything pertaining to the Home Office in their safes, I gather?"

"No. Yet that does not mean they are necessarily telling all of it. I am convinced in certain situations; one such as these, the victim may not come forth with a full explanation of events, if you know what I mean. Still, it would be a bloody shame. I'd hate to contemplate what it might mean; still, I feel that I cannot justifiably let it go."

"Bloody Hell!"

"Really Acworth, you are beginning to sound a trifle wearying constantly repeating yourself."

"Sorry old man. Let me investigate this, I will get back to you as soon as I find something. That damn deed needs to be found straightaway. Not to mention my personal duties. I am already a month late in coming, but with the recent activities of our thief, the trail will be hot."

"As much as I would like to see this matter resolved, and of course that of your as you said personal life, you must first head to The Gables. Find the list, Acworth. This other can wait. As for your charges, I am sure you will find them safely ensconced in Devonshire; so, you see, my friend, you'd be killing two birds with one stone."

Acworth wearily rose from his chair, shook Beaumont's hand then slipped out into the darkened corridor. Beaumont would wait, as was the practice, five or ten minutes before exiting the tavern.

Reaching into his pocket he pulled out a crown, tossed it to the lad holding his horse. Taking the reins, he mounted Magnus. Giving a command, he swung about, at a gallop disappearing into the fog-shrouded night.

Chapter Four

Cara lay back on her bed, arms spread high above her head, spoils from tonight's, as well as the previous two adventures, were spread hither and yon about the bedspread. It was becoming easier and easier. Not that the prey lacked fewer wits than Huntington, for they did not. She was more adept at controlling her emotions and that made a world of difference.

For the first time Cara felt free, oh she knew there was a long way to go before she would be finished. However, she felt confident that once the monies were raised to save Wonderland as well as the other Danforth properties, she would raise enough to finance Rex's enrollment to Eton and with a little luck, put something away for the girls as well.

Seventeen hundred pounds—the amount left after dispersing monies owed to the estate manager along with a letter stating his assistance was no longer required. Four times the amount of her dowry in three soirées!

She'd done it!

Life was grand!

If she remained undetected, all would be well. Perusing periodicals and society columns for a sign of Rose's reported thefts, Cara was relieved to see all was as she assumed. No man would willingly admit to a liaison with his wife hosting a party just outside the study door. Men, of their class especially, always kept mistresses but to carry on right under their wives' noses in such a public arena would be the scandal of the century.

Permitting herself a quiet gurgle of satisfaction, she got up to eradicate the evidence, storing it in the bottom of her trunk. She spied the notes at the bottom. Should she dispose of them? What could they mean?

Even though she could not make heads or tails of the notes on a whole, she all but ruled out blackmail. What could anyone have blackmailed her father for? As to why her father would sign something and to find that something in possession of men who had already taken from him... It didn't make sense.

Something was familiar about those numbers; balderdash; she wished she had the foresight to bring her father's journal.

Clearly, Cara hadn't known the man her father had become since coming to London almost three years ago.

Quickly, she made the decision to hold on to the incriminating, or at least what she assumed were incriminating, documents until she could cross reference them with the account book back at Wonderland.

Walking to the escritoire, Cara sat, neatly unfolding what was readily becoming a worn piece of vellum, her list; taking the tip of her quill she placed a check beside the next name on the list.

Grabbing the stack of invitations, she slipped out the one for Sir Alfred DuPont's fete. Running her fingers thoughtfully over the gold-embossed lettering, she plotted out her next mission.

By all accounts, this one should be a breeze. She'd seen Sir Alfred roaming eye on more than one occasion. Refolding her list, Cara placed it back in the secret compartment of her desk. She didn't think Rex, in his quest to discover the truth, would search her room but…one could never be too careful.

A glint of light shone through the heavy crimson drapes, sunrise, time to get a few hours' sleep; she had promised to take the children to Astey's today. She'd read somewhere that its amusements should not be missed. It could have been in one of the many periodicals she read. She wasn't sure at this point which one, she had read so blasted much lately, researching her marks, their lives, their homes, their families, their jewels, anything that could recommend her quest getting her safely ensconced in their private rooms where she would be able to work her magic.

It really was magic, in way; she thought as she pulled back the covers then climbed into bed. For what else but magic could have drawn them out of the hole in which their father submersed them? She would remain an illusion appearing and disappearing without a trace.

When she had enough, secured enough, Rose would disappear forever, allowing Cara to once more reign in Wonderland. Well… at least until Rex came of age and took a wife. The thought made her wince. Where would she be in five, ten or even twenty years? Living off her brother? That thought left a bitter taste in her mouth.

Not that Rex would mind, in truth by the time she'd seen to his schooling and the girls' come outs, she would well and truly be on the shelf. A spinster.

As sad and lonely as the prospect made her feel, she knew there was no help for it; she had responsibilities, she would have to console herself with being the doting aunt instead of the loving mother she had always dreamed of. Allowing the self-pity to run its course, Cara closed her eyes hoping her dreams would console her.

***

Roland leaned back the chair letting it rock on its hind legs as he contemplated the situation. All of Thomas' correspondence lay open on the desk; he wondered who would have gone through his letters, as he recalled the children were small enough that they would not be the least bit concerned with it and as to the dismal lack of staff about the place that left only one person who could have opened it. Mrs. Brown, the housekeeper. Or had someone else been in Thomas' study? He would have to question Mrs. Brown later; if nothing came about, he'd broaden the search once he returned to London.

Sifting through the opened letters, invoices, missives, and messages from members of the home office, Huntington, DuPont, they would all have to be decoded in hopes of finding answers. There was something odd about the lot of them.

At last, he found what he was searching for, another veiled communication that would make very little sense to anyone at first glance. It wasn't that it was more extensive than the other eleven he had found the fact that the only signature, which appeared, was a giant D in the bottom right-hand corner. Briefly, he scanned the note decoding words he discovered in hopes if would lead him to the location of the list. What bothered him was whether these eleven members, or past members, of the Home Office were accomplices in the trading of secret information. The other questions surrounding all this would have to wait until he made sure the record wasn't in the hands of the enemy. Once he was back in London, he would go to Hatchard in search for the travel periodical supposedly concealing the list.

Roland took a few minutes to reflect on the overall atmosphere of The Gables, while he bundled the letters. Run down. Worn out. Stables emptied. Crops in need of planting and the grounds in need of a thorough tending—the only staff an elderly housekeeper.

One person to care for this great seat; the place though old and worn wasn't dirty or outrageously unkempt. There was a sense of pride behind the picture of loneliness, the neglect. Someone had loved this place nurturing it as best as they could. Could Thomas have been so low on funds that he was unable to care properly for his manor? His lands? His children? Where the hell were they anyway? Didn't children usually run? Jump? Play? Weren't they always about when visitors came?

Come to think of it, there was no noise at all; one could have heard a pin drop the whole time he was here. For more times than he could count, the thought jumped into his mind before he could stop it. Something wasn't right.

Leaning forward, Roland spotted a cream-colored piece of vellum on the floor. Picking it up he glanced at his own words, a letter to Thomas some time back. Someone wasn't happy about this particular communication, as a matter of fact if the wrinkles had anything to say for themselves, they indicated that whoever read this letter was quite upset. The letter was written in the heat of the moment when Thomas first informed of his decision of guardianship.

He recalled writing it; the last thing he wanted was come back to England being faced with added responsibility of four small children when he had neglected his own estates. He was twenty-eight now. Two years passing didn't necessarily change his outlook one wit. Fate, however, had seen differently. Once this business was finished, he would have to see to his charges, staff and lands then find a wife to look after it all so he could get on with his life.

He would talk to Mrs. Brown in the morning to find out exactly where his charges were. She could introduce them all. He wished reverently he had discerned more about the family he had inherited. They were young and, in his arrogance, he assumed, another family member would take charge of them in his absence.

Damn! Why hadn't he learned more? Frankly, it was simple. In the scheme of things, the importance of four small children seemed minimal. What in God's name did that say for him? He still couldn't believe Thomas had never changed his will after receiving his letter all those years ago. He felt a tug in the region of his heart attributed no doubt to yet another failure involving family.

Roland's parents had died when he was seventeen, too young to properly care for his title, estates; his uncle had taken over for him seeing that not all was lost as he escaped into somewhat reckless behavior. In and out of gaming halls, drinking till all hours of the day or night could not banish the image of his parents' boat in the Channel sinking before it could be rescued. He was supposed to be on that ship.

They were headed to view the recently purchased tea plantations in Ceylon. Roland couldn't be bothered, stating he would rather enjoy life after Oxford before taking on his father's role. It was a battle to which his father grudgingly surrendered, allowing him the time allotted of their journey. One year. Upon returning, Roland would take up the reins learning to care for the ducal estates. Six years later, submersed in crime, Beaumont offered him his only means of staying out of Newgate.

"Work for the crown or rot," he said. Funny how over the years he had come to value Beaumont's opinion, so much so that he would rather die than disappoint him. So, he came home, had done his duty, was still doing his duty. He had to find out about those children! He could not bear it, that, if in his negligence they had come to harm. Slamming his fist down on his own words, Roland hollered for Mrs. Brown, the conversation couldn't wait until morning.

***

Getting Sir Alfred alone was proving to be a bit of a problem. It was getting close to midnight, as a lot of the partygoers were at their strongest just after midnight, it allowed her to make good her escape without detection, if she was forced to hang about longer, it was possible that someone may see her exiting.

More than a little anxious about the outcome of tonight's events, Cara began to circulate, trying to discover the study on her own. If she could get inside, mayhap she could find a secondary route should she need one. Passing one person or another, Cara acknowledged them each with a brief nod of her gray-veiled head. She tried not to move too much for this veil was decidedly shorter than the others, coming just barely to the tip of her elegant button nose.

She pulled her hair back tighter so none of her blackened tresses could be seen; for some reason in all her precautions she felt a sense of unease. Making her way through the throng, Cara breathed a sigh of relief when she finally entered the hall. The lady's retiring room was to the right, she had been there a couple times tonight already to make sure she remained unrecognizable. She didn't remember, as she peeked into the open doorways along the way, anything that resembled a study, most likely it was one flight down; so far, the only person who had had a study on the same floor as the ballroom was the obnoxious Sir William. Her body gave an involuntary shudder at the thought of Sir Williams's thickset hands. His hands she had managed, it was the rest of Sir William that she had abhorred.

Cara tossed the unwanted memory aside; she had more than enough to worry about tonight with her nervousness growing; she could not afford to devote any time to past jobs that turned out all right in the end. Her musing halted as she reached the bottom stair. Looking about she saw no one, turning she headed away from the entry. Cara spotted a closed door at the end of the long corridor, picking up her pace, she hurried to it, grasped the knob. Hastily she placed an ear to the door. It was no use. She could not hear anything through the solid oak.

She could not stay in the hall. Mind made up, she gave the knob a twist, quickly entering the dimly lit room.

Cara silently closed the door, and the room was bathed in darkness; she waited for her eyes to adjust to the dim light that trickled through a window on the opposite side of the room. Silently, she made her way deeper into its darkened recesses; looking around she tried to orientate herself with her surroundings. Bookcases lined the three windowless walls, in truth it was more of a library than a study, she'd read Sir Alfred was a collector of fine books. One, which he was famous for, was an authenticated logbook of a pirate captain, supposedly containing a detailed map of a West Indies Island showing where Spanish treasure was buried.

Those who believed the treasure really existed believed it had never been claimed as it was buried too near to the time of Captain Bundy's capture, and subsequent introduction to the hangman's noose. Most believed it was nothing more than an unsubstantiated legend. Cara didn't know what to believe, quite frankly she didn't care; her only significant interest in the bloody book was a means to enter Sir Alfred's safe.

"Aha! I've got you now, m'cherie. Where have you been, m' petite fleur? I have been waitin' an age for you!"

Cara could not breathe. It was all she could do not to fight. *Bloody hell!* She cursed silently as she realized she has just discovered the whereabouts of one Sir Alfred DuPont. *Think, damnation, think*!

"Sir. Kindly unhand me or I will scream!"

"What? Who the hell are you, what are you doing in my study?"

"Your study?"

"Of course, this is my study, who's else would it be?"

"Oh, my dear, Sir Alfred?"

"None other. Now who pray-tell are you, Madam?"

"I…oh yes, pray forgive me, sir."

Cara took a step back, sinking into an elegant curtsy.

"Mrs. Rose Black; I am pleased to make your acquaintance."

Cara raised a gloved hand. Sir Alfred looked at it, helped her rise, didn't let go. "I have heard of you, m' petite fleur. Yes, yes indeed. Come let us shed some light to see if my memory serves me correctly."

"Pray, sir, that is not necessary. I have clearly taken a wrong turn. Please forgive my impertinence. I will leave directly."

"Nonsense!"

He pulled her to the desk, with eager little steps, holding her there as he found and lit a single taper standing at the corner of his desk. Lifting the candle aloft, a soft glow illuminated her form.

"Ah, yes, it is you Mrs. Black. Beautiful, just as I remembered, now what was this about a wrong turn?"

"I needed air, Sir; the balcony was so very crowded. It is quite a crush and I thought perhaps if I went through the front door, it would be rudeness beyond the pale. All these rules… I find them so terribly difficult to remember." Cara touched a hand to her veiled brow. "Things are so much different in the city then in the country. I need not tell a man of your obvious refinement such things. Pray forgive me. I was exploring."

"Ah. And what Madam did you expect to find in my study?"

"I didn't know at first it was your study; I mistakenly took it for the library sir. I have read how terribly fond of books you are; it is said you have one of the best collections in all of England."

"It must be terribly tiresome in the country to have worried your pretty head about my collection?"

"True. The country is oftentimes quite tedious; Mr. Black was more concerned with his periodicals than anything else. So, you see when he met his great reward, I was absconded with nothing more than periodicals. So, I read. I'm truly sorry if I upset you."

"No not at all, my dear. Why don't we sit, discuss literature? It appears I have some free time. Since my, ah…appointment didn't show."

"I must admit it is ever-so-much quieter here. I think sir;" Cara inclined her head toward the leatherbound couch. "I would like that over-much."

Sitting down, silence reigned. It appeared that Sir Alfred didn't know where to begin.

"Sir? May I trouble you for a glass of sherry?"

"Huh? Oh…why yes, my dear, spirits, what a clever notion."

Sir Alfred stood up and walked back over to his desk, taking the top off the decanter, he poured a generous amount of amber colored liquid in each.

"I am afraid brandy will have to do; it seems I am all out of sherry."

Turning, he walked spryly back to Cara. Cara took note of his slight frame. He was as old as her father, mayhap even a little older. His dark-rimmed spectacles sat elegantly on his fine, noble nose. All in all, he was a good-looking man. She thought back to when she met his wife, such a dragon; Cara hadn't spent long with her at all. With a wife like that, Cara almost sympathized. Almost.

"Thank you so much, Sir Alfred, it's just what I needed," she said as she raised the glass for a sip. Sir Alfred followed suit though he seemed to have a bit of difficulty swallowing. Tension hovered around him like a thick fog.

"Mrs. Black." His parched throat crackled, he cleared it, tried again.

"Mrs. Black, I fear I must ask a favor of you."

Cara's brow shot up in question.

"You see it…ah…you see my dear, here in the city, it is not…how should I say…?"

"Sir Alfred, I find it best, in the country that is, to state what is one's mind. Therefore, I would not be offended in the least if you would just come out, say what it is you have to say."

Alfred took his handkerchief from his vest pocket, mopped his sweating brow.

"Thank you, Mrs. Black, mayhap that would be best. I know you must have realized by now why I wasn't in the ballroom with my wife. I cannot let this get out; you understand?"

"Perfectly."

"I mean should my wife ascertain…what? What did you say?"

"I said I understand, Sir Alfred, you may count on my discretion in every way."

Sir Alfred calmed; the tension that was building magically washed away with Cara's words.

"Thank you. I am indebted."

"Think nothing of it, Sir. I know I shan't."

"But you do understand I am honor bound to repay you for your generosity. It binds the pact; I am sure even in the country you have such things."

Cara took her time pondering the thought, Sir Alfred stared intently; Cara brought her head up abruptly. "I have it! There is one but one thing I can think of… that is of course, if you are willing. I am sure you will find my request; how should I say…easy to accommodate?"

"Name it, fair lady, it shall be yours. That is…"

"Have no fear, Sir what I want will not, shall we say, get you in more hot water? I wondered if I might see the famed treasure map I have read is in your possession."

Sir Alfred nodded. "That, indeed, was a simple request and my pleasure."

Standing, he walked toward the wall of books. *Oh no, don't say the man keeps the bloody book on the shelf!* Cara began to worry; she didn't need a book from the bloody shelf she needed a safe. As she started to plan her next step should this tact fail to produce what she needed, she was startled by the sound of wood scraping against wood. Raising her head, she saw Sir Alfred disappear behind the wall. *The Safe!*

Straightening her back, she listened to the somewhat muffled sounds behind the open bookcase. Snapping open her reticule, Cara retrieved the vial inside. Opening it, she dumped the contents into Sir Alfred's drink. A few seconds later, Sir Alfred emerged, setting the worn book on the table in front of her; Cara gently opened its historical pages. Faded script demanded her attention; the size and design were written by a bold albeit untutored hand, her fingers caressed the discolored paper. She wished she could leap into the pages, into the past. A sensation significantly stronger than anything she could have felt for a chest full of the finest jewels.

Lost in the wonder of the ages Cara hadn't noticed her companion had vanished into a totally different world.

"Sir Alfred?"

No answer came. How she would have preferred to keep looking at the captain's journal but alas, she had a job to do. With one final gentle stroke,

Cara closed the tome. Extricating Sir Alfred's cravat, she carried the volume back to the safe.

Damnation! How had he opened the safe? What book triggered the mechanism? Replaying his hand movements in her mind, her hand rested on Gulliver's Travels, could it be so obvious? She tipped the spine towards her and sure enough the soft click of the mechanism sounded. She placed a black rose on top of the remaining contents, sighing she closed the door and made her way out of the room.

***

Roland was worn-out. The last thing he wanted to do was attend a bloody social gathering. After arriving in London, and a too long debriefing at Beaumont's behest, all he sought was his townhouse and his bed. Tomorrow he'd have the list. Hopefully.

Now on top of everything, he had to track down his bloody charges. After questioning Mrs. Brown, the answer to the noiseless manor was apparent; the children were gone. The housekeeper refused to enlighten him as to their whereabouts, she spoke in terse rambling sentences regarding the townhouse Thomas owned; he had been aware of the property as he told her, still she was adamant that he should do his duty properly and look in on the house and the staff.

As to who the children were with or who had given them permission to leave or even where they were or with whom? Nothing was forthcoming; she said she was being of assistance, yet she hadn't given Roland one clue let alone respond to one question with a straightforward answer.

There were no portraits of the children. Odd. And the abominable Mrs. Brown would not so much as divulge their ages, saying only they had taken care of themselves for a respite. "They be back when they're good and ready, not before, now do check on Danforth House when you reach London, it's as good a place as any to start by my reckoning, although that Thomas…"

She didn't have anything good to say about Thomas, at least not in the recent years. It seemed peculiar; the man, he remembered would not have disowned his family. At least he didn't think so. Though Roland could not be certain as all his dealings with Thomas were, more or less, pertaining to the agency. Damn! If the man really did do all that Mrs. Brown accused him of, then those poor children needed someone. Even he would be better than no one at all.

Handing his top hat and gold-tipped walking stick to the butler, Roland was about to remove his cloak when a flurry of gray satin knocked him backwards. He grabbed for her shoulders, steadying them both. Lightning bolts shot up his arms. All he could see was the top of a dark gray satin bonnet, decidedly out of date, of which he could attest because the whole outfit was out of date before he had left England. She was solid; willowy; he could feel the tension in her soft-rounded shoulders. His senses were engulfed in honeysuckle, cinnamon, and cloves, a scent so intoxicating it sent another jolt straight to his loins.

"Beg your pardon." It was a sweet almost breathless whisper. Like her scent, it gave the impression of down carried forth on a summer breeze, swirling, hovering; demanding your attention…except they weren't outside. His loins tightened even more. Bloody hell, he was too long without a woman. Her voice spun around in his head. He was inebriated. Forcing himself to step back, confirming, by telltale signs of widow's weeds, that she was in mourning. She wriggled, he immediately let go of her shoulders, said not a word as she turned to the butler, retrieved her cloak.

"Leaving so soon? The best of the party has yet to begin."

"Ah… Yes… I am afraid so, yes. An emergency. If you'd kindly remove yourself from the door, *Sir*, I really must depart."

Her voice flowed, low, breathlessly, as though she were speaking words in her lover's ear. The resonance did unexpected things to him. Never could he remember a time he was so instantly aroused. Fastening her cloak, she pushed onward without another word, leaving Roland wondering just who this walking contradiction was. He was sure of a couple things, first she was lying, about what he didn't know, but he was sure of it. Secondly, *she was no widow!* He'd stake his newfound reputation on it.

Roland was awhirl with the contradiction minutes later when he rounded the corner into the ballroom. Amylia Stapleton, the Duchess of Greyley, came forward, smiling, "Roland, darling, when did you get home? You naughty boy, you didn't even send around a note. I swear you are more devilishly handsome then I remember. Come, come, my boy, walk with your dear old aunt, tell me what you have been up to in those wild lands of yours."

Roland couldn't remember the last time someone referred to him as a boy, but God how he had missed it.

"Old? I think not. In fact, if you were single, I'd snatch you up in a heartbeat." Roland's lips curved as he bent to kiss her cheek. Amylia blushed. She should have expected nothing less from her wild nephew. He held his arm out to his aunt, as she placed her hand upon her sleeve, "Madam, I should be honored to walk with you. Shall we?"

Roland told his aunt as much as he could about the last three years. She listened with an affectionate ear, asking questions, thanking him more than once for returning home. Roland owed his aunt and uncle a great deal, for while he was running wild; they were taking care of his responsibilities. The act was never spoken of aloud or established in any way, but Roland knew his uncle was behind Beaumont's initial contact and subsequent assignment.

He had tried his best to keep in contact with his uncle while he was away. Thanks to Beaumont, he was able to converse at length about the Fairhaven estates. Beaumont had spent countless moment tutoring him on all that was forgotten prior to his recovery, a mild term to say the least, as well as all he had missed in his imposed banishment.

Deep down he knew it wasn't exile, and he had enjoyed the assignments but the older he got, the more he regretted his previous actions that had forced him out of his beloved England.

Even now, he devoured every morsel Beaumont fed him. And was confident with each aspect of being the Duke of Fairhaven. A title that up until now he never heard in connection with his own name it would take some getting used to, being a peer of the realm.

***

He watched with a discerning eye as Acworth led the hostess about the ballroom. Danforth had trained him; his father had said. He was the Home Office's top decoder. It proved they were getting close. A flash of anger crossed his face, *Thomas and his bloody tricks*. Had he given his father what he wanted, he would have been able to ditch the old man. Now he was forced to wait, to do his father's bidding until he had what he wanted, whatever the hell that was. It would have been a hell site easier if he had more information to go on, he thought irritably.

Father had taken Thomas out of the picture; he was no longer any consequence. Plan A was over, but his father spent little time switching to Plan B. His amour? The little widow that appeared shortly after Thomas departed. She had set up residence at Danforth House, never went out during the day, arrived late for soirees, and left surprisingly early. What was she up to? Father wanted her, or least the information he felt she could provide.

He'd get the widow and the information too; if Acworth was here to stop him or found it first, he would take care of him as well. His father would want to know of Acworth's appearance in London. In the meantime, he felt sure it was best to keep an eye on Acworth; they may have a need to know his weaknesses.

Chapter Five

Cara reached the safety of her bedroom; her breathing was erratic, her heart still pounding. Her mind whirled with images of the most handsome man she'd ever seen. She could still feel his hard-muscular body pressed up against her.

What was the matter with her? She had barely touched the man! Still, she could not overlook the tidal wave of emotion that had strummed throughout her body from the very first. The heat. And when he spoke…oh Lord!

Cara paced her bedroom in a vain attempt to control the spiraling sensations. She hadn't wanted to go out tonight, the Duke of Greyley wasn't one of her marks; still, she had had to go. If there were repercussions from Sir Alfred, she needed time to prepare.

Unfortunately, Sir Alfred spoke of his loss. Fortunately, the story he told, whether he believed it or not, was that the culprit came in after he had fallen asleep. He had made no comment of being engaged in a conversation with Mrs. Black at any time throughout the evening.

Still, Cara had been decidedly tense all evening. Feeling as though she was being watched. The sensation was potent. Eerie. Just thinking about it sent chills down her spine. When she spied Sir Alfred coming toward her, she panicked. What if he knew? Losing herself in the throng of people she made her way to the door just short of a run.

Head down, she scurried toward the foyer, heart pounding wanting only to be away. Coming to an abrupt halt slamming into a barrier blocking her path… a very warm barrier. With strong hands that reached out to steady her.

A smell; fresh and clean, reminded her of the countryside around her beloved Wonderland. Hard, warm, and as sculpted like the finest of statues. Without seeing his face, she knew he would be handsome, his chest, as well as the rest of his body scant inches from hers, oozed masculinity. An air of danger, she had never yet met a man who could with one touch send her emotions flying; he was paradise and all things that went with it. Her mind screamed.

Danger! Stop this instant Caralyn! You cannot do this! You have a purpose; until it is completed there is no time for idiotic imaginings that stood little chance of becoming a reality.

Plopping onto the bed, an unladylike jounce that would have made both Becky and Robby proud, Cara hugged the down-stuffed satin pillow to her breast, trying to impede the unwanted aches in her heart and unwelcome thoughts in her head.

Two thousand pounds, the take on the last four jobs combined. The staff was paid, and more than ample stash was left; the mountain would continue to grow. There were seven jobs left, six of which she hoped to complete within the next fortnight. The seventh would be a little more difficult. If she could complete it at all…

Maxwell Liberton was currently out of the country. After making discrete inquiries, Cara knew Liberton had left almost two months prior, as to when he would be back, was anyone's guess.

She needed a break, a trip to Hyde Park or better yet a carriage ride into the country. A peaceful picnic, away from prying eyes… yes, much better. Forcing herself to undress, she climbed into bed for some much-needed rest.

"This is perfect. Is it not, Cara?" Becky scampered about arms spread wide drinking in the sunshine like a dark daisy. Robby was an extension of the bright rays. Laughing, playing in the same carefree manner as they did at Wonderland.

Even Rex seemed to relax. The constant holding true to proper decorum had taken its toll. Cara didn't think Rex realized it, however, even he, who has matured so much so rapidly, was more at ease bordering on carefree.

Cara's heart swelled, she wished they could stay longer. As it was, she had only a precious few hours. All too soon, she'd need to be back to work.

***

Roland walked through the open doors of Hatchard, it was a bright glorious day, as such, the doors were spread open allowing the gentle summer breeze to spread about the book-lined space. Making his way to the third row, just to the right of the entrance, he turned, walking to where the section on travel began. Quickly, he searched for the periodical mentioned in Thomas' message. Amazing how the man could be so crafty yet so simplistic in his choices.

It wasn't simplicity for which Thomas was famed; therefore, it stood to reason that it was Roland's extensive tutelage that enabled him to discern the hiding place so swiftly.

Still, he found it hard to believe that, with a little diligent work, someone else could not have decoded the missive. As far as he was concerned, this missive wasn't near the quality he remembered. The other messages he had found signed by various members of the home office were also coded therefore someone else had to have known how to use the code. Either that or Thomas himself wrote those letters to himself, which didn't make any sense. Why go to all the trouble of forging signatures and posting letters? On the other hand, why would anyone else know the codes? There were a lot of quirks that didn't make sense and each of them screamed for further investigation.

Thomas was an excellent teacher. Patient, clever and kind. Roland's mind once again turned to his charges. He could not believe the wicked things Mrs. Brown alleged, leaving the children to fend for themselves in utter seclusion for three years? He must find them. The sooner the better. Once he had the list, he would contact Beaumont, and then broaden his search for his charges.

That was another thing that didn't quite fit. Thomas was high up in the agency when Roland had left, still he would not have been entrusted with a list of agents, their assignments; such information was always divided, spread amongst the higher ranks of the organization to ensure safety. Each assignation was coded in the briefest communiqué possible, always placed with different people so that if the information should be needed, due to death of the Director, it could be found.

Nevertheless, no one aside from the Director himself should know the full whereabouts of all the agents at any time. Why did Thomas have the complete list? Did he keep his own personal record instead of destroying the information once it was coded, as was practice? He would have to demand that Beaumont tell him all he knew classified or not. He hated working half blind.

Spying the West Indies Travel Guide, Roland quickly looked around before taking it from it place on the shelf, over a month had gone by, would it still be here? Roland felt the front cover for any sign of a rise in the paper or an opening that may have previously contained such material as a missive. Nothing. Damn!

He flipped through the pages, nothing slipped from their grasp. Carefully, he caressed the back, no definite rise, but… there was a slit at the bottom of the back-page's binding that didn't look as if it should be there.

Roland smiled. He scanned the aisle before retrieving his dagger from its sheath in his Hessians.

Taking a deep breath, he carefully inserted the blade, running it to the top; detached, he peeled back the inner layer. Fastened to the layer was a piece of paper, an exact fit to the back cover, Thomas must have pilfered the magazine then put it back after inserting the paper, re-stitching it back to the binding. Clever. Original Thomas. So, if the way in which he concealed the information was Thomas-like then why were there so many other contrary factors?

He had to discover the truth. Something wasn't right, and damn, how he hated not having all the information. Taking the paper, now carefully folded, he placed in his coat pocket. Smoothing down the page, he placed the periodical back on the shelf, leaving as quietly as he entered.

Installed in his study a short while later, Roland grabbed his pen and scribbled a quick note to Beaumont. He rang for Dobson, his butler and all-around man of affairs. Dobson had been with him on many assignments, an excellent butler, though that wasn't his sole purpose.

Dobson was batman to his uncle when he had served his country twenty years earlier; remaining loyal to his uncle and later, Roland. He had traveled with Roland ever since; butler, valet, confidante, investigator and second, pledged to protect The Duke of Fairhaven and had done so many a time. Much of what he had learned came from Dobson.

Roland finished sealing the message just as Dobson arrived.

"Your Grace?"

"Deliver this to the Earl. Wait for a reply."

"Yes sir."

Dobson came forward, taking the letter in a flash that belied his years, he vacated the room, closing the door and once more shrouding Roland in privacy.

Removing the list from his jacket pocket, Roland smoothed the page on the desk. He browsed the words it contained.

At first glance no one would notice it contained secret information. Only someone with access to Thomas' previous tutelage, such as himself or the person to whom this missive was meant, could so easily break the code. Did

Thomas really fall so far that he had trained another person in the code? Roland had a tough time believing it.

Taking a sheet of vellum, Roland began to decipher the series of jumbled words, which to the untrained eye resembled a letter written at the hand of a madman. Roland smiled as he systematically counted out then wrote the third letter of each word. An anagram within and anagram. Good old Thomas. Why had he thought that this would not take him long to crack? True to form, this missive would take the remainder of the day.

As much as Roland couldn't afford the time it would take to decode the information, he would not be sorry for it; there was always a special sense of excitement that overcame him while he worked out every detail and the pride of accomplishment when the task at hand was completed, knew no bounds.

Even if he had known beforehand what that information should be, there was always the question as to if he was correct. Knowing this, he forced from his mind all thoughts that didn't pertain to the task. Thoughts of Thomas' odd behavior or Beaumont's neglected answers, of course, his charges, *ah the damnable disappearance of his charges*, all would have to wait. He would need his wits to ensure no mistakes. One miscount could destroy all his hard work; the hell of it was that he would never even know about the error. Roland sighed as he returned to the task at hand. The job needed to be completed before he met with Beaumont.

***

Cara was feeling rested. Even forty-eight hours out of the limelight of the ton was a blessing to one, not use to the pace. Night after night of balls and soirées had taken their toll. This little break was the medicine to cure her weakened focus.

Cara checked the nursery making sure all was aright with her brother and sisters. She would be isolated in the study for some time planning her next job and to ensure peace and quiet meant spending time with her siblings before she locked herself away.

"Cara!" Becky and Robby rushed toward Cara for an embrace.

"Goodness girls, you've had nothing but my full attention for the past while, as much as I enjoy your affection, I must say you are being a tad dramatic about the whole thing. Quite overdone. Makes one wonder if mayhap we should have skipped the trip to the theatre? You are far too adept at acting without encouragement."

The girls pulled back, identical horror-struck expressions lit their faces. Rex and Cara looked at one another nodding solemnly. Cara was the first to laugh.

"Oh Cara, you were only joking."

"Of course, imps, how could I restrict something that evidently has taught you so much?" Cara raised a brow and the girls dissolved into giggles.

"Are you going out tonight, Cara?"

"I'm afraid so, imps, I just stopped by on my way to the study. There are some things I must deal with before I get ready for the evening."

"You will tell us all about it, won't you?" the girls asked excitedly.

"Don't I always?"

The girls' pretty heads bobbed up and down, black curls bouncing about their cherub-like faces.

Rex stood, walked to the window and looked out; his hands embedded deep in his pockets. The sun kissed his hair causing blue hues to shimmer. Pushing the girls toward their studies, Cara silently made her way to Rex. Placing a hand on his shoulder, she waited for him to glance her way.

"Whatever is the matter, Rex?" she whispered.

"Just thinking."

"So, I gathered, what is it that has you so preoccupied?"

"I don't like it, Cara, you know that!" he hissed.

"Yes, Rex, I know. It cannot be helped. This whole conversation is getting a little old, don't you think? I've answered all your questions. Now please, for the love of God, just drop it."

Rex nodded then turned back to his desk. "One day Cara, I will not be too young to know the truth, like it or not you will tell me, or I will find out on my own." He sat, picking up his history book.

Yes, Rex, of that I have no doubt, but by then, it will cease to matter, Cara thought.

This would be the trickiest job she had ever contemplated pulling off. She searched high and low for information on Mr. Evan Stevens; she had come up empty-handed. He was a collector, and in certain circumstances she would have been able to use that to her advantage; apparently, according to Tibs, he was a collector of such objects no lady would be interested in.

She had only assumptions to go on that indicated he would be fascinated by an intimate meeting, that being he was a friend of her father's and most likely a rake of the lowest class, though Sir Alfred DuPont had proved her theory to have more than a few holes… she had lucked out with Sir Alfred, plain and simple.

The Duke of Huntington was a great initiation into the profession she had chosen, Sir William Bradmoor was just as demanding, but she garnered enough from the previous night to aid her; Viscount Morley was an insufferable bore, his interests in his current hobby, bottled ships, made him an easy mark.

What worried her was that one day, she would have to locate and open a safe. Picking the lock would pose no problem. Heaven knows she picked enough locks to get at the children when they were playing their games. She was very adept with her hairpins. Still, a little practice couldn't hurt.

Cara walked to the door, it locked from the inside. She would have to be on the outside to pick it. Mayhap it was best to try upstairs where Tibs would not be able to easily spy her kneeling before a locked door. A knock came on the door, putting an end to her musing. "Enter."

"Miss, while you were out, a gentleman dropped 'round. He left his card."

Was Cara mistaken or was Tibs' voice more frosty than usual?

"I would have given it to you earlier, but quite frankly, I didn't know if you wanted the children to be aware of the caller." Tibs handed Cara a small calling card neatly penned with the title 'The Earl of Beaumont'.

"Who is this man, Tibs?" Cara asked without looking up.

"I—"

"The truth if you please. I can tell by your tone you are acquainted with the man."

"I believe he and your father had some sort of relationship."

"When was he here last?"

Tibs looked thoughtful for a moment then said, "I believe he was here about a month before your father, ah…departed, Miss."

Cara took that piece of information and stored it away for later. She was about to excuse Tibs when he continued.

"Your father, Miss? He refused him admittance. I don't believe he sent around a note in response to the gentleman's card either. Though he may have delivered a message in person."

"Thank you Tibs. That will be all... Oh and Tibs? Don't say anything to the children, if he comes back when I am not here, they are not to meet, is that understood? Should you remember something else about the man, please let me know immediately."

Tibs nodded his agreement and left. Tapping the card against her index finger, Cara paced ...Beaumont? He wasn't one of the men mentioned in her father's correspondence, why would he come here? Why would he leave his card?

There was something Tibs was not telling her, she would have to question him further when she had a bit more time.

Cara headed to the library, finding a copy of Peerage she opened it. The binding groaned from too little use, after all this was a book intended to adorn everyone's, who was anyone, library but not used. Cara began searching the crisp pages for the Earl of Beaumont's family. Any information she could find was bound to be helpful; she would check the periodicals as well. On that thought, she made her way back the study.

Damn! It made no sense. What would this Beaumont character want with her father's children? How would he even know they were in residence? For that matter, how or why would someone of his ilk, even associate with her father? There was absolutely no information on him in the society pages.

The only thing Cara could think of was that their so-called guardian had sent him to check up on them, and if that was the case, she was right in telling Tibs that Beaumont should not meet the children. As soon as they had any sort of clarification on them, the lot of them would be packed off and sent back to The Gables, as much as she wanted to go home, now wasn't the time.

Shaking off the numerous questions, she focused on the job ahead nothing interferes, mayhap when she was finished and was ready to return to Wonderland, she would contact Beaumont and find out exactly what felt so suspicious about his visit.

Cara walked into her room. Taking the skeleton key from the pocket of her day dress, she placed it in the lock, no, no, no, this was not going to work. The other times she was confronted with a locked door, the door was locked by someone on the other side thus the key was removed, how was she going to pick a lock with the key plugging the bloody hole?

The door was out, now what? The trunk?

Perfect, Cara thought with a smile. Closing her bedroom door, she knelt beside the trunk, reaching behind she guided her hand sightlessly under her mattress until she felt the cool iron key. Good, it was still there. Rex hadn't found her hiding spot. Leaving the key where it was, she removed a hairpin, a couple of strands bounced free from their confinement, she pushed them unceremoniously behind her ear.

With ear pressed to the trunk, Cara shut her eyes, inserted the pin, moving it gently up and down back, forth until she'd slipped the tumblers. With a decidedly hushed click, the lock sprung.

She hadn't lost her touch. She doubted very much if she could lock it with her hairpins; promptly she decided that if she must break into a safe, she would simple close the door leaving it unlocked.

There were not as many people here as at the previous balls, to her, it was more than enough. Cara was having a hard time getting her mark alone. As she worked her way through the crowd, Cara stopped only when necessary, trying not to make herself too available to conversations. The hour was drawing close. Cara knew she would have to find a way to cross the bridge that impeded her. Still, she had no idea what interested Mr. Stevens.

Taking a champagne from the passing footman, Cara did what any other woman would do in her place, she took a fortifying sip, a deep breath, plunged forward right into Mr. Stevens.

Her hand jostled, the champagne slopped over the side onto Mr. Steven's evening jacket; gasping in horror, Cara said, "Oh, my. I am so sorry sir. I keep telling myself I have no place here. Are you alright? I do hope your jacket is not ruined. One moment. Hold this please, or what's left of it. I believe I have…oh yes, here it is right here."

Cara took her handkerchief, dabbing at Mr. Steven's sleeve, head down she tried to contain the chuckle. The man must think her absolutely mad. In truth mayhap she was. A small giggle escaped her; thankfully, Mr. Steven's mistook it for a cry and case of distraught nerves.

"There. There. Mrs. Black, is it? It is all right. Never fear, my dear. Here, let me take you away from this crush so that you may get yourself under control in private."

Cara ceased her caterwauling. Without lifting her head, she nodded her consent. Mr. Stevens took her hand and lead her from the room. Her periodic sniffs caused Mr. Stevens to place his hand over hers in a gesture of comfort.

If this side of him was any indication at all, Cara's hopes for a liaison were out the window.

All wasn't lost, Cara remembered their elderly gardener. He wasn't of Mr. Stevens' class, yet his temperament was the same; whenever Cara or one of the other children was hurt, he would babble and soothe. Uttering complete nonsense, anything to drown out the sound of the ensuing cries.

The closer Mr. Stevens got to the Ladies Retiring room, the more Cara sniveled, letting out the occasional muffled wail for good measure. True to form, Mr. Stevens walked eagerly, something told her he would have run, if possible, past the room down the long corridor to what Cara hoped was his office. "Where... Are... We... Going?" Cara said between sniffs.

Mr. Stevens patted her hand. "It's all right, child. I find a wee nip at a time like this quite the thing. Let's go somewhere more private; I'll leave the door ajar. All will be quite proper. Shhh."

Cara's head jerked. Head bowed, she followed obediently.

Once inside, Cara's mind worked frantically. How do you get such an upstanding gentleman to go against rules of propriety? The door needed to be closed. If it wasn't, anyone happening by could see him passed out or her removing the contents of the safe.

Quickly scanning the room, Cara left Mr. Stevens in favor of a spot next the window. Dropping her head into her hands, she let loose a howl so akin to a banshee, Mr. Clark would have been proud.

Flustered, Mr. Stevens' hurried footsteps sounded with an undeniable click as his heels hit the oak floorboards. Coming up behind, he stopped and with more force than necessary, solidly patted her back. Unaware, her head hit the window before she could brace herself.

She didn't have to feign the "ouch" as her forehead hit the pane, turning it to her advantage, she wailed even louder. It would have been funny to be able to see the look on Mr. Stevens face as he started spewing nonsense, anything to make her stop.

Worried someone might overhear the distraught woman, he strode to the other side of the room and closed the door. Cara's varying sniffs, moans, and banshee calls continued until a nerve-racked Mr. Stevens wrapped her hands around the glass.

She took a sip. "Thank you. You are so kind. Especially. After... After... What... I did to you. How countrified? I don't dare go back out there."

"Countrified? Whatever are you talking about, my dear? I have seen you at countless parties since the summer-season began. I have yet to see you behave undignified. No doubt you will be a paragon by the time the true season is upon us. You are being far too hard on yourself. It is the bad light. I keep telling Mrs. Stevens we need better chandeliers in the ballroom; so easy for one to take a misstep. Yes, it is quite all right, my dear, you simply lost your footing that is all. Do not fret any longer over the subject, that's it you just keep…"

Cara listened as he droned on. Keep talking, Mr. Stevens, I am sure you will tell me something I can use. Listening intently, every time it looked as though he would stop, Cara would sniff. Like oil to a lamp, Mr. Stevens would be fired up once more.

Normally, there would have been a danger of falling asleep. Her reading of Mr. Stevens's personality was right on the money, in fact, the more he talked, the more Cara stuffed the handkerchief in her mouth to keep from laughing aloud. Such a mixture of boyish enthusiasm and old age proprieties made for a humorous companion.

"Oh, dear Mr. Stevens, you are too kind. I hate to ask, but could I trouble for just a tad more, I feel I have myself quite under control but would like another before I must go out and face all those who might have seen my unseemly behavior."

Mr. Stevens rose, leaving his glass half-full on the table before her. Cara reached into her purse, extracted the vial, and quickly emptied the clear liquid into his drink. Resettling herself on the couch, Cara decided to throw caution to the wind.

"You mentioned collecting guns; is that a hobby en masse in the city?"

"I did?" His head snapped around, clearly shocked at the topic he had chosen to converse on.

"No doubt, I picked up on it because my late husband was a bit of a collector himself. I am afraid I do not know much about them, you named a double loader, is that correct? I must admit my curiosity has gotten the better of me. What did you mean by double loader?"

"Oh dear, I really shouldn't have said anything, it is not a proper tête-à-tête when one is in the company of such a fine lady."

Cara waved off his comment.

"Please sir, think nothing of it. I am not one to dwell on propriety. To be truthful, I don't think I would be able to forget such an exciting tidbit if I tried. Please may I see it?"

"Well…" He hesitated clearly torn between the urge to show off his new toy and the possible repercussions from indulging in such an event with a lady.

"I promise sir, I shall not mention our conversation to anyone. No one will ever know. And you will allay my curiosities."

"I suppose it couldn't hurt just to look."

Tossing back his head, Mr. Stevens finished the remainder of his drink in one gulp. A gentleman would never have downed that much at once. Cara hoped it was a sign of the havoc she'd played on his nervous system. Not long after, he opened the safe and retrieved a three-inch high red cedar box, resembling one of her father's cigar boxes.

"I keep most of my guns over the mantel in the Cigar Room. It was an additional parlor that I managed to coax from Mrs. Stevens when we first bought the town house years ago, this one, it is very precious to me, not to mention costly. I am quite proud to be the owner of such a fine piece of craftsmanship."

She stared at the pistol, wondering what on earth to say that would sound intelligent enough to keep the blasted man talking or, more to the point, drinking. Though he was a kindly man, he hadn't made a pass of any kind toward her, proving far more difficult than his lusty predecessors.

"I admit I know little of guns, sir, as I am an avid learner of all subjects so I must say this is a great treat." There, she managed to say something intelligent without actually commenting on the dreadful weapon. She gave him her best please tell me more look and was not disappointed when he started to speak.

"Yes. Yes. It was quite ingenious. My own personal design it took a fair amount of coin to bring about its existence. It is the only one of its kind thus far…" He prattled on about his hopes, dreams of the future seeing the pistol, his pistol, in the hands of any gentleman worth his salt as he helped himself to another drink.

Cara was seriously considering finding something with which to conk the man over the head with. Not that she wanted overmuch to hurt the fellow, but he was taking so dreadfully long to pass out, and she was impatient to go about her business. Listening about the Stevens' Double Loader was not in her plans for the evening.

73

She had to add another batch of draught to his brandy and soon.

Mr. Stevens set down his drink, giving in to a silent plea; he removed the pistol from its haven. He was a man in love. Holding it. Caressing it. Cara suppressed a shudder. She hated weapons; guns in the hands of anyone could do such great harm. Guns in the hands of idiots…frankly, there were too many idiots.

Placing herself between Mr. Stevens and his drink, she opened the vial dumping the contents into the glass; if this didn't knock him out, she might very well be forced to hit him over the head with his own gun.

Bucking up her courage, she turned, glass in hand. "Mr. Stevens, sir, you have been so kind to me. Do you think I might be able to hold it? That is, of course, if it is safe." She prayed it would work.

"Of course, it is safe, my dear, I haven't had the chance for an alchemist to prepare a combustible ball to fit the chamber. Not something one would normally show a woman, but I am inspired by your interest. Please be my guest. Hold it. Feel its weight in your palm. Precious is steady. Balanced to perfection."

Placing her hands around the cold metal of the pistol, she focused on the pearl-encrusted handle as Mr. Stevens sipped and watched, watched and sipped. *That's right sir, just keep drinking.*

Cara didn't know how much time had gone by when finally, Mr. Stevens made his way to the settee, settled down, his eyes drifted closed before she could count ten; she was hit with the sudden feeling of despair that she may have given him too much. Quickly, she offered up a prayer that he would wake hale and hearty on the morrow, if not sooner.

Putting "precious" delicately back into its case, not knowing whether to trust the cold metal. Upon closing the box, she tenderly removed Mr. Stevens' cravat, taking both she walked to the safe.

She grabbed the cash. As always, since finding the first document with her father's name, she searched for anything that resembled the previous three. Triumphant, she found the small piece of paper tucked inside a ledger at the back of the safe.

Closing the scarf up nice and tight, she made her way to the door. She was about to turn the knob when she heard the distinct sound of footsteps about the hall. The sound wasn't far away, with every beat of her heart, it was getting louder. Louder meant closer. There was only one room at the end of the long corridor. It was the very same room in which she now stood. *Damnation, it looked as though she were going to have to purchase a new cloak on the morrow.*

Spinning on her heel, she made her way quietly to the window, releasing the latch she hitched up her skirts, crinolines and all above her knee, she stuck her stocking-clad foot through the opening. Like a thief in the night, which in fact she was, ironic, she thought with a smile. She really was getting quite good. Now just one more leg and she'd be out of sight before anyone entered.

Chapter Six

It was well on its way to the witching hour. All of London, or at the least the elite, was in full swing. People entering and exiting one soirée after another on their way to see and be seen. Roland had never particularly cared for the ins and outs of his stature nonetheless; right now, it suited his purposes to see.

He had spent the better part of the night ensconced in a private meeting with Beaumont.

Beaumont had stopped by Thomas' townhouse. A rather crusty butler, one of whom he had seen many times before with Thomas, a trained member of the Organization, that tidbit he had remembered, stated there was no one home at present. The statement could mean the occupants were in fact out, where he hadn't a clue, or they were avoiding callers. Neither of which made his life any simpler.

While Beaumont had tried to take care of the posing problems with his charges, he spent the rest of the day and the better part of the evening decoding Thomas' list.

The list made not one lick of sense. Names contained within were not of active agents. Enemy spies would determine the information was fraudulent. Quickly. Was Thomas buying time?

Although a spy may realize he or she did not carry the all-important list, it would take a little time to deduce. Even for someone as trained as Roland, it had taken nearly six solid hours. Would the decoder find what Roland had? If not, how much time would it take before that was determined? Thomas had to have been vying for time. Roland spotted the connection right away. The names enclosed matched some of the members of the Organization. Names seen previously on letters sent to Thomas.

Puzzling indeed. It merely raised additional questions. He'd had a chance to decode the messages to Thomas; even decoded they were nothing but babble. Mystery surrounded those damn letters as well.

How were that many people able to code when the Organization employed few? The answer was simple there isn't. Therefore, Thomas must have sent those missives to himself. Why? For what, purpose?

Beaumont could not or would not shed any light on the matter. Roland was pissed. They couldn't classify his assignment complete. If they did, they were fools! Roland knew Thomas in a way few people did. And what he knew told him there was more.

Roland's mind whirled. The most resent happening, connecting those same names was the thefts. Whether it would be sanctioned or not he would find out. He was a peer of the realm. About bloody time that started working in his favor.

Striking out from the Cock and Crow headed a quick stop at his townhouse for a change and a word with Dobson sent him immediately to the only gathering being held by someone related to the Home Office.

Mr. Evan Stevens, Esquire.

Various members of society strutted and preened for the title of head cock or hen. Doing his duty, he conversed, skirting details regarding his time in the Colonies and veering, diplomatically, to safer topics like the weather. He was very adept at avoiding issues that were better left alone. Right now, his ties to the Organization were one of those issues. People could suspect as much as they liked but until there was concrete evidence, he had the upper hand.

Standing on the terrace, Roland poured over his thoughts everything a jumble of confusion. Briefly, he reflected about the people with whom he had met none of them struck him as the thief. Oh, they were crafty and cunning, for that were the way of the world. Given another set of circumstances, he didn't doubt any number of them could be his thief. Just not this time… He had an aptitude for reading people, which was dead on the money. It had had to be.

Nothing made sense. He was sure that if the thief were out tonight, he would have been able to spot him, however, he hadn't.

Leaving the vine-covered terrace, he walked amongst the gardens. The cloud covered moon cast a soft glow. The path led throughout flower and yew lined walkways. Designed for comfort, the sweet scent wrapped around him easing some of the tension of the last forty-eight hours.

The cloud moved and the moon glinted for but an instant on a flamboyant marble cherub standing in the center of an open giant clamshell; his arm held a small urn tilted at a forty-five-degree angle gently dribbling water into the shell below.

Roland stood watching the water trickle, the soft light of the moon making it sparkle. He heard the soft fall of a footstep on the lawn. It could have been any number of lovers taking advantage of the foliage. Though if that were the case, he would have heard the footsteps one after the other. He didn't.

Making his way from the fountain, Roland silently sped around to the back of the mansion. He didn't know what led him to that exact location but the tightening in his gut told him mayhap he hadn't missed his thief after all. Air caught in his lungs as he spied a long shapely leg resting on the ground below a window. The owner of the leg had yet to appear. Still, there was no mistaking it. His thief was a woman.

The familiar tightening of his loins told him more than any investigation ever could.

The Widow. She had affected him like no other. It was searing, immediate. And it was happening again. Staying close to the wall, Roland quickly made his way to the window. He arrived just as the second portion of her lowered itself through the window.

Seizing her wrist, he spun her around facing him, back to the wall. For a second, she was too startled to fight but only for a second; when she did, he was ready. Grasping her other wrist, he pulled her arms high above her head; pushing in close, he pinned her to the wall. Anger flared in her eyes; he could tell the exact moment that she was going to scream; he allowed no sound to escape her mouth; his lips came down ravishingly to take possession of hers.

Cara could no longer think; the most intense heat surrounded her. Fire erupted in her abdomen, spiraled throughout her whole being. She was light-headed; her heart was beating faster than a stampede of wild elephants.

His breath was warm. His soft lips belied the hardness of the body pressing against her. She should push him away. She should slap him. She really should, and yet, all she wanted to do was move closer melting into his warmth letting the flames devour her. His tongue passed by her lips. Cara gasped, and then his tongue was in her mouth; she could taste him. His taste was a mix of champagne and cigarillos, musky and sweet, utterly male.

Cautiously, Cara mimicked him, exploring as deeply as he. She felt him groan more than hearing it, for it was quite possible he made no outward sound at all.

The hue and cry were raised from the other side of the window, as quickly as his lips had captured hers, he released her. Cara's head was still spiraling when he hauled her through the shadows toward the cover of the trees. Helplessly, she followed.

Vaguely, she noted how silent he moved. In a league of a predator, a black panther, stalking his prey soundless and swift. Apprehension skittered down her spine. It had nothing to do with her fear or the adventure and everything to do with the man who held her captive.

For the sake of preservation, Cara followed silently, it wasn't that she had instincts or training for this sort of thing; thankfully her slippered feet made not a sound as she tried to keep up.

Who was he? Her savior, her knight in shining armor? Surely if he suspected anything untoward, he would have turned her over to the bellowing footman.

He hadn't.

The further away from the house lights, the less Cara could see. She wished she could rip off the veil covering her face; the moonlight wasn't strong enough to allow her to see where she placed her feet, let alone the surrounding area. She hated the fact that she would have to rely on someone other than herself. A stranger. Cara listened to the distant sounds trying to make out whether they were calling for the watch. It was hopeless. She could neither hear, nor see adequately.

She had vacated before she was seen, therefore, the footman most likely assumed his master was ill when he would not awaken. Possibly calling for the aid of a doctor.

Hastily, she replayed the events of the evening. Did she leave any tracks quickly detectable? Aside from the open window... *Think.* Mr. Stevens' missing cravat, that's one they were sure to notice but hopefully, they would be too intent on reviving the man to consider that piece of evidence.

Of course, once his safe was opened the black rose would be seen, the cash missing, would someone open it? No. It would be safe until Mr. Stevens was up... she hoped.

Ares pulled her through a gate at the rear of the property. Noiselessly, he closed it behind them. They were in an alley. There were cobblestones beneath her feet, and she could make out the distant orbs of light cast off by the lanterns that lined the main thoroughfare.

Cara cleared her mind of past dilemmas she could do nothing about and concentrated on the present. She was with a man she did not know, could not trust. And they had gone far enough. Reaching the end of the alley, they rounded the corner; Cara dug her tiny feet into the cobbles.

If she thought to stop him, she was mistaken. However, suddenly having his companion become a dead weight did force him to slow his pace. She planted her feet once more and pulled with all her might. Finally, he stopped.

Catching her breath, she tilted her chin and stated as chillingly as she could muster. "As invigorating as that little scene was, Sir, I must excuse myself from the next act. You have managed to spirit me away from a stage in which I—"

"Where you were sneaking through a window?" He finished accusingly.

"I wasn't! I was simply… I needed a bit of fresh air."

Wishing she could see his face better, she rallied her thoughts to reply when he spoke, his voice icier than hers.

"Is that the best you can do? I would have thought someone of your talent, training, would have invented a more plausible excuse then lack of fresh air."

Cara stamped her foot; what in the name of Venus was he talking about? Someone of my talent?

"I haven't a clue what it is you're talking about. For all I know you could have pulled me through that window just so you could have your way with me."

A bark of incredulous laughter erupted from him.

"You're getting better, love, nevertheless, I still don't buy it. You know full well you were well and truly out of that window before I detained you."

"I know no such thing!" Cara hissed.

"Don't you?"

Cara could just imagine the cock of an arrogant brow; she didn't know how she could see it with such clarity in her mind, but she did. Then a faint memory, slight though it was, plagued her.

"I know you!" It came out like an accusation when in truth it was nothing of the sort.

"Ah, Love, you do remember. I am flattered indeed. I knew you could not forget me."

"Now what in Hades are you talking about?"

This time he did chuckle. Holding her steady with one hand his other came up, his thumb smoothed over her recently kissed lips. She forced herself to step back when everything in her urged her to move forward. His features hardened. His hand dropped away. Cara suffered the loss. What she wouldn't give to be able to explore him further. To have him explore her, touch her.

"Come." His terse demand cooled her ardor.

"I will not! I thank you, Sir, for untimely assistance. But I fear the night is at an end. I am fatigued. I'll return for my coach."

"No. You will come. Now. On your own accord or I will carry you. Make no mistake in this, widow. Time is wasting; if you are so tired then come."

"You insidious oaf, I tell you I will not go! You have no right! Damn you! Unhand me this instant!"

He shook his head.

Keeping the restraining hand on her wrist, he placed her hand in the crook of his elbow, brought the other down on top, securing it there. Fuming, Cara forced herself to plan an escape. Best follow now, meekly, hoping that before they had gone too far, he would drop his guard.

In submissive silence, Cara walked beside her captor. Any passer-by would think nothing of the seemingly casual stroll; Cara didn't fool herself into thinking she was free to walk away.

Silence surrounded, darkness closed in, as they left the main roadways of fashionable London. Where was he taking her? She trembled as he led her deeper into the darkened alleyways. Remembering the uneasy feeling that came over her when Daniels had taken her to Mim's Apothecary. In the dark areas such as that would be even worse, fear gripped her overriding her silence.

"Stop. Wait. Please. Where are you taking me?" She hated the begging.

"Shhh." It was meant not only as a command but as a form of comfort as well. Cara shuddered. Still frightened, her temper ignited.

"No! I have been cooperative. I don't know who you are or where you are taking me. I have behaved a far sight more honorable than you."

"I said be quiet. I will tell you everything when we are off these streets. It is not safe to stand about yowling like a wet cat."

Cara didn't care for the analogy, but she kept silent. He had to stop eventually. He was right. If the foul-smelling refuse was any indication, this was not an area to be in longer than necessary.

Thankfully, aside from dodging the occasional man too heavy in his cups or sporadic guffaws of shadowed bodies huddled in nondescript recesses, they encountered no trouble. Her stomach churned at the stench, she was thankful for the veil that covered her face keeping her identity a secret, shutting out all save the shadows.

It was getting late, Daniels would be worried, her feet were sore from the cobbles, and wet with God knew what. Compiling her list of woes Cara felt justified for her dreadful temper.

They came to a halt in front of a darkened doorway. She could tell they were about to enter the back door of some establishment. A bawdy house or a pub, most like; that knowledge did nothing to ease her tension. The odor of smoke, urine and alcohol took precedence. Lewd calls, squeals and giggles made her feel uncomfortable. She moved closer to tall muscular warmth, which for now was her protection. His arm came, tightened around her oddly making her feel safe.

There was no sign of light as her companion steered her safely to a door thirteen paces down. Cara heard the man yank on the handle opening the door before she was propelled forward in the darkened room. It was tiring not being able to see. She was at an enormous disadvantage, for even if she could escape, which way did she go?

She stood listening to his footfalls about the room; he was quiet for a man of his size. Cara heard a scratch and the distinct smell of sulfur before a light flared to life. Silhouetted, the combination of lantern and veil made him appear more Lucifer than Ares. Dark, mysterious, dangerous. How could one look cause Cara's heart to hammer? She couldn't see him, but the brief look of days ago was etched in her mind. He had taken the place of her faceless knight in her dreams. But he was no knight.

"Why am I here?" Cara demanded with enough frost in her voice anyone should have scattered to do her bidding.

"Lift your veil," he ordered with the same chill.

"I don't think so."

"You will. For now, just sit." He pulled out one of the well-worn chairs from under the table.

Cara stared at the chair. Her eyes shifted to the table, back down. Then as if it hit her all at once, she looked about the room. There was no bed. It seemed strange since she was sure they had entered some sort of tavern. At least she knew she hadn't been brought here so that he could have his wicked way with her.

She didn't know exactly how she felt about that. She should be happy. She should be relieved. She wasn't. Amongst all the emotions running full tilt through her, happiness wasn't one of them. *Get a hold of yourself.* Maintain control; if that didn't work, she could always smash him over his arrogant head. Gently.

"Don't even think it. Now come. Sit. You will not be going anywhere just yet, my dear."

Cara glared at him through her veil. Damn the man and his insight! Slowly, she made her way to the chair, sitting she fluffed her skirts about to rally her defenses. It was bad enough when she thought he might try to take advantage of her but with no bed in sight that could not possibly be the case. There was only one thing Cara could think of and suddenly, she felt sick to her stomach.

***

Roland watched as she seated herself with stylish precision. He sensed she wasn't as collected as she would like him to believe. Good. He wanted her on edge. If he had ever learned one thing from being in the field, it was to gain the upper hand and keep it. The simplest way was to keep your opponent off guard. Saints! The way his body responded to her; she could have the upper hand if she wanted.

Yet another clue she was not the widow she claimed to be, for naught but a virgin would be so naïve as to not know her own power and how to use it. Roland waited for her to comply with his first command; after several seconds, he repeated the order.

***

Time passed slowly; Cara heard the words, frantically wondering if there was any way to keep identity a secret. Unfortunately, she could not think of a single thing. She was caught. Thousands of times she had rehearsed the dangers involved in such an undertaking. Still, it didn't mean she was prepared for the reality. Slowly, she removed the hatpins and one by one set them on the table. Lifting the veil off her head, she placed the hat on the table as well. Tilting her chin, she forced herself to look straight into his eyes.

"Well?"

"That's much better. Thank you. One hates having a conversation with a companion he cannot see."

"Conversation?" Cara's replied haughtily as her body tensed even more. She pinned him with stormy eyes.

"Don't you mean interrogation? I have been brought here against my will."

"You have been brought here so we can discuss your recent activities and come to some arrangement."

"I haven't a clue what you are referring to, sir. As I believe I told you back at The Stevens' residence. You have made a dreadful error. One I am sure you will want to correct immediately by escorting me back to my carriage."

"Mistake? No. As to going back, I shall take you myself, *Dear Widow*, but not…just yet. You see there are some very important answers I need. They involve a few papers, documents if you will; sensitive documents to be exact; you my dear have them. I want them."

Cara placed her trembling hands on her lap. Sensitive documents? He must mean her father's promissory notes. Why would he want those? She was about to question him when he continued.

"No bother denying it. I am one of the best, and you my dear are very readable. Yes, you have what I need. So, what do you say?"

"You're a bloody bastard!"

"Uh, uh… no name calling, our association will run much smoother if you accept that your fate, as well as your immediate future rests entirely in my hands."

Cara slumped back in her chair. What was she going to do? What did he want of her? If she was well and truly caught, why did he bring her here instead of Bow Street? There was no way out. She had to comply, if only to buy time. The outcome may depend on it. She was still running over the pros and cons, so engrossed in her thoughts that when spoke his voice startled her.

"Your name?"

That she could answer. "Mrs. Rose Black," she said neutrally.

"So, you are a widow?"

She swallowed, wetting her bottom lip, "Yes."

Though he didn't believe her, he was willing to let it go; noticeably her real name would be of little importance at this juncture.

"How many thefts have you committed?"

"Five, including tonight's."

Roland watched carefully reading movements and facial expressions as he questioned her. She was quite easy to read with her veil off for even though her eyes were shrouded in darkness, her body language suggested her nervousness. Swallowing before speaking, pointed answers, hands hidden beneath the table. She was scared but she was telling the truth, or at least part of it. Five thefts. That meant she had started when Beaumont had guessed. What possible ties to the organization could this woman have? What possible ties to the French? Her tone contained no foreign accent. Who was this mysterious woman?

"What did you take?"

"Only what is mine by right," came her simple reply.

"Yours? How so?"

"I will not answer that Sir. I cannot. You could not possibly understand the situation I face."

"You'd be surprised, my dear Rose, just what I can comprehend. But unless it becomes necessary, I will not press for your reasons. I must ask to see what you scurried away with tonight, and you will need to show me what you had obtained previously. Also, what you may acquire, in the future, that is until you, obtain the information I seek."

"What information do you seek?"

"That, Madam, is none of your concern."

"How can it not concern me? You tell me I must show you my gains, yet you do not tell me why. What word do I have that once I show, you will not slit my throat, leave me in a gutter? You are obviously not from bow street, or you would have turned me in already!"

Roland burst out laughing. What a vivid imagination! Her eyes squinted at him from across the table. Smothering a chuckle, he plunged ahead.

"Madam, allow me to introduce myself. Fairhaven. At your service… I am worth more than your spoils; the crown values me."

"I see no point in turning you in, what you have taken has hurt no one and although I am a member of peerage, I too feel a lot of them have more than they need. So if you can help me…" He let her digest that information before continuing. "As for leaving you in the gutter, well that option is still open for discussion; I fear I would not be the one to wield the knife, trifle messy, Lord Dobson, that's my valet, would tear me limb from limb; he so detests it when I come home covered in blood. Has a hell of a time cleaning it up." He shook his lowered head somberly.

Cara picked up her hat and flung it at him; hatpins fell to the floor with little clinks. It would have been nice to have something heavier to hurl at the bastard. Making fun of her. So, what if he worked for the crown; that didn't mean he wasn't a killer. And Fairhaven, what kind of name was that?

Deep down Cara knew he wasn't a murderer. For some odd reason, she trusted him. Getting up she began to pace the room. Running off in her mind, every foul word she'd ever heard to calm down. While bloody Fairhaven sat there laughing at her stress; "fair my ass". She didn't realize until his laughter doubled that she had said the last out loud.

Tears trickled from Roland's eyes, smoothing out the crumpled hat he set it neatly on the table. He could not remember when someone had made him laugh; she was succeeding at every turn, not only that, for the first time in a long time he felt human.

It was a glorious feeling.

Previously, he worked without emotions. Emotions hindered one's ability to do one's job. It endangered lives, his and countless others. He was finding it difficult to maintain a detached air in the face of such candidness.

"Rose. Calm down. Let me put it this way. If what you are doing is so important someone else must be involved. No, don't deny it. I won't even ask for whom, you need these things. I am quite sure by this brief conversation, I can safely say there is no possible way you are working against your country."

"You can't possibly have ascertained that in this short time? No one is that good Sir!"

"So, you are working against your country?" He raised a knowing brow.

"Stop putting words in my mouth! That's not what I meant; you well know it!"

"Well?"

"Well, what, damn you?"

"Are you working against your country?"

"Oh, for the love of St. Peter. No!"

"Good. Then I see no reason why we cannot work together."

86

"You don't? I do. You have given me little information, aside from your name, why should I trust you?"

Roland placed a hand over his heart feigning injury. "I'm wounded. Truly I am."

"Bastard."

"There's that name calling again. I thought we were over that?"

Cara huffed, pacing the room like a caged tiger, when in fact she was more like a caged kitten, waiting to be devoured by a tiger. Through gritted teeth she ground out, "fine".

"That's better. And for the record, I'm not."

"Not what?"

"A bastard; my parents were married upon my conception."

Cara made a sound akin to a ferocious purr and Roland laughed again.

"Now this really will go faster if you sit and listen, then I can get you safely back to your carriage. You're tired, I'm tired…it really would be for the best, come on, Rose, sit down. I promise to be less painful than Bow Street."

Knowing she had little choice, resignedly Cara walked back to the table; sighing she looked him in the eyes, waited for her newly appointed boss to finish.

***

Cara regarded the elaborate gathering, trying to follow the snippets of conversations going on about her, yet concentration was impossible. All she could think about was the deal she had made with the Devil the night before. She gave up listening to the ebb and flow of discourse from those around her. No longer offering simplistic responses to remarks directed her way her mind returned to the events of the previous evening.

Several hours had passed since she and Fairhaven had parted, in that expanse of time, the world, as she knew it, had tipped off its axis. Even the floor seemed to tilt slightly as everything shifted, she had to fight the impulse to grasp the nearest potted palm to keep from losing her balance.

Nothing was the same.

With his ultimatum of prison or country in her mind, Cara tried to keep hold of the only thing she really had any influence over anymore. Herself. Her mission. Her family. All because of the pact she had made with the Devil.

Fairhaven stood across the room; subtly, he tipped his flute toward her. Cara tried unsuccessfully to stop the immediate fluttering of her stomach, a response she was coming to associate with the Devil himself; she gave a tight-lipped smile, a brief nod in acknowledgement. Anything more would not do, for they had not been formally introduced.

**

Just look at him, so smug. Damn him, if it wasn't for the preservation of her family she would not be in this mess. Not that she wished ill on her family in any way, shape, or form. So, in essence he really did have her where he wanted her. Curse his eyes! The one fact that had made Cara smile was that he had yet to ascertain her identity; hopefully, if she played the few cards he handed her, in the correct order, he never would.

She would do as asked, serve him and her country, even if she didn't the how or why. It mattered little at this point anyway. She would see he'd have no reason to investigate her background. All he wanted was a chance to read whatever documents she could remove from the safes, well not all documents apparently… only the one concerning her father's gaming debts. What he wanted with those was a mystery but so long as he stayed true to his word, allowing her to keep her hard-earned spoils, she would not balk. After all, all she really needed was the money, now that she had recovered the deed to Wonderland.

Convincing him anything she removed could not affect her country had been fruitless. She wasn't a trader, she wasn't committing treasonous acts against the crown, she wasn't selling information to foreign governments, she was only a small-time thief, and in the grand scheme of things it really wasn't all that much. Her twisted thinking appeased her aching conscience. Resigned, Cara vowed she would do this, the only other choice was Bow Street.

Time to work. Spotting her quarry, the roly-poly Sir Jacob Smythe. Straightening her spine and steeling her nerves she left the group of acquaintances, maintaining polite conversation along the way, as she nonchalantly intercepted her unknowing mark.

Roland watched as Rose made her way around the room, she was attired in a black velvet gown, a few years out of date; the cut left little to the imagination. The tops of her ample breasts looked as though they would spill out of their confines at any moment, his mouth watered as an uncontrollable feeling twisted his insides. Her veiled head gave an air of mystery rather than sorrow, her plump luscious lips were an allure for any man with a breath left in his body.

. Roland had watched as Sir Jacob eyed the mysterious beauty all night like she was a stack of bonbons meant to be devoured. The thought rankled. He knew this was what Rose wanted, no, needed to portray if she was to continue succeeding. Knowing this didn't calm him one wit.

He was glad for her veiled face; for they kept from sight her dark stormy eyes and beautifully contoured face that called to him like a siren. He had vowed the night before to take a better look in the daylight. Somehow, he didn't think she would be any less alluring.

Watching her work, he was surprised at the amount of faith he had in her abilities. Automatically, he knew she would be successful. Probably in record time too, that thought brought a smile to his lips. Who ever thought the new improved Duke of Fairhaven would happily aid and abet a known criminal? At least he now had permission from the organization.

When he conveyed his plan to Beaumont, his superior had been less than thrilled.

Come dawn, a sure sign that he was up the better part of the night thinking about Roland's idea, Beaumont sent word he should proceed. Anything for King and Country…

Watching Mrs. Rose Black work, he had to admit, she was good. He didn't believe for one minute that she'd given him or anyone else for that matter her real name or status, but it made little difference. He needed her, or more specifically the papers she lifted from her marks, hopefully it would shed light on so many of his questions. *By the Grace of God, I'll clear Thomas' name,* he declared silently.

He didn't know what it would be like to be guardian of small children. At some point in time those same children would be old enough to venture out into the hungry masses of the ton. When that happened having a name, they could be proud, a name untarnished by treasonous acts would be imperative. Rumors could follow a person and their children forever.

Three years; still there were whispers of his escapades; his less than pristine conduct none of which would be as bad as treason. His aunt and uncle had to endure worse. He had taken Beaumont up on his offer and left these shores all those years ago. They had remained listening to the tales of his debauchery on every wagging tongue.

He had to plan for the future. He may not have liked the idea of Thomas leaving him in charge but now that he had little choice, he would do his damnedest to ensure no breath of scandal would touch them.

And where in the hell were his charges? The card Beaumont left when he called around had been ignored. No reply sent. *Well, they would not ignore him.* For on the morrow the Duke of Fairhaven would assume his rightful place at Danforth Manor.

Rose's hand gently brushed Sir Jacob's arm. Taking it, he kissed her palm, placed it in the crook of his arm, and led her out of the room. As Roland edged closer, he heard false laughter as they rounded the bend. Lingering long enough to hear a door open and close, he slowly ventured down the same hall.

Counting off the paces, he listened carefully at each closed door for the sound of Rose's voice. Reaching the end of the hall, he made his way back to the front foyer where collecting his cloak and hat from the eager butler, he made his way out into the night.

Roland waited for the door to shut firmly behind him before veering sharply to the right. Silently, he made his way around the massive dark red brick structure, which was the Baron's London home. Excessively overdone, like so many of the lower peerage up-starts, his place screamed money, announcing to the world at large that he was worthy of any and all companionship. It was enough to make one sick.

He paced out the approximate footage, running parallel with the interior foyer and corridor running past the exceedingly rare main floor ballroom. A tribute no doubt to the Baron's very hefty late wife enabling her to entertain without having to climb the stairs.

An answer to why the Baron had sired no legitimate offspring. In all likelihood, his wife could not make it to the bedchamber on the second floor.

The Baron himself was no better than other previous members of the Organization. He had let himself go. One of the worst, Roland recollected. Anyone spying on him would easily liken him to an overcooked, brightly colored Easter egg.

Chapter Seven

Lights had yet to illuminate any of the windows. Praising himself for his foresight, Roland counted off six of the eight windows, most rooms being equipped with at least two separate panes. He parked his body to the left of the sixth. Blocking out all other sounds, he homed in on the seductive timber of Rose's voice.

She was something.

She could lead a battalion of men to their graves with nothing more than a look. He could attest to her looks, but her smiles... What would it be like to see her smile? Honestly. Her smiles were strained, rehearsed. As if terrified to let her guard down.

He had yet to see her really smile, though he guessed it would hold a sense of mischief and pride.

What he wouldn't give to see her eyes, the eyes told a lot. He was sure hers would speak volumes.

Remembering the one brief sincere smile she had graced him with, only fueled his determination to discover more. Too bad he conceded to her request not to accompany her to her carriage. For him it was a missed opportunity. For her it was yet another sign she had something to hide.

Tonight, he would see her carriage. He would finally find out the person inside the Rose Black guise. He didn't know why it was so important, as he mentioned, it mattered little to job at hand.

She wrongly assumed that once the job was over, he would allow her to go on as before; unfortunately, he couldn't. He wanted to get the chance to know the mysterious woman who set his loins on fire with a simple word and a brief touch.

After thirty minutes of listening to Rose prattle on about this and that stroking the man's insufferable ego, all was quiet. Roland, normally a cool-headed quick-thinking agent, trained for the most impossible of situations contemplated killing the bloody victim as Rose lavished her attentions on him. She was damn good for a virgin. Roland had another wayward thought. Just where and how did she glean her experience? With a vile oath, he left the window and rounded the front of the house to locate and install himself in Rose's carriage before he made himself a candidate for bedlam.

Now, which one was hers?

Cara listened intently for any sound in the hall; making sure, the coast was clear, she slipped out and silently closed the door. Stopping by the ballroom in search of her boss, she used the term loosely, took only a second. Much taller than most, he would have been easy to spot, even without the flutter in Cara's stomach. No flutter. He was gone.

"Your wrap, Madam?" With a nod, the butler turned to retrieve her cloak. Speaking briefly in hushed tones to the waiting footman who promptly left to get Daniels, he handed her the wrap. Cara thanked him before descending the front steps with the aid of the waiting footman.

Daniels, hat pulled down low, stayed in the driver's box, while the footman hurried her inside. The footman closed the door; the carriage rattled as it pulled out of the drive all before Cara managed to seat herself. What was the blasted hurry?

Trying to set herself to rights in the darkness, she fluffed her skirts and removed her veil, setting it aside. Stretching out her legs in front of her, she smoothed her wrinkled gown. Tibs would have a fit if she appeared at the door like a windblown waif.

Her toes connected with something across from her and an all too familiar flutter in her stomach brought with it a certain amount of terror. What the tarnation? Opening the curtain, a crack hoping there would be enough light to aid her, she peered across the darkened expanse of the interior.

Sure enough, there slumped in the corner, was the exceptionally large, very sculpted, sleeping body. What the hell was he doing in her carriage and how the hell did he find it. Frickin' spies, she hoped the carriage was the only thing he managed to find out. *The nerve!*

It was a good thing they had not taken the Danforth carriage, if they had, the jig would have been up.

So, he found a way to get his answers tonight, maybe he didn't trust she would be found on the morrow, but she had promised she would come by and show him everything.

The blasted man sought her out to question her and couldn't even stay awake to do so. She ought to hold back all information she gleaned when the conceited oaf awakens. It would serve him right.

As the carriage turned out on the main thoroughfare, Cara snapped closed the curtain taking a little of her frustration out on the velvet swatch while she debated the wisest course of action. Should she awaken the beast? Or let him slumber?

The two ideas warred with each other as Cara silently waited for the outcome. She would like him to answer how he determined which carriage was hers? He didn't know her real name so therefore, one would assume he would not know her conveyance. The man had some answering to do when he awoke.

Sticking out her foot, Cara nudged his leg with the toe of her slipper. When nothing happened, she pushed again a little harder. Still, not so much as a snore. Cara shrugged her delicate shoulders; with a small chuckle she thought it really was too bad she didn't have another rose in her possession. She would stick it in his lapel right before she got home, then… then what? She didn't even have the man's direction.

Speaking of home, they should be getting close. The coach should be slowing down; instead, it seemed to be picking up speed. Cara lifted the curtain to peep out the window, she could no longer see the lights surrounding Carlton Lane, frowning she worried her lower lip. Something wasn't right.

Hoping for an optimistic outcome, Cara prayed Fairhaven had simply given Daniels other instructions. If that were the case, she would have to wake the bloody nuisance to determine their destination.

Cara drew her foot back and kicked for all she was worth. Still nothing happened. Jumping up, she stepped across the small aisle, placed her hand on the back of his seat. Leaning over the body, she patted his cheeks, each pat becoming more of a slap, as desperation set in, Cara began shoving at his chest. Nothing. Absolutely nothing.

Cara quickly removed her glove, letting it fall where it may; she pressed her naked fingertips to Fairhaven's mouth. There was the slightest wisp of warm air passing the otherwise stationary lips. Cara sighed, pent up relief flooded through for a moment, at least he wasn't dead. Running her hand over the contours of his handsome face, Cara worked her way, slowly, to his forehead. She could feel the signs of a bump covered with a sticky residue, which she could only assume, due to the lack of light in the carriage, was blood.

Someone had hit him! Hard! That was it, alive or not, Cara couldn't help herself—she screamed.

At the first chord, the carriage lurched forward unencumbered by heavy London traffic, throwing Cara down on top of Fairhaven. Their bodies were joined from the thighs up. At this angle, Cara's head was level with Fairhaven's, as thoughts of where the hell they were going running through her head she tried to think. Where was Daniels? Daniels would not be driving hell bent for leather out of London…with her? Not to mention Fairhaven knocked out back here. Controlling the inclination to scream again, Cara inspected the shadowy face of the man beneath her.

Such full lips, so soft… The thought appeared as if out of nowhere. What could it hurt? Surely, he would not notice, she thought as her lips descended to his. The small kiss seemingly stirred him to life, for just as in Sleeping Beauty, Fairhaven moved slightly. It was enough; Cara brought her head back a bit, "Fairhaven?"

Cara put her face closer again trying to see or hear any other sign that he was finally coming around. "Fairhaven?" she called to him softly, a little louder; her fingers moved of their own accord smoothing the severe lines in his face as the carriage careened seemingly out of control. Cara was tossed back and forth, when her head slammed into the wall of the carriage, she lost what little sympathy she held for the man beneath her. "Fairhaven! Damn your hide. Wake up!"

Roland stirred; he could hear Rose's voice, feel her weight on top of him, her loins pressed into his moving slightly back, forth pressing deeper into him. She felt so damn good. She fit him perfectly, just as though they were made for one another. Not wanting the dream to end he refused to open his eyes. Relishing in the feel of her lips on his, her hands on his face, her fingertips on his brow, this was so much better than any of the dreams that had come before. So real… he could feel her breath as she spoke softly to him, her essence, cinnamon and cloves, surrounded him. She was his siren; this was her call. A call he would gladly answer.

Vaguely, he heard a thump, and then Rose was yelling… At him… He couldn't bear it; if he didn't do something soon, the dream would end. Reaching out his hand he grasped the back of her swanlike neck, bringing her mouth down on his, taking her words into his mouth. For a brief while she relented, with a moan from both parties, she kissed him back. He slid his

94

tongue into her mouth; she drew back. With all her might, she brought a closed fist into his ribs, no small feat in such close quarters; still she managed to gather enough strength to wind him. It wasn't so much that it hurt but something in the back of his mind questioned a dream of his making striking him. Dreams don't hit...do they?

"What pray tell are you thinking? I do not care Sir, who you think you are. I will not be treated in such a manner when our very lives are hanging in the balance. Now, kindly release me, you officious oaf! Get up! Someone has made off with us in my carriage; it is entirely your fault!"

Roland released Rose; she scrambled to her feet, leaving him bereft.

She stood as best she could, the floor swaying beneath her. Finally, she settled in the seat opposite, glaring, willing him to rise and to get them out of this mess. A mess, entirely of his making, she was sure. After all, she'd committed several jobs, and no one had tried to make off with her. Not that is, until she met, and joined forces with the mysteriously handsome oh-so-dangerous Fairhaven. He was to blame for all her woes! And she had kissed him! Again! She fumed silently.

Roland gingerly made his way into a sitting position. The speed of the carriage was the least of his worries. Head spinning. Stomach nauseous, churning like a ship tossed about in a storm. There was enough banging going on, one would think someone was in there erecting a bloody monument.

It was complete stupidity on his part, to have wound up like this. Cradling his head in his hands as though it were made of the most precious substance known to man, he tried to put Rose's words into perspective.

"Rose," he croaked, clearing his throat. He tried again.

"Rose. What happened? Say again. Slowly. And, if you have one ounce of compassion, do it softly."

Taking a deep breath Cara ordered her thoughts, it would be best to comply with his wishes if they were to ever get out of this somewhat sticky situation.

"I completed the job. Was escorted to this very carriage. My carriage..."

"Rose, love, your voice is rising."

Grumbling, she began again. "I'm not your love," she hissed. "Now, where was I? Oh yes. You were inside, I didn't notice right away. Not until after we started moving. It was so blasted dark when I discovered you. I assumed you were sleeping... I was quite put out." Cara thought she heard him smother a laugh; she couldn't help hoping he'd choke on it.

"Once I noticed your *exalted* presence, I tried my best to awaken you. You would not wake, the carriage was moving faster and faster, farther and farther away from the city, I began to worry, you would not wake up. Oh Gawd, Fairhaven, someone has kidnapped us! And I don't even think this is my carriage."

Her voice finished on a high note, but she didn't cry. Though Roland suspected she was remarkably close to tears, he watched as she hugged her arms about her middle tighter and tighter as though she wished she could climb inside herself.

She reminded him of a small kitten curled in upon itself to ward of harm off the unknown. The sight, silhouetted as it was, hurt him more than her tears ever could. His heart constricted. She didn't trust him. No, he argued with himself. It was incredibly wise on her part, still the knowledge hurt like hell. Roland swore he would have her trust if not a whole lot more before their relationship was through.

"Rose," Roland said gently as he carefully let go of his head, reached across the aisle to grasp her hand. She was hesitant to place her hand in his. He gently coaxed until she relinquished the death grip on her body and placed her ungloved hand in his.

"Come," he said, as he pulled her across onto his lap. She was skittish until he expressed the need for quiet conversation. She settled, stiffly, and listened.

"I promise you; I will get us out of this. We must wait for the brigand to stop. As soon as he does, I will take care of him. I give you my word, love. I need you to be strong, no don't fight me, if I wish to use endearments know that it soothes me as much as it does you. You would not be so heartless as to deny me this, would you?" After a moment Roland could feel more than see Cara's head give a small shake; still she remained stiff in his arms. Fine. So be it. Soon enough, he would have her snuggling into him just as he had dreamed.

Cara tried focusing on Fairhaven's face, there wasn't enough light to see his eyes, or read his expression. All she had was the sound of his voice. Mesmerizing. Soothing. It comforted even though it should not. She didn't know him well enough to stake her comfort on him, or put her life in his hands, however fate and circumstances hadn't given her any other choice.

Cara didn't know if he could read her uncertainties but while her mind was in turmoil, he spoke in soothing tones as if gentling a young colt. She was exhausted, relaxing she closed her eyes.

Feeling the tension seep out of Cara's body, Roland hoped she was beginning to trust him, if only for a little comfort. Gently his hand massaged circles over her back while he admired the sleeping beauty in his arms.

She'd been through so much; any other woman would be reduced to vapors, unless of course she was trained. Knew what to expect. That was one prospect Roland hoped not to face. He would not let her go. *What if she is a spy?* Doubt niggled. Sighing, he tilted his aching head back against the seat. If she were, he would deal with it when the time came.

The sounds of the carriage slowing caused Roland to wake. It was time to put their plan in motion. He'd have to wake Rose.

They had been traveling for some time; through the crack in the curtain Roland could see sparse hints of light. Almost dawn. They had been out all night. In most other circumstances that would mean marriage; Roland did not feel anxiety about the possibility. At least then he'd finally find out her real name.

"What are you smiling about?" Cara asked the last remnants of sleep attached to her already husky voice.

"Nothing. Nothing at all… Look, do you remember everything I said?"

"Yes. I am to wait until you give the signal then I am to pitch a fit."

"That's my girl. You can do this. I just need you to get one of them inside. There are sure to be at least two, I cannot see anyone going to this trouble and not planning ahead… Rose, you will have to trust me…Can you do that?"

"Yes. I really have no choice, do I?"

Roland's lips curved. "No, you don't."

Cara moved to the other side of the carriage; it was easier to move now with the coach going at a slower pace. Once settled she said, "My driver, Daniels, what do you think they have done with him?"

"I'm sure we will find out soon enough. The vehicle is slowing; we should meet our captors shortly."

Roland checked his Hessians; his knife was still sheathed within. Thankfully, the fools never thought to check him for concealed weapons. They had taken him down easily, too easily, Roland reflected. They probably thought him not much of a bother. Let them. They would soon find out differently.

The carriage came to a stop. Waiting, both listened to the creaks and moans of the coach as the driver alit and spoke to another. Straining, they tried to hear the conversation outside hoping to ascertain how many men there were.

Fairhaven told Cara there would be two, possibly three, brigands to contend with once they reached their destination. Explaining that most likely the carriage would stop with the doors parallel to the doors on whatever building they were to be held in. Lessoned the chance of altercation and escape.

Cara didn't know how he knew. He said it with such confidence she had no doubt in his abilities even if she had previously found him knocked unconscious. Besides, she had no alternative. Alone, she would have been at a loss in this type of situation, it wasn't the same as when she was confronted by Fairhaven. Then, she could see her captor. This was vastly different she hadn't seen anyone, knew they were violent from what they did to Fairhaven and still she had no idea what they wanted with her.

Only two voices came from the other side of the wall. Cara raised a brow; Fairhaven shook his head, indicating they should wait. Their words were muffled, hard to understand; their thick accent confirmed they were hired thugs. Footpads would not have gone to such lengths to secure their bounty; anyone going to such elaborate attempt would have to have money so as not to get his hands dirty. Roland had seen it before. Many times.

Birds chirped, ringing in the morn. As much as Cara loved wildlife, she wished them all to perdition. She was losing focus, but Fairhaven seemed to do amazingly well, another sign she didn't know the man across from her. He stated she was to adhere to the instructions; not to deviate from their course; if something should happen, he didn't mention what, she was to follow his lead. He went so far as to tell her not to be frightened. Cara couldn't help thinking he was warning her of his actions, and not of the men outside.

Roland listened intently; he could tell by the look on Rose's face she didn't comprehend the exchange. He was having some difficulty hearing but not enough to hinder his plan of attack. There were two men outside with a guard inside waiting for the prisoners to be escorted in. That would be the man waiting for their superior. The carriage handlers would oversee getting them inside. Then, as far as Roland could tell that would be the end of their job. They talked of departing immediately to dispose of the coach.

The conversation ended; Roland could hear one of the men. He was large, for the grass crunched beneath his weight. Heavy or untrained, neither of which was a surprise.

Pressing his ear closer, Roland waited for the sound to disappear indicating he was far enough from the carriage for them to carry out their plan. Rose wasn't trained; therefore, he needed the element of surprise, and hopefully having only one man to deal with would provide the edge. If he were feeling better, he would gladly taken them both on. As it was, if he had to deal with two, someone was going to be killed. Killing was nothing new to him, he knew of numerous ways to dispose quietly of unwanted villains. Rose was different and he feared her reaction.

The door swung open. Roland gave a nod before he slumping back. He watched Rose through closed lids. She lay back in her seat holding her stomach, moaning. As instructed, she would continue until she enticed the captor through the door.

"It is time, 'ome." A booming voice heralded.

Cara looked up slowly, "I cannot. Something is wrong. Please I need help." She grabbed her stomach again throwing herself forward in the process; sounds of retching came from her, as her slender frame rocked with ferociousness.

Roland fought the urge to laugh, what a good little actress, his Rose. The man looked in the carriage; wearily, when he pushed at Roland's leg, he didn't move. Apparently deciding it was safe, the man heaved his leg up. He was short, round and grungy taking a considerable effort to climb. Angrily, he spouted thick accentuated insults about frail ladies, paltry few shillings and whether it was worth the effort. He must have decided a few shillings was better than no shillings at all; greedy by nature he realized he wouldn't be paid for producing a hurt or ailing prisoner. That was incentive enough to get him into the carriage.

Bending over Rose, he placed his hands under her arms poised to lift her out of the carriage.

Roland silently stepped behind; grabbing his neck in one hand his fingers came hard and quick into the man's jugular, something he had done hundreds of times before; to his credit the man's eyes drifted back with nary a sound and Roland let him slip to the floor.

Cara stared at the man slumped down taking up most of the floor of the carriage. She knew enough to school her features before looking up, this was what he had meant, she was sure of it now. Fairhaven wasn't a man to be trifled with, suppressing a shudder. She looked up, for directions as to what was to happen next.

"He's not dead, he will awaken shortly." Removing his cravat, he handed it to Rose. "Bind him," he said.

Cara cursed herself for not being able to hide her fears. Fairhaven noticed it, his hardened face, the ice in his voice told her all she needed to know, he thought she was disgusted by him. Cara swore she would make it up to him; surely, she could not let him go on thinking she feared him or what he did. Nothing could be farther from the truth.

Cara secured their unconscious captor as Roland slipped quietly from the carriage. Had she not been watching him go, she never would have heard him leave. She still found it amazing how someone of his size and presence could move so swiftly, silently.

Not knowing what to do at this point, Cara used her own judgment; if Fairhaven was going to be upset about it then let him. She would deal with that later. Running her hands over the thug's coat Cara found what she sought. Digging into the grimy pocket she retrieved his pistol. She still disliked the cold metal, but she would do whatever was necessary to aid in their survival. Tucking it into the pocket of her cloak she climbed over the sleeping man. She needed to get outside. Being cooped up inside that carriage for so long, caused every bone in her body to ache she needed to stretch her legs; if Fairhaven questioned, that would be her excuse.

The door on a small, long-forgotten shack stood open, all other openings had been boarded up a long time ago, wood weathered with the ages. The interior looked dark against the bright light of day. Cara strained to see Fairhaven but could not. Making her way quietly she slipped the last few steps, undetected, to the door.

Peeking around the corner, she peered inside letting her eyes adjust to the dim interior. On the floor just inside the doorway, another man, most likely the other coachman, lay flattened on the ground. Cara pulled out the pistol; not knowing whether it was loaded, let alone how to use it; she leveled at the man while she crossed the threshold.

Roland heard the creak before spying Rose coming through the doorway, he forced down a smile noting the death grip with which she held the gun…a gun currently trained on an unconscious man. He would have laughed outright had his insides not been knotted with fear that she could very well hurt herself.

Not wanting to startle her yet wanting to let her know everything was secured and she could put down the gun, Roland made his way silently about the room, coming up behind her, he grabbed the gun.

Cara didn't wait to see who had grabbed her gun; all she could think about was if someone was about to get her gun then something must have happened to Fairhaven. Coming up with her hand she bashed her unseen assailant in the face, grabbed his hand and bit down. He let out a fierce growl thankfully dropping the gun. Stamping on his foot for good measure, she quickly retrieved her weapon, spun around leveling it at the cursing man.

"Damn it! Rose, put down the friggin' gun!" Fairhaven roared.

"Fairhaven?"

"Who in the blazin' fires of Hades did you think it was?"

"I thought you were… well… one of them. What do you mean coming up on me like that? I could have killed you."

"Hardly. I doubt very much you know how to use the blasted thing!"

"I know the concept."

"Oh yes, the concept. Pardon me."

"Don't you use that tone with me, I thought you were hurt."

Roland took misplaced pleasure in the image of Rose standing there shaking with worry for him, but he was more than a little concerned that if she didn't put down the weapon, she would be the one doing the hurting.

"Rose. Please put down the gun or give it to me."

"No."

"Excuse me?"

"I said no. I am still angry at you."

"Angry? Or are you frightened? Is that why you are holding me at gun point?"

"I am doing no such thing! I am not frightened of you…you…pigheaded arrogant jackass!"

"Then put it down. We don't have time for this, as you well know."

Cara did know. The fact that he was correct made her even angrier. Pointing the gun at the floor, she walked to Fairhaven and handed him the gun, butt first.

"Happy now?"

"Much. Now come here."

Roland grabbed her about the waist, pulled her close. His body thrummed a mixture of unspent passion she released in him every time he looked upon her no matter the situation, the adrenalin from his victory coursed throughout his body spreading like a wildfire. One kiss, just one kiss then he would get back to business.

He brought his lips down on hers with such brutal force she on the verge of fighting him a wave of insight flashed through her mind. He wasn't angry, as she first feared, he was excited—beyond excited, in his quest to fulfill his needs, he came to her. Knowing this she relaxed her lips, opened her mouth giving him permission to take what he so desperately needed.

Heat unfurled through her body, a tingle, she moaned, pressed closer as if being part of him would stop the burning ache inside. Fairhaven pulled her closer; she could feel his erection through the layers of clothes they wore. It wasn't enough, again she moaned in protest.

Roland knew this had gone too far, he was close to exploding in his breeches if he didn't slow the pace, then it came to him exactly where he was, why; slowly his probing tongue left hers, he placed his chin on her head. She nestled in close, her head on his chest. *She felt so right in his arms.*

Breathing labored, they stood in silence waiting for it to slow before attempting to speak. His hands moved up and down her spine he pulled her closer not willing to release her. Savoring the scent that was cinnamon, cloves, and uniquely Rose. He chuckled. Rose. She smelled nothing like a rose.

"Why are you laughing?"

"I was just thinking how un-rose-like you are."

"Whatever do you mean?" Cara asked with a trace of indignation.

"Well, mayhap not completely un-rose-like, you sure have thorns."

Cara huffed, pulled out of his embrace, resorting to a crisp manner to mask what she really felt inside.

Roland wasn't fooled. He knew he was in for it. He didn't know what devil made him egg her on so, he had to admit he loved her fire almost as much as he loved her…shaking his head at the wayward thought, Roland said, "I have one of the men, tied in the back room. I wanted to question him before we leave, I doubt very much that he knows anything, but it is worth a try. Would you like to come, or would you prefer to stay here?"

Pulling herself up to her full height, she raised her chin. "Of course, I shall accompany you whatever made you think I would not want to be there?"

Eyes firmly adjusted to the light, Cara didn't wait for an answer as she turned on her heel, headed for the room in the back without bothering to see if Fairhaven followed or not.

Roland shook his head, smiling like the lovesick fool he was, he followed.

They hadn't been in the room for more than thirty minutes, as Fairhaven figured the man knew nothing about who had hired him and his friends. His only orders were to abduct a woman in widow's weeds then bring her to the appointed location. Fairhaven was taken simply because he has been in the wrong place at the wrong time. Asking about the wrong woman. Daniels was rendered unconscious so the carriage switch could be made, they had left him lying on the ground amidst the other carriages or so he said.

The footman was on the payroll. Fairhaven said he would try to find him, question him, but he was most likely an extra hired for the event. Quite often for gatherings such as these, temporary servants were hired in, it would have been quite easy to install a felon in the ranks and be none the wiser.

It was a relatively simple plan; executed quite well considering it would take all three brains to make one complete. Roland had to admire the three nitwits. He hadn't credited them with that much intelligence.

After finding Rose's carriage—which by the way they made no mention as to how they knew it was hers—they had rendered Daniels unconscious and took up his spot waiting.

Fairhaven had made his way around the carriage yard, asking for the carriage that belonged to the woman in mourning; he was subtle, often speaking with the drivers getting his information without much fuss. After all he hadn't wanted anyone to remember, to have it bandied about that he and Rose were having an assignation, he hadn't even used Rose's name. He had the misfortune to stumble across the hirelings; they became worried at his questions, making a quick change in plans. After clubbing him over the head, they had callously dumped him in the coach.

When Rose left, she was ushered so quickly to the carriage, the fact that her family logo wasn't on the door never crossed her mind.

They were brought here, destination unknown, a rundown abandoned hunting lodge, most like, to await further instructions those of which had yet to be delivered.

They could have stayed for the instructions to come, but presently with the worst diverted, they decided to get back to the city.

Rose would be missed. Rumor would follow. Roland first destination once they got back to London was Beaumont's. He had to decide whether Rose should go with him, something told him she would not take kindly to being dropped at home. Wherever home was.

The ride back was a good four hours, most of it was spent in silence, Cara had refused to be seated demurely in the carriage she wanted to be outside with Fairhaven in the driver's box. She needed the strength that came with being in the countryside. Beautiful wildflowers dotted the farmer's fields, birds, no longer a nuisance, twittered as they flitted about, all brought her the sense of inner peace she so urgently needed.

She watched a pair of squirrels fighting over an acorn, smiling when the smaller of the two won out. Fairhaven held the ribbons in his strong hands guiding the horses down the country lane. They had had some time to rest from their night journey, aside from their first burst of speed when they had left London most of the drive was spent at a sedate walk or trot, so as they approached an inn, Fairhaven stated they need not stop unless she was tired. Cara had shaken her head, and they continued.

The last thing she needed was to have to sit across the table from Fairhaven, and act as though nothing had happened. Though nothing had, everything had and that made all the difference. If she were the widow she portrayed, she'd throw caution to the wind, ask him to appease the ache she felt deep inside. Would it really be so bad, she was resigned to spinsterhood anyway? What would be the harm?

Chapter Eight

Just before noon, on the outskirts of London, Fairhaven wordlessly reined the team to a halt. Wrapping the ribbons about the brake, he turned his serious countenance to Cara.

"Why are we stopping? What's wrong?"

"I thought it best we decide what to do before entering town. There is sure to be some talk. I doubt anyone aside from the people at home know that we were out all night, I don't believe anyone would have seen us leave together, but all things considered—"

"No, I don't believe so," she interrupted anxiously.

"Rose; you must know, that…" Fairhaven plowed his fingers through his hair; worry and something else creased his brow. "Rose, if things should, happen, I will make this right."

Cara waved away his comment.

"There is no need to look so worried, I am a widow, what I do or not do is of no one's concern but mine. Surely you didn't think I would drag you to the altar—"

Fairhaven cut her off, "You wouldn't be dragging me anywhere."

Skepticism in her eyes, Cara's brow rose in disbelief.

"Alright, it is true I have had no prior interest in marriage, I must admit I have never been faced with circumstances such as this. There are far worse things that could happen."

"Far worse things?"

Cara could not believe her ears; she'd dreamed of a marriage proposal for the better part of her life. Now it became even more important since it seemed likely that she would never receive one; but never once in her dreams had she sat before a handsome man and listen to him tell her there could be worse things. Where exactly did that rate her? Somewhere between catastrophe and annihilation. Or was she slightly higher, an accidental mistake perhaps?

Fairhaven's hand pulled over his exhausted features, back through his hair, making him look younger, more Rex-like. He was clearly having difficulties with whatever he thought he should say or do, Cara wasn't about to let him insult her further.

"Please, Sir, pray do not say another word. I am a widow," he strangled a snort— "No Sir, all I need is a few hours' sleep and a hot bath so if you would be so kind as to get these beasts moving, I would like to be away."

Roland stared at her, both annoyed and amused, a combination he felt almost as much as the sexual tension she aroused when she was near. The statement hadn't come out right, for some reason he was worse than a tongue-tied schoolboy.

He would have liked to tell her he'd be honored to marry. He also knew saying the correct words now could very well could have him picking himself up from the ground below. It mattered not. There would be time to woo her before their assignment was over. If all else failed, he could hire the thugs he knocked out to spirit her away until she came to her senses. That brought a smile to his lips as he untied the ribbons, unleashed the brake, and clucked to the horses. Out of the corner of his eyes, he looked at Rose, still steaming over his botched proposal.

"When we get into town, I'll have to drop the carriage and horses off at the stable yard, we can take a hackney back to your place."

Cara mumbled, folding her arms over her chest; she turned to look out over the edge.

They were too close to London, the road too well traveled for there to be scenery therefore Roland knew it for what it was…. a direct cut. So be it. He continued as though she'd done nothing of the sort, more or less to amuse himself than for any other reason.

"After I drop you at home, I'm sorry to say I will not be able to stay, I will send round a missive of when I will be available to go over the information you have gathered. I have an appointment, some relocating; I haven't been back in London long. After I'm settled would be the best time for us to proceed, the next soiree is not until tomorrow, if I have my days right, so I will make sure to contact you before then."

Cara refused to so much as look at him as he prattled on about one thing or another, as if she cared that he was seeing someone as soon as they got back in town. It was probably his mistress; every one of his rank had a mistress. She was most likely the reason he could not see his way to marry. Well, no matter; it wasn't as if she sought to marry the arrogant lout.

Fuming over his impending visit to his mistress, other words started to register slowly in the one-sided conversation. So, he was going to escort her home was he, huh! Not bloody likely. Luckily, the exchange of carriage left her identity a secret; thank St. Anthony for small miracles.

She didn't know—well she did know just didn't want to admit it, especially now—why this man had her tied in knots. Rattling off, mentally, all the curses she knew, she had managed to block out everything but the presence of the man beside her, once finished she started again.

Roland maneuvered the coach into the first Coaching Inn they found, climbing down he came around to Rose's side, assisted her in alighting from the driver's box. She graced him with a small tight-lipped smile, a small nod of thanks. Anything more would have been a delight but totally insincere. She needed time to cool off. Roland understood that. He'd give her space then try again.

Perhaps after seeing Beaumont, he'd have an ally, not that Beaumont would support him in his love endeavors but his position for the crown and the circumstances surrounding the lovely Mrs. Black may entice him to step in. In his role he could possibly convince the stubborn woman to act as Roland's fiancée for the sake of her country.

After all it was his duty to solve the mystery for the Organization and to do that, he must protect their ace. The best way to protect the ace was to keep it as close to one's sleeve as possible. Yes, a couple subtle hints, Beaumont would fall into line giving Rose no alternative. Mayhap, in such close proximity Roland would be able to win her heart.

"I must go in, see the man about the carriage, maybe he has information. You'd like to come I presume?"

Fairhaven was already reaching for her arm when Cara took a step back.

"No thanks, I will wait here. I love the fresh air; I am loath to be cooped up again if only for a little while," Cara said, with a winning smile.

Roland heart flip-flopped. Nodding, stating he'd be back shortly, he turned on his heel toward the office.

Once he was inside, Cara immediately made her way back out to the street, hailing the first hackney; she gave her direction and stepped inside. *She would contact him if, and when she was ready.*

When Roland emerged from the manager's office, there was no sign of Rose. Damn! He shouldn't have left her alone. Her sweet answer, her smile dripped in honey when she felt nothing but vinegar, should have told him something was up.

Damn! The vixen. Damn her hide! Sneaky. Sly. Beautiful, vivacious... she was everything he wanted, and have her, he would. Shaking his head, a wave of admiration flooded him. Smiling, he walked to the curb and hailed a cab.

Cara was still smiling as she climbed the back stairs into the townhouse. She had the driver drop her at the alley in case Fairhaven decided to hunt for her conveyance home. Walking down the narrow stretch, she could not help feeling a combination of loss and wonder at being able to give a government-trained man the slip. Oh, she had managed to keep identity a secret, but at what cost.

If only his proposal could have been real.

The truth that she got away undetected had to have been his hurry to see his mistress. Yet he had offered to marry her. Laughable. Compared to his "appointment", he hadn't a care about her or where she went. So be it. She'd started out this adventure knowing she had but one purpose. Resigned that she would have to be content remaining a spinster. The thought rankled even more than it did before.

Maids covered shocked expressions quickly as she entered the kitchen through the back door. To them, her rumpled state and the fact she had been out all night made her the fallen woman. She'd best get used to it. Knowing the servant grapevine, undoubtedly many of her father's acquaintances would hear of it as well.

It was a good thing no one would associate the fallen daughter of Lord Danforth with the widow Mrs. Black. That should buy her enough time to do what needed to be done. Help England, help her family and get back to Wonderland before their guardian came for them. Explaining just how or why the family was in London would not be easy. Explaining how a girl of nineteen with nary a come out could be brandied about as a fallen woman was something Cara didn't want to contemplate.

Taking the servant stairs, she hurried to her room, hopefully escaping Tibs. She would think of a way to handle him, just not right now. She required a believable story, before seeing him. Did Daniels make it home? Did he say anything? Was he alright? She prayed he was.

108

Closing the door to her room she removed her cloak, giving the bell a yank. She sat waiting for Lucy to come. A bath and rest would set her to rights. Lucy would see to them without question or condemnation.

"Good morn', Miss Cara. Water is heating, I thought you might like a bath; Mrs. Leeks will send the footmen with it, when it's ready. Shouldn't be long."

"Thank you, it has been a dreadfully long night, I need rest but there is no possible way I can climb into bed like this." She motioned with her hand. Lucy's eyes followed her hand, the mistress's gown was badly wrinkled, the hem soiled, the tips of her fingers dirty with traces of what looked like, blood? Keeping her mask in place, she gave a quick bob. "I understand, Miss."

As Lucy went about helping her out of the soiled clothing, Cara feared she had seen more than the others had, either that or she knew more; at any rate Cara needed to know how far that information would spread.

"Lucy?"

"Yes Miss?"

"Did Daniels make it home safely? Is he here? Is he alright?" She hesitated with each word wondering if there was a better way to phrase her questions. There wasn't.

"Yes, Miss, he and the team came in about three, aside from a bump on the noggin, he was just fine. Mrs. Leeks tended him. Miss, might I say, no one has said anything, I mean the staff here of course no one knows, some truths some fiction but fact or speculation; not one word will leave this house without your say."

A band tightened about Cara's throat. What Lucy said, or didn't say rather, let her know they cared. She had the backing of her father's staff. For once she didn't feel completely alone. Not trusting her voice, she simply smiled sadly.

Twenty minutes later, Cara was in the tub soothing away her aches. Eyes closed she was beginning to relax when Rex called for her.

"Cara. Cara. Open up we need to talk."

The thinly veiled demand couldn't be missed. Sighing she wondered what to tell her little brother. Mayhap some of the truth would be better than trying to avoid everything, eventually lying would only lead to trouble with his cleverness.

"Just a minute Rex, I will be right out," she answered resigned to her current course. She stepped out of the tub wrapped her robe about herself then walked slowly into her bedchamber. Rex was sitting on her bed, kicking imaginary fluff about the floor with the toe of his polished shoe. Head bowed, he looked so much older than his eleven years. Cara's heart constricted. This was all her fault.

Walking to her bed, she sat down bedside Rex, laying her head on his shoulder, she reached for his hand "I'm sorry, Rex, I thought I could handle this. I really did. I didn't want you to worry; I can see I have only made things worse. Tell me love, what is it you would like to know."

Rex toyed with his sister's hand. Now that he was faced with her telling him the truth, he wasn't so sure he wanted to hear it. He was sure he had most of the puzzle pieced together anyway. The only thing left was to say it aloud. He took a second to steel himself. He was the man of the family; he would have to make things right. Being a coward was no way to accomplish that.

"We are in trouble, aren't we? I am not an idiot, Cara, I knew from the start you didn't come to London to acquire a husband. So why did you? My only guess is that it had something to do with father's will; are we broke, is that it? I cannot believe he would leave us to our own devices. I realize that we only have each other as far as family goes, but I would have thought if he felt anything for us, he would have arranged for a little guidance, a little help until I was better equipped for my role. Did he care so little?" The last was said around a large lump in his throat.

"Of course, he cared. He loved us. To answer your question, yes, he did name a guardian. A Mr. Roland Acworth. But it is almost two months since Father died, no word has come." Cara didn't tell her brother about the note. Let him think their father's will had given her the name she had come to hate.

She prayed for Rex's sake; the absentee guardian would show making everything all right. Though it would be hard on her she would not allow her brother or sisters to think their father hadn't cared.

"Then why? Why are we here, instead of at Wonderland waiting for him, it's possible he's sent word? There are so many reasons why he couldn't have stepped forward. Mayhap he was out of the country? Did you think of that?"

"Yes, I thought of it." She hesitated. She knew Acworth was coming from the Colonies but again, she could say nothing without indicating the wayward guardian's letter. No way she would tell him. It would break his heart.

"Then we must go back."

"Soon, Rex. I promise." Cara could not be more specific than that.

"Why can be ready to leave on the morrow?"

Cara sighed; this was the part she dreaded telling him, she had no choice, with any luck, he would feel better in knowing.

"Although I didn't come to London to find a husband, the trip did have purpose. I cannot go into detail. My quests have led me into a bit of a government dilemma, so I have been asked for assistance. I need you to trust me a bit longer."

Rex looked at her incredulously. He didn't believe her. Cara worried she would have to invent a lie after all, but his gaze changed. She prayed for him to see honesty in her yes, when he did his expression turned to one of interest. He nodded.

"I don't suppose, being government, you can tell me anything?" he asked, his brow rising hopefully.

Cara's lips curved affectionately, "I'm afraid not, that is until we are back in Wonderland, then I will tell you all the tales of my adventure."

"That's why you weren't home last night? You were not hurt? Like Daniels?"

"No. I wasn't hurt as you can plainly see. I was dirty, tired—I am still tired, as soon as you agree to watch the girls, I am going to sleep." Cara kissed his cheek.

He patted her hand, rose and headed for the door. "Goodnight Cara."

***

Roland stared at the front of Thomas' townhouse; his luggage would be sent over as soon as he talked to the staff. Ascending the stairs, he grabbed the brass knocker rapping it against the solid oak. He heard sounds echoing from within as he stood waiting to be permitted. The door opened to reveal, Tibs' Thomas' former man of all work, turned butler, eyeing him suspiciously.

Roland knew him well.

"Well, Tibs? Am I to be invited in?"

Tibs, expression masked, bowed, backing away from the door.

"Your Grace. This is a surprise. The master…"

Roland pushed past before he could say anything further.

Shutting the door, Tibs turned to take his hat.

"I am aware. Please, we can discuss it later, perhaps in a more private setting. As for the "Your Grace", it isn't necessary. You and I have known each other for an exceedingly long time. How have you been, old man?"

Tibs looked taken back by the question, though he shouldn't have; Roland had never hidden his scorn for ceremony; the past three years had not changed his outlook. Nine chances out of ten, Tibs had hoped Roland had changed. Tibs was a stickler for ceremony. Well, tough.

After placing Roland's hat on the mantel, Tibs returned, "Quite well, Your Grace, thank you for asking, and you, Sir, how have you been? It's been three years if I recall rightly."

"You have it right. Shall we go to the study?"

"The study? Of course, Your Grace, please follow me."

Roland followed down the long-marbled corridor. The townhouse was very much as Roland remembered, richly appointed, tastefully done, a home any man would be proud to call his own. He thought back to when he was at the Gables, he had feared Thomas had fallen on rough times. The townhouse still stood in grandeur, again things weren't adding up.

Tibs closed the door and waited for Roland to seat himself on the other side of the desk before sitting in a chair in front of the desk. Roland could tell right off that someone was using the office since Thomas' death. The desk was strewn with papers.

"Forgive my impertinence, but why have you come? Surely you must be aware the master is no longer with us?"

"Though newly returned, I am aware Thomas is gone. As a matter of fact, it is the reason for my visit. Have no fear; you and I can and will converse freely?"

Roland tidied a small area in front of him while he pondered his best choice of words. Tibs looked like a lost lamb, not knowing if Roland was sheepdog or wolf. According to Beaumont, he had remained out of the loop since Thomas' death, possibly before. Yet if anyway could help him answer the questions in this mess, it would be Tibs.

"I don't know if you are aware, I just returned to England to fulfill my role as guardian to Thomas' four youngsters."

It sounded as though the duke hadn't a clue who his charges or how old they were. Not know if he should correct him, he remained silent.

"I was at The Gables. I found no one in residence. Mrs. Brown wasn't very helpful to say the least. So, I have spent the better part of my time back home trying to track down four small defenseless children. You do see my dilemma, do you not? You wouldn't happen to know where those children might be?"

Roland raised a masterful brow; he knew very well where the children were. He'd heard them when he arrived. Would Tibs try hiding them as well? For that purpose, he had not brought his belongings. He wanted to know who he could count on should the need arise.

Tibs swallowed, noticeably uncomfortable.

"They are here, Your Grace," he said at last, "they showed about two weeks ago."

"Thank you for your honesty, Tibs. Who accompanied them?"

"Accompanied them?"

"Yes, Tibs. I assumed when Thomas left me guardian, the children had no one else…"

"That is true, Your Grace, right sad it is."

"So? If they had no one else, how did they come to be in London?"

"Mr. Farley brought them in the country carriage, Your Grace."

"Who's Mr. Farley?"

"A farmer, Your Grace. Lives close by. I was given to understand that he helps out from time to time."

"Where is he now?"

"He went back to the country."

"When?"

"The following day."

"So, who has been in charge of the children?"

"The staff. Do not fret, Your Grace; the Master prepared us for any event. We are managing the matter quite well."

"Thomas didn't spend much time with his children recently."

It was a statement, not a question and to Tibs there was no right answer. Master Thomas had cut ties with his family out of love and protection, though he doubted a man with no family would understand this. Tibs said nothing. Answer only what is asked, that was beginner course interrogation.

The old batman was in a conundrum; eventually Roland would figure him out. He wasn't lying, but something in his manner suggested he wasn't telling the whole truth either.

Tibs prayed the duke would not ask to meet the children. It would be best if he simply went on his way. He needed to speak with Daniels; he could seek him out after the duke left. On the duke's next words, Tibs knew his prayer would go unanswered.

"I think it is time I meet the children."

"Yes, Your Grace."

"And Tibs, do not address me so in front of them, I do not wish them to feel intimidated."

"Yes, Your Grace."

"Fine. Fetch them. I'll meet them in the drawing room."

"Yes, Your Grace."

Rising, they exited together. Tibs went left toward the servant stairs. Roland went right toward the drawing room back toward the entry.

An elegant room fit for serving tea and cakes to the fashionable ladies of the ton. Roland grimaced. He wasn't one for entertaining, though surely it would be in Rose's taste if he could find the blasted woman. He talked to various hackney drivers none of which remembered anyone of her basic description, a very basic description. It hit him like a knee to the groin; he couldn't say for certain what she looked like. Oh height, weight, curves, luscious lips, soft skin, delicate cinnamon and clove scent, but anything that would describe her to someone else, he didn't know.

He wished he'd spent more time looking into her eyes or studying her full face instead of her profile on the drive back. All in all, it was a good sign. For the first time in his adult life, he hadn't wanted a woman simply because of her pretty face, he wanted Rose for herself. Just her. Her very essence surrounded him like a cloak, a yearning that would appreciate over time.

His aunt and uncle shared a similar love.

Roland may be young, but he was old enough to know what he wanted. And he'd get it. He already picked the rose, now all he had to do was find it, de-thorn it and bring it home.

At the sound of little footsteps, he buried his thoughts and turned.

"Your...I mean, Mr. Acworth, Sir? Your charges," Tibs managed before stepping aside.

"Thank you, please stay a moment, I shall need introductions. It wouldn't be proper for me to introduce myself to such lovely young ladies."

114

Looking at the trio, he smiled. Running on instinct he walked to the first young lady, girl about ten or eleven, he'd guess, funny, he thought they would have been younger. She stood beside another, her mirror image who was positioned next to a boy of the same age. They all had the same black as midnight hair, the same startling blue eyes. Aside from gender, they were in fact perfect replicas of one another.

Roland had known Thomas had triplets, he had to admit he hadn't known what to expect. Certainly not this, he was astounded. The same. Right down to the dimples in their cheeks. The boy didn't smile; if he did, Roland assumed he would have dimples too. The boy would be the toughest to win over. He eyed Roland as though he were a fox in the henhouse.

"Mr. Acworth, may I present Miss Rebecca-Dae Danforth," Tibs said, his tone stately.

Becky flushed, feeling ever so important as the smiling man said, "Pleased to meet you," he then bowed and kissed the back of her hand. It tickled and she giggled.

"Becky. You may call me Becky," she said.

"I'd be honored; you may call me Roland, unless you find Mr. Acworth more satisfactory."

Becky shook her little black head; Roland let go of her hand and moved to the next little one in line.

"Miss Roberta-Dawn Danforth, Sir."

Roland repeated his movements.

"And you, charming Miss? Do you go by Roberta, such a lovely name, or is there a shorter term you prefer?"

"Oh! Yes, Sir!" Robby said.

Roland raised his brow in question making Robby realized she hadn't told him; the thought made her giggle. "Sorry, Sir, it's Robby. That's what all my friends call me; well, it is not that I have many friends in the country, everyone lives so dratted far away, and I have… oomph!"

Robby couldn't finish due to her brother's warning elbow to her ribs, but she was too excited to care.

"She talks too much. They both do. I am Thomas Rexley Danforth III. You can call me Rex. But only because it is shorter," Rex said with dignity.

"It is nice to meet you, Rex. You may call me Roland, not because it's shorter, I hope we can be good friends, and my friends call me by my given name."

Roland let him process that thought for a moment.

"If I am to be outnumbered by females, it would be nice to have another man in my encampment. What do you say, Lieutenant?"

"Were you in the war, Sir?" Rex asked hostility forgotten in light of this delightful discovery.

"You might say that. So, what do you say, can we call a truce for the betterment of England?" Roland thought it a rather good line; he'd be wise to use it on Rose—when he found her.

"Yes, Sir," Rex answered hesitantly, his thoughts brought back to the present.

"Well then, Lieutenant, here's our first problem. I was under orders to greet four Danforths, I see before me only three, where might I ask is our other little damsel in distress is?"

Rex smiled, thinking of Cara as a damsel in distress. She would never admit such a thing, even if Rex knew she was, but she certainly wasn't little. Before he could answer, Tibs interjected.

"I am afraid she's under the weather Sir, she is abed. Might I suggest it best to leave her to rest?"

Roland was at a loss. What to do? Should he go to the nursery? Call for a doctor? Had a doctor been consulted? Was the girl frail, prone to illness? Worry must have shown on his face for Tibs went on.

"Do not worry, Sir, Mrs. Leeks and Lucy, the upstairs maid, have her well in hand."

"All right then, Tibs. If you're certain."

"Yes Sir, I am," Tibs said most definitely and prayed that would be the end of it. Thankfully, it was.

"Tibs, I think I would like to spend some time getting to know my new family. You may go."

"If there is nothing else then Sir?" Tibs said, turning to leave.

"One moment. Have the housekeeper—Mrs. Leeks, was it? Have her send some refreshments. Tea and cakes, I should think. I shall be entertaining."

"Very well Sir."

Once a weary Tibs was out the door, Roland turned to the children.

"Well ladies, gentleman, shall we have a seat and get to know one another?"

The girls nodded and plumped themselves rather hastily on the settee; Rex watched them and Roland with an expression far too grave for one so young.

"Did you mean what you said about family?" Rex asked seriously.

"Why yes. Does it bother you that I want to think of you as my family?"

"That depends."

Rex crossed his arms and tapped his toe. The gesture was familiar to Roland but for the life of him, he could not see Thomas doing such a thing and as he had only just met the children, he was being foolish, plain and simple.

"On what?" Roland asked a hint of amusement lurking in his eyes.

"On why," Rex said instantly.

"Ah, I see. You are already an incredibly good Lieutenant, 'question the motive of thy enemy', only I am not the enemy, and the reasons are quite simple."

"Then what is it?" Rex demanded, not giving an inch.

"I have no family. My mother and father, like yours, are deceased. I was never blessed with siblings. So, you see, you"—Roland waved to encompass all of them— "are all I have."

"All? What about aunts? Uncles? Cousins?" Rex raised his ebony brow.

"You are quite intelligent for your age; what are you ten? Eleven?"

"We are all eleven. And you didn't answer my question."

Roland's lips twitched; he was a smart one. Protective too. Roland could suddenly see himself as a father figure to these small children. And amazingly enough, he was enjoying it.

"One aunt, one uncle, two cousins who are married and no longer reside in London. My aunt and uncle come here for the season then they depart for Greyley Castle once the legislature is closed."

Rex seemed satisfied with Roland's answer, gracing him with a smile. Again, Roland had a feeling of familiarity, and just like another; this little boy smiled all too infrequently. That had to be what was reminding him of Rose. Not that she was ever far from his thoughts.

This was a little boy with far too much on his shoulders. Roland would see what he could do about bringing some fun back into their lives.

"Who's up for a tour of the park after tea? Such a lovely day should be celebrated out of doors."

Three black heads bobbed in agreement but said nothing as Mrs. Leeks bustled in with tea and poppy cakes for all.

Chapter Nine

Cara woke feeling more herself than she would have expected. More tired than she realized, she had slept straight through to the following morn. Lucy had come in earlier to open the curtains, now the unsympathetic morning sun streamed into the room. Cara didn't mind, the sun seemed fitting. It transformed her room into an inviting haven and after yesterday, this refuge was what she needed most.

She didn't usually have anyone bring her hot chocolate or breakfast in bed. It was a sin to burden the staff when she was able-bodied enough to go down to the dining room. This morning, Lucy had brought a tray of hot chocolate and toast prior to her waking. It was a nice treat. Cara positioned herself before reaching for the tray. It felt awkward and the thought of eating in bed sat about as right as the silver platter, wobbling and slopping chocolate all over.

A knock sounded as she finished. Setting the tray aside she called for her siblings to enter. There were but a few people who would come to her room. Mrs. Leeks, Lucy or one of the children, if not all three given she had been sleeping for over twenty-four hours. Lucy had come and gone. Mrs. Leeks would presumably be busy so that left... Cara smiled as all three poured through her bedroom door like a tidal wave.

The girls were all giggles, hiding secrets. Doubtless they wanted to surprise her with one of them. She truly hoped they hadn't done anything to the staff. After being cooped up for days, anything was possible. She must try spending a little more time with them outdoors. Children needed fresh air and sunshine.

Becky and Robby whispered happily back and forth as they plunked themselves upon the bed. Rex was smiling and quiet. But there was something... Cara couldn't put her finger on it. Tipping her head from side to side, she studied him. Possibly... could it be her little brother looked a little more child-like than usual? Preposterous! But the more she looked, the harder he smiled. He looked for the entire world as if his face would burst with sunshine.

"Good morning to you, hellions."

"Morning Cara," they chorused. Rounds of "Did you sleep well? Are you hurt? Are you sick? Why ever did you sleep so long?" came from the girls with the rapid speed of a bullet from Mr. Stevens' *'precious'*, until Rex silenced them with one of his fierce looks.

"I am fine, I assume that you have all came in here to tell me something. I do hope you haven't dropped the wash water on passers-by from the nursery window," she said.

"Becky, I told you there was something we forgot to do," Robby admonished. The girls giggled and rolled their beautiful big blue eyes.

"Our Problems, Dear Sister, Are Over!" Rex announced with relish.

Cara felt a tingling of unease.

"What do you mean our problems are over?" she asked. Belatedly, Rex remembered his sister was not party to what was going on.

"It doesn't matter anymore, Cara. We can go back to Wonderland now," Rex said.

"What did you do?" Cara said, sounding more accusing than she had meant to. The look of happiness fell from three cherub-like faces. Cara immediately felt kicked in the stomach.

"I'm sorry. I didn't mean to snap; maybe I am feeling a little off. Please forgive me. What are you all so excited about?"

The girls looked at their brother, afraid to forge ahead lest they get snapped again, Cara sighed, "I really am sorry," she pleaded.

Looking from the girls to Rex, now off the bed pacing the room his hands shoved deep in his trouser pockets. *He looks like a barrister*, Cara thought admiringly. He will do well in the House of Lords.

Braving the front, they all tried to speak at once. The look Rex gave his sisters reminded Cara of a high-appointed judge quieting an assembly. Immediately, they fell silent. Cara smothered a giggle, for Becky and Robby were never truly quiet but they were as hushed as they were going to get. Knowing this, Rex began.

"Mr. Acworth has arrived," her brother stated with as much admiration as if Zeus himself had descended upon them. Apparently, he was taken with the dratted man already. Good God had the entire world gone to salt while she slept? He, who never trusted anyone; leery around strangers; self-contained around his sisters, he was now a pillar of approval for Mr. Blasted Acworth!

Cara fighting to slow the racing of her heart and whirling of her stomach, managed to squeeze the word, "When?" past her constricted throat.

"Yesterday, while you were sleeping."

Figures.

"No one woke me?" Cara knew she sounded like she was whining but it couldn't be helped. Her only other choice was to be as ferociously livid as she wanted to be. And she couldn't do that, not in front of her siblings.

"Tibs said it would be best to let you rest; Mrs. Leeks would not have allowed us anywhere near your room if we tried. It wasn't until this morning, after we all had breakfast that Lucy said we could come."

Cara didn't know why Tibs, or Mrs. Leeks would keep the children from her. It was almost like they wanted to keep her away. But that was ridiculous! They could not have anticipated how she would act toward their new guardian, she in truth she herself did not know.

"Where is our guardian now?"

"He left after breakfast," Rex replied.

"He was here for breakfast?" Cara's voice cracked.

"Yes, I just told you we all had breakfast together; were you not listening?"

"I assumed you meant the three of you, possibly Mrs. Leeks. But I did not know that man was included in one of the numbers. What in the devil was he doing here for breakfast?" she thought aloud.

"Doesn't one normally have breakfast upon awaking?" Rex was clearly losing his patience.

"You mean he stayed here!" Cara yelled.

"Of course, he stayed here!" Rex yelled back. Brows drawn down in a perfect V. "He's our guardian, where on earth did you think he would stay?"

"Oh, yes, Cara. Isn't it wonderful? He has not had much practice with children, or at least that is what he said, he doesn't look very old, wonderfully handsome. Did he not look wonderful, Robby?" Becky praised.

"Oh, yes," Robby breathed.

"Wonderful. He surely is. You should have seen him, Cara. Most wonderfully handsome and he told the most wonderful stories. He even took us on a wonderful trip to the park, we walked and talked and fed the ducks. He

121

even had us eat in the dining room, not like when father was home, and we all had to eat in the nursery. He called us his family," Robby added.

"He did tell fascinating stories, Cara. He has led a most interesting life; Becky and Robby have the right of it. He seems wonderful..." there was a slight uncertain pause before he finished, "he really seems to want us."

They were hooked. Each one of them in his or her way, in less than twenty-four Godforsaken hours, had become infatuated with their guardian.

Cara worried her lip; she felt a sharp jab in her chest. She was jealous, she could handle that, what she couldn't handle was the broken heart this charmer would leave behind when he no longer 'wanted them' as Rex so enthusiastically put it.

She had little doubt he intended to walk in and out of their lives just like their father had. Appearing and disappearing at will. Like a phantom, well she wouldn't stand for it! She'd be ready for him when he returned. Battle lines would be drawn, and God help the saint who crossed them!

With an exceeding effort, Cara managed not to let her feelings show.

"Did Mr. Acworth say when he would return?"

"Not exactly." This came from Rex.

"But he will. Said he'd meet us later today. He may have been more detailed with Tibs; they were in the library when we came up."

"Then he may still be there. Out, all of you. I must get dressed."

Cara dressed hurriedly, a floral day dress, buttoning in the front she would not have to ring for Lucy. Finishing, she went in search of Tibs. Hoping she'd find Acworth.

"So, he said he would be back for dinner?" The wheels in Cara's head were turning; she shouldn't confront him at the dinner table, would he be back before then?

"Yes, Miss Cara, that is what he said."

"I have a dinner invitation—I could cancel. I must go to The Earl of Salisbury's Soiree—as long as I'm there by—" Ticking off her agenda out loud, Tibs interrupted.

"I beg your pardon, Miss Cara, don't change anything. What if he sends word, he cannot make dinner? Then you have cancelled your plans for naught."

"You may be right."

Cara was struck with a horrible thought.

"Tibs, are you trying to delay me from meeting Mr. Acworth?"

The question shocked Tibs, not because it wasn't true but in fact because it was.

"Miss Cara, how could you think such a thing?" Tibs said, looking guilty.

"Mayhap, because you are sending me out instead of to my room."

"Miss Cara, I have never done that!" Tibs said indignantly.

"No, you haven't. Not with words, at any rate. But I have been the object of quite a few steely-eyed paternal gazes of late. Never mind, that is neither here nor there. I will persevere as I must. Now. When will Mr. Acworth's things arrive?"

"His Gr...that is, Mr. Acworth stated his things would arrive this afternoon."

"Which room has Mrs. Leeks given him? Might I suggest the room at the end of the hall, it's on the second floor overlooking the garden? The one that looks like it was fashioned after some unkempt Roman mausoleum. I realize it would have to be cleaned, we really must get names for these blasted rooms; it would be ever so much easier, I suppose Mrs. Leeks could have some of the footmen take the boxes to the attic, then the room should be aired, I guess..."

"Excuse me, sorry to interrupt."

"Yes, what is it?"

"The room you're referring to has a name, it's the storage closet. And as to Mr. Acworth's room." Tibs could not hide the wry humor in his voice or his eyes. She really was too much. The storage closet, indeed...

"Why do I get the feeling I am not going to like this?"

"Mr. Acworth has requested the same room he stayed in last night. I believe he said he found it very much to his liking."

"And what room did he stay in last night?" Cara asked hesitantly knowing she was not going to like the answer.

"The Baron's old suite."

"You let him stay in Father's room?" Cara almost yelled.

"He did request it, Miss."

"Well, he will have to be moved! That room connects to mine! He must go!"

"Miss, be reasonable, there is no conceivable way we can go against his wishes. What if I speak to Mrs. Leeks and have you moved to another room? The one overlooking the garden perhaps?" That he said it with a straight face was a detriment to his years of training.

"Very funny! You will do no such thing! I was here first, and I have no intention of giving up my room for…for that blasted man!"

"But Miss Cara, there is no other choice, protocol dictates…"

"Damn protocol!" Cara shouted. "The door can, will be locked immediately. Is that clear?"

"Miss Cara, that will not solve the problem once he meets you."

"What do you mean *once* he meets me?"

"I believe Miss, that Mr. Acworth is under the assumption that all the *children* in this household are kept in the nursery."

"WHAT!"

Cara slammed her hands down on top of the desk, and then as realization hit her, she sunk back slowly into the chair. *The man didn't even know the age of his charges, oh Athena help me.*

Tibs swallowed, he had known this wasn't going to be easy. He should have been honest with His Grace and Miss Cara, but he couldn't. He needed time, something wasn't right, it could be mere coincidence or speculation on his part, but he needed to be certain. First Daniels was attacked, then Miss Cara taken and now, not more than a few hours later an agent for the Organization shows up. Why? He had known there was more to her nightly outings. Husband hunting didn't fit with who Miss Cara was. He knew it, Daniels knew it, even the Master, God rest his soul, had known it. Thus, they were well prepared for Miss Caralyn's arrival, just in case.

The Master had read his daughter well.

Their instructions were to watch over her, protect the children, but to let his daughter run her course. 'Cara's like a runaway team. She'll beat the odds as long as no one steps in her path,' the Master had said. 'Just protect them all, until their guardian comes. He will know what to do.'

When questioned, Thomas said he could not reveal the guardian's identity until he was certain. Certain about what Tibs and Daniels never knew. Thomas has been dispatched before they learned everything including the name of the guardian.

Then yesterday, Roland Acworth, Duke of Fairhaven, stated with all certainty that he was the appointed guardian for the children, he had no documentation, only his word. It was up to him and Daniels to determine whether his word was true.

Miss Cara was their only ace in the hole. His Grace not knowing there was a person of Miss Cara's age and ability within the household worked to their advantage. If His Grace wasn't on the right side, then they could tell Miss Cara what they knew, dispatching her and the children to safety. For now, though, the safest place for all of them was right here, with two of the Organization's trained members on staff.

All they needed was a little time, so they could investigate. He hadn't worried so much when Beaumont called, for although he didn't like the man for building a case against Thomas, he didn't think Beaumont would be one of the double agents. He was married to the Home Office.

Acworth on the other hand had been out of the country for three years. Undercover. That kind of deep assignment had turned more than one good man. No, they needed time. Another twenty-four hours at least to figure out what to do, until then they needed to keep their aces buried.

"Tibs?" Cara said again, a little louder than before.

"What? Oh, sorry Miss, I was wool gathering, what did you say?"

"Tibs, how much sleep have you had?"

"I'm all right Miss, pray go on."

"I asked if that was all the instructions our guardian left you with."

"Yes, that's about it. Wait for his things; install them in the Baron's suite of rooms."

"All right then. Do what you must. If he shows before I leave, send someone for me; I'll be in the nursery. Do you think you can find another driver for me on such short notice? Perhaps I should take a hackney?"

"That will not be necessary. Daniels is faring much better; he will be most put out if you do not allow him to escort you."

"I should like to talk to him myself. Have him come to the nursery when he has a spare moment. Oh. And Tibs, get one of the footmen to watch the door, you need rest."

"Yes, Miss. Thank you." Tibs acquiesced knowing his time could be better spent elsewhere. Leaving the library, he found a footman to tend to his duties and went in search of Daniels.

"Have you found them?" Beaumont inquired.

"Yes, they were at the townhouse. Can you believe it; some farmer named Farley helped get them here? According to Tibs, it was the brainchild of the eldest. I cannot wait to meet this particular paragon."

"But I thought they were all about the same age?"

"Tibs must be up to something."

"I figured as much. Tibs never liked me, now that I have made it known throughout the Home Office that I am investigating Thomas…well I can only imagine his feelings about me are even stronger. So now that you have found them you will be sending them back to The Gables? We must get on with our investigation."

"I won't send them away, lest ways not right now. It would be cruel, just having met. I gathered last night they miss their father greatly. I know what it is like to be young, without family…" He shrugged.

"I can continue just as I did before; the only thing that has changed is my address. Besides, I couldn't move them even if I did want to, the eldest is sick."

"Sick?"

"Yes, when I arrived, I met three of the four; we spent a pleasant day together given the circumstances. Got on famously. The fourth, Caralyn, was abed sleeping. Tibs assured me it was nothing apparently Mrs. Leeks had it well in hand. Then this morning, she didn't come down for breakfast, I asked Mrs. Leeks if a tray was sent up to the nursery, she said no. That means the little tyke has not eaten since yesterday. She cannot be well. I intend to find a physician, have him look at her first thing tomorrow."

Beaumont considered his friend very closely as he talked. "You are jumping into this mire rather quickly, old friend. One hopes you do not find quicksand."

They both laughed.

Together in Beaumont's sitting room, they were at ease. Even as messy as it was. Beaumont's profile to a tee—desk piled sky-high with papers, letters, Home Office paraphernalia. Roland was sure some of it hadn't even been opened.

"I say, old chap, doesn't the maid ever clean in here?"

"Hold your blasphemy! I'd never find anything if they came in here."

Laughing, it was an easy carefree companionship friend-to-friend, man-to-man. Normally, their time together was overflowing with business, secret tense and somewhat terse exchanges held at the Cock and Crow. This afternoon what Roland needed to discuss wasn't of the highest secrecy. He needed to secure Beaumont's assistance before seeing Rose tonight.

There was no way she would miss this job. It had all the makings of an excellent take; Salisbury the fool never liked banks. Kept his worldly possessions close. Rose would have done her homework; no matter how mad she was at him personally she'd show.

"No luck in finding the elusive Mrs. Black?" Beaumont asked breaking into his thoughts.

"No. She will be at the Earl of Salisbury's ball tonight. We can catch up with her there. Do you have evening clothes from this century?"

"I have no need. You know I don't go out if I can help it."

"Yes, I do. But I am asking for you to don those much-unused historical pieces and help me apprise Mrs. Black of our plan."

"Me? Help you with a woman? Oh, this is rich. I thought you said you could manage it?"

"Amusing. I would have, had I been able to find the chit. My time has run out. Blast it anyway!"

Beaumont chuckled, "I do believe this paragon of virtue has you tied in knots, my friend." Beaumont looked at the snarl on Roland's face and laughed again.

Normally, he wouldn't dream of meddling in people's lives. He hated meddlers if it wasn't for the fact that he had taken a special interest in Roland, interfering all those years ago? Roland had become a special project for him. Why quit now?

A man needed a wife. The sooner the better and with four little ones, the timing couldn't be more perfect. The only thing Beaumont wasn't sure of was whether or not a widowed thief would be the best match. It seemed marriage lay ahead, somewhere. It wasn't as though he wouldn't benefit from the union. She'd be an asset to the Home Office. She had, and was still, proving her worth.

She had eluded one of England's finest, thwarted him at every turn. She could give as well as she got. Even in a hostile situation she'd behaved as well as any trained agent. She was green but she had raw talent. A rarity. Yes, this could definitely work.

By Roland taking a wife who enjoyed the game, he would be less tempted to leave the Organization and play nursemaid to four children.

Too many agents left; burnout was high, the death rate even higher. It wasn't the easiest job one could have. The pay in most cases simply wasn't worth it; one had to be in it for the thrill. And when a man wanted a family, well, that was the end of the game. Agents like Acworth were hard to come by, he was damn good at what he did, finding a replacement would be damn near impossible.

"Sounds as if you would actually marry the chit."

Roland, who was lost in his own plans, smiled. "Would that be so bad?"

"No, I suppose you'd need a wife with them four wards of yours but, come-now, man, a thief?" Beaumont raised a brow of a true skeptic. It was what Roland would have expected.

"That is my problem not yours. Will you help or not?" Roland replied in a no-nonsense tone. The subject of just what Rose was or wasn't, was none of Beaumont's concern.

Beaumont sighed, feigning resignation.

"Yes, I'll help. Have you any plans?" Beaumont leaned forward, pushing some of the clutter out of the way.

Roland laughed. *What a mess.*

Cara was back in the carriage. The Earl's soiree was next on the agenda for the evening. The Huntington's supper invitation was a dreadful bore. She had only accepted out of some sense of misplaced guilt she carried about her first job. Liking Lady Huntington made the night a little easier.

It took forever as the carriages progressed slowly down the few blocks separating the two mansions. Cara would have loved to walk, but it was against protocol and Daniels would never have allowed it.

The streets hummed with activity; streetlamps cast a celestial glow. It was so different from the countryside Cara loved; still something of city life called to her.

Cara had read about parties such as these, seen the mansions in paintings. They were a part of her imagination. Now? Now she was here, though the tension was enormous, she still felt the allure. She couldn't help wondering if she would enjoy her chosen profession if circumstances were different. Like a game preformed out of fun rather than necessity.

Suddenly she was appalled the direction her thoughts were taking. Sure, she'd always longed for adventure. What girl didn't? For the most part she found her adventures in books, Mrs. Radcliff's Gothic tales or Shakespeare's handwritten works. Even the tales of history held appeal.

The reality was what started out of necessity, was becoming something, she enjoyed. It was a crazy notion, really, one that would never happen.

Slowing to a snail's pace entering the courtyard, the coach stopped. Cara donned her veil and waited for Daniels to climb down to assist her. The man was almost as stubborn as she. Suggestions of another driver were adamantly refused. Both he and Tibs were acting peculiar. Daniels appeared dressed like a footman instead of a driver; Tibs explained she was to be handed from carriage to door, personally.

Overprotective? Absolutely.

It could have been as they said, not wanting to take any more chances with her safety, admitting they were correct, would mean believing she was in more danger. She wasn't ready to do that, but she complied with their demands just the same. If anyone thought it unusual for the personal escort to the door, no one remarked; Daniels left her in the hands of the Salisbury's butler before disappearing back into the night.

Making her way slowly to the receiving line, Cara realized how early she was. Normally, she avoided them by coming late. Tonight, in her need to escape the Huntington's' dinner party, she was faced with the task of curtsying, smiling, and furnishing inane comments to each; hoping that none would grow teeth and bite her at a future date.

All day she had tried not thinking of Fairhaven. She was past fuming. His botched proposal was given out of duty. Out of honor. And honor was something she was unfamiliar with when it came to men. Honor could cost dearly. In this case, what could cost Fairhaven could very well give her what she wanted. Him. She could admit that now. In truth, she had thought of little else.

Still, she could not marry him, not as Rose Black. Was it possible he'd be willing to marry Caralyn Eve Danforth? *Aye, sure, and mayhap you're dreaming.*

It would be grand, not needing their so-called-guardian. Insufferable. Absentee guardian. She was still incensed. He hadn't the decency to show all afternoon. She wondered if he disappointed the children by not appearing at the appointed supper hour. She should have stayed.

Cara stood, poised at the top of the long stair. It took but a moment to prepare for the descent. The murky waters below, churned her stomach. Anxiety or anticipation? Tonight, she was Rose Black. *Time to swim with the sharks.* Pasting a smile on her face she took her step.

A shark eyed the tasty morsel. He would consume her if he were given the chance. And he would be. She had slipped from his grasp once; next time he would be prepared. Yes. He'd plan better and father would be here to assist him. Goddamn nuisance trying to act alone. If only his father would tell him what he wanted instead of ordering him about. His gaze was immersed on her lips as they curved seductively as she slowly made her way to the ballroom.

He imagined her smile was directed at him.

She'd have to be a pretty thing, better endowed than his current mistress, if she ever removed that veil he'd know for sure. Her body was luscious and even if her face wasn't, he meant to try her. Father said Thomas had a taste for finer things. His woman would be no exception.

Once she was no longer of use, he'd keep her for as long as she could please him, moving discretely he tried to ease the lower portion of himself that was being strangled by the confines of his breeches, the boundaries of his thoughts. Damn her. He would have the wench if it were the last thing he did.

Roland watched the widow, his body tied in knots. He was a predator of great proportions. He loved the thrill of the hunt as much as he liked the reward of the kill. Killing wasn't what came to mind when he thought of Rose. She would be his. She, alive and well, passionate and desirable, would be his reward.

Cara never noticed the two pairs of eyes; she was busy trying to look regal as the fear of falling headfirst down the stairs played on her mind. Though the sadistic thought of laying ass over teakettle in front of everyone kept a misplaced smile upon her face.

Roland, Beaumont on his heels, pushed his way through the throng of people blocking his path. Various times Beaumont stayed his friend because someone directed a question his way. He could give a rat's ass about their questions, answering with some unconscious and noncommittal remarks he forged onward. It had been forty-eight hours since he had seen her. Almost. He had spent most of his time counting every minute. Beaumont muttered something about looking too anxious. He agreed. Still, it was difficult making his feet and heart obey.

An eternity later, Roland and Beaumont arrived at Rose's side. She was already surrounded by hordes of dandies vying for her favors. Well, be damned if they were going to get the chance, Roland cursed silently.

The crowd parted to make way for Duke of Fairhaven and the Earl of Beaumont. Rose's lips curved in a mischievous smile. Leaning closer to one of the dandies, she whispered something. They laughed. Roland would have gladly killed the bastard.

"My dear Mrs. Black," said the dandy on her left, "allow me introduce His Grace, The Duke of Fairhaven, and his comrade in arms, His Lordship the Earl of Beaumont." He finished with a smug lift of his lips.

Cara hadn't heard anything past 'His Grace, The Duke'. *Oh... My... Gawd! He's a Duke! A Duke!* Cara was numb with shock. *Oh, my Gawd, he's a Duke. I turned down a bloody Duke. I could have been a Duchess.*

How she managed to keep a pleasant smile on her face while her stomach was strangling her throat was astounding; Fairhaven reached for her hand, routinely she gave it to him. Bringing it to his mouth, he placed a kiss directly on it instead of the few customary inches above. Heat burned through Cara like a wildfire. Adding unladylike sensations to her already scattered wits.

"A pleasure, Mrs. Black."

Did he know what he was doing to her? Dreams from the previous night rushed forth; Cara blushed, hoping it would stop at her cheeks.

Roland enjoyed the play of color fusing Rose's body; even in her widow's weeds, he could sense her nipples pucker. No, she wasn't as immune to him as she would like him to believe. That would work in his favor.

Roland reluctantly yielded her hand to Beaumont; he had held it far longer than was proper but since they would marry, it was of little import.

The man with Fairhaven kissed her hand, as Cara tried to remember his name. When it hit, Cara returned to her senses. What was Fairhaven doing with the Earl of Beaumont? The very same man Tibs had warned her against. Comrade? Were they friends or something else entirely?

"A pleasure Madam," he said softly.

Cara's mind was racing, she tried to sense something to dislike about the Earl. There was nothing. He seemed the perfect gentleman. Damn! Looking from one man to the other, Cara still had the presence of mind to include the various other members of the party in her gaze.

Redding seemed different now, almost possessive. There was something not right with the young man. He had conversed with her, looked, no, watched her. Maybe that was what was so unsettling? It really didn't matter; she would not be around much longer.

As conversations progressed, a quiet exchange seemed to take place between him and Fairhaven. It wasn't pleasant. Was the young man infatuated with her?

Beaumont had to admit he liked Mrs. Black. He had been prepared to dislike her, but her forthrightness was like a breath of fresh air. Covertly, he watched her, he could not put his finger on it, but as Roland had first said, there was something. He concurred. There was more to this widow than met the eye.

Cara soon made her excuses leaving Fairhaven and the others in search of her dupe, the enormous bag of wind known as the Earl of Salisbury.

Roland and Beaumont broke away from the dandies. They had only held court for Rose's sake. Now they would assume their positions in case Rose needed assistance. The Earl of Salisbury was known for his hatred of banks. He was known to keep large sums in his home. Not so unusual for an elder member of the top ten thousand, what was unusual was that the Earl constantly broadcast it to anyone who would listen. The fact that the fool hadn't been relieved of his wealth long before this was a miracle.

Still, there were other reasons the man's luck held. Damian Wortherley wasn't a man to be trifled with. Elderly he might be. Weak he was not. He didn't think Wortherley would attack a woman. Rose hadn't divulged everything about her work. He knew only that she rendered her prey unconscious; he prayed she would do so quickly. Before coming to harm.

Chapter Ten

An hour later, Cara left by the front door of the mansion. She could retire tonight. She would never have to do this again. A jolt of awareness hit her like a lightning bolt. She didn't want it to be over. It might have had a lot to do with not seeing a certain Duke ever again, but Cara feared it was more than that.

At midnight Daniels was waiting for her to emerge. He knew the approximate time Miss Cara departed. She was her father's daughter; she would not deviate from her schedule.

Giving her his arm, he led her down the front steps, across the courtyard where the team awaited. Tibs and he decided it would be in their best interest to get Miss Cara back to the townhouse as soon as she was done. Timing was of the essence. Cara needed to be home, installed in her room and preferably asleep before His Grace came back for the evening.

A runner was sent with a message from Tibs, stating that The Duke and The Earl had gone out shortly after dinner. Daniels was on alert; he hadn't seen His Grace arrive but that didn't mean he wasn't in attendance. The carriages could have impeded his vision, or they could have arrived earlier, as they had to come from The Huntington's. Either way, he was sure to go to his club afterwards, which meant he had a little time to get Miss Cara home before they would meet face to face.

George, Mrs. Leeks' grandson, quickly handed down Cara, ushered her into the townhouse. Cara thought they were taking her protection a little too far as Tibs met her taking her cloak.

"Did you have a good time, Miss?" Tibs inquired.

"Why yes. Tibs, I did. Thank you," Cara said, thinking it odd for Tibs to ask.

"You must be very tired; I sent Lucy up to your room," Tibs said, pushing.

Cara eyed him; something funny was going on and she was going to get to the bottom of it. Tomorrow. Tonight, she was in fact truly tired. Salisbury, the renowned eccentric, was not frail. Pompous. Overbearing. Lecherous. But not frail; she would have to seriously consider revising her definition of old and eccentric.

Climbing the stairs slowly, Cara stopped as she did every night of late to admire the paintings on the wall; so many reminded her of Wonderland. The lush green fields, the well-trimmed gardens; for the first time she wondered if her father had them commissioned because he too missed Wonderland.

It was asinine, really, if he missed his home all he had to do was come back. No, she was tired; that was why her mind was reaching toward the maudlin. Lucy was in Cara's room. The bedsheets were already turned down.

"I didn't pour you a bath, Miss, Mrs. Leeks felt it would be best if I waited till the morrow, you just recovering an' all." Lucy's head bobbed up and down as if she stood in front of Mrs. Leeks agreeing all over again.

"No, I suppose you are right, Lucy; please just help me with these buttons, then you can go. I can manage the rest myself."

Lucy nodded, and with quick efficiency unhooked the back of Cara's dress. Then bid her goodnight. Cara finished with her toiletry donning a fresh night rail. Sitting on the edge of her bed, she took down her long waist length hair and began the arduous task of combing it. With each stroke, she contemplated the behavior of her servants.

It had to be something to do with that man. It just had to be. Putting aside the brush, Cara went to the door that connected her room to Mr. Acworth's. Turning the key, she quietly opened it. The room was empty, except for a trunk standing at the end of a massive oak bed, a much bigger one than her own bed. It was a masculine room. Cara decided as she walked in further; the pieces of furniture were big and bulky, though not gaudy.

She could picture her father in this room, the person her father use to be. He too was bigger than life. Though not gigantic in stature, his persona was that of a God. When he spoke, everyone listened.

Sighing, Cara walked to the wardrobe, opened the doors and peered inside. For no reason save curiosity, she inspected each article of clothing. Mr. Acworth was a big man. Big in stature, the breath of his shoulders, the length of his pants to the extra pair of gleaming Hessians standing at the bottom, everything was large. She wondered again if he showed up at supper.

Familiarity engulfed her senses. Holding the garment to her nose, she sniffed. Tired as she was, she could not put her finger on any one thing. She returned a jacket to its hanging spot and shut the door. With one last look about the room, she exited. After plaiting her hair, she blew out the candle, soon falling into an exhausted sleep.

Goddamn it! She'd given him the slip again! Roland stood in the newly appointed study, casually nursing his third drink. It hadn't helped. Nothing helped. When he and Beaumont noted Rose exiting the Earl of Salisbury's library, they made their way to the front door, meaning to detain her long enough to have their conversation.

It seemed everyone wanted a word. Then, the bloody butler couldn't find their cloaks. All bluster and apologies but by the time they left the mansion, it was too late. Rose was nowhere in sight. Beaumont, the damned fool, had laughed and slapped his knee. Curse his hide; Roland would have loved planting one in his smiling face.

Roland searched; Beaumont followed. Nothing. She had disappeared like a puff of smoke. If it weren't for the pumping of his heart and tightening of his groin, he would have thought these past days nothing more than an illusion.

Taking a seat in front of the fire, Roland peered into the fiery liquid hoping to find an answer. It was deathly quiet. The servants had retired. The children were asleep. All should have been serene, yet a torrent of frustration raged within. Another night Roland would not be allowed sleep. He stared deeper into the flames contemplating everything, Rose, Thomas, Beaumont, the Home Office, Rex, Becky, Robby, Cara. Yes, Cara.

She was still not well enough to join them for supper.

Beaumont had enjoyed meeting his wards and they him. Stories were shared, with interest and laughter. Beaumont, to his credit would have made an excellent father. Roland had seen a different side of him tonight. He read the longing and his heart went out to him. What secrets hid behind the workaholic?

Something woke her. Cara lay listening; only silence reigned. She didn't know what jolted her awake. Beating her pillow, she tried to get comfortable. After about fifteen minutes of tossing and turning, Cara knew sleep would not come without aid. Tossing back the covers, she headed in search of warm milk, and a book. Anything to fill the silence and allow her to go back to sleep; she needed sleep if she was to confront their guardian come morning. This not knowing had gone on long enough.

Cara didn't bother with a candle knowing her way down to the kitchens. Entering the hall, Cara stopped long enough to glance at the door to the Baron's suite. She didn't know what time it was, but if he had entered his room, she would have known it.

No doubt he was out carousing and gambling. She wondered what Fairhaven was doing. She pushed away the unwelcome answer as she angrily started toward the stairs.

Going first to the kitchens, she found a jug of this morning's milk and poured it into a pot on the stove. The last embers were still hot enough to warm her milk though it would take a bit. While waiting, she went in search for her newest Mrs. Radcliff novel. Now where in Hades had she left it? The library? No—she wasn't in there. The parlor? Possible, she'd check there first. Lighting a candle, she hurried to the parlor.

Roland heard the footsteps outside the door before the handle turned. He was in no mood to see anyone. Was it one of the children? It would be of immense importance for them to seek him out. Maybe little Cara had taken a turn for the worse? He hadn't even met the young one yet; he would tomorrow, whether she was well enough or not.

The door opened; Roland stayed facing the fire.

"Come in, child. Did you have a nightmare?" he said, his tone comforting.

"Fairhaven?" Cara couldn't help herself it was out before she could think better of it.

Roland stood so fast he sloshed brandy all over himself. "Rose, damn it! What are you doing in my house? Where the hell were you tonight? Beaumont and I searched all over hells acre and could not find you!"

"Your house? What the hell are you taking about, *Your Grace?*"

Roland took out his handkerchief to wipe away most of the spills.

"Answer me," Cara demanded. "What are you doing here?"

Roland set down the cloth, with a speed Cara should have anticipated but didn't, he was across the room, grabbing her arm, pulling her closer to the fire.

"Damn you, Fairhaven! Damn you. Let me go!" Cara yelled.

"Hush up, damn you; do you want to wake the whole damn house?"

Cara tried to get a hold of her temper; she wiggled in his grasp, and it only served to tighten the bands that bound her. He had both of her hands in one of his. He was a big man.

"Damn you!" Cara hissed. "You're him, aren't you? Don't try denying it! I'd know your scent anywhere! Just when in the hell were you going to tell me?"

"Rose, for the love of… Calm down. I haven't been able to speak with you for two damn days, not my choice by the way," Roland hissed back. "Now what was it I was supposed to tell you?"

"That you're him! You bastard! I cannot believe this!" Cara stamped her foot into the rug.

"What are you talking about? You damn well know who I am."

"No…" Cara's head started shaking frantically. "No…I don't…I didn't…Oh Gawd," she finally croaked.

Roland lit a candle. Bringing it close to her face, for the first time he saw her glass-like silver, gray eyes, "Holy Shit!"

"Exactly!" Cara ground out.

"Who are you?" Roland demanded.

"I should think you'd know one of your own wards, *Your Grace*," Cara said snidely.

"My ward? You are mistaken. My wards are four children. You are no child!" he accused.

"Three."

"Three what?"

"Three are children, eleven years in age to be exact, the fourth, *Your Grace*, the fourth, is nineteen!" Cara yelled.

Roland felt the earth open up. It threatened to swallow him whole. This woman was his ward. The woman he loved and wanted to marry was under his protection. Holy Mother of Christ! What was he going to do now?

"It can't be? Thomas would have been…"

"Twenty-one. He would have been twenty-one when I was born, yes, I know. And in case counting is not one of your stronger points, *Your Grace*, I am eight years older than my siblings, *Your Grace*, is there anything else you'd like to know, *Your Gra*—"

Before Cara could utter another 'Your Grace', Roland's mouth came down on hers, effectively swallowing all further comment or thought. Cara tried to fight the wave of passion that engulfed her, she could not, and before she knew it her body betrayed her, moving closer and seeking the warmth that only Fairhaven could give.

Her mouth opened beneath his. His tongue swept in bringing with it the heady taste. Cara moaned, moving closer still. Her hands, no longer restrained, worked their way through his hair bringing him closer; his roamed over her hips up her waist and across her taut nipples. She burned as if she were on fire, "Fairhaven," she whispered breathlessly. "Oh, God."

"Hush, love, hush," he said smoothing her hair, her head snug against his chest. After what seemed like an eternity in bliss, Roland pulled back. Taking Rose—no, not Rose, Caralyn—taking Caralyn by the hand, he led her to the chair by the fire. Pulling her down on his lap, he held her there when she tried to get up.

"No, my love. Now, we will have our talk."

His hand stroked slowly, quieting her as effectively as a jumpy colt. When she calmed, she looked at him with those silver-gray eyes, Thomas' eyes, Roland cursed himself for not seeing it before. Not seeing her before.

A gentle finger traced her eye. "You have his eyes."

"A curse," she spat.

Roland could sense the hatred in her voice. Hatred so strong it could only come from great hurt. They had to start somewhere. Her hatred for her father would be as good a place as any.

"You hate him."

It was a statement not a question; the answer surprised even Cara herself.

"I want to…but I can't," she finished on a whisper.

Roland kissed her forehead.

"Why?"

"He left us. He left me."

"Rose, sorry, I mean, Caralyn…"

"Cara."

"What?"

"Cara, everyone calls me Cara."

Roland smiled at that.

"Okay, Cara. I don't think he wanted to. No. Let me finish. I have known your father for a long time. He was a good man."

"No."

"Yes. He was. I don't know what happened to make him leave you, I only know he didn't want to, how could he? I wouldn't."

"You're just saying that you weren't here. You couldn't possibly know," Cara said denying the small flicker of hope that ignited in her heart.

"No. You're right, but I can tell you this. The investigation, the one Rose was helping me with, I think that when we find the answers to the Organization's questions, we will also find the answer to this."

Deflated that he was unable to give her concrete proof this instant of her father's goodness, Cara sagged. "I hope you're right," she whispered. *Please God, let him be right.*

They sat in silence until the sun peeked through the distant horizon. "Go to bed, Cara. We'll talk again after you have had some sleep." Roland made do with a quick peck on the forehead as he pushed her up out of his warm lap. She was beautiful, even pale and tired as she was. All night he had wanted to kiss her again, take her under him, and bury himself deep inside her. He didn't. Now he cursed himself for being an even bigger fool as he watched her hips sway softly back and forth outdoor.

Roland made his way to his room. Stripping off his cravat, shirt, breeches, he climbed naked into bed, letting the coolness of the sheets soothe his impassioned body. He wondered where Cara's rooms were. Obviously, not the nursery.

"Who'd do such a thing? That's what I'd like to know!" Mrs. Leeks' animated voice came from the direction of the kitchen. Cara had a sinking feeling as she walked through the dining room, entering the kitchens from the front, sure enough there was Mrs. Leeks scrubbing her new-fangled stove. *Oops*, Cara thought.

"Can I help you, Mrs. Leeks?" Cara asked innocently.

"Naw, Miss Cara. I almost have it. Breakfast will be a little while. 'Annot cook on when there be burnt curdle everywhere. The others awake?"

"No, Mrs. Leeks, never fear. I appear to be the only one about."

"Not so."

Cara turned to see Fairhaven leaning against the door jamb, arms folded over his chest, mischief in his eyes. Her stomach tightened.

"Ach!" squawked Mrs. Leeks.

Tibs entered the kitchen from the servant's door. "Your Gr…that is to say, Mr. Acworth." Tibs looked from Cara to Mr. Acworth and back again, neither missed the look of guilt clearly written on his face.

"Tibs, since breakfast will be delayed, I think that Miss Danforth and I would like a word with you." Roland looked to Cara.

"Quite right, Your Grace," Cara said sweetly.

For an instant Tibs looked like he would rather be anywhere but in the kitchens with the two people he had been trying to keep apart obviously joining ranks against him. Schooling his features, chin raised, back straightened, once he again looked the part of the regal butler, he nodded.

"Yes, Your Grace, Miss." He waited for them to take the lead out of the kitchen.

"So, this is why you have been letting me sleep undisturbed, ushering me out the door when you would sooner, I stay right here at home," Cara said from her perch on the windowsill.

Tibs looked as though he would rather be swimming in a cesspit. So far, answers hadn't been very forthcoming.

"I think it would be wise to answer the Lady, Tibs. I for one would like to hear what you have to say." Roland's gaze stabbed the errant butler's bowed head from behind the desk. Tibs sat in front staring at his folded hands, not uttering one single word to confirm or deny his guilt.

"Well then, let me see," Roland said and paused for effect, before counting off the infractions on his fingers.

"You led me to believe Caralyn was naught but a child, led me to think she was ailing, when in truth she was recovering from her kidnapping…"

Tibs' head shot up. "You know about the kidnapping, Your Grace?"

Roland didn't answer, instead he charged ahead; with the addition of each violation, Tibs cringed as if the death knell were ringing with every word.

"…And you led Caralyn to believe I hadn't inquired about her welfare, when in fact, I had been sick with worry. I hope that's all because as you can see,"—Roland held up his hands, fingers up. Cara bit her lip to keep from laughing— "I am swiftly running out of fingers. Caralyn, do you have anything to add?"

Tibs was saved from answering by a knock on the door.

"Enter."

The door opened, revealing a guilty looking Daniels on the other side.

"Ah, Daniels, do come in. We would so hate for you to miss the party," Roland jibbed, brow raised. Cara coughed suspiciously into her hand.

Daniels entered, closing the door and took a seat next to his accomplice. Sorrow-filled eyes looked upon Cara before turning their attention on the man in front of them.

A little after one, a subdued Tibs answered the door. The Earl of Beaumont had arrived.

"They're in the library, My Lord, if you would follow me," Tibs said, laying the Earl's hat aside.

"They?" the Earl questioned.

Tibs didn't answer, only turned, and led the way down the corridor.

"The Earl of Beaumont, Your Grace."

"Thank you, Tibs. Please have Mrs. Leeks bring refreshments," Cara said.

"Very well, Miss," Tibs replied, with a bow.

Cara felt the weight of Beaumont's stare. Turning, she met him look for look.

"I'll be damned! The widow!"

"That's what I like about you, old chap. You're quick on the upswing," Roland chirped. "Have a seat before you faint. And don't stare so, didn't your mother ever teach you it was bad form?"

Beaumont made his way to the closest chair, his eyes never leaving Cara's face. "By Jove, she has her father's eyes," he said to no one in particular.

"Right again. Your good today, I do believe that's two for two."

"Oh, Fairhaven, do let the man be," Cara admonished.

Beaumont expected Roland to put the young chit in her place, instead he found him staring, and smiling, like a love-struck fool.

"Since His Grace seems to have lost his manners, let me introduce myself," Cara said, coming to Beaumont's side.

Roland shook his fog-clouded head. "Terribly sorry. Allow me. Beaumont, Miss Caralyn Danforth. Thomas' eldest daughter."

"A pleasure to meet you, again, My Lord." Cara smiled ingenuously.

"And I you. Again, that it is," Beaumont flung back.

"I guess I do not need to tell you the reason for the urgent dispatch this morning?" Roland stated.

"No, I don't suppose you do. How are we to progress with this little turn of events, I ask you?"

Cara went back to the windowsill; Roland refused to tell her anything stating that they wait for Beaumont to arrive, so they spent most of the morning, after talking with Tibs and Daniels, in the nursery with the children assisting them with their studies.

Now Cara was anxious to hear more about proving her father's innocence. As the conversation progressed around her, she listened with half an ear for some morsel about her father. None came.

Her thoughts turned to Fairhaven. Nights such as last night spent in quiet solitude could not happen again. He was her guardian; it went against the very dictate of society for her to remain under the same roof. Therefore, there was only one thing Fairhaven could do.

Send them back to Wonderland. Alone.

Oh, he would come, visit from time to time, not often, and not without a proper chaperone. How could her father have left them in such a tangle?

He was good in his choice, so much that the children would come to love their guardian and he them. What of her? She could not allow herself to love him, not the way she longed to, and just like that, because of their situation the children would miss out on the benefit of having a father figure. How would they look at her knowing it was her fault yet again that the man they loved stayed away? Worse yet, she feared it was too late. She already loved him.

"…So, if your aunt sponsors her and she stays there until the wedding I cannot see any problem. The investigation could go on, as an affianced couple you would be welcome anywhere together and our precious little thief would not have to be sent back to The Gables. We need her here, Acworth."

Cara caught that. "What!" she cried, stunned. "You cannot possibly mean for the two of us to marry? It's—it's unthinkable! A farce! He's, my guardian!"

Roland had wondered if Cara was paying attention, obviously she was at least in part. Her reaction angered him. He knew she felt the same way about him as he did her. Marriage was the only plausible answer. One look at the stubborn tilt of Cara's chin told him she would be anything but reasonable. Ignore her, he told himself, she'll come around, he'd see there was no other option.

"Fine. How long before you can get the special license?" Roland asked.

"I should have it in two possibly three days at the outside. When can you have Cara's things moved to your aunt's?"

"She'll be there within the hour. We will, of course, halt our activities until after the wedding."

"Your aunt and uncle will smooth the progress significantly, I should think," Beaumont said, as he thought of all that would need to be done.

"You cannot be serious!" Cara shouted. Jumping up from the windowsill, she paced the floor angrily.

"I will not do it! I will not marry *him!*" Cara's head shook forcefully back and forth. "You can't make me, us, do something neither of us want to do!"

"Who said I don't want to marry you?" Roland interjected.

"You can, you will, my dear girl," Beaumont intoned neutrally.

"What?" Cara glared at the man she was coming to like. Just went to show she lacked better judgment. "Who do you think you are? You cannot order me about!"

"Oh, but I can. I need you. The Home Office needs you. England needs you. For this reason, you will do as I say," Beaumont said strictly.

"Or what?" Cara yelled, stamping her foot on the plush carpet.

"Or you can say goodbye to your siblings, your home, your possessions, and say hello to Newgate. I suppose there is always deportation. I should think Newgate the better choice; you would want to be close enough for your family to visit…"

"And to think I was starting to like you." Cara sniffed.

"Well, what is it to be?"

"You haven't given me a choice!"

"Oh, I have, dear girl—become a Duchess or a criminal. One should think the choice a simple one."

"OOOOOO!" Her fists were clenched, and her voice quivered with anger.

Roland watched the exchange with a mixture of horror and humor. It was nice to see someone get the better of Cara for a change. God knows he hadn't been able to. He knew he must stop the drama going on around him, humorous as it was, if he let it continue, he'd have a devil of a time getting her to like him once they were married. Smothering a chuckle, he jumped in.

"Cara. It isn't as bad as all that. If, once the job is complete, you decide you cannot come to love me, I will give you an annulment. You will be free to walk away."

Cara glared at him. How did he expect to get an annulment, even if he could keep his hands off her and not consummate the marriage, what of her? She wanted his touch. Damn the man!

"Fine. Now that everything's settled, could you go pack a few things? Please. I will take you to my aunt's house as soon as you're ready."

With a sniff Cara turned on her heel, slamming the door behind her. The sound echoed, bouncing off every wall in the room. Roland couldn't help it— he laughed.

Cara heard the boisterous sound of male chauvinistic laughter coming from the library. It only served to fuel her already raging temper. She'd show him! Yes. She'd marry him. For even that was better than prison. Slightly. She could go without touching him. Hadn't she gone nineteen years without touching a man? What's another couple of days, weeks—she swallowed hard—months? Damn him! Dratted man! Cursed man! Arrogantly handsome man—OOOO, how she would like to scream!

She'd like nothing better than to wrap her hand about his well-muscled neck, kiss…no…kill him. Yes, definitely kill him.

Fuming, she slammed open the door to her room, grabbed her suitcase, and started flinging everything inside, not caring one whit that some would be wrinkled beyond repair.

Lucy stood off to one side, afraid to approach. Frankly, Cara didn't blame her. She was in no mood for civility. Finally, out of fear for the wardrobe, Cara thought, Lucy came forth, removing what Cara had carelessly thrown in the case. Quietly, she began to smooth, fold, and repack. In silence, they worked together to get the job done.

"Do you really think you should be laughing?" Beaumont asked, his laughter now completely under control.

Roland puffed, trying to gain control of his emotions, "Yes. Well. I do believe…I have finally pulled one over on her and…and lived to talk about it." Another fit of laughter struck him, doubling him over his desk.

"You gave her the impression she could have an annulment. After I played the bad guy, forcing her to accept what you wanted all along. I cannot believe that when this masquerade is over, you will simply let her go?"

"I… Won't…have to," Roland said between gulps of air.

"But you said…"

"I know what I said. There is no way she will be able to stop me from consummating the marriage. Therefore, old chap, she will have no grounds for an annulment."

"You honestly don't mean to force her—do you?"

"Of course not!" Roland snapped, enraged his friend would think such a thing. "She loves me. I know she does. She's just not willing to admit it. Let's face it," Roland sobered. "Thomas did her a bad turn, leaving them. She's afraid. But I'm not leaving soon, she'll realize that."

"And you expect to make up for years of her father's neglect overnight?" Beaumont elevated his brow, his expression filled with doubt. "It can't be done, I tell you."

"Notice, my good man, I didn't say that I would refrain from trying to change her mind?" Roland said seriously.

Beaumont looked as though he were lost.

"I fully intend to have her in my bed. I will not force her; I have learned a thing or two about seduction and I intend to use it. All of it."

Beaumont grinned. "Ah, so you plan to seduce your wife."

Roland grinned back. "Of course. I wouldn't have it any other way."

Beaumont stayed long enough for another drink then he was off to call in a few favors and obtain a very important, special license.

Roland sat at the desk, penning a note to his aunt. Next would be a missive to Henry Gomersal, Thomas' solicitor. He hadn't had the time to go over Thomas' will. But now that he intended to wed Thomas' daughter, Beaumont suggested he contact the man and finalize matters with the estate.

Once done, Roland called for Tibs. "Have a footman take this directly to Mr. Gomersal. And this other is for my aunt. Have him go there first."

"Yes, Your Grace," Tibs said sheepishly.

"Tibs, have a seat. Thank you; this won't take a minute. I wanted to say that I appreciate all you have done for my wards. I will not hold your actions against you, nor Daniels, you had reason to do what you did. Forthwith, I should like to be consulted." Tibs still looked unsure.

"Now is not the time to go into detail, although I feel you can help interpret what is happening. Things will progress much faster if you are open and honest with me. I understand you may not trust me. But please remember, Thomas did. I'm asking for you to help."

Tibs gave a slight nod, the only indication that he may be revising his earlier assessment of Roland.

"I am to wed Caralyn in three days' time, sooner if I can manage it. I'd like the opportunity to clear Thomas' good name while I serve my duties for the Home Office. All I ask is that you and Daniels both think hard about the month prior to Thomas' death; give me anything that you may or may not feel relevant. As his son-in-law, I assure you I do not want to taint his name but repair it."

Roland allowed Tibs time to reflect upon what it was he was saying. The spy business could be damnable tricky and obtaining allies devilishly hard. He hoped that Tibs could see and hear the sincerity in his speech.

"I will speak with Daniels, Your Grace. What time would you like to meet?"

"After dinner. I have some errands to run, and I think you and Daniels need time to refresh your memories."

Tibs nodded. "Very well."

Roland watched him walk out; before the door shut completely, it opened again. A resigned-looking Cara stood on the other side, debating whether she wanted to enter. Roland's heart clenched. If she weren't so bloody obstinate, all of this would be much easier.

Chapter Eleven

Slowly, she closed the door and approached him. Head bowed. He'd almost relent just to see her smile.

"I assume you are packed, ready to be introduced to my aunt?" he said quietly.

Cara responded with a stiff nod. She didn't look up. Refusing to look into his eyes. If she did, she'd crumble. Knowing she would be lost in a beautiful sea of blue. She was saddened by what was to be and what could never be. A mountain of confusion erected within, growing by the minute, and she could not seem to focus enough to see her way out.

She had thought about little else. Any way you sliced it; someone would lose. With an annulment, she'd lose her siblings, be forced to move out of the family home. She would lose Wonderland. She'd lose Fairhaven. If she didn't go, the kids would lose a man they were coming to know and love. They needed a man. Roland could provide what her father so callously had taken away. It wasn't right that she should deprive them of yet another father.

If she stayed married, Roland would lose his freedom. Tied forever to a woman out of duty and honor. A woman he didn't love. A woman he would come resent.

Roland knew he shouldn't touch her. It would only anger her and make matters worse. He clenched his fists in an effort not to reach out.

"I sent a message to Mr. Gomersal, hopefully, we'll hear back soon and will be able to meet with him. Would you like to be present?"

He didn't say *before the wedding*, but it hung there between just the same.

Cara remained stoic but shrugged her delicately rounded shoulders; there was nothing the solicitor would tell her that she didn't already know. On the scale of happenings, it barely registered.

Her could-care-less attitude pushed Roland to his limits; coming out of the chair, he was around the desk and behind her, in less than a heartbeat. Considering how fast his heart was beating…it was damned fast.

He pressed in close from behind; he didn't care if it angered her. In truth he now hoped it would. He wanted a reaction. Any reaction. Some sign that she was still the same woman he had fallen in love with. An indication that he could breech the defensive wall she had so quickly erected. She remained inflexible.

Cara caught herself before she sighed, he was so close, she had to force herself not to move, not to turn into his welcoming embrace, and take what was offered. He did it because of duty, because of honor, because to him it was the right thing to do, and he had no choice. That was not the way she wanted him.

Funny, when she thought of her father and how his honor-less actions had hurt them, she had prayed for their guardian to be different. Now that he was, she hated it.

Roland leaned closer, running a finger over the base of her neck, he could feel her heartbeat quicken. Relief flooded within him. She wasn't immune. She was angry. Fighting him the only way she knew. So be it. Bringing his lips closer to the tender skin beneath her ear, he let out a warm breath. She shivered. She didn't know how much that little action told him. Feeling confident, he whispered, "Time to depart. Have you said goodbye to the children?"

His voice was low and husky, a breath of words. He could be saying anything; it still would have set her aflame.

"Yes."

It came out slowly almost dreamily. Roland was tempted to ask just what she said yes to. Pulling back without kissing her, he headed for the door.

"Coming?"

Blinking, Cara shook her head to gather her wits. She was in trouble. He was far more experienced than she, and he had just proved he could turn her to jelly. She would have to be always on her guard, spending as little time alone with him as possible, or she would never survive.

Roland was waiting in the hall. He made donning a cloak the most sensual experience Cara had ever witnessed. He held his arm; Cara placed her hand just above. She would not touch him. She would not.

Tibs closed the door before allowing himself the small pleasure of a smile. Miss Cara had met her match.

All too soon, they were being admitted into Greyley House. The home of Amylia and Anthony Stapleton, Roland's aunt and uncle; Cara had been there before. It seemed like a lifetime ago when she had attended only to find information concerning Sir Alfred.

She had left in a hurry, running headlong into her fate.

"Thank you, Roberts," the woman said. Smiling, she came forth to embrace her nephew. It was a comical sight. Her blond head scarcely reached the end of Roland's knotted cravat. After what seemed like an eternity, as nervous Cara was, Fairhaven was released. Still holding his hand, she turned her cornflower blue gaze to her. Cara fought the urge to squirm.

Fairhaven intervened, "Caralyn, this gorgeous beauty is my Aunt Amylia. Aunt Amylia, Caralyn Danforth, my fiancée."

Amylia cast a flushed look toward her nephew. Cara was glad for the respite.

"My nephew has a silver tongue. Pay him no mind, my dear."

Amylia smiled invitingly. She really was beautiful. Cara smiled.

"Dear Caralyn, it is a pleasure to meet you."

Cara curtsied. "And I you, Your Grace."

"There is no need for formality, Caralyn; please you really must call me Amylia. I do declare you'll give my dear nephew seizure, Your Grace-ing me. He simply cannot abide ceremony. I fear I have completely given up trying to reform him."

Amylia cast Roland a look of mock disapproval, shaking her head.

Fairhaven leaned forward, waggled his brows and kissed her cheek.

Amylia blushed, ushering them to the sitting room giving herself time to regain her composure.

Cara sat. Not knowing what else to do, she looked about the room. Every nook and cranny spoke elegance. Wall hangings of an assortment of colors and designs accentuated the deep brown walls and golden draperies.

Louis XIV furniture was strategically placed about to offer convenience and welcome visitors. The plush Persian rug was the same hew as Lady Greyley's golden colored hair. Was it called the Gold Room? Whatever its name, Roland's aunt looked like a queen, the parlor her throne designed to correspond with her best features.

"…Is that not, right? Dear?"

Cara realized Lady Greyley was speaking to her. "Um. I am sorry, Your Grace, my mind was elsewhere."

"That is understandable, I was just explaining to Roland that if the wedding was to be in less than three days, we do not have time to sit and sip tea. We must start immediately. We will have to go shopping, Lord knows we won't be able to acquire everything a young married woman needs in such short time, but with Madame's help, I am sure we can purchase enough to tide you over for the first week or so of your marriage.

"We'll need a church. There will be outings you will have to attend. Together." She slanted another look at her nephew. We must plant word so there will be no wagging tongues. Let's see, have I forgotten anything?"

"Thank you, Your Grace…"

"Amylia."

"Thank you. Amylia. I am sure I could use all the help I can get but there are several things on your list I can do without."

"What things would that be, dear?"

"Nothing, Aunt Amylia. She will need everything you suggest. Except for the church, I had thought perhaps your gardens. That is if it's okay with you."

Roland looked at Cara for a moment; there was a glimmer of something in her eyes, appreciation, perhaps. He knew she would not want to be married in a stuffy church, for her the outdoors meant life. Hopefully, being married amongst the blooming abyss, she would come to realize their union too would blossom. Flourish just as his aunt's garden did.

"Why, I think that's a lovely idea, dear! What do you think, Caralyn?" Amylia clapped her hands quickly a couple of times, all the while watching her soon-to-be niece carefully. Something was stressing the sweet thing. Knowing now would not be the best time to voice her misgivings, she decided to remain silent until Roland's departure.

"I think the gardens would be lovely." Cara stopped, fearing she'd say too much, or perhaps show too much.

Amylia saw the flicker in the girl's eyes, though quickly covered, there was a longing. *So that is the way the wind blows.*

Amylia felt relieved, for a brief time she worried Roland was forcing the young woman. Though it would be out of character for her nephew to *have* to force any woman, he wasn't beyond doing just that to obtain what he wanted. And he wanted Caralyn.

So, what then was the girl's problem? She needed to get rid of Roland; he was making things worse.

"I'll show Caralyn to her room now and help her pick out something to wear tonight. Almacks. That is where you should make your début, my dear. While you have a nap, I will contact Sally Jersey and arrange everything. She'll be only too willing to help; she just loves a good romance. Come now, let's show your fiancé to the door. I'll tell Claire to prepare your bath."

Amylia rose. Roland knew he was dismissed. Rising, he offered his hand to Cara, who deep in thought placed her hand in his. She was overwhelmed, all this was moving so fast. And Lady Greyley was like a hurricane blowing in, reshaping everything all at once.

Cara bit down on her lip to keep it from trembling; she was tired. That was all. She was a big girl, she didn't mind being left alone, in a strange house, with people she'd just met—really, she didn't. Being left was nothing new to her.

Reading her thoughts, Roland placed a finger beneath her chin, raising her eyes to his; softly he whispered it would be all right, he'd be back soon. Brushing her lips lightly, he was gone.

Lady Greyley showed Cara to her rooms, then immediately vacating so she could have her bath. Cara sent the maid, Claire, on her way she could undress without assistance. She needed to be alone.

Claire must have been sent up shortly after they had arrived. Cara's things were already hanging in the wardrobe. The copper tub stood filled with steaming water, next to inviting fire. Though the room was exceedingly warm, Cara felt chilled to the bone. Mayhap that was the reason Amylia had it set. Jadedly, she removed her clothing and stepped into the steaming water.

She sat back, letting the water seep into her bones. The chamber must have belonged to Roland's cousin, a daughter, for it was too personal to be used simply for housing guests. The bed swathed in white linen and lace, had puffy pillows piled three high across the top. Little pink buds with trailing green vines dappled the fabric. Bed curtains hung completely to the floor on the side closest the window. The other was held back with lace ties, invitingly.

Carpet was so white, Cara cringed at the thought of dropping something on it, thick and soft; she vaguely remembered her feet sinking into it as she'd walked across the floor.

Long deep rose-colored drapes adorned two floor-to-ceiling windows, the deep color chosen to block out more of the sun. She closed her eyes, allowing her body, her mind, to be swept away by the very serenity it represented. Peace.

"Miss Caralyn, please wake up. His Grace will be angered if you catch a chill."

Cara opened her eyes to find Claire standing over her, towel in hand. Cara stood, while Claire wrapped it around her. Mechanically walking to the bed, Cara climbed in. She would apologize to Claire for her rudeness when she awoke. With that, she was sound asleep.

"How's our guest, Claire?" Lady Greyley asked.

"Just fine, Madam. The poor dear is tired, found her asleep in her bath. I woke her only to move her to her bed. There she still sleeps."

"Let her sleep for a couple of hours. We will not have to get ready till eight, wake her at seven with a tray."

At seven-fifteen, a cheery Amylia floated into the room.

"How are you feeling, dear?"

"Fine, thank you. It is a lovely room. Peaceful."

"I'm glad you like it dear, it belonged to my daughter. She, like you, loved the outdoors. Her and Ian reside in Scotland. I miss her so."

"Why Scotland?" Cara asked more to make conversation than for a deep-seated need to know.

"I prayed my Beth would find a nice English Lord." Amylia chuckled. "Difficult to the end, she lost her heart to a highlander. Ian is a good man, and he makes my daughter happy, but he must remain in Scotland much of the time. They visit a couple of times a year, still it is not the same as having her here."

Cara thought of her father and had to agree.

Amylia saw the look of longing that struck Caralyn's countenance. Promptly, it was pushed aside. This was a girl well used to hiding her emotions. Had Amylia not been watching closely, she might have missed it altogether. Looking to change the subject, Amylia started readying Cara's clothing for the evening.

Together, they bustled and trussed and laughed. Cara couldn't help feeling lighthearted, she had not wanted to like Roland's aunt so much, but it was exceedingly nice to have a friend. They talked about all kind of things from blooms to blunders while the woman put finishing touches on Cara's bun.

"You look quite divine, my dear. Roland will be the envy of every gentleman in London."

Amylia's smile, and good humor was infectious.

"Just London?" Cara inquired with a smile.

"You are a devious one, very well then, all of England," Amylia said with a flourish, causing Cara to giggle like her sisters.

The woman instantly transformed into a girl. Amylia couldn't help hoping that Roland would be able to nurture the impish side of Caralyn for years to come.

"Are we ready then?" Cara asked.

"Yes, Anthony is having the carriage brought around. Roland is to meet us at Almacks. I cannot wait; he will be speechless when he sees you. And Ro is never speechless."

Amylia linked her arm companionably with Cara as together they glided down the stairs. Roland's uncle stood at the bottom, love for his wife clearly written all over his face. As they neared the bottom, he handed them both compliments though Cara noticed he didn't look at her. His eyes remained riveted on his wife.

She wanted that kind of marriage. One filled with enough love to stand the tests of time. Her heart ached with bitter resentment. Anthony assisted the women with their cloaks then offering an arm to each, he escorted them to the waiting carriage.

"I will be the envy with two such beautiful women on my arms," he stated, straightening his spine and puffing out his chest.

Roland's day had been going wrong from the moment he returned to Danforth House. Closeted in the library, making plans for the evening, the door swung inwards with enough strength to hit the wall noisily.

"Where is she? Where have you taken her?" Rex demanded as he charged over and stood in front of Roland's desk.

"Hello Rex. It is nice to see you too," Roland said calmly.

"Where is Cara?" Rex demanded once more.

Immediately confirming Cara hadn't spoken to her siblings prior to leaving. Rex stood in front of him, four feet ten inches of fuming grandeur that spoke Lord of the manor…a very irritated Lord.

"Rex, I was about to send for you, how very clever of you to seek me out, saved a great deal of my time. Thank you. Please have a seat."

Rex eyed Roland suspiciously. Eventually shrugging nonchalantly, he took a seat in front of the desk. Perched on the edge of the seat, he sat his small, booted foot tapping silently on the carpet. He looked ready to hurdle the desk, should the need arise, to pummel his guardian. Roland choked back a laugh, a minute terrier confronting a massive wolfhound. He would never win, of course, whether it was lack of good sense or outright courage, he would stand his ground.

"Well?" Rex said, at last bringing Roland out of his musing.

"Yes, quite right. Well, we—that is to say, your sister and I—wanted to speak to you but were unable to with the girls present."

"Why?"

"Your sister has consented to becoming my wife. We wanted to ask for your blessings, of course, you being the head of the family and all."

Rex raised his small black eyebrows and pursed his lips in thought.

"Cara doesn't want a husband," he stated.

"Oh?" Now it was Roland's brow that rose.

"Yes. I want to speak with her. Where is she?"

"Rex, Cara gave me no indication she was averse to becoming my bride." The small white lie tripped off Roland's lips with ease. "In fact, she's so excited, she forgot to tell you of her departure to my aunt and uncle's house. At this very moment, they are preparing wedding arrangements for tomorrow next. So, you see, very soon, your sister will soon be back under this very roof where she belongs."

"Why? Why would she marry you? She's only just met you. And you, her."

This was going to be a might harder than Roland had originally thought. Convincing Rex though would be the hardest task; hopefully, he would get by the girls without difficulty.

"Rex, I assume with your intelligence that you have known about Cara's escapades prior to me mentioning it now?"

Rex gave a small hesitant nod.

"Very well, then you might know that your sister and I have been working together for some time. True, I did not know she was your sister, but we did develop an attachment to one another. Therefore, under present circumstances, it is in our best interests to wed."

"Not good enough."

"Then look at it this way, Cara is an eligible unwed woman living under the same roof as a bachelor of no relation. Few options are available to us that the ton would not frown upon; one, we marry which is what we are intending to do. Two. Cara relocates to another home, somewhere safely away from me."

"Three,"—Rex interrupted— "you relocate."

"Not possible. Though Cara is of an age to wed, she is not legally old enough to act as your guardian, nor was she named as such by your father."

"Why do you care what the ton thinks? I am sure if you asked, Cara would not give one fig about what the stuck-up ladies of the ton would have to say."

He just wasn't letting up; he was worse than a bloody dog with a bone. *And here he'd thought Cara would be hard to convince.* He could not divulge the danger Cara was in or that he needed her for the Organization. But there had to be something that would convince him it was for the best.

"It's not the ton. Think about it, Rex; who means more to Cara than anything else, who would bear the punishment of her actions in years to come?" Roland waited watching Rex's face while he was deep in thought. He saw the moment true understanding when it crossed the boy's face. He paled. Swallowing, the word came out squeakily, "Us."

Roland didn't answer. The boy turned whiter fighting the demons of age and helplessness. He knew only too well what those demons felt like, the death of his mother and father was something he had never been able to forgive himself for. Knowing no words would help him, he rose, walking around the desk, he placed a comforting hand on the boy's shoulder.

"She cares for you?" This came after about ten minutes of complete silence. The question startled Roland.

"Yes, I believe she does. And I,"—Roland swallowed nervously— "I care for her a great deal. I will care for her, Rex. I will stay true. On my honor."

With a nod, Rex rose and left. Roland poured himself a generous helping of spirits. Swallowing it in one gulp, he let the burning sensation chase away any leftover doubts before heading to Almacks.

155

Cara stood beside Amylia and Anthony, nervously awaiting the arrival of Beaumont and Fairhaven. Several intrigued people flocked to the Duke and Duchess of Greyley seeking an introduction, some of which Cara had relieved of a few hundred pounds or more.

She was proud of the way she handled herself. It made the situation easier knowing she had two consummate actors from which to follow their leads. They had rehearsed the story on the carriage ride over.

According to Lady Greyley, Beaumont had managed to plant the evidence needed to give credence to their tale. As confused as she was, she realized their story was believable. Her father, having worked closely with Roland, had arranged a marriage between his eldest daughter and his friend, prior to Roland leaving for America.

As Roland would be gone for some time and Cara was not of an age to wed, their betrothal was left secret. It coincided with the story of Roland's guardianship nicely. Now with the death of Cara's father and Roland's immediate guardianship, the marriage was to be arranged posthaste so the family could get on with their lives. After all, three years was long enough for any engagement.

Not everyone received the tale tonight, but it would pass quickly through the ranks. Sally Jersey dispatched the information to anyone who happened by. Cara's reputation would not be tarnished, as Lady Jersey put the spin of young love into the tale more so with each passing. No one would dare question Sally Jersey. After all, it simply wasn't done.

She felt him before she saw him, the familiar fluttering in her stomach told her what her eyes missed. He had arrived. It was all Cara could do to stand in quiet elegance as her instinct to run to him reigned.

Roland spotted her beside his aunt and uncle. She was an ethereal vision in dove gray silk. The dress gathered high under her lovely breasts, cascading to the floor like a shimmering waterfall. She was unencumbered by the many stays that were all the rage. She was a vision.

Her raven black hair was gathered and held at the top of her head, a few tendrils curling fell about her oval-shaped face.

"I say, why are you stopped? Thought you were all fired up to see your fiancée?" Beaumont, who had just finished righting himself after running into Roland's back, peeked around Roland's shoulder.

"Odd's Blood, Acworth, she is much too beautiful for the likes of you," he said, as he clapped Roland on the back.

"She is. And she's mine. Forever. I refuse to let her go."

Roland inhaled, as if trying to pick up the faint scent of cinnamon before setting forth once more.

They danced, they talked, and they laughed. It was a carefree evening; one Cara had dreamed about many times. Amylia had said to forget the lot and enjoy herself. There would only be one more night of her brief come out. She decided to take pleasure to the fullest, keeping the memories close when she no longer had a place among society.

Either by divorce or annulment, she would be shunned by all polite civilization. She could manage it, but what of her brother and sisters? Could they? Unconsciously Cara worried her lower lip thinking about what might become of siblings once this muddle was over. To free Fairhaven, she would have to taint her reputation thus ruining prospects for her siblings…what a tangle.

"What's the matter, sweeting?"

His voice brought her back to the present.

"If you persist in looking at me like that, where all and sundry can see, I fear no one will believe you want to marry me."

She had forgotten they were in the middle of the dance floor. Cara took a quick peek around; sure enough, her downtrodden looks had caused more than one questioning eye. Forcing a smile on her face, she looked into Roland's eyes, as always, she was lost on contact. No one watching would have any doubts now. Oh, how it was hard, looking into the eyes of the man you loved, knowing you could not in good conscience have him.

The dance finished, and together they made their way to the punch bowl. No one bothered to stop them. There were general nods of acknowledgement along, envious looks from women Cara could not name and sly looks from the men. She ignored them all. *Stop it!* Cara cursed her awareness, mostly jealousy toward the women. There would be time enough to think things through tomorrow. She heard Amylia's voice "*Just give yourself up to the dream. Be happy.*" Pushing unwanted feelings away, Cara promised herself she would do just that.

All too soon, the night ended. Beaumont having his own agenda quit Almacks saying he would contact them the following afternoon. Roland, with promises of seeing her tomorrow for a drive in the park, family in tow, gave her chaste kiss on the forehead.

Not exactly the type of kisses a girl dreams about, Cara recalled bitterly as they entered Greyley House.

Chapter Twelve

Sitting in the open carriage, touring Hyde Park was wonderful. The sun beat down with nary a cloud in the sky. The copious scent of flowers masked other various objectionable aromas associated with the large number of animal's present. To Cara—a country lass at heart—those faint aromas reminded her of Wonderland, though she doubted others of her exalted circle would find anything wondrous about hot horseflesh and moist droppings.

The girls, naturally, were bouncing in an unladylike fashion. This was their first ride through the park, people approached often to have a word with the returning Duke of Fairhaven. Introductions were performed. Men talked of horses, laws, and copious other male-related topics which Cara found more interesting than talks of weather, latest fashions, or hottest gossip contributed by the ladies.

No one mentioned anything unusual about Fairhaven's fiancée, not that they would. Still, that didn't mean there wasn't talk. Cara's nerves were stretched like a bowstring; the last thing she wanted to do was embarrass Fairhaven, so aside from polite smiles that made her cheeks ache, she did and said naught.

She really wasn't cut out for a life in the limelight.

Roland noticing Cara's unease and readily agreed when the girls asked if they might get down and walk. Rex, of course, said nothing. Cara didn't know if he was just being Rex or if perhaps something else was bothering him. This would be an excellent opportunity to talk to him.

Roland pulled the landau into a side lane, handed the reins to the waiting groom before assisting the ladies. With Cara on his arm, the girls forging on ahead at a rapid pace, they walked the cobbled lanes of Hyde Park. *Like a family*.

Rex followed sullenly.

Roland led Cara to a bench not far from the path Becky and Robby were already heading down. She could see the pond, a family of ducks gathered chancing to be fed. "No. I can't, I should stay close to the girls, and they might fall in," Cara said, without enthusiasm for she really did want to talk with Rex.

"Never mind that, you look dead on your feet, not that you don't look beautiful, I can see to the girls. You rest; we can't very well have you falling asleep at the altar," Roland joked.

Cara didn't think it was funny. She had had next to no sleep the night before, the way her thoughts kept plaguing her; she doubted she would get much sleep tonight. *Especially tonight.*

Cara smiled tiredly, "Thank you."

Roland placed a kiss on her gloved hand and went in pursuit of the girls. Rex stayed, sitting next to Cara. His legs dangled, swinging back and forth. The action so childlike she knew immediately something preyed heavily on his mind.

"Don't you want to see the ducks?" Cara asked hoping he wouldn't.

"Not particularly."

Swing, swing, swing, went his feet. Cara knew if she didn't pull her eyes away, being as tired as she was, she was likely to go into a trance. Forcing her gaze upward, she looked at Rex's bowed head.

"What is it, love?"

When he didn't answer, she covered his hand with hers and squeezed gently, giving him the strength to confide in her.

"Do you love him?" Now he did look up, his gaze boring into her.

She felt like a specimen under a microscope. Choosing her words carefully so as not to offend. She swallowed.

"I…" She swallowed again. "I…oh Rex," she said knowing about this, she had to tell the truth. "I do. Very much so."

Rex looked at his sister. He couldn't remember ever seeing her quite this nervous. Her blush was nice though. He didn't think he'd ever seen her blush either. She was always contained, always a leader. Even after their father had died. Now, she seemed to share more, almost like she knew she didn't have to be the pillar of strength any longer. Was their guardian, her fiancé, responsible for this younger side of his sister? He didn't know.

"So, you will be happy together then? This, this marriage, it is what you want?" Rex gestured with his hand in the direction of Roland and the girls;

160

Cara's eyes followed. She watched Roland contributing to the unladylike manner of the girls by unceremoniously swinging them around. Skirt billowing like sails, they were red from exertion and laughter. He smiled down at them, not caring one whit what others may think.

Could she be happy? Was this what she wanted? Before she could stop the breathy longing from escaping aloud, it was out, "Oh, yes."

Rex looked at his sister; she blushed, adjusted her bonnet hoping it would cover most of it. Then Rex did something so totally out of character, Cara almost fell off her seat. He hugged her. Right there in the middle of Hyde Park. Where anyone could see. He didn't seem to care; as for Cara, she felt the warmest of feelings run clear through her heart.

Roland, girls in tow, made their way back to the bench; looking at Cara, he cocked his head in question. When Cara nodded, his lips curved. This was his hope all along, no doubt. Obviously, since Cara hadn't spoken to the children about her appending nuptials before leaving Danforth House, it had been up to him. She felt a small twinge of remorse for making him contend with her siblings. A very small twinge.

She gave her hand to Roland; placing it in the crook of his arm as he piloted the entourage back to the waiting landau.

Overall, it was a lovely day and as Roland dropped Cara off at Greyley House, she could not help feeling a pang of regret at his landau, pulled by the team of magnificent, dappled grays, pulled away from the drive.

Amylia placed a gentle hand on her shoulder. Cara let the warmth of newfound friendship seep into her. She felt so blasted cold. They were to go out again tonight; Cara wished she could cry off. Though staying at home with her thoughts did little good. She still had to come up with a solution, thankfully all talk of robberies, or investigations had ceased. For the moment, she wasn't fool enough to think that once the wedding vows were said, their investigation would not resume on schedule. What she didn't know was how she was to pull it off when her mind was cluttered with so many other things.

Cara allowed Amylia to pull her from the drawing room window to a lounger not far away. Before she knew what was happening, Amylia pressed a glass of sherry into her hands. She swallowed, willing it to warm her. It did. Apparently, it also loosened her tongue, for she said, "I love him, you know."

Amylia nodded knowingly.

"But...I can't marry him." Cara set the glass aside, kneading her hands.

"Why ever not?" Amylia said fearing she knew the answer.

Cara shrugged, "It would be different if he was marrying me out of love—I've always dreamed of love."

Amylia smiled inwardly; it wasn't as bad as she feared. Though she could not tell Cara that her nephew already loved his bride-to-be.

It would be wasted breath. And Cara would not believe her. Amylia thought back to her own days when Anthony had said everything but the right thing. Evidently, her nephew was no different. Still, there was but one thing to tongue-tie a charming man.

Love.

She knew her nephew could be heavy-handed, too used to getting what he wanted. When he wanted it. Without a doubt, he had entirely botched the job.

Rushing things.

That sounded like Roland. Always in an all-fired hurry.

"So, what will you do?"

"I…" Cara's voice broke. The rest came out shrilly, "don't know."

Amylia arose so unexpectedly, Cara jumped.

"I'll tell you what you will do." Amylia stabbed the air in front of her as her voice raised with each word. "You will do as you're told! You will have faith! And you will make it right!" Amylia lowered voice, again sitting next to Cara.

"Now. This is what you will do. You will marry my nephew tomorrow, just as planned. Then my dear, you will win his heart. Is that clear? You can do it!"

Cara didn't answer, only stared eyes as big as saucers. *The woman must be mad.*

"I am not crazy. I am experienced. When His Grace and I married, I was caught between the desire to love him and the wish to kill him simultaneously on a regular basis. For a man of words, he frequently said the wrong thing. At first, I was ignorant. I didn't understand." She paused waiting for her words to sink in.

"I soon learned, as you will, that men are as thick as a block of cheese. Content, and even somewhat intelligent when playing their games, talking of races, the markets, and more; but throw into that equation, fire, passion and love, and the block of cheese loses any stiffness it ever had."

She said warming to her topic. She placed a finger on her chin in thought, "my nephew is no different. But Caralyn, Darling, you are more than halfway there. He admires you. Desires you. Use that. Turn up the heat, the cheese will melt, and you can mold and shape it into what you want the block to be. Don't you see?"

Cara was tired. No. She didn't see, was Roland cheese? Oh God, how she needed some quiet time alone. Amylia was so inspiring with her tone, but her words made not one lick of sense, except, of course, for Roland desiring her. Could she turn that desire to love? She blushed as her thoughts turned to what she would have to do to seduce Roland's heart.

"There is no time to be missish. Buck up, girl, do you want a real marriage or not?"

Cara tried unsuccessfully to pull herself together; placing her hands on her cheeks she tried to cool the visible embarrassment. She nodded without thinking.

"What, what's this?" Amylia mimicked the nod.

Cara cleared her throat, straightened her back, and said, "Yes, I do," as determinedly as she could.

"Good. Much better. Now, now we can begin."

Cara's mind was whirling with all Amylia was reiterating. Could it be possible to make her soon-to-be husband fall in love with her? It would be the answer to her problems.

Amylia headed out of the room, made for the stairs without waiting to see if Cara followed. In Cara's room, Claire waited to assist her for their evening of dinner and dancing at some friends of the Greyley's whose names had slipped her mind. Little wonder, with everything else in there, it was decidedly crowded.

"You may go, Claire. I shall aid Miss Caralyn."

"Very well, Madam." With a quick bob to both ladies, the maid was gone.

"Now, let's see. Madame Beauchamps sent over more dresses while you were out. I had Claire put them in the armoire."

Swinging open the doors, Amylia surveyed the contents. Light blue, lavender, gray, Cara's silver wedding dress, *ah, here we are*, she pulled a deep burgundy gown from the rack.

"This," she held the gown up and twirled, "will be most magnifique."

Cara stared, horrified, "But...I cannot go out in that! It is a dress for a married woman."

"Which you will be. Tomorrow. No one will comment. Now come. Let's see how it looks."

Cara still wasn't sure; she should be in the light hues and demur cut fit for an unwed woman. Even that was a stretch, for in all actuality, she should be in black mourning her father. Amylia must have read her thoughts. She really seemed to be getting unnervingly good at it, Cara reflected. Just as good as Fairhaven. Was the whole family touched? Oh hell.

Amylia chuckled, "It is your face, your eyes, your expressions, they show all, my dear. Though there is a little gypsy blood running through Roland's veins, I doubt very much that it would allow him to read your mind, or we wouldn't find ourselves in this tangle to begin with."

Cara chuckled at the thought of Roland sitting in a darkened tent with a crystal ball in front of his waving hands.

"Makes a funny picture, doesn't it?" Amylia said daring Cara to say otherwise. She couldn't. Instead, she stood walking closer to Amylia.

"Well, I guess if one wants to be noticed then that is definitely the dress to do it. Though I'd be happier if only Roland would notice me in the process."

"Ah, I am afraid this is a case you cannot have your cake, eat it too. You will need the eyes of others upon you if you know what I mean?"

"I don't see how I can make Roland jealous when he does not love me."

"You don't? Well, Roland is, as his father and father's father was, possessive. Acworths protect what is theirs. And you, my dear, are his."

Cara wanted to object, and then she realized that in the eyes of the law, and God, as of tomorrow, she was. In her heart she already was. She didn't much care for thought of being a possession. Mayhap she could work on that—after she secured his heart.

Amylia helped Cara out of her walking dress, a practical, beautiful confection made of soft yellow cambric. It came with a matching parasol and gloves, which, much to Amylia's dismay, Cara could not bring herself to carry or wear on their outing. She was well used to the sun.

In fact, she liked the sun and the few freckles it brought forth on the bridge of her nose. She would not be a diamond of the first water, her skin wasn't as pale as it should be, and her brownish-black hair had streaks of color infused from the sun and, worse yet, red highlights.

Amylia efficiently trussed her up in her corset and stays; all too soon Cara was bound tight in the deep red gown. Coming around the front, Amylia surveyed the dress with a critical eye. Shaking her head, she pondered the neckline. Cara had requested the décolletage not be too low. Unfortunately, modesty wasn't on the menu this evening.

Walking to the bell, she gave it a yank. Soon Claire appeared.

"Claire, please fetch my sewing kit."

Claire disappeared into the small dressing room, returning a moment later with a small wicker basket.

Amylia pointed to the offending neckline. "Lower it."

Claire turned down the material a good half-inch then looked at Amylia. The tops of Cara's breasts were clearly visible now. Amylia shook her head.

"Lower."

Cara screeched, grabbing for her gown, "That is too low, it is…indecent!"

Amylia swatted her hand away. "Change your mind?"

Cara shook her head and Claire lowered the gown another half-inch. With Amylia satisfied, Claire quickly basted the neckline.

"Thank you, Claire. You may go." Claire set aside the sewing box, curtsied, left.

Cara tried to avoid looking at her image in the mirror. It was no use. The combination of the claret-colored gown and the bareness of her chest, whiter against the dark fabric, had a hypnotic effect. She could not turn away. When she breathed, her breasts threatened to spill out. Flustered, she said, "Oh my."

"Yes, absolutely stunning, it is definitely missing—just a moment, I will be right back."

What would Roland say? What would he think? Would he be upset? Would he want to rip the offending garment off her? Oh my, Cara blushed clear to her toes.

Claire came in the room followed by Amylia carrying a red cedar box. Claire asked her to sit and arranged her hair in a sophisticated elegant topknot. Amylia handed Claire a silver ribbon, which she promptly threaded through Cara's hair. It added a special something. The picture was complete. Cara stared into the mirror looking upon a beautiful stranger.

"I'm pretty."

"Not just pretty, my dear. Ravishing. You give yourself too little credit. There is something missing, I was going to give you these tomorrow as they will look lovely with your wedding dress, but I think it would not hurt to wear them tonight as well." Amylia removed a chain of black pearls, with a black diamond teardrop pendant hanging down from the center and matching black diamond teardrop earbobs.

Cara gasped. Never had she seen anything so beautiful or so costly.

"The Fairhaven Family jewels. Normally, Roland's mother would present these to you on your wedding day, as she is no longer with us; I have kept this in trust for the future Duchess of Fairhaven and that, my dear, is you. No. Don't cry, you will make your face all blotchy, totally ruining all my hard work. That's it, smile, you are even more beautiful when you smile. Here now, let me help you put these on."

Roland came in the Danforth carriage at seven o'clock. Anthony, Amylia on his arm, Roland, Cara on his, led their cloaked ladies to the awaiting coach. At Amylia's edict they were all ready and waiting, Cara's dress covered, before Roland arrived.

Coming into the front parlor, he looked toward the waiting party. "Am I late?" he asked. Anthony hid his smile as he downed the remaining drops in his glass; there was no stopping his wife when she was on a mission. Although no one had seen fit to confide in him, one look at Caralyn told him his lovely wife was up to something.

"No, we are just excited to be away," Amylia lied smoothly.

Roland nodded; his eyes fastened on his fiancée. She glowed. Everything about her was radiant, he could not remember seeing her thus, and his heart skipped a beat. It was a good thing they were to be married tomorrow; he didn't know how much longer he could walk around in such a dangerous state.

She looked different. Confident. Happy. He offered up a silent prayer that her happiness meant they could consummate the marriage. She smiled. He groaned quietly. Walking to her, smiling like a love-struck fool, he grabbed her and there in front of aunt, uncle, and whomever else cared to see, he kissed her.

Cara stiffened, propriety flashed in her mind, and then with a moan she melded to his demanding mouth. His tongue swept in. He tasted her. When had he last kissed her like this? He wanted to keep going to never stop. His uncle cleared his throat; Roland reluctantly released her lips.

A dazed Cara stared up at him. Roland kept a possessive hand on her waist. Though his aunt and uncle were in the room, Cara was thankful for the lack of proper decorum that kept her knees from buckling beneath her.

In the carriage, she used the traveling time to prepare for when she must give up the security of her cloak. The carriage halted in front of the Heatherington home. Cara had made a point of finding out the names of people hosting the party so she would not embarrass herself or her companies upon entry.

Walking into a well-lit entrance hall, Lord and Lady Heatherington came forth to take their hands in welcome as the butler took their things. Cara stood, Roland at her back, waiting her turn to greet and be greeted then rapidly followed Amylia while Anthony and Roland gave their thanks.

Lady Heatherington came forward, leading the ladies to the parlor as the men followed talking of a future hunt planned at The Arthurbee's country estate.

Lady Heatherington waxed on about supper, a small affair, with only twenty in attendance, prior to the ball, in which, another *small amount*, of one hundred or so was attending.

Cara didn't know if she would ever get used to the idea of a small amount being one 'hundred or so', her lips curved, and head bowed ever so slightly elegantly mimicking Amylia in grace and demeanor. She listened, periodically adding tidbits to the conversation as they awaited the rest of the guests.

There were about ten already seated talking gaily in the parlor, with about six more to show before the dinner bell would ring. Cara prayed her stomach would hold out until then. She had had little to eat over the past two days as her worries had overridden her appetite. Now with Amylia's advice and subsequent backing she was feeling her appetite return full force.

She looked about, finding Roland still cosseted by the fireplace conversing with his uncle. Others had joined the conversation. Apparently, there was a lot to be said about hunting.

Roland felt Cara's eyes on him. He hadn't looked at her since they arrived, trying to cool his ardor with talk of hunting and fishing. He would be all right if he just didn't look at her, he told himself. Then he would not feel like throwing her down. Making love to her, now, in front of everyone.

Before he could stop, he turned in her direction, their gazes meeting. It was a mistake of catastrophic proportions. *Who the hell let her come out dressed like that!* As if he didn't know, his eyes searched out his aunt from across the room. She returned his gaze, smiling innocently. *Damn. Damn. Damn!*

Quickly, he looked about the room; his were not the only set of eyes straying to his fiancée's daringly bared bosom. Making his excuses to his smiling uncle, obviously in on this little joke as well, *damn him*, and the others present; he made his way to his fiancée, putting a possessive arm around her waist.

Propriety be damned, if they thought he was going to just leave her to her own devices while every gentleman present ogled her, as society was wont to do, they had another think coming.

"We must talk."

Cara looked up for the first time since Roland had turned into a thundercloud and blown his way to her side. His arm felt like a metal band securing her. She didn't know how to feel about that. Scared or excited? She swallowed, and then cursed herself. She hated the simple action that showed her weakness.

Roland knew that just above, on the runway overlooking the ballroom, the Heatherington's much beloved artwork was displayed for all who ventured. Many did. But the night was young, and there, they would be assured a little privacy.

Placing Cara's hand on the crook of his arm, Roland quickly told his aunt where they were headed, rather than trying to sneak off, their disappearance being noted in an unpleasant manner, and led a tentative Cara out the door.

Amylia smothered a chuckle. Poor girl looked like a lamb taken to slaughter. She'd learn. Eventually.

Roland said not a word, body rigid, as he walked the path to the runway.

Slowing his steps for Cara, she sensed, with great unwillingness. He was the hunter separating his prey from the protection of the herd. She prayed she would be up to the battle.

He stopped before the first painting, Rembrandt's *Return of the Prodigal Son*. Cara didn't know much about artwork; but this work was priceless. She stared at the image in silence. An old man held a kneeling man, the prodigal son, while onlookers watched in sullen silence. The browns and reds flowed together, making the images lifelike.

With what she had been told of Roland's youth, he could be a prodigal son, had his parents lived to see his decline and return to society. That was a conundrum for had his parents been alive; Roland most likely would not have gone wild. Where would he be today if his parents had lived? Would he be married? Married to some beautiful diamond, holding a babe, their babe, in his arms?

Cara didn't like the feeling she got with the image.

"You wanted to speak with me, Your Grace?" Cara asked innocently. She would much rather get this over with than dwell on what might have been. For in the images running unwillingly through her mind, she wasn't the woman on his arm.

"Your Grace?" Roland said with a sneer. "I thought we were over that?"

"I was only being polite," Cara said, offended.

"If you wish to be polite, you will call me Roland, especially when we are alone. If that's too difficult for you, Fairhaven will do," he snapped.

"All right. Roland. Whatever is the matter? Is it about tomorrow? Have you changed your mind?"

"No."

"Well?"

Roland turned to face her. He ran his fingers over her much-exposed bosom; Cara shivered as heat pooled inside her.

"This," Roland said; he dipped his fingers beneath the neckline, running the tip over her aching nipples.

"This?" Cara's words were a murmur as she fought to control herself.

"Yes, my love, this. I don't ever want you wearing anything this low again. Is that clear?"

"Is that an order, *Your Grace*?" Cara shot back.

He moved like lightning, pinning her to the wall with his large form. Without warning, his mouth came crashing down on hers in hungry urgent appeal. His hands roamed freely about her burgundy, gown-clad body. Over her nipples, where he stopped long enough to encircle each one until she was writhing beneath his touch; she wiggled as his legs insinuated themselves between her pinned legs, he pressed his knee against her, where the heat pooled, moved it in a circular motion in rhythm with his tongue swiping in and out of her mouth.

Her heart was stampeding in her chest, her breathing short and shallow. His kisses. The corset. The dress. Pressing in on her. Heat spreading like wildfire. Her heart pounding, faster and faster, she couldn't catch her breath. Then, all went black.

"Whatever did you do to her?" Roland's aunt demanded.

"Nothing. I…" It was no use. Her lips were still red from his kisses. Her gown was creased. He felt more than a little foolish and a whole lot more helpless. This was hardly like stealing a cookie from a cookie jar; he couldn't help feeling young and immature under his aunt's accusing glare. An ardor-cooling finale—not the conclusion he would have liked, but a finish, nevertheless.

Lady Heatherington did her best to keep things quiet with her guests as Amylia and Anthony took care of the problem on the runway. Roland held his limp fiancée in his arms, while his uncle looked very much like he was laughing behind his hand. Roland glared at him; instead of stopping, he only laughed harder until tears silently dripped from his eyes.

Amylia chastised her husband as she waved vinaigrette beneath Cara's nose. She wouldn't have figured the girl to be of such a delicate constitution.

"Will she be all right then?" Roland asked carefully, fearing his aunt's wrath.

"Yes. Just so you know; I blame you—"

Roland said something that sounded to Amylia like 'without a doubt' after a stern look at her nephew, she dismissed it, "but, there is possibly more to it than your prowess. Cara didn't have lunch before you hurried her off to the park; I do believe that she skipped tea as well, knowing we would be dining out. I think a mixture of starvation and fatigue…ah, look, she is coming around.

"Caralyn dear, can you hear me?"

"What happened?" Cara asked groggily.

"You fainted, dear."

"But…I never faint!" she said crossly, trying to sit up.

"Be that as it may, you do, you did, and you have. Now, let's see about getting you under the power of your own feet. Shall we?"

Roland lifted, and then carefully set Cara's feet to the floor, staying close. Cara got her bearings. Aside from the world being a little askew, she was fine. Minutiae leading up to the blessed event, if one can call it such, immediately put her in a dreadful blush.

"I think," she said turning to Roland, "I'd like to go home."

Roland was about to concede when his aunt jumped in.

"You will do no such thing. No one knows what happened here except an upstairs maid, Anthony, and me. It will not only look frightfully rude if we were to leave before dinner was served, but it would also give way to all kinds of vicious talk. No. We will stay. Pull yourself together, girl. Now."

Cara turned back to Amylia ready to lay vent with her temper, when she caught sight of another maid coming their way. She reined herself in, nodded, and murmured, "Very well, if I must."

"*We* must. Now let us go down, everyone should have arrived by now. Let's see if we can hurry along the dinner bell."

Anthony, now in control of himself, Amylia on his arm led the way back down to the parlor. They arrived just as Lord Heatherington and his wife were leading the guests into the dining hall. With a knowing look, partially disgusted, Lady Heatherington motioned for them to follow.

Dinner was an enjoyable affair; the courses came, went in number, footmen placed at strategic places around the table served each course as it arrived. Leek soup, buttered mushrooms, roasted pheasant in orange and ginger sauce, parsnips, yams; the list was endless, undoubtedly quite good. She was ravenous. Eating as daintily as she could, she found it hard to keep up with the conversation around her. Next time, she would make sure she ate something before going out to dinner.

The man she had seen on countless occasions, as Mrs. Black, Lord Redding, sat next to her. Every time she tried to take a bite, he spoke causing her to place her utensil back down, to answer him lest she be rude. She wasn't used to the slow pace, conversation between servings, small servings at that, the whole process was taking forever.

After dinner, the ladies, led by Lady Heatherington, repaired to another room while the men sat with brandy, cigars and with any luck, more tantalizing conversation than Cara was made party to. The evening progressed, more guests arrived, and soon they were all in the ballroom. Cara tried her best to keep a smile on her face while dancing and talking but all she wanted to do was go back up to the runway and have Roland kiss her senseless again. Literally.

Well, mayhap not the runway; in the carriage on the ride home or at the door and inside the door. Before long, her feelings had her flustered with no way out. She couldn't wait to go home.

Chapter Thirteen

The big day arrived. Cara sat in her bed eating toast, drinking hot chocolate, and trying frantically not to let her nerves get the better of her. She still found it hard to believe she'd fainted, right in the middle of…while he was…Oh Gawd. How would she face him? The rest of the evening was spent avoiding intimate conversations with Roland, afraid of what he might think of her, likewise for Amylia and Anthony.

She made a hasty exit upon arriving home. No kisses, such as the one that had kept her so preoccupied most of the evening, no, instead she fled like a coward. She set aside the rest of her toast as her stomach started doing flip-flops, threw back the covers, and with a resigned sigh forced herself into the bath Claire had kindly arranged with her breakfast. There would be little point in hiding. If Roland didn't come and haul her down, sure enough Beaumont would, Cara reflected bitterly.

Claire helped Cara out of the tub and into her wedding dress. With the final touches to her hair, her jewels in place, she was ready. The woman staring back at her through the mirror could do anything, she told herself. Anything, including making her husband fall in love with her.

Claire had no sooner gone, the door opened, Cara hoped it wasn't Amylia. She had yet to speak with her regarding her case of the vapors. How much had she seen? How much had she guessed? It was all so frightfully embarrassing.

Rex, Rebecca, and Roberta stood into doorway, frozen. The girls, for once, were completely silent as they stared at what must seem to them as a princess. Cara ushered them close, pulling them together for a group hug. The girls were first to pull away. Unusual.

"What is it?" Cara asked thinking they might be upset that she was marrying the one man they both cared for. Her fears were put to rest when they girls started chirping about wrinkling her dress. Cara chuckled. Relieved.

Rex backed away.

"You're certain you wish me to give you away?"

"You are head of the family. It is your place."

"Right then, I guess we should be going. Lady Greyley told me I may take you to parlor; we are to wait by the French doors for the piano music. That will be our key to enter the garden."

"We get to go ahead of you," the girls said together.

"We are to toss rose petals. Oh Cara. Isn't it just grand? You look just like a princess in a fairytale."

Normally, Rex would have rolled his eyes, just as Cara herself did, this time he nodded in agreement.

"I don't think I have ever seen you so beautiful."

A tear escaped Cara. She was turning into a regular watering pot, a fragile creature even given into fainting. If it didn't stop soon, she was sure she would hate herself inside of a sennight.

Rex took Cara's arm, led her out of the bedroom, down the corridor, *I wonder if this is how it feels when they lead one into Newgate?* Cara laughed at her folly. Surely it wasn't as bad as that. She had come to terms, had a plan, was resigned to making this marriage work come what may, and the *may* had better be her husband's heart. She would settle for nothing less.

Roland stood at the makeshift-alter, Father Baird in front of him. His aunt had outdone herself. She turned the gazebo into center stage, stationed at the end of a cobbled walk, in the center of the garden. Cherub fountains dribbled water giving a serene, almost ethereal sound to the surroundings. Fresh cut flowers of every kind imaginable, from her very own gardens, filled the air with their heady bouquet. Guests gathered around each side of the walk to witness the bride as she entered.

Becky and Robby gently tossed rose petals as they came down the aisle. She would be here soon. His eyes never left the door. Miss Perryweather played the bridal march as Rex, with Cara on his arm, slowly floated toward him.

Roland's breath caught in his throat. The vision was most exquisite. 'A moonbeam fairy in shimmering silver'. No white gown for his bride but silver, to bring out the sparks in her fathomless opaque eyes. He would enjoy losing himself in those depths for many years to come.

Her gown fell from a scoop-necked bodice to her toes in a tapered unembellished line. The soft material flared at her feet ended with a small train in the back. Long white gloves with black beads and silver thread covered her arms to the dress's short, puffed sleeves.

She wore no veil, fearing that should she been seen in something so close to the former Mrs. Black costume, someone might make a connection. Her hair was fashioned in a simple topknot, with hundreds of silky ebony curls falling down her back to her waist. Once again, she wore the Fairhaven jewels. The color and setting both rare and lovely, yet many of the former Lady Fairhavens had not the coloring to accentuate them so beautifully. It was the darkened hue of Cara's skin in which they rested that highlighted the gems, making them appear extensions of her eyes.

She walked slowly toward him; her sparkling gaze fastened with his. The mischievous smile she sent him caused a wave of love, and something else, to wash over him. Roland hardened, quickly adjusting his jacket just in case. He beamed like an infatuated schoolboy. Knowing he was totally captivated with her and not caring. Let the world think what they liked. He was in love with his wife. So be it.

Roland's uncle stood to the right of him. Rex would stand there as well. Aunt Amylia stood in place instead of preceding Cara down the aisle, as was the custom. The girls stood next to Amylia, and of course, Cara his stunning bride would soon be standing next to him. Hand in hand.

All happened as rehearsed within the boundaries of his mind. Father Baird spoke, the guests quieted to hear the responses of the bride and groom. Silent tears of joy hovered in Cara's dusky eyes, making them shine.

She promised herself she would not cry. Her voice vibrated, and her hands shook as she repeated the vows, vows that would link her to this man, no matter what happens, throughout this lifetime.

When it was his turn, Roland stared deeply into her eyes. Cara hardly heard the words, so lost was she in the desire-filled blue pools. What was he thinking? Was he happy? She wished she knew. How much was desire? How much was admiration? How much was honor? Was there any love there? Could there be? Amylia thought so. Grabbing on firmly to that thought, Cara smiled at her husband.

It was finally over. It was done; they were man and wife. Roland's mouth came down on hers, she felt the strain in his muscles; the very effort it took to keep the kiss light, still, she was dazed, and her knees were weak when his mouth left hers.

They turned to the sea of well-wishers. A small ceremony planned by the Duchess of Greyley must mean no less than sixty for Cara realized there were far more people than she anticipated. Odd, she didn't remember passing so many people on her trek down the aisle; but then she had been so nervous she had sought out Roland's comforting form. Her eyes had never wavered. Now, standing en masse, her shaky confidence, faltered a little bit more. Were they judging her? Measuring her worth? Did they find her lacking?

Pasting a smile on her face, Roland shook hands, made introductions and accepted congratulations on their behalf. Most of the time, Cara tried to remember the rules. She was a Duchess now. Did she curtsy to the Lords? The Ladies? How should she address them?

Roland noticed her unease, without so much as a word, his hand tightened on her, refusing to let her dip, she was his wife and she'd bow down to no one. *Except with him.* Possessively, he ran his thumb over the curve of her waist. Filled with manly pride when a shudder ran through her. She desired him, she may not know what it was, the passion that ignited when they were together, but he'd teach her. He loved her. Without a doubt she would come to love him too. It would only take time.

He prayed he would not have to remain celibate; it would be much easier to show her he worshiped her—well if he could worship her.

The Duchess of Greyley herded everyone to the dining room for the elaborate wedding banquet, the crowd waiting, allowing the groom to lead the bride through the French doors first.

The dining room was awash with blossoms, a breathtaking sight indeed. Carnations not roses, of every color imaginable, filled small silver pots along a table set with Sevres chinaware. Roland was given the head of the table, which had really been the middle of the side of the table. To his left was the Duke of Greyley, Rex, and Antoine, the Duke's son, Roland's cousin, up from Yorkshire. He was followed immediately his pretty petite wife, Hermione, with her doll-like face and golden curls she was the picture of classic beauty. Nameless others sat carrying around to the other side of the table.

Cara sat to Roland's right, next to her was the Duchess of Greyley, Rebecca, Roberta, Elsabeth, Beth for short, the daughter's whose room, Cara had used the two previous nights. She wondered how Beth made if from Scotland in time for the wedding, word would have taken longer than that to get there, when she questioned Amylia, her face had glowed.

"She and Ian are purchasing a property in Dorset, so that Beth may stay in the country when they are in England. It was quite a surprise when I received their missive; I immediately sent word for them to come to London immediately. They arrived this very morning."

"Ah, how wonderful for you, mayhap with their own estate in England their visits will become more frequent."

"One can only hope," answered the Duchess glowing with happiness.

Conversation went on around the table as the footmen brought forth dishes of coddled eggs, roast ham, scones with sides of fresh gooseberry jam, toast, bangers, potatoes, the list was endless. And unbelievably delicious.

At the end of the meal, Roland thanked everyone for coming, took his bride, his charges, kissed cheeks, shook hands and ushered them all out the awaiting Danforth carriage. Inside Rex, Becky and Robby chatted wildly about all they had seen and done. Cara smiled maternally grateful for her well-behaved siblings. They had done well. Normally children would not have been allowed to dine, at least not at the head of the table, but as they were so important to the day and to Cara, Roland thought it only right they had a place among the elite.

Cara joined in on snippets of conversation, worrying about what lay ahead. She decided that if Roland wanted, she would share his bed. If—he wanted? She wasn't completely naive in the ways of men; he kissed her with passion, looked at her with desire. Would he want the marriage consummated after telling her she could ask for an annulment? Had the annulment been a way out for her, or for him?

The previous night's woolgathering had brought forth new insecurities. She had to trust that Amylia was right. She sneaked a peek at her husband, what was he thinking? What did he want? What was best for him?

Roland turned, meeting her gaze, she tried to see the answers to her many questions. She could not. What she did see gave her faith. His blue eyes shimmered with a familiar light. Suddenly, foolishly, she wished it were time for bed.

Shortly after arriving at Danforth House, while the servants united in the Blue Room giving congratulations to the new Duke and Duchess of Fairhaven, there was a knock at the front door. Moments later, Tibs announced in a frosty accent that the Earl of Beaumont was waiting 'His and Her Grace' in the study.

"It is your bloody wedding day," he muttered.

The children were given the day off from their studies and took themselves off to the backyard to play, as Roland and Cara made their way to see Beaumont.

Beaumont didn't spend time offering best wishes, instead he got right down to the business at hand. "It's been too long, necessary of course, but too long nonetheless, we must get back to the investigation. Where are the papers you acquired as Mrs. Black?"

Cara stared at Beaumont for a moment, she hadn't seen this side of him, she saw him as a friend, and then as a villain; she hadn't imagined this intricate business guise.

"They are in my room, at the bottom of my trunk." Feeling she must explain herself, she said, "I assumed they were gambling markers, I kept them to show Rex the folly of playing with high stakes." She shrugged.

Neither Beaumont nor Roland appeared interested in her reasons, they only wanted to see the damn papers, and said as much, so Cara hurried off to her room to retrieve them.

"She still has her own room?" Beaumont raised a brow. "My, my, your restraint amazes me."

"Don't get all full of yourself, old man. She had the Baroness' old suite and as it connects to mine…" Roland paused. "Let her have her haven. I have the only key, and no intentions of locking the door. Ever." Roland's lips curved smugly. He didn't need to add that if he had his way, the only time she would spend in the Baroness' suite was when she was dressing.

The door swung open, and Cara immediately tossed the pages on the desk in front of Beaumont. He picked up the scattered pieces of paper, looking them over before nodding. Cara could tell he saw more than a jumbled mass of words and numbers that she assumed to be amounts owed.

Handing the papers to Roland, his eyes scanned each document carefully, setting them aside with an excited flourish, he reached into the drawer withdrawing another piece. A full sheet filled with writing. In the other drawer, he found a blank piece and set it beside the others then as if he was no longer aware anyone else was in the room, he began scribbling on the fresh sheet, eyes jumping back, forth from one page to another.

Beaumont looked on in anticipation. Minutes ticked by on the mantle clock, Cara couldn't stand it. "What's going on?" She was instantly chastised for her outburst, feeling like a scolded child, she went back to the window seat and waited.

She was about to depart when Roland yelled, "I've got it!"

Beaumont sat up. "Record time too, I'll wager, good work, lad!"

Cara found it hard picturing Roland as anyone's 'lad'; she had to chuckle. They were like a couple of kids at Christmas.

"Well?" Cara asked.

"It was as I ascertained, my love, your father, he ah—well, that is to say."

"Roland, for Christ sakes! Go ahead. Tell her! She is married to you after all, I do think that she has a right to know the kind of life she will be involved in, from time to time that is, only when needed, of course," Beaumont added, clumsily.

"What is he talking about? Roland? Tell me what? What kind of life? Do you mean spying?"

"If you two could remain silent longer than a minute, I will explain," Roland said lightly. "You already know about the work for the government. I, like your father, and Beaumont, here, belong to an organization, known as the Home Office. We are a network of trained individuals with the sole purpose of protecting England's interests, so yes, it does involve spying though we prefer being dubbed agents.

"I am a decoder; I decipher encrypted messages for benefit of England; I was trained by the best man the Organization ever had. Your father."

"My father was honorable? He—he was good? Then why…?"

"I don't think your father did what he did because he wanted to. I think, or at least I had thought—Hell, I don't know, I guess mayhap I believed he was forced. I still do but I have no proof.

"Beaumont called me back home to investigate. His information led him to believe that your father was playing deep in black-market. With Napoleon gathering secrets for his growing forces, you can see how important it was, and is, for our whereabouts to be kept in strict confidence. Years of work, planning, placement, and lives would be lost."

"A person could make a healthy sum selling secrets," Beaumont said.

"But nothing fit," Roland said, exasperation clear in his voice. "When I returned and started my investigation, there were things I noticed, because of my close association with your father. His death struck me as suspicious. I mean, what better way to dispose of someone who was no longer useful. When I searched The Gables—"

"You were at Wonderland? When?" Cara interrupted.

"Wonderland?" Beaumont asked.

"The Gables," Cara clarified, not caring if he understood.

"I went there directly after meeting with Beaumont. A couple of weeks ago now; I needed to look at his correspondence; I had hoped to find my charges at the same time." Roland smiled.

Cara blushed.

"They weren't there, amazing that. I did find some clues, so the trip was not a total loss, yet what I found only served to add more questions. The missive that contained the location of the secret information was easily deciphered, not at all Thomas' best work. Rather sloppy in fact. And that wasn't your father's style.

"Then upon decoding the information obtained from Hatchard's, I recognized immediately that it wasn't agent placements as we, Beaumont and I, were led to believe. Instead, I was faced with a list of men. Men associated with the Home Office. Currently these men, or at least the three who had come forth, were being robbed."

Cara swallowed. "By the Widow Rose Black."

"Yes, though we didn't know at the time, the men avoided all talk about the incident that would provide the kind of proof we considered necessary. Still, something inside would not allow me to let it go. So, attending soirees hoping to catch him in the act."

"You thought the thief to be a man? But that night, you knew I was coming through the window. How? I was a woman and even I didn't know I'd have to escape from a window."

"It was fate." He smiled. "I was late, due to another meeting with Beaumont; I feared I had missed you. I left the terrace to walk about the gardens when I heard a sound. I went to investigate and spotted someone coming through a window. I didn't know until I focused on a delectable stocking-clad leg that it was a woman. You were my thief. What I didn't know was whether or not you were an agent."

"So that's what the interrogation had been about. You thought I was a French spy?" Cara said, flabbergasted.

"What interrogation?" Beaumont asked, not having been party to this particular detail.

Roland ignored his question.

"You were incredibly good, my dear, I could not see you as a spy, but you did manage to deflect a lot of my questions, so I couldn't be certain. It wasn't until I seen you handling a gun, the day we were abducted, that I knew for certain you weren't. That led to more questions, which were only recently answered."

"Finding out that I wasn't Rose Black but Caralyn Danforth," Cara said following most of the conversation.

"So then, you were drawn back to the events surrounding my father, you think he was murdered," she said as she ticked off on her fingers, "you think he buried the agent information in pieces about the Organization so that whoever tried to employ him would have a devil of a time getting his hands on the list even if he managed to get the coded message, the message at Hatchard's, before you. My father trusted you. That is why he set you up as our guardian so that if anything happened to him, he'd have a trained man to protect us."

Cara pressed on, her mind spinning with possibilities as Roland and Beaumont looked at her with a mixture of amazement and admiration.

"You are beautiful!" Roland said at last coming to give her a quick peck on the cheek, "and gifted." Another kiss.

Beaumont cleared his throat. "Your wife has stumbled upon some interesting details. I say we part company for today, it's almost supper; we can meet again tomorrow and formulate a plan. Shall we say one?"

Beaumont looked back, shook his head in mock disgust as Roland was once again kissing his bride. As this was no gentle peck on the cheek, Beaumont made his way silently out of the room. He'd send a note.

Roland lifted his head. "I wish it were time for bed," he whispered. He tucked a stray curl behind Cara's ear, pausing long enough to smooth her earlobe between his fingers. The caress had Cara moaning once more, as Roland's lips descended to hers.

A knock sounded, Cara tried to jump back, but Roland wouldn't allow her to. He moved to her side and yelled "Enter" toward the door.

"Sorry to bother you, Your Graces, there is something you must see." He took the paper from beneath his arm. Handing it to Roland, he waited for them to read the article.

"My God! That's father's attorney!" Cara gasped.

"It may mean nothing," Roland said, trying to assure her as best as he could.

"You don't really believe that. What other reason would someone have to break in? Roland, he didn't even practice law anymore!" Cara broke away and began pacing.

"Tibs, were you able to use the time since the paper arrived to determine anything substantial?" Roland inquired.

"As a matter of fact, Your Grace, I did. I spoke with the footman I sent with your letter. He spoke to an elderly housekeeper; she told him that Mr. Gomersal wasn't in, so he left the letter in her possession."

"Did you happen to investigate matters outside of the house?"

"Yes. Daniels and I were able to establish a few more details. The robber, according to Bow Street, who marked the case as common housebreaking, struck the solicitor on the head rendering him unconscious. His doctor has been reported to come and go every few hours. Apparently, his patient, still unconscious; the prognosis is not good. He may or may not wake. His advanced age will be the deciding factor."

"As to the break-in; according to the housekeeper, a Mrs. White, nothing was taken while his chambers were turned upside-down. Papers everywhere. Daniels asked if any other part of the house was touched. The answer was no."

"So, whatever they wanted was presumably in the study?" Cara said. "I wonder if they found it."

"Did Mrs. White tell Bow Street about this?" Roland inquired.

"Apparently so, Your Grace. Daniels' informant is a runner. Bow Street feels they may have left after rendering Mr. Gomersal comatose, worried about someone else happening upon them."

"But that's crazy!" Cara shrieked. "If they were worried, why would they have taken the time to search the place? Did the study even have a window or did the supposed breakers vanish through the wall?"

"Very good, Your Grace." Tibs said visibly impressed.

"Yes. You're right again. Calm yourself; Bow Street tends to make sticky situations worse. If they are not worried then let them remain so, for now."

Tibs nodded in agreement.

"I think it's best we send the children out of the city, Your Graces. Daniels would be able to care better for them at The Gables."

"Oh Roland, the children—do you really think they could be in danger? Wouldn't they be safer here with us?"

"Normally, I would agree, but to date, we do not know enough about the situation. I'm sorry, love; in this case I think Tibs may be right. Anything somebody would search for is right here. What if someone came looking and found the children awake? No. I really think we should employ a governess and send them with Daniels to The Gables."

"I should go to the Governess agency then. Interview some candidates. I don't want the kids to be handed over to just anyone."

"No, Cara."

"No?"

"No." Roland turned from his wife to Tibs. "Send a missive to Beaumont. Tell him Cara and I require a governess for the children, *a highly trained* governess."

Tibs' face was alight. "Quite right, Your Grace. That, no doubt, would be the best."

"What do you mean *highly trained*? Roland, if you think for one moment, I will let you put some bossy old woman in charge of my brother and sisters, you'd best think again. They do not need some crusty old battleax attending them, especially with everything that is going in their lives right now! So much has changed, they need—"

"Easy, my love," Roland chuckled, "I am not going to have some 'old battleax' take care of them. By trained I mean she will have other, shall we say, abilities."

"You mean like a bloody bodyguard? You don't think they will be any safer at The Gables, do you, and still, you insist on sending them away?" Cara charged.

Tibs thought again that this union would be an interesting one, all told. He hoped to live a good long life, just so he would be around to watch. A butler had so little fun these days.

"What are you smiling at?" Cara said as she turned on Tibs.

His face straightened immediately. "Nothing, Your Grace. Should I fetch Beaumont then?" He looked to Roland for guidance. When Roland nodded,

Tibs reluctantly left the confrontation. He grinned unrepentantly; no doubt he'd hear about it.

Cara was fuming, why separate her from the children, she had been their protector for so many years. She was still their protector. It galled her that no matter where they went, for the time being, they would not safe. It was her fault. She paced silently fuming until she came face to face with a warm brick wall. Bands of steel tightened around her.

"This is not your fault—any of it. I will not have you blaming yourself. We will keep them safe. I promise."

Cara looked into Roland's deep blue eyes, before she had a chance to say anything, his mouth was on hers, wiping away everything from her mind. She hated this. She loved this.

Roland needed to taste her. He needed it like an addict needed opium. Running his tongue along her lower lip, Cara opened willingly, his tongue swept in, and he feasted. She sparred with him—savoring his taste as much as he was drinking hers. Her hands climbed, tantalizingly slow, up over his shoulders to link around his neck.

Her fingers entwined his long hair pulling him closer. His hands roamed freely the luscious curves of her body as he pressed his engorged shaft against her. She moved her hips, instinct rather than knowledge, and her naively seductive response affected him more than any trained courtesan.

"We should…" Roland rested his forehead on Cara's, catching his breath and tried again. "We should get ready for dinner."

"Yes," Cara said, but didn't let go.

Finally, Roland took a step back. Distance was what they needed. No not needed, it was what the situation called for. He wanted to ask her if she would come to him tonight, but he feared she'd say no, so he said nothing as he left to change.

By the time Cara made her way back down to the dining room, her thoughts were once again her own. Ignoring the three questioning faces of her siblings, she made her way to the head of the table. Leaned down and kissed her husband on the cheek.

His lips twitched, he winked.

Lowering her mouth to his ear, she said most seductively, "Nice try, I have no intention of letting you hire anyone until I meet with her. Make sure you have Beaumont send this paragon over."

She smiled, sauntered to the end of the table where she took her seat. Tibs cleared his throat, unsuccessfully choking back a smile. As he watched Rex, Becky, and Robby stare at their sister like she'd suddenly grown three heads.

Roland looked at her, a spark of respect and something else Cara wasn't quite sure what, in his eyes. Being the focus of attention, when it was one's own family who was staring, wasn't so bad. Cara ignored everyone as she raised her hand, the duty of the Duchess, giving the signal to begin serving.

All was quiet while the footmen settled all dishes at once, instead of one paltry serving after another. It was a family dinner, simple and carefree. Tonight, would start a tradition in their family. The footmen departed and in order, everyone served themselves.

Cara dipped her spoon into her pea soup, lips puckered outward; she gently blew cooling it before tasting. Her pink tongue sneaked out occasionally catching the odd dribble collecting in the corner of her mouth.

Roland watched in agony, leaving his food untouched. Damn! Even watching her eat was erotic.

The kids chatted about all that had happened. The wedding, the luncheon, their new great aunt and uncle and cousins, the people, and the attention, Cara caught snippets of the conversation but stayed out of it until Rex commented that they could now return to Wonderland.

Cara dabbed her lips with a napkin. "Yes. I think you all will be returning to Wonderland before long. Would that please you?"

The girls were excited instantly, telling Roland of all Wonderland offered, Rex shushed them immediately. "What did you mean 'you all', we are *all* leaving London, aren't we? Together?" He looked from Cara to Roland then back again.

Cara sighed. She should have chosen her words more carefully. "Well," Cara started. Helpless, she looked to Roland for guidance. There was no help from that quarter; probably he was still remembering his rumored confrontation with the head of the family. So be it, she could handle her little brother.

"Rex, there are some things Roland, and I must deal with. We wished to send you on ahead. I have made appointments to interview some governesses. Hopefully, one of them will be suitable enough to send with you, to care for the girls. I was eager for you to get everything ready so we could introduce Roland to the Wonderland we all love."

Well, it wasn't the best attempt with her nervousness and careless wording, but it seemed to work. Rex smiled, even blushed a little and immediately excused himself from the table. The girls rose, tagging along after him. Tired, they said.

Cara watched them depart, Becky and Robby arguing about the need to go to bed at eight o'clock in the evening.

"He got the wrong impression, you know."

Cara's eyes snapped from the door to Roland. "What do you mean?"

"I mean, he thinks your attempt to soothe him was an attempt to get rid of him."

"That's absurd; if he thought I was trying to get rid of him, he'd be angry. You saw him he was smiling, blushing even, he wasn't mad."

"Yes, my dear, he was smiling; just because he is young doesn't mean he is not a man. Yes, he was blushing because it is often hard to hear about your sister's sexual needs—"

"Stop right there! Don't you dare say it...Oh..." Cara covered her flaming face. "What should I do?" she said helplessly.

"Nothing, for if you hadn't given him the impression, I am sure I would have, if for no other reason than to avoid his lecture. For a child, he is exceptionally good at lecturing."

Cara looked up to see Roland shudder and they both laughed.

Roland stopped laughing, his blue gaze turned to fire.

Tension quickly gripped Cara, picking up her glass, she took a hasty swallow. She choked. Roland was out of his chair in an instant. One hand rested on the table beside her while the other smacked her on the back. Cara finished coughing, covered his hand with hers. "Thank you."

Roland turned his palm, grasping her fingers he helped her up from the chair. "There is a cure for things that frighten you."

"What is it?"

"Confronting it."

Silently, he led her up the stairs. Depositing her outside her door, he turned, she watched him enter his room. Lucy was waiting, all smiles. "Your Grace," she said adding extra depth to her curtsy, "I cannot believe I am ladies' maid to a Duchess." Realizing she probably shouldn't have said as much out loud, she blushed.

"Lucy," Cara said trying to put the girl at ease, "I am the same person I was yesterday. Do not treat me differently or I fear I shall have nightmares living up to your expectations."

"Very well Miss, err, I mean…"

"Madam, I am a married lady, Madam is fine, Lucy. Or Cara if you're feeling bolder."

"Thank you, Madam," Lucy said, coming forward with Cara's nightgown.

Cara sighed. It was too much to hope for that the girl would finally be comfortable addressing her by her Christian name. Maybe in time.

Cara turned her back so Lucy could undo her buttons; realizing she was staring directly at the connecting, swiftly she turned away. Sending Lucy side-stepping, still holding onto the clasps. Once finished, Cara sat back to the door, while Lucy brushed her long locks, another indulgence she wouldn't normally request. It took longer and tonight she needed time. She closed her eyes, letting the feel of the bristles soothe her.

Roland stood quietly at the door. Cara's head lay back over the chair, her beautiful swan-like neck arched invitingly. Her beautiful eyes remained closed. *What was she thinking?*

He waited for Lucy to notice him then put his fingers to his lips. Walking silently, he took her place without missing a stroke; Lucy let herself out of the connecting door, and Cara was none the wiser.

"Mmmm, that feels good, like floating on a cloud. Have you ever lain on your back in the lush green grass to watch the clouds, imagining you were on them?"

"No, but I could. As long as you were there beside me." Cara's eyes popped open. Her husband's lips were on the curve of neck and her thoughts fled.

"Oh, my…" Cara purred, closing her eyes once more.

Roland's tongue followed a path to her ear. Cara shivered with delight. She arched back. Her natural instinct fueled his passion. Taking her openness as a sign, Roland worked his hands under her giving her time to protest. When she remained silent, he stood and in one fluid motion set off to his room. He had been prepared to let be if that was what she wanted. He came only to show her what she would miss. Being here now, he didn't know what he would have done if she had said no.

Chapter Fourteen

Laying her down on the bed, *his virgin sacrifice*, he stood staring down at her flushed cheeks as slowly, he removed his remaining clothing.

Cara protested being left alone until her senses registered that he was still there, standing above her, disrobing. At the first sight of his naked chest, she reached for him.

"Not yet, my love," he whispered, as he undid his trousers. Opened but not removed. Cara was taunted by the sight of black curly hair that disappeared just below the opening of his waistband. Reaching out, she made to grasp the top of his breeches.

He was quicker, ensnaring her hand so she could do no further damage. Leaving his pants on was for his protection as much as it was hers. For as soon as they came off, he knew he would take her. She must be ready first before allowing her to touch him, he had dreamed of her touch but tonight he was already too far gone.

"No Cara, not tonight, my love," he said, bringing his head down to her raised hand.

"But why?" Cara asked.

"That, my innocent one, I will explain another day. Trust me in this."

Roland lowered her hand. Taking the tie of her robe, he slipped it from the knot. Taking it in his mouth, he sucked it.

Cara watched with interest; her curiosity urging him on.

Taking the moistened tip, he ran it over Cara's fiery skin. She shivered with delight as her normally glassy gray eyes turned the darker shades of a brewing tempest.

Laving her gown-clad nipples made the material doubly see-through as her breasts tightened and pushed against the cool wet fabric. Her back arched, pushing more of herself into his hungry mouth. There he feasted, from one to the other, until Cara was writhing beneath him.

"Please." She didn't know what she was asking for. Unquestionably, there had to be more to *it* than this. She'd read many books, obviously, all delicately jumped over some very important missing pieces. She was quickly finding out her education wasn't nearly what it should be. This intense fire that burned within her stoked and rose. It never ebbed. Something else had to happen; no one could be expected to go through life this way. It was cruel.

Roland's hand slipped beneath her night rail, stroking her bare legs, caressing her thighs. He cupped her center, massaged his palm against that one intimate spot. She arched her back, her legs parting automatically.

"That's it, my love, let me show you what you long to know," he murmured.

His fingers stroked between her thighs, fueling a fire that already burned red-hot, she writhed, desperate to grasp that unknown just out of her reach. She moaned. Words beyond her, begging for something only her husband could give her.

Roland's mouth covered hers, drinking in her excitement and feeding off the adrenaline that comes from knowing you are pleasuring the woman you love. He caressed her damped folds in rhythm with his tongue; she clung to him, her arms tightening around his neck, and the flames built so fast, so hard, Cara thought she might melt.

Then…she did. Moaning, she stiffened in his arms; her whole body vibrated as her body exploded. Hot pleasure flooded her; rippling across her skin, her body sparked, awakening her internal senses.

Roland grabbed the neck of her gown; wrenching it apart, he tore the garment in two. Cara, still in shock from her climax, didn't even notice he had shed his trousers. Then he was there, where his hand had been, where he had shown her so many wondrous things. He was pushing into her. She could feel his tension. He fought to go slow.

Cara wanted nothing more than to feel the fire. She wanted to experience that great burning within, once more. She wrapped her legs about his hips, bucked against him, impaling herself. She screamed at the sudden jolt of pain.

"Deuce! Cara, I wanted to go slow. Are you hurt?" Roland remained still, buried deep within her.

Cara took a few short breaths. "I'm fine. I wanted to be on fire again. I didn't want to wait. Did I do something wrong?"

Roland chuckled, "No sweetheart, you did nothing wrong, we'll just stay like this until the pain stops. There will only be pain this once and I promise it shouldn't last long."

He kissed the tip of her nose, her cheeks, her eyelids, and finally her mouth. Cara could feel the heat building once more, she felt itchy, knowing it was only the beginning, she rubbed her hips against his; slowly, he began to move in and out of her.

The fire built, this time when Cara's climax hit, Roland followed her over the edge into the flaming abyss.

Their bodies tangled, still joined, Roland rolled to his side taking her with him. Cara's fingers played about his nipple while she caught her breath.

Roland ran his fingers through her long dark locks. "Your hair feels like silk, I remember wanting to touch it almost from the first time I saw you."

Cara chuckled. "How could you have even seen my hair? It was under a veil."

"I guess it was my runaway imagination. From the moment you ran me down in my aunt's foyer, I wanted you."

"But...you didn't even know me."

"My body did and that was all that mattered. The night I saw you sneaking out the window."

"Hmmm." Cara turned to look into his laughter-filled eyes.

"I couldn't say it in front of Beaumont. I knew it was you. Your body called out to mine before you had emerged fully from the window."

Cara's head shot up, she blushed for she had had the same reaction only she didn't know until this very moment what it truly meant.

Roland pulled her head down for a kiss; reluctantly, he left her warm haven. Getting up from the bed, Roland went to the washbasin to dampen a cloth. Coming back, he gently smoothed the last traces of her virginity from her body. Placing the cloth back in the basin, he returned to her, curling up behind her in spoon fashion, holding her tight. Soon, they were both fast asleep.

Cara could feel the penetrating warmth of mid-morning sun. It must be late; she didn't want the dream to end. It was so perfect, the loss of her maidenhead, it was everything...no...it was more than she had ever imagined. For until last night, she'd never really known how wonderful making love could be.

Though, was it making love, when only one of the participants was in love? She didn't know. If what Amylia said was true and she should know, then this was the way, or at least part of it, that would secure the ultimate treasure. His heart. And nights like the one before were not a heavy burden to bear.

Sitting up Cara spotted her robe, her night rail, tattered, torn, hopefully Roland got rid of it before someone saw it. She wondered if it was proper for a wife to wake up in her husband's bed; worrying her lip, she swung her legs over the edge of the bed. She winced. Giving herself a moment, willing her sore muscles to relax, Cara breathed slow steady breaths. Finally, the initial soreness left. She reached for her robe, put it on and walked through the connecting door into her room.

Lucy was there, waiting, as was a tub of steaming hot water. A bath. How wonderful!

Lucy came over, taking Cara's robe; she waited for her mistress to step into the clove and lavender-scented bath.

"There you are, Madam," Lucy crooned. "You just lay back now; I'll fetch you something to eat." Lucy patted the top of Cara's head, left the room. Cara burst into a fit of giggles. Lucy wasn't much older than her if at all and here she was treating her likely a badly abused child. It was too much.

Returning a short while later, tray in hand. Lucy set it down, looking about the room. Nodding, she went to Cara's chair and carried it back to the tub, "This should be the right height." She went back to get the tray then placed it on the chair, nodding once more. "Will there be anything else, Madam?"

"No, Lucy, thank you. You may go. I will ring if I need you." Cara offered her a gracious smile. Lucy bobbed a curtsy and left.

Cara nibbled the toast, sipped the tea, thank goodness Mrs. Leeks didn't send chocolate. She preferred a bitter attack on her taste buds first thing in the morning. Perhaps Mrs. Leeks felt chocolate was for children; now that she was married, she was no longer a child. Whatever it was, Cara was thankful for it.

Quickly, the water cooled, forcing Cara to get on with the day. She dressed in one of her new walking dresses, one that buttoned in the front so she would not have to disturb Lucy.

Amylia had picked out the pattern. The fabric, a cool lawn, yellow speckled with tiny blood-red rosebuds. It was fast becoming one of her favorites.

That done, she hurriedly brushed her hair, twisted it into a loose topknot, rioting tendrils cascaded in wisps about the side of her face, she shrugged.

Pinching her cheeks for a hint of color, Cara went in search for her husband. There was much to do today: finding a governess, preparing the children for their journey back to Wonderland, meeting with Beaumont—with a sigh of anticipation, Cara speedily descended the stairs.

"Tibs, have you seen my husband?" Cara asked reaching the bottom step; Tibs was stationed at his usual post next to the door.

"I believe he has gone out, Madam."

"Gone? When?"

"Better part of an hour ago, Madam."

"Did he leave a message for me? Word of where he went. Anything?"

"I'm afraid not, Madam."

"Oh." A frown creased Cara's brow.

"Is there a problem, Madam?" Tibs inquired.

"No. No, it is all right. I'm sure I will see him when he returns."

"Right you are, Madam." Tibs turned back to the door.

"Tibs, are the children in the nursery, or outside?"

"I believe they are in the garden, awaiting the new governess."

Cara's brow quirked. "Awaiting? Did Beaumont send word he was sending someone over?"

"I believe so, Madam, at least that is what His Grace told the children before leaving."

OOO, that man! It sounded as though the woman was already hired; well, she would just see about that! Cara turned on her heel and went in search of her siblings.

Fuming, she stepped out into the glorious sunshine. Closing her eyes, she tilted her head back soaking in its soothing warmth. She could hear the girls giggling not too far away, Rex was sure to be with them, if not playing, then watching, shaking his head at his sisters' follies.

Taking a long deep inhalation of fresh flower-scented air, Cara lowered head, opened her eyes and went in search of her family.

The garden wasn't large. In fact, it held nothing in comparison to the beautiful landscaped, if sadly neglected and overgrown, gardens of Wonderland. Still, it was a small piece of the country in a city that had more places, which smelled of, refuse and other disgusting things often wafting their way into civilized neighborhoods. She wondered how anyone could simply shrug off the offensive odor as though it didn't exist.

191

Surely the winter when the season was in full swing and the weather was cooler the smell would not be as bad, still for the people who didn't take residence in Bath, Brighton, or other country abodes, during the summer months, it was amazing they didn't wander about with cravats tied tightly about their noses.

The girls were chasing a butterfly as it happily danced over, around and through the pansies, chrysanthemums. Occasionally camouflaged by the colorful flowers, the girls squealed with delight when it re-emerged right before their eyes.

Rex, for a change, was smiling, he seemed to be doing that a lot more lately. Maybe he realized the extent of the dire straits they were forced into or mayhap with their father gone he had felt he had no right to his childhood, either way, one look at him now enjoying these simple pleasures told Cara she made the right choice. At least for her family.

Cara sat on the bench watching the children, Rex taking interest in a spider spinning a web between two branches of a rosebush, caught an ant between his fingers he placed it on an already weaved portion of the web. "I think she's going to have babies," he said, as if it explained his sacrifice.

"Oh, lovely, little spiders all over the place. I can't wait," Cara said with an over-exaggerated shiver.

The girls looked up made no comment as they watched their butterfly. Rex laughed. "Should I feel that way about my nephews or nieces then?" Mischievousness lurked in his blue eyes, making them sparkle.

Cara turned fifty shades of red, she was sure as her face heated. "That is hardly the same thing," she retorted, fanning herself.

"I know." Rex shrugged. "But it is nice to see you blush."

"Thomas Rexley Danforth III, what a terrible thing to say! You are not to make comments about a lady's blush. You...you are to ignore it. That is the gentlemanly thing to do."

Cara realized her mistake when Rex went into a fit of laughter; he was egging her on, the nerve of him! She glared until she too, was overcome by giggles. Becky and Robby, butterfly forgotten, joined in.

Tears streaming down their faces—three black heads of hair glistening in the sun—was how Roland found his family when he followed the laughter through to house to the garden. Standing, he watched, his heart swelling with pride and yes love as he watched and counted his blessing for the family he'd almost thrown away. How could he have ever been so foolish? To turn down such a treasure would have been madness.

Walking over, Roland placed his fingers under his wife's chin, raising her face, he placed a gentle kiss upon her lips. "You are well, I trust?"

Cara's cheeks reddened. "Yes. Quite well. Will you sit?"

Roland sat next to Cara one arm over her shoulders as he watched the children as they began playing once more. "This is nice though I fear we will not have much longer out here; Beaumont and Miss Pebble are on their way."

"Miss Pebble?"

"The new governess."

"You mean, a candidate, for surely you would not have gone ahead without me and hired one. I do believe you value your life a little more than that, Your Grace."

Roland chuckled. "Yes, I do but I also value the lives of your siblings, therefore, Beaumont will bring only the best with him. There will be no need for further interviews, besides, I can think of other areas that your, um, talents can be put to use."

"My talents?" Cara inquired softly. "I'm sure I don't know what you're talking about."

"Dare I say?" Roland teased.

Cara blushed, elbowing him, she wasn't used to the sexual byplay, though she found it immense fun, it was also terribly embarrassing to be carrying on so in front of the children, whether they could hear it or not.

"All right, I will leave those particular talents to be detailed later. For now, we should discuss what we are going to do about Mr. Gomersal."

"Is that where you were? Is he awake?" Cara asked hopefully.

"I spoke with everyone again. I didn't go to Mr. Gomersal's. I didn't have to. His doctor said he was still unconscious. His son has been contacted and should arrive within the next couple of days. Once he does, I think we should see if he is able to find anything. Until then, there are still missives to locate and decode."

Cara leaned her head on his shoulder. "Do you think it is wise to start on the investigation with kids still here? I don't know about you, but I would feel safer once they were out of the way of immediate danger."

Roland kissed her forehead. "Me too."

"Excuse me, Your Graces; the Earl is awaiting you in the Blue Room."

"Thank you, Tibs. Have Mrs. Leeks prepare tea and cakes."

"Is she here Cara? Is she pretty? Is she nice?" the girls screamed excitedly in unison.

"Girls, cease! Hollering like hooligans is likely to have her running the other way, pretty or not." Roland's smile belied his words; the girls giggled.

"Come, my love. We'll beckon the children following your approval of the governess. *And you will approve*," he whispered the last.

Cara knew she had no choice in the matter; however, as Rex was watching them like a hawk, Roland's wording had been for his benefit. Linking hands, they walked back into the house.

"Ah, there you two are. I have brought Miss Pebble, she's highly trained, no one better for the job, I must say, what do you think?"

Miss Pebble sat on the settee a picture of serenity; she was young, mid-twenties, dressed in drab gray, auburn hair was pulled back in a severe knot. She looked like the perfect Governess. Now, was she? And would she be able to manage the role of bodyguard.

"I am more than capable, Your Grace," Miss Pebble said, her voice soft, more than adequate for making children feel comfortable.

"I'm sure you are, I wasn't thinking of your Governess skills."

"Nor was I speaking of them, Madam."

Cara heard the challenge in her voice. Who was she to question a trained agent? Cara tossed out several questions, rapid-fire answers were shot back. Nibbling her lip, she looked to Roland; when he nodded, Cara turned back to Miss Pebble. "Thank you. Thank you both."

"Where are the children? There are three, aren't there?"

Roland answered, "Yes, one boy two girls, all eleven. They are in the garden, so it is safe to talk."

"All eleven?"

"Triplets," Cara clarified.

Beaumont cleared his throat noticeably in a hurry to get down to business. Cara and Roland took a seat next to each other; Beaumont sat next to Miss Pebble on the settee.

"After you left yesterday, Tibs brought me a copy of the Times; I assume you read the article pertaining to Mr. Gomersal?"

Beaumont straightened. "Yes, I will investigate—"

"There is no need, Tibs and Daniels took care of that quarter. I was back talking to several of the people this morning. Gomersal is still unconscious; the doctor doesn't know if he'll wake, therefore his son has been sent for."

"I still don't understand why Thomas would use Gomersal; the man is retired. Damned strange if you ask me," Beaumont said.

"Perhaps, he felt he could trust no one else," Miss Pebble interjected.

"Why would my father not be able to trust another attorney, Miss Pebble?"

"Well, I haven't been given all the details, but if Thomas' blackmailer was English instead of French, he may have been leery of anyone in current contact with the Organization."

"You mean my father feared an insider?"

Roland contemplated the thought. "That does make sense, don't you think, Beaumont? Thomas' actions over the past three years seem to indicate that he was distancing himself from the Organization, maybe even his family. Though we have informant's information about the French, there is no sign yet of Thomas being in cahoots with them. In fact, we have only hearsay that the French are even involved."

"It's a place to start. Have you managed to find anything more out about missives?"

"No, I wanted to meet with you before contacting the remaining names on the list."

"Which are?"

"Maitland, Hampden, Lawson, and Liberton."

"Mr. Liberton was out of town, to be returning around the end of the month," Cara said, with an absent wave of her hand.

"Previous research, my love?" Roland waggled eyebrows.

"As a matter of fact, yes," Cara said, smiling.

They spent the next couple of hours going over what they needed, the missives being the first on the list, Miss Pebble's duties second to that. Cara took Miss Pebble out to the garden to meet the children while Roland and Beaumont finished up.

"You have a lovely home, Your Grace," Miss Pebble said as they walked through the back of the house.

"Cara, please."

"All right, Cara, I am Megan."

Exchanging a smile, they walked out into the garden.

"They are usually very easy to find, one has only to listen for the sound of laughter to know where they are." Cara cocked her head. Meg did the same, grinning as she heard the excited giggles.

They followed the sound of merriment down the graveled path between a series of rose bushes. Suddenly, Megan stopped, cocked her head, and peered as though something had caught her eye. Carefully, she separated the outer bushes. Cara held her breath, she didn't know how much Megan knew, would she connect the handsome black roses to…

"These are beautiful; I don't think I have ever seen a black rose. May I?"

"I'd rather you didn't," Cara said, rather sheepishly.

"Oh?"

"I will explain later if I can, how about one of the others?" Cara suggested quickly.

Megan gave her a questioning look. "I brought that bush from The Gables, my mother cross-bred various types, coming up with a rainbow of colors. Though you will find the garden in much need of attention, I have tried to keep it up as best I could. By the time you arrive, they should be in full bloom; feel free to help yourself."

Megan nodded. "Thank you."

"Cara, is this her? Is she to be our Governess? Cara, she is very pretty."

Megan blushed at the compliment, staring down at two beautiful cherub-like faces. Big blue eyes stared back. She smiled. "Hello, my name is Miss Pebble. You are?"

"I'm Becky, this is Robby. Rex is back there, feeding a spider. He says she is going to have babies. Lots and lots of them, how many babies do spiders have?"

"Girls," Cara admonished.

Megan chuckled. "It's all right. If one doesn't ask questions, one never learns. Spiders have hundreds of babies, not right away; they hatch from eggs. Then the babies spin their own little webs, not in a design just a thread, the passing wind picks them up and moves them to another area so that they can start their own lives."

"So, they never get to know their mother?" Becky asked.

"No. They leave as soon as they are hatched."

"That's like us, our mother left us as soon as we were born," Robby said.

196

"Girls, please go and bring Rex over to the bench so I can make proper introductions."

The girls skipped over to their brother.

"Where did you learn so much about spiders?"

"My secret is out."

"What secret is that?"

"Why, that I am a blue stocking, of course." Megan's mouth went into the shape of an O, her green eyes got huge in mock horror.

They both laughed.

Sitting on the bench, Cara introduced the children, given names and nicknames. Megan said it would be a while before she would be able to tell the girls apart but with time, they would do well. That statement led Cara to believe that she would be with them for a very long time. Good or bad, she hadn't decided.

"How long do you think we will need your services?" Cara inquired quietly as the children made their way inside to get ready for dinner.

"For as long as I am needed," Megan replied.

"After?"

"After if there is nothing for me and you still fancy my services, then I'll stay. I enjoy children."

They sat for a while getting to know one another, without either one really mentioning anything about themselves, when Megan checked the watch pinned to her lapel. It was getting late.

"We should go to the nursery. There is a lot that needs to be done before tomorrow."

With that she called the children and like ducklings to a mother duck, they followed behind.

They were on their way. Roland insisted on an early start to ensure they would be safely installed at The Gables before dark. Cara would miss them. She stayed on the front step waving until the carriage could no longer be seen. She had never been apart from them. Aside from the two nights at Amylia's and then she hadn't been more than a couple blocks away. Silent tears rolled down her cheeks, it was for the best. It truly was. They would be safer at Wonderland with Daniels and Megan.

"Come, Cara, let's go inside, they will be fine."

"I pray you are right; I cannot get over this awful feeling," Cara said tearfully.

"Then we had best finish up here quickly. The sooner we are done, the sooner we can be with them at your precious Wonderland."

"Why are we just sitting here, I hoped you had brought me here for some purpose. Did you find the Widow like I instructed?"

"There." The man's finger pointed in the direction of a townhouse.

"That's Thomas Danforth's, is it not?"

"Yes."

"So, it was as we expected, his paramour has taken up residence. Who's the man she is with?"

"Are you a fool?"

Liberton reached across the carriage lightning fast and planted his fist into his companion's face.

Redding brought his glove to his lip, enough to stop the trickle of blood.

"You're a bastard. No wonder you can't get anyone to work for you."

"A bastard, yes. You very well may have the right of it, though I believe my mother was married to a man by the time of birth. Some of us," he snarled across the carriage, "are not that lucky."

"What the hell are you raving about, old man?"

"Careful, son. I would hate to have to even out your sneer. Now. Talk."

"She is not his paramour. She is Miss Caralyn Danforth, or at least she was until a couple of days ago. Now, she is Duchess of Fairhaven, ah I see the Fairhaven name still rings a bell even if you can no longer recognize the face."

"So, what happened to the widow?"

"The widow disappeared the same time the Duchess appeared. You figure it out."

"So, they brought Fairhaven back into the fold."

"Fairhaven never left the fold. Not from what I hear. He was stationed in the colonies, with that being a loss, I assume they called him back to catch bigger fish. You have made some powerful enemies, Father."

"It is only one enemy I am concerned with, now what else were you able to find out? What about the list? Anything? Is there a stir in the Home Office? Who are they pointing fingers at?"

"I had hoped to have more to go on when I arranged for the abduction of the widow, the local blokes I hired to see to the job, truly botched it. Of course, it took me a bit to discover the identity of the widow. There has been so much activity with the wedding I could not search the house. I discovered Thomas may have left important documents in the hands of his attorney, a chap by the name of Henry Gomersal…"

"Henry Gomersal, are you sure?"

"Yes, why?"

"Gomersal used to be the lawyer for the agency before retiring some years ago. Damn and blast, I would have liked to use Thomas to further ends. I wasn't nearly close enough to my goal."

"You should not have killed him until we had the list. Or is there some other reason we are doing all this? I could oversee things more efficiently if you would tell me what this is all about," Redding hissed.

"Let us be away before we are discovered. We can discuss what to do on the way."

Obviously, the conversation was closed for discussion as far as his father was concerned, Redding silently seethed. He had tried for years to be what his father wanted, for some reason he always fell short. Now this, was he after the list? The woman? The Home Office, what?

Roland stood to the left of the curtain; he watched an unidentifiable black carriage start down the road.

"Are they gone?"

"For now. Undoubtedly, they will be back."

"Did you notice them when we were loading the children in the carriage?"

"No, not until after Daniels pulled away. I suppose they could have been there before."

"But what? What are you thinking?"

"It was probably a fact-finding mission, nothing more."

"Then they know the children are alone."

"Not alone, Cara, they are with two very highly trained agents."

"Yes, yes, they could decide the best way to get the information is to get to the children."

"Yes. I have thought of that too. That's why Daniels is switching the coach at Greyley House. Even if whoever is behind this knows we are married, chances are they looking for the Danforth or Fairhaven coach, not one belonging to the Duke of Greyley."

"So, you anticipated this?" Cara asked in awe.

"A good agent must be prepared for any event. Being as how we do not have all the pieces to the puzzle, it is best we keep all our bases covered."

"Still, they will know of The Gables, what is to stop them from going there?"

"Nothing, I'm afraid. At least if they are at The Gables, Daniels and Miss Pebble will have an arsenal at their disposal, and don't forget Tibs will be leaving shortly to ride back up. There is no better in a fight than Tibs."

"But Wonderland has no weapons! If you are counting on guns and ammunition, you are sadly mistaken. There is nothing there I tell you."

"Is there not, remember my dear, when in battle, the best weapons are the ones that not necessarily inflict the most damage, but those that can be used to your best advantage. Wonderland is full of nooks and crannies. Hiding could very well be their best weapon of all."

"Still, something doesn't feel right." Cara twisted her hands back and forth in her lap.

"Excuse me Your Graces, this just arrived." Roberts, former newly acquired footman promoted butler, walked regally into the sitting room, instead of simply handing Roland the note, it sat in the center of a silver tray held in front of him. Roland took the note, sending Roberts on his way.

"I miss Tibs already," Roland said opening the letter.

"Shhh, he'll hear you," Cara scolded with a smile.

"It's too bad Dobson was needed elsewhere; I really would have preferred having one of our own men here."

"Roberts is one of our own men."

"I meant an agent," Roland said, looking up from the note.

"Well, of course you did, how foolish of me," Cara said throwing her hands up into the air. *Agents, agents, agents*... "What does the note say?"

Roland smiled, it never ceased to amaze him how the slightest show of her anger could affect him so thoroughly.

"It's from Beaumont; he requests the presence of Duke and Duchess of Fairhaven at a small fete this afternoon. In Newmarket, of all places; he will be here at one. We are to be ready."

Cara looked at the clock; it was still early, barely nine.

"Whatever would be in Newmarket?"

"A fete there surely means a fundraiser of sorts for the Jockey Club."

"And the Jockey Club is?" Cara asked.

"A group of men with nothing better to do than race about the countryside. What else?" Roland's lips molded to a roguish smile.

Once again, Cara could not believe how handsome he was.

"But why would we want to attend something like that. Are you a member?"

"Me? No. Though a lot of the members are, shall we say, well-connected, and your father was a member."

"He was?" Cara was clearly shocked.

"Yes, he was. Let's go into the study and work on the notes; if Beaumont intends to draw someone out, we will need to be prepared."

Cara had never been to the Newmarket tracks. The lawn was set with huge tents in case of rain, though there wasn't a cloud in the sky. An enormous oval could be seen stretching into the distance, she wanted to get a closer look, but Roland had told her it could all be seen from the stands, most people use opera glasses, but the naked eye would do fine if you had nothing better at your disposal.

Only one portion of the track was beyond sight, entering a stand of trees in the southwest corner where riders and horses would be invisible for a few moments. "Usually," he said, "whoever went in the victor rarely remained so on the other side."

Cara didn't need to him to tell her that jockeys would quite often use a bag of tricks in order to off-seat their opponents.

They wandered about seeing and being seen. That was the most important part Amylia had told her. The Duke and Duchess of Greyley had followed behind in their closed carriage. Cara tried to remember the names of the people as she passed; there were approximately two hundred in attendance, a fair turnout for a fete held out of season. When she made comment of this Amylia laughed. "My dear, racing is never out of season."

The setting was almost carnival like in appearance, former-racing champions stood placidly in portable pens, manes and tails braided, some with flowers others without. Their coats shone in the afternoon sun making them look every bit the champions they were even without even moving.

Cara had never seen so many wonderful animals. She loved horses, always had, but when the grooms were taken from Wonderland so was the riding horses. All they had now was a couple of older mismatched bays used for pulling the coach. Again, Cara fumed at the unfairness of it all. No matter the circumstances, she and her siblings had been forced to miss out on what should have been simple pleasures.

A sleek black thoroughbred caught Cara's eye, the sign on the gate read Night Dancer, Winner of the Pennington Cup '09 and '11. He was so beautiful. As she approached, he whickered. Speaking softly to him, he snorted and brushed the ground with his hoof.

"I see our good Night caught your eye. He is a beauty, is he not?"

Cara turned to see Lord Redding standing next to her. "Yes, he is very grand. How have you been, My Lord? I don't think I had the chance to thank you for coming to the wedding. I had no idea you knew His Grace."

"I was there strictly as an escort, Your Grace, but I thank you all the same."

Roland watched his wife make her way closer. The beast looked agitated but made no attempt to attack. These portable fences would be nothing to a horse like that if he wanted out. He saw another beast approach, this time outside the fence. He said a few words then departed.

"Beaumont, did you ever check into Lord Redding? I swear that man bothers me."

"He bothers you, my dear friend, because on three occasions now he has been seen talking to your wife. He is of little consequence, I assure you. He is too young, too inexperienced to plan something of this magnitude. Look. He is moving on, now wipe that scowl off your face, this is a party."

Roland forced a smile in place and went to fetch his bride. She looked beautiful standing there in deep navy blue. She was excited when she dressed stating that she had thought it frivolous when Aunt Amylia forced her to buy a habit because she thought she would never have use for it. Her matching blue riding hat naturally tilted to one side, launching a single long dark blue feather downward to graze her shoulder.

Her hair was tucked up beneath the hat, except for a few escaping tendrils making her look slightly mussed and very desirable. She stood unmoving, murmuring soft love words to the big black. Even to a horse, she gave her unwavering loyalty. He found himself wishing for that same strength of affection, that same steadfast loyalty, the kind that came with undying love. He'd never thought himself a romantic, not that is, until Cara had made his heart sing. Now he knew he would do anything for her love.

"Penny for your thoughts."

Standing behind her, she could feel the heat of his body through their many layers of clothes, though it was electrifying and intense, Cara felt something stronger... Shelter? Protection? That was it. He was her protector. Her very own White Knight coming to save her, she leaned back into his solid form.

"Come to save me from the beast, Your Grace?" Cara whispered, jokingly.

"Which beast would that be I wonder, the one with two legs or the one with four?"

"Two legs? Oh. Surely you cannot mean Lord Redding. He came only to gloat over the beast being his."

"He was at our wedding too; I have barely spoken with the man. He makes me uncomfortable. I would appreciate it if you were not alone with him."

"Roland, we are amongst hundreds of people. What could he do to me here? Besides, he said he came only as an escort to the wedding. If you remember, he has only been with me, Cara, on that one occasion. The other times it was Mrs. Black."

"All right, my love, but please—"

"Yes, Roland, until this mess is cleared up, I will be extra careful. Now did you come to berate me?"

Roland rubbed his thumb in circles over her gloved hand. "No. I came because I cannot bear to be separated from you. Why this one?"

Cara didn't ask what he was talking about. "Because he has sleek lines, his coat is as black as a moonless night, he is a harness of unleashed power, and because if you look into his eyes, he is alone."

Roland squeezed her gently then turned her back toward the crowd. "Let's make the rounds, sweetheart." Giving her his arm, they walked and talked gathering information, then departing bits that would soon draw out their adversary.

Chapter Fifteen

It was late when they returned home from Newmarket. Roberts was waiting for them at the door. "This came while you were out," he said, handing them a note.

Roland took the paper on his way to the study.

"Brandy?"

Cara closed the door. "I'll get it. You read."

"It's from Tibs; they made it safely there by supper. Everything appears fine, Mrs. Brown, the old bat—"

"Surely it doesn't say that?" Cara said, aghast.

"No, I improvised. Apparently, she is not sufficiently satisfied as to our marital status and has told Tibs such. He did not go into detail, saying only that Miss Pebble is currently smoothing things over."

Cara handed Roland his glass then turned toward the other chair, thinking better of it, she plopped herself lightly onto his lap instead.

"You really are bad, you know, calling Mrs. Brown an old bat. Not very kind at all."

"I thought you liked my bad side," Roland said bouncing her up and down.

Cara's lips trembled. "It has its moments." She winked. "But I must say if today is any indication, those moments are very few and far between."

"Are you feeling neglected, my love?" Roland asked to bring his lips a breath away from hers.

"Not neglected. Lonely."

"Let me see if we can rectify that."

His hand cupped her cheek, it felt firm and warm, it smelt of sandalwood and leather, and the scent teased her senses making her mouth water. Her body hummed with awareness. As he leaned closer, his scent surrounded her, enticing her to burrow closer to that hard, male body; she tangled her fingers in his ink-black hair, kneading the soft, thick strands.

Their lips met, like paradise, his lips soft against hers, skilled as always, coaxing her to open for him.

He pulled her closer with his arm, his other hand sliding from her cheek to the back of her head. A soft mew of pleasure escaped her as she clung to him. Her head swam with pleasure. She could barely breathe. Her blood roared through her veins like a familiar wildfire, her body came to life and rattled her already thrumming senses. Her breasts were swollen, the nipples so hard they were painful as they pushed against her layers of clothes.

Standing with her in his arms, Roland walked slowly and carefully, his mouth still on hers, to the door. Balancing her was no small feat but he managed to do so without any sign of wear. Silently, he carried her up the stairs to their chambers.

Depositing her in the middle of the gigantic four-poster bed, he left to dismiss Lucy. Returning, he closed the connecting door before coming to the bed and removing Cara's dainty leather boots.

Cara wiggled her toes, though she still had her stocking on; Roland leaned forward and nibbled, winning a delighted squeak from her as she squirmed to get away.

Helping him with the rest of her clothes, then with his, they tumbled into bed, where Roland could show her once more, how un-alone she really was.

"You are so beautiful." Trailing a finger over her skin, he playfully bit her soft creamy shoulder. She grinned at him, snuggling her nose into his chest. Her hand hovered over him, learning that landscape of her husband. Every crease of his hard body was hers, hers to enjoy, and hers to pleasure.

She ran a finger around his nipple and was rewarded with a tremor. Feeling more confident, she traced a path down, connecting with each rib, to the indent of his naval, lower still. When she reached his engorged manhood, she encased it with her hand, something wicked in her told her to stroke him as one would stroke the neck of a sleek stallion. His breath hitched, confirming her instincts. She stroked with a cadence she'd learned the night before, building up momentum.

Roland turned, allowing her this. The torment was surely enough to kill him, but she deserved the right to be his equal. To explore him and please him as he would her. He swallowed hard, hoping her curiosity would be satisfied quickly.

Cara kissed the pulse where it beat in his neck, the more she stroked the faster it beat. It was beating, right now in this moment, for her. She moistened her lips trailing damp kisses, down his body. She licked and suckled his nipples; they hardened just as hers had done. Naughtily, she pulled on the small hairs surrounding them before continuing downward.

Roland had his eyes closed, his fists clenched tight at his side, knuckles turning white, but he was in control. Cara wanted to break him. She wanted to have him squirm for her as she had for him. To need her…want her, with absolutely no thought for anything else.

She poked her tongue into his navel, tasting the salty sweat gathering there, and then lower. When she looked at the tip of his rod in her hand, it was glistening with a drop of moisture. She licked it. Roland's eyes flew open, his hands making a grab for her. Cara agilely evaded capture.

"Cara," he breathed, "you cannot. I cannot. I want you too much."

Cara looked into his deep blue eyes; lips bowed. "Can you ever want too much?" she asked before her mouth covered his manhood. She feasted, licking, suckling, tasting his salty essence. He felt satiny soft, yet he was so hard. She moved her mouth in an up and down motion, leaving her hands free to roam his body.

His manhood jerked; his whole-body shook; instead of crying out, Roland ruthlessly grabbed her pinning her to the bed with his body. Cara laughed.

He entered her with one swift powerful thrust, not taking the time to prepare her. The sudden fullness took her breath away. Cara encircled him with her legs, as Roland's thumb found that special nub; he rubbed quick and hard over it, as he pushed frantically in and out of her.

Cara was on fire; all she could think about was finding her release. She met his hips burying him deep inside her. When he moved outward, she mourned the loss. He was trembling, holding back, waiting. Cara felt the fire spread through her body, she arched her back, screamed in ecstasy as her climax rocked her very core. Roland roared like a lion before embedding himself deep within her, flooding her womb with his seed.

When breath returned, he asked, "Did I hurt you? I tried to control myself. Lord help me, what you do to me is criminal."

"Shhh, you didn't hurt me, it was wonderful. Did I make you lose control?"

Roland chuckled. "Do you doubt it?"

Cara smiled exhaustedly. "Not anymore." Yawning, she kissed his chin. "I'm glad. Can't stand that blasted control." Then she was out, fast asleep, leaving Roland no chance to comment.

He moved off her, bringing her into his embrace, he held her close, protected. Not alone. Placing a kiss on the back of her head, Roland drifted to sleep with the beat of her heart beneath his hand.

Cara was warm; a cooling sensation lingered over her body firing her from the inside out. Firm hands stroked her, soothed her; cherished her as she fought to open her eyes. She gave up the fight, opting to drink in the sensations still so new to her.

Roland had awakened with the dawn. Lying beside his lovely wife for at least an hour, he watched her sleep. Her hair twinkled like rubies where the sun kissed it. Her lashes were crescent moons on her cheeks, dark and full as if painted with a master's brush. Twenty-four freckles dotted a path across the bridge of her nose, spread out in a delicate V formation.

Lying on her back, head twisted to one side rested on her soft hands, pillowing her right cheek. She was the perfect model of a woman-child. In that pose, she portrayed innocence and trust of one so young contradicted by womanly curves. Not willowy. Not his Cara. She was curvilinear. He loved that best of all.

The smell of cloves and lavender lingered. A soft natural aroma, not the potent scent caused from heavy perfume. He appreciated that she was unlike most of the ladies today, bathed in layers upon layers of varying rose fragrances.

He watched her chest rise then fall with each breath more of the covers slipped from her. Standing to attention, dusky nipples pebbled, was she dreaming of him, or could she sense somewhere in her subconscious that her husband was looking at her? Wanting her.

She had four small freckles on the soft curve of her right breast, eight on the other, possibly more hidden beneath. They seemed to call him, to taste them; did they taste of cloves? Without waking her, he began to slowly taste each delicate little freckle.

Moving his way down, he checked for more, knowing it would be futile. The sun brought out freckles; there was no chance of sun getting to these nether regions. Though it wouldn't hurt to check. Sliding the covers off his wife, Roland licked his way from the first brownish speck inward and down around each nipple, until they puckered even more. He kissed a trail to her navel, stopping to swirl his tongue.

She smelled of sex, their fluids had mingled the night before emitting an aroma, as strong as the call of opium. His tongue gently flicked. He took a deep satisfying breath at the succulent alcove of her womanhood. Positioned between Cara's legs, resting them on his shoulders. She moaned at the loss of his tongue but didn't wake.

Spreading her open like the petals of the rarest flower, Roland lowered his mouth. Licking from the nubbin in downward motion, he felt Cara stiffen, she moaned and arched, giving him better access.

Cara came awake with a start; this wasn't a dream—she tried to sit up. "Roland, don't."

His only answer was to secure her legs so that she remained lying flat. Open to him. Then he sucked. Cara's whole body quaked and bucked beneath the onslaught of his mouth.

"Roland, please," she begged, her air getting short, she feared she'd pass out. With a scream, her body convulsed. Shaking from the aftermath of such a vicious climax, she was still panting when he entered her. In one rapid plunge, he reached her core. Cara could hardly keep in time with his movements. So urgent was his need. She opened wider, wrapping her legs about him, giving what she could.

With her hands she grasped, squeezed his nipples, the contact soon sent him over the edge, for the first time she watched as his back arched making himself go as deep as he possibly could. The muscles in his chest seemed to jump. His black hair was mussed falling over his closed eyes, the cords in his neck stood out.

Soon Cara could no longer focus on her husband's good looks as the fire that was raging within longed for another discharge. Reaching her arms about his neck she pulled herself off the bed high enough to suckle his hardened nipple; he roared, jerking as together they sought the stars.

Much later that morning, Cara and Roland sat in the study, penning notes to three of the four remaining parties, requesting that they call on Roland as soon as possible. The notes themselves were simple, for if they should tumble into the wrong hands or God forbid one of them were on the wrong side, they didn't want them knowing what they were up to.

First to send word back was Mr. Burton Lawson, Esquire. He was the current attorney for the Organization. Roland's note to him led him to believe that he needed his services on a personal level, therefore with the prospect of representing a Duke and fattening his bank account, he jumped at the chance to come. His message stated he would be honored to drop by, today at two.

Next to respond was Viscount Hampden, 'Hammy'; Roland had gone to Oxford with him. They hadn't been friends then, and though he had no great compulsion to be friends now, he led him to believe he would like to further his acquaintance. His note requested Roland's presence at Gentleman Jackson's, around four o'clock.

There was no word from Baron Maitland.

Roland left just before lunch, to check on Mr. Gomersal's condition and stop round to question Maxwell Liberton's staff regarding his return.

The doctor's prognosis was the same. Mr. Gomersal would awake in his own good time or not at all. Roland had the chance to meet his son, Henry Gomersal Jr. while he was there. He explained his association with Mr. Gomersal and secured the younger man's word that he would look for any documents that were address to him or his wife. If he found anything, he would bring it over personally. Before leaving, Roland left his current direction plus knowledge of The Gables in case locating the material took longer than their stay in London.

Cara paced the sitting room; it was close to two o'clock, the appointed time for Mr. Lawson to arrive and Roland wasn't back. What could have happened? She knew his destination, when he left, he felt confident he would be back in time for the meeting. Cara could see a hackney approaching the drive; it was sure to be Mr. Lawson. And Roland wasn't here. She left the window pacing harder; she didn't know if she could do this.

Pull yourself together. She scolded herself, *calm down, sit, greet the guest, and give Roland's apologies, as a good wife should, entertain him with tea and cake. Keep his mouth full and his mind busy and Roland would arrive shortly. If not try to discover anything that may help, then kill Roland when he returns.* Yes, Cara thought as she forced herself to sit on the settee, just breathe.

"Mr. Lawson to see His Grace, Madam," Roberts intoned from the door.

"Send him in, Roberts, His Grace will return shortly. Have Mrs. Leeks prepare refreshments."

Bowing, Roberts took a step back allowing Mr. Lawson to proceed into the parlor. He was a short bald man with big thick gold-rimmed spectacles that perched precariously on the end of his nose, looping a little to one side. His cheeks were flushed with what Cara hoped was excitement and not imbibing, as he came forth.

He executed a bow with flourish, taking Cara's proffered hand. "Mr. Burton Lawson at your service, Your Grace."

"Mr. Lawson, how kind of you to come so quickly," Cara said taking her hand back. "Won't you sit; have a cup of tea with me while we await His Grace?"

"I'd be delighted."

As if on cue, the housekeeper came in bearing a tray.

"Thank you, Mrs. Leeks, I will pour."

With a curtsy, she took her leave. Cara poured while she watched the little bird-like man's eyes dart around the room. Was he nervous or looking for something?

"You have a very nice residence, Your Grace," he said, at last giving Cara an opening.

"Thank you, Mr. Lawson, we quite enjoy it. How would you like your tea?"

"Plain is fine, Your Grace. Did His Grace say when he would return?" Mr. Lawson appeared to be nervous. Fidgety.

"He is aware of the appointment, sir; I am sure he will return as quickly as possible. Do you have another appointment elsewhere perhaps? I know my husband received your direction from the Earl of Beaumont, you must have some very influential clients; does it make for an interesting career?"

Mr. Lawson looked up startled, and then seemed to recall he was addressing a Duchess, she was beyond being reproached.

He smiled. "You misunderstand, Your Grace."

"Oh, dear me, I'm so sorry."

"No, please don't be. I do work for Mr. Beaumont in a roundabout way though I rarely get a chance to meet the people I represent."

Cara's brow crinkled in confusion. "You don't? How then do you know they need representation?" Cara was thankful she didn't have to feint the confusion or the interest in her voice.

"Quite simple really, they send a missive and I reply in the same manner."

"But then why did you so readily agree to meet with my husband?"

Mr. Lawson blushed but was saved from answering as Roland came into the room, "Lawson, I presume?"

"Yes, Your Grace."

"Fairhaven, if you please."

"Very well, Fairhaven," Mr. Lawson said coming to his feet to shake Roland's hand.

"Please be seated, Mr. Lawson. Thank you. I requested your presence, as you are a well-known attorney, were you acquainted with Baron Thomas Danforth by any chance?"

Something flickered in his expression, quickly covered; he replied, "On occasion, Your Grace, mayhap if you could be a little more specific, I would be able to elaborate."

"Very well. The late Baron Danforth was my wife's father. I was given the role of guardian upon his death. Presently I have no legal papers pertaining to such, only a letter written to me years ago when I was overseas. As I expected some word from an attorney of his passing as to my subsequent duties, you can imagine my dismay when no one contacted me."

The bird-like man nodded, clearly eager to help, Cara could not get over how easily Roland could weave a network of truths and lies to obtain his goal so easily. Did he do that with her as well? Shaking away imaginings she had no time for, she listened to the ongoing conversation.

"…So, I have done no prior work for the Baron."

"Is it possible, Mr. Lawson that Danforth left you in possession of any material, no matter how odd that may help in my quest?"

"No. No, wait. There is a small note he left in my care. Could that help?"

"Could you describe it? Of course, I would most likely need to see it to be certain, could that be arranged Lawson?"

"Well, it was really nothing, a few dates, some figures. Originally, I thought he gave it to me by mistake for expenses and such incurred, when it should have gone to Weatherby. However, when I took Weatherby the document he noticed my name clearly on the paper and informed me I was mistaken. I took the paper back, evidently without knowing why I had it to begin with. I placed it back in Thomas' file I had meant to contact him, but before I had the chance, he—died."

He turned uneasily toward Cara, "So sorry about your loss, Your Grace."

Cara acknowledged him with a smile, as she wasn't currently dressed in mourning, she could not by rights let her true emotions show. It was Beaumont's idea. He said, "If father had cut ties to the family, it was best that the family appeared not to mourn him, a falling out could last years. Anyone worth his grain of salt would be able to draw their own conclusions from how his family behaved."

"Is it at your office, Lawson?" Roland asked, his mind still on getting that note in his hands.

"No, Your Grace, I keep company files at home, in case of burglary."

"I have another appointment this afternoon but should be free around six; if you give me your direction I will stop by when I am free."

Roland really left no room for Lawson to say no, so the man agreed. If reluctant, he didn't let it show as he gave Roland his direction and confirmed he would see him at six o'clock. Then he took his leave.

Once the front door closed, Cara turned to her husband, "Why were you late? Did something happen? Oh, Roland, I was so nervous I thought I would have to question Lawson alone, surely, I would have made a complete muck of it. You did marvelously well. I am extremely impressed. Did you find out about Liberton? Is he back…?"

Roland listened to her rattle questions then with a brief smile, he silenced her in a way that was proving to be most useful. She made a small mew of protest before wrapping her arms about his neck with the mew turning into a moan.

When she was completely dazed, his mouth left her, his thumb smoothed the soft skin of her cheek. "I got caught in traffic was all, the regent must be planning something, there is an overabundant number of carriages lining the streets."

Cara, still unable to form an intelligent thought, simply said, "Oh."

Roland couldn't help smiling.

"I met with the doctor about Gomersal; his condition is the same, though he does not appear to be getting worse. His son, Henry is in residence. I have him going through his father's papers in hopes of finding something of consequence."

"Liberton is a different matter. He wasn't in when I called around. His staff informed me he was expected back any day. I got the impression he's been away for some time."

"Since just after my father's death," Cara said absently.

"What?"

"I said—"

"I know what you said, Sweetheart. How do you know this…let me guess, research for Mrs. Black? It strikes me as odd though; you wouldn't happen to know the exact date, would you?"

"No, not exactly. Mrs. Huntington was a wealth of information even Rose couldn't get that information without making it look suspicious, a widow new to town."

"I see your point. I will send word to Beaumont. I want Liberton investigated."

"Do you think he could have killed my father?"

"It is possible. If so, we must know."

A shiver ran down Cara's spine. Roland reached out to comfort her.

Beaumont was there within the hour. "I used all resources available, this Liberton didn't exist, or at least I can find no sign of existence past the last three or four years. I have submitted his description to Lord Renfrew to pass among the Organization. Hopefully, something will turn up soon." Beaumont stopped briefly reflecting on his conversation with Lord Renfrew. "He did seem a mighty put out about the thing. I hope for our sakes Liberton is in at least some small way connected to this game."

Roland took his cupped fist and tapped himself thoughtfully on the mouth. "There is something about that man that bothers me, has since the beginning. His disappearance alone is unusual, his reappearance even more so, the fact that the man had no life prior to, what was it, four years ago? He must be dirty. I'd stake my reputation on it."

"We will keep a man on him."

"Is Dobson returning soon? It would be just the job for him. Liberton's not likely to recognize him."

"He should return in another week or so, hopefully with some good reports from our borders."

"I don't see why you would send one of my best men away in the middle of an investigation. It wasn't well done of you, my friend."

"Don't look to me when you cast blame. The orders came from the top."

"Renfrew? Isn't that a little odd?"

"Who can say with Renfrew, I fear the man is getting dotty. Still, till the board forces him into retirement, we as lap dogs must obey."

"I did discover, an amour, in Liberton's resent past. It is worth checking out; you know how men are in bed."

"You think he might have let something slip?"

"Quite frankly, yes. And for the moment she is our only lead. You'll look into it?"

"I will." Roland said with a determined nod.

Beaumont was pacing the study like a caged animal.

Roland knew he had more on his mind then he was letting on, hopefully since their earlier clearing of the air, Beaumont knew better than to hold back relatable information pertaining to the case. So, Roland could only assume it was something else that was bothering his old friend.

"Want to talk about it?"

Beaumont sighed shaking his head. "I'd best take my leave."

Considering the matter dropped, Roland acquired the information for contacting Liberton's amour. With Beaumont gone, Roland penned a note to Mrs. Isabelle Dupries of number twelve Coventry Lane. Liberton's former mistress.

Chapter Sixteen

Amylia called round just after Roland and Cara had finished their noon meal. Her suggestion of shopping for the children was a hit. It had been four days since the children had departed, and aside from one note from Tibs saying all was well, there had been no word.

She missed them terribly. It was more than a trifle boring, sitting. Waiting. Roland remained closeted in his study decoding messages. He had gone to Mr. Lawson's, obtaining yet another note. Met with Beaumont daily; sometimes she was included; most of the time she wasn't.

He scheduled another get together with Viscount Hampden at his club on St. James, of course ladies weren't allowed on St. James Street, notorious for its gentleman's clubs, so once more she would be left out. With everything on his mind, she hated to complain, but it hurt not being trusted to share these important pieces of the puzzle.

Their nights were filled with glorious lovemaking. She'd taken up permanent residence in his suite, only going to her own room to dress. Roland often sent Lucy away, helping her, which usually led to even more lovemaking, this time in her bed, and thus a later start to the day.

She lived for those minutes. She found herself falling deeper and deeper in love. In those moments, they would become one. One body. One soul. One mind. In those times, she imagined Roland loved her as much as she loved him.

Other times, when the insecurities of the day hit her outside the walls of their private rooms, she wasn't sure.

Cara's mind kept churning her fears bubbling, as they strolled about Bond Street and Pall Mall.

Amylia babbled; Cara offered snippets, but her heart wasn't in the conversation. Turning into the doorway of Madam Beauchamps boutique, the little Irish woman with her forged French nuance came forth, fake red curls bouncing almost as much as her greatly exposed, ample bosom.

"Bonne journée, Madame Greyley, Madame Fairhaven, bienvenue. Bienvenue! It is so good to have such excellent patronage grace my modest boutique. What can moi do for such lovely ladies, hmm? I made you a new wardrobe, non? Is it not so?"

"Madam Beauchamps, you are kind," Amylia answered.

Cara simply stood trying hard to stifle the laughter she felt bubbling to the surface over the Madam's rather terrible French accent. She still couldn't believe that an Irish washerwoman could turn out to be one of the richest designers of the age. Simply by pretending she was something she was not.

Amylia had told her the story after their first visit when Cara had inquired about her odd enunciation. Amylia had chuckled. Subsequently telling all.

Madam Beauchamps, formerly Alice Clark, was a friend of sorts to Amylia; of course, back then such a friendship could not be acknowledged publicly. The very idea of a gently bred English lady consorting with the likes of an Irish commoner would have caused a scandal of gargantuan proportions.

So, in secret they met, Alice did Amylia's alterations making her look beautiful enough to catch the eye of Anthony Stapleton and in return Amylia taught Alice the finer points of economics combined with a smattering of French. It was a match made in heaven. Amylia got her man. Alice got her shop. "La Boutique pour la Tonne Délite".

"Deux filles, how magnifique. Come. Come. Let us choose the modèles et copies."

They spent the remainder of the day choosing from fabrics of all colors, and patterns of all designs. Madam Beauchamps was to make twelve outfits for each of the girls, everything from play dresses, day dresses, walking dresses, party dresses, and underthings.

When Cara tried to call a halt to Amylia's spending of Roland's money, Amylia said to her, "Don't be dippy, my dear, it is your money too. You are his wife. When was the last time the children had new things? Didn't you tell me it was well over three years?"

Cruel of her to use the children but Cara couldn't argue with Amylia's logic. She was no match whatsoever. Agreeing, they headed home. It was six o'clock. Rex would have to wait for another day.

As Cara climbed the steps to Danforth House, a young scraggly looking lad charged up the front steps.

"Why, hello," Cara said, before the boy hastily ran her over.

He looked up, big brown eyes in the center of a dirt smudged face. When he grinned, he was missing his two front teeth; Cara pinned him to be no more than seven or eight. His hair was shoved under an equally dirty chimney sweeps hat; she prayed the little boy wasn't a climber. His clothes were covered in grime. Cara tried urgently to see beneath the dirt; was there any burns? It was hard to tell.

"Do ye live here, misth?" the boy said, having a challenging time talking around his two missing teeth.

"Why yes, I do. Can I help you with something?"

"I'th goth thith lether for thith addreth." The boy held out the letter.

"A letter? I can take that, one moment." Cara reached into her reticule pulling out a shilling. The boy stared at the coin with hunger in his eyes. Cara handed him the coin. "Here you go and thank you for bringing the letter."

"Aye," the boy said, giving it to her. Then in a flash he disappeared back the way he had come.

Cara turned to find Roberts standing, door open. She walked through, handing him her things. Once done, she took the letter with her to the Blue Room.

Sitting on the window seat, Cara took the vellum turning it in her hand thoughtfully. It was addressed to The Duke of Fairhaven care of the Danforth House address. The writer had a flowery hand. Definitely a woman's hand; Cara felt her gut clench, bringing the paper to her nose, she sniffed…the paper was doused in a rose-scented perfume. Cara felt a knife stick in her heart. And twist.

Holding back the tears her wild imagination was forcing her to shed; she tapped the paper against her fingers. It was sealed with a simple blob of candle wax. No symbol appeared within the mold. Picking at the wax, Cara debated opening it.

"Sweetheart, you're home. Did you have an enjoyable time with Aunt Amylia?"

Cara jumped, dropping the letter. It fluttered to the floor. Cara watched it descend; time seemed to stop as it hovered to the corner of the Axminister carpet.

"Cara?" Roland asked his voice tinged with worry.

Cara's head snapped up, jumping off the seat, she bent to retrieve the letter.

"This, ah, that is to say, a boy delivered this." She stuck the offending piece of paper under his nose.

Roland took the letter, amazingly enough, or mayhap not amazing at all, he recognized the delicate flowery scroll. He tucked the letter in the pocket of his coat. Cara stared at him, a question in her eyes; he had to tell her something. But what?

He opted for a partial truth. "Liberton's mistress. Beaumont wanted me to question her. Undoubtedly, it is confirming a time and place to meet."

He watched the color return to her face. The life in her eyes, gone but a moment ago, came flooding back.

Thank God.

If only she would speak to him, confide in him. If only she loved him as much as he loved her. He desperately wanted to help. But until she spoke her fears aloud, he could do nothing, and he wasn't about to jeopardize what little ground he had gained. And that included telling her about Izzy.

They had been married only a week, and with everything that was happening around them, it wasn't any wonder she could not give her heart the time it needed to love freely. *Patience, Roland. Patience. She will come to love you in time.* It was okay, she was here with him; he would the rest of their lives to win her.

Cara chuckled uneasily, "I…" She looked at her hands as they were to fault for her invasion of privacy. She shook her bowed head. "I'm dreadfully sorry."

"You have nothing to be sorry for, love. Don't give it another thought."

Roland pulled her into his arms, just holding her. Soothing her, as one would sooth a child after a nightmare. He kissed the top of her blackish red curls, ran his hands over her back, repeatedly, until bit-by-bit the tension flowed from her body.

"Dinner is ready to be served." Roberts announced from the doorway.

"Tell Mrs. Leeks we will be in shortly."

"Yes, Your Grace." Roberts bowed his way out going in search of Mrs. Leeks.

Dinner was a quiet affair, each barely discussing the events of the day before lapsing into awkward silence. Cara knew it would take some time for the feeling to return after being summarily twisted by jealously. She kept telling herself Roland would elaborate; mayhap even take her to meet

Liberton's mistress. He cared for her enough to put her mind at ease. Didn't he?

Immediately after dinner Roland shut himself in the study, Cara, he assumed, would be reading. He noticed her with books in hand more than once this past week. It is good she is doing something she enjoys while he was so wrapped up in this investigation.

Knowing she was at home, or out with his aunt, put his mind at ease. She was safe. And would remain so. Then when the investigation was over, he'd take all of them, children included, away. He had thought frequently about the perfect wedding trip.

The memory of Cara standing on the front stoop waving to her siblings made him realize they could not go away for a long period of time without taking the children with them. They would have to take a governess; mayhap Miss Pebble would agree to stay on. France was one of his favorite places but with the turmoil there it wasn't safe. Spain was out as well. With Napoleon putting his brother Joseph on the throne Spain had its fair share of upheaval.

Roland's father had invested in some tea plantations in Ceylon. He'd never been there. Mayhap it was time to check on things. The wildlife alone would be something for them to remember. Knowing his father, as he did, there was sure to be a quaint villa big enough for all of them. Later when upheaval had quieted; they could go to France or Spain, alone. It was closer. Their time away would be shorter.

Roland put his musing aside; reaching into his pocket he retrieved the letter he'd put there earlier. Mrs. Isabelle Dupries. Cracking the seal, Roland opened the message scanning the words carefully. Though he knew what they would say as soon as he saw the hand in which it was written.

Bella. Or Lady Belle as she liked to be called currently. Back when Roland knew her, she was humble but dazzling Izzy O'Claire. Nineteen, full of spunk and curious about her body, his body. Her only other obsession was with the stage. Roland's affair with her lasted nearly two years, enough time for her to find her way to treading the boards. At the end of their liaison, she was in the limelight. Her vanity became too much for one man to bear. Her narcissism, sexual hunger and greed, had her dangling upwards to five men at a time from her little finger. Roland was young enough or mayhap smart enough, though that would have been a stretch, to realize he no longer wanted or needed to be the fifth fish on the hook.

He didn't look forward to this meeting. Damn Beaumont. He must have known who Isabelle Dupries was before he had suggested he talk to her. Why in the hell didn't he say something? Unfortunately, now, Izzy wanted him to resume their friendship.

Five years. Five years since he had seen her last. Roland felt nothing at the thought of Izzy except possibly, revulsion. Sighing, he threw the letter into the fire. Standing there, he watched it burn.

Cara sat in the upstairs parlor, reading, or at least trying to. She couldn't get Roland or the letter out of her mind. Immediately after supper, he had given her a peck on the cheek before going into the damn study. Again. Again, he'd shut her out.

She hadn't seen him read the letter, meaning of course, he wanted to read it in private. If it was really nothing, then why couldn't he have shared it with her? And that look. The look he got on his face when he looked at the writing. Shock. Surprise. Quickly covered but she had seen it nonetheless.

She didn't like this feeling. Jealousy. She had always thought herself beyond such a base emotion. Obviously, she was wrong. For right now, she would like nothing better than to confront the writer of that note.

She'd like to put her hands around her throat and squeeze the very life out of her body. She couldn't. Could she? *Of course, you can't! You're letting your imagination get the better of you. Roland would not cheat on you and if he did, surely his mistress wouldn't send a note to the house where his wife would be able to intercept it.*

But what if his mistress didn't know he was married. The ceremony was quick, quiet, and not long ago. What if Roland was so busy initiating his new wife, conducting an inquiry, he hadn't told her. It would mean he had been seeing his mistress while he kissed her. And like a fool she had allowed him to do more! Throwing the book across the room, she rose. She'd confront Roland, make him tell her at least show her the letter.

Mind made up, she frantically took the steps back down to the study. Damn. It was empty.

"Roberts? Roberts!" Cara raised her voice.

Roberts came into the study, worry plastered on his face. "Is something the matter, Your Grace?"

"Where's my husband?" Cara asked, her tone as normal as possible.

"He has gone out, Your Grace."

"When?"

"Just moments ago."

"When moments ago? Oh, never mind! Just send Lucy for my wrap. I am going out. Be quick about it. Hurry. I must catch him."

Roberts left in a rush. Soon, Lucy was at the study door with Cara's requested items in hand.

"Your Grace, I brought my things as well. You did want accompaniment, did you not, it *is* getting late."

"For God sakes, Lucy. I don't have time for this. I'm a married woman. That ought to afford me some rights."

Lucy paled. "Yes. Your Grace…"

"Oh fine! Come along then. I'm wasting time. Roberts? What conveyance did His Grace take?"

"He had me call the Danforth carriage, Your Grace."

"Fine. Lucy."

With that Cara swept out the front door like the hounds of hell were snapping at her feet. She ran to the street, Lucy barely keeping up. Cara could see the carriage rounding the bend at the end of the street. Quickly, she hailed a hack.

"Follow that carriage; that one, rounding the bend. There is extra in it if you keep it in sight."

Cara jumped unladylike into the coach. Gawd, it felt good to do something unladylike. Lucy followed her in, mouth almost trailing the floor.

"Lady Fairhaven!" Lucy said, gasping for air. "This is not at all proper!"

"*Lucy*," Cara warned.

Lucy closed her mouth with a snap, forcing her lips together to keep from issuing another lecture to her mistress. The hack slowed; the driver must have gained enough space to keep a watchful eye on the Danforth equipage.

Cara relaxed; she would not lose track of Roland.

As much as her heart ached at the thought of catching him with his mistress, her adrenaline pumped for the thrill of the chase. Roland's appointed meeting time had left little room for speculation; sitting back she waited for the hack to stop, doubts hitting her tenfold.

Did she really want to know if Roland had a mistress? Did she really need to see how much more beautiful she was? How much more desirable? Experienced? What if she were caught? What excuse could she give for following her husband when all husbands had the right to keep a mistress, and most did?

The coach stopped. It took only a second to decide her path. She'd come this far; there was no turning back. Better to have loved and lost…Oh hell…no one could force her to believe that drivel.

Cara opened the door, jumping unceremoniously to the gravel below. Hack drivers rarely assisted someone from the carriage, if they did, it was at a snail's pace. She would not wait. Could not wait.

"Wait here," she said to both Lucy and the driver.

They were in the theatre district. Coventry Gardens in its entire splendor stood before her. Couples strolled casually among the pathways. There were not many, by Amylia's standards, but there were enough to keep her sufficiently concealed from Roland, furthermore if she wasn't careful, enough to make her lose sight of him.

She scanned the area for a glimpse of her husband. There in the distance she saw him striding down a path. Grabbing her skirts, she rushed to catch up.

He turned when he reached the side of the building. Cara followed discretely. She ignored the beautiful flowers that on any another occasion she would have stopped to enjoy; walking past a water fountain of two cherubs, one pouring water from an urn over the head of the other; she gave it no more than a passing glance and marched on.

Roland crossed the back lawn, entering the maze situated at the end. Cara allowed a bit of time, then followed.

She listened carefully to the sounds around her. Hearing footsteps, she stayed close to Roland, not wanting to lose him in the various twisting-turns. She made note of each turn, repeating the directions over and over in her head so when the time came, she would be able to exit without trouble.

It was something she'd taught the children when they were small. Part of Wonderlands' beauty was the dense forest which surrounded the back of the property. At its center was a stream; they'd fished and played in the cool water. Each time they took a different route, it was part of the adventure. The mystery. Each time the one who could remember the exact route back got the first choice of cakes. It was nothing more than a game, but Cara was thankful for it.

Cara rounded the last bend. Roland had stopped. Before anyone saw her, she ducked back around the hedge.

"Oh, Row, darling, I knew you would come back to me. Did you miss me as much as I missed you?"

Cara could hear the swish of skirts Roland started to answer but was cut off. Cara peeked back around the hedge. The woman, dressed in a flaming red gown plus hair to match, had her arms wrapped around Roland, her mouth pursed tightly to his. Roland's hands rested on her hips. Cara's eyes narrowed. He was squeezing her hips. Cara stuffed her hand in her mouth lest she cry out like the wounded animal she was. She'd seen enough. Turning, with all the speed she could muster, tears streaming down her face, she ran.

Back to the waiting hack, back to Danforth House. Back. Back. Back. Back to her old room, back to being alone.

"For Christ Sakes, Izzy! Let go of me!" Roland roared, peeling Izzy's pathetically thin body off his. He pushed her away with enough force he sent her stumbling backward. She caught herself before she fell on her overly stuffed derrière.

"Row. Whatever is the matter with you? You called me, remember? Or do you like it rough now?" Izzy said, anger showing.

"I called you because I wanted to talk. Talk. Nothing more. What we had was long ago. Five years long ago. *And* when it ended, I felt nothing more for you than pity. That, my dear, hasn't changed."

Izzy sniffed, crossing her arms under her chest in a deliberate maneuver; her tiny breasts popped up over the indecently low neckline, Izzy always was a showgirl. Too bad she never did have much to show. Her nipples winked at him, no longer covered with fabric. Roland turned his back, sickened by the display.

"Cover yourself. What you have I don't want."

"You wanted it well enough to write."

"As I said, I want answers. Truth be known, had I known it was you, I wouldn't have come."

"You don't mean that!" Izzy pouted.

"I couldn't mean it more. I'm married…"

"Lots of men are married, Row," she said, hope ringing clear in her voice.

"You didn't let me finish. I'm married. *And I am* very much in love with my wife."

"Oh, how pathetically droll. I am so sorry for you, darling."

"Yes, quite. But there you have it. Now are you going to answer my questions, or do I leave?"

Finally, confident he had managed to get through to her, he turned back around. Izzy was now covered, though she didn't look like she was going to be of much help. She was clearly pissed. So be it.

"Tell me about Maxwell Liberton. Before you get any ideas, Izzy O'Claire, remember I knew you before you were Lady Belle or Mrs. Dupries; I could do or say things as peer of the realm that would have you treading the boards in Whitechapel."

"Don't you threaten me, Mr. High and Mighty. Your little slip about you loving your wife could come in extremely useful if I chose to use it."

"You'd be dead. Now, this is getting us nowhere. I want to be away from here, so talk."

Giving a heavy sigh, Izzy eyed him. He wasn't joking; he would really kill her if she hurt his precious wife. Fine. Liberton didn't pay well. Not for what he expected, in truth he wasn't her lover either. He was a watcher. He brought her his son. He'd watch her please him, by methods he dictated, while he was stationed in the room above with a young lad she hired to help with chores.

The whole thing was a little too much. But the one time she voiced her opinions over the use of Robert or the coin he offered in return for her services, he had beat her so soundly she couldn't leave the house for a month. Several times since, she'd thought of being rid of him, yet she feared him. Now was her chance. He deserved what he got, the sick twisted bastard.

"Fine. What do you want to know?"

Cara threw herself onto the bed crying; her heart felt like it had been ripped from her chest. She couldn't breathe, her stomach rolled at the thought of Roland there, in the maze, right now, with his ladylove.

How could she have been such a fool?

She had believed Amylia when she said that he would come to love her. How could he love her when there was someone else in his life?

Cara had only a quick glimpse when she was pressed up tightly against Roland, and she was classically beautiful. Her hair shimmered like spun gold; she'd bet her eyes were blue too. Not the deep soulful blue of Roland's eyes but the ice blue eyes of a porcelain doll.

What was she compared to that? Black hair tinged with red in the sunlight instead of classic black with blue highlights. 'Cinnamon' her mother called it.

Who wanted to be likened to a spice? Even Cara's figure screamed cinnamon roll. Oh, she wasn't fat, but she was short. Her curves were far too curvy. She didn't even like cinnamon rolls!

What was she to do? She couldn't go back to Wonderland, at least not yet. Besides if she did, he would only follow her there. She needed time. Time, she didn't have. What would happen when he returned home tonight? Would he come to her after making love to his China doll?

He wouldn't dare!

Something in Cara screamed that he would. He would think her none the wiser for his extracurricular activities. She should not have been. She could have gone on thinking she was doing everything right. Everything to make his heart hers, she would kiss him good-bye, welcome him home, make sweet love to him and in between he would be with her.

Well, she wouldn't have it!

Cara angrily flung her pillow across the room. It felt good to throw something, to exert her anger-ruling frustrations on inanimate objects. Getting up, she looked about the room, for something else to throw. Her eyes met with the connecting door. Stomping over to it, she flung it closed. The resounding shudder of the heavy oak made her smile. The sound echoed about the room.

It never should have been opened!

Bending, she peeked into the hole, where once there was a key. The key. She no longer had it in her possession. Where was it? Roland. Damn the man. Cara stomped to the wardrobe. She pushed against it. It would take most of her strength and a lot of time to move. She didn't care she'd do it.

Putting her back into it, Cara grunted straining against the weight of the heavy oak closet. *Push damn you! Push!*

Bit by bit, inch by inch, the wardrobe moved. Finally, it was in place.

Taking a step back, Cara watched it, expecting it to move or be moved. It stayed fast. With a nod of satisfaction, she collected an empty candleholder, several novels, and an empty bedpan to set on the bedside table.

Roland left Izzy, standing in the middle of the maze. He had what he needed. Now all he wanted to do was meet Beaumont so he could get back home before Cara went to bed.

She had been up in the drawing room, reading when he had left. He hoped what he had to do would not take long. It had. Over an hour with Izzy had been hard even when she was his mistress, over an hour with her now…suffice to say, it was a hell sight worse.

He sniffed. Damn, he smelled terrible. Roses. Goddamn roses. Now he had one more reason to hate the offensive toilet water.

He'd need a bath.

Beaumont was waiting for him at the Cock and Crow when he arrived.

"What took you so bloody long? The runner arrived at my house with a message stating you were meeting Mrs. Dupries at nine o'clock. It's now eleven."

"Believe me. I know what time it is. If I could have dragged the information out of that strumpet, I would have. It wasn't as though I wanted to meet my old mistress."

Beaumont chuckled.

"You bastard! You did know. Odds Blood, Beaumont, you could have at least told me. I thought I was penning a note to a mistress—Not my old mistress, mind—it was written with an air of seduction to ensure a meeting would be forthcoming. Do you have any idea what it was like to receive a perfumed answer back? Handed to me by my bloody wife?"

Beaumont paled.

"Sorry old man, I didn't think of that."

"Obviously."

Beaumont, still sitting down, for a change, watched Roland paced the floor. Mayhap he had made a big mistake by not telling him; no, had he told him, Roland would have refused to meet with the bloody woman. And they needed answers. He had nothing to feel guilty about. But he did feel guilty.

"I hope Cara didn't get the wrong impression," Beaumont said meekly.

"Oh, she got the wrong impression all right. I found her sitting on the window seat so wan, one would think she were dead."

"Christ! You did put her to rights though?"

"She didn't read it. Course, she didn't have to. The bloody thing was drenched in rose water and had my name scrolled larger than life in flowery script. I told it was a meeting. Information about the case…"

"But she believed you. Didn't she?"

"I don't know. Beaumont, I swear if you have done anything to jeopardize my marriage, friend or no, I will have your bloody hide."

The venom in Roland's voice said it all. Beaumont shifted in his seat and hastily got down to the heart of the matter.

Roland left the Cock and Crow just after midnight, heading for home. He felt drained. He needed to feel Cara's arms around him. Feel her body beneath his. She would cleanse away the remnants of the filth left behind by Izzy's lecherous hands and Beaumont's treacherous schemes.

Roberts was at his post, Roland relieved him for the night going into the study for a glass of brandy. Roberts parted, though rather reluctantly. The chap seemed downright cold to him, in fact. Mayhap he didn't like his promotion. Roland made a mental note to speak with him in the morning. Downing the brandy in one gulp, he quickly left to find his bed and, more importantly, his wife.

Quietly, Roland opened the bedroom door. It was wholly dark. The drapes drawn, no candle lit. He disrobed silently, slipping into bed. He rolled over, reaching…

What the hell?

Cara must have gone to sleep in her own room, still unsure of going to bed without him. Roland sighed. Throwing back the blankets, he headed for the connecting door. He'd get her and bring her in here with him. Where she belonged. Tomorrow morning when they were making love, he would explain to her that going to bed before him didn't mean she slept in her old room.

He wanted her here. Waiting. He needed that.

The knob turned easily; Roland inched the door… The door was stuck. It opened barely an inch, no more. There was a flicker of light. A candle. Roland called softly.

No answer. Grabbing his robe, he went out into the hall.

He'd use the other door.

Cara heard noise in the other room. She was used to his soft footfalls; aside from the occasional brush of his foot upon the floor he was silent. She had been listening for that brush. There was silence for a time, then he tried the door. It when it connected with the wardrobe.

Mayhap he would give up.

He called her name, softly, once, twice…then silence.

Her heart pounded in her chest. She ached. Her stomach churned. Please give me strength to send him away, she prayed. She loved him so much. Wanted him so badly.

He has just come from her.

The door to her bedroom opened. Cara didn't bother waiting to see if she had the force to turn him away. She grabbed the candleholder, bringing back her arm; she waited for just the right moment, and then hurled it with all her might.

"What the hell…?"

"Get out! Now!"

One book.

"Cara?" Roland pleaded, confused.

"I said. Get out…"

Two…

"Of my room…"

Three…

"*Your Grace…*"

Four…

"Before I have Roberts throw you out!"

Cara screamed at the top of her lungs. She knew the servants most likely heard. She didn't care. Her voice was frightened and yes, wounded. She hated that. Why couldn't it have sounded strong?

Roland was mystified, was he a candidate for Bedlam? He came home with nothing on his mind but his wife and her arms, and now…this?

The candleholder, for he could look at it now lying on the floor next to his feet, had missed his head by a sliver. Now here was Cara sitting on her bed screaming for him to get out. Throwing books to punctuate her words, her aim going increasingly off course. What had he done? Worry tightened his gut. Beaumont. Damn him.

"Cara, please love," he begged.

Cara threw her newest Mrs. Radcliff novel. It connected with his middle; she was rewarded by the sound of air being forced out. Unconsciously, she smiled.

Roland looked down at the book. It had caught him off guard. Really, it wasn't so big, catching his breath he looked up to make sure it was his wife sitting there. It was. And she was smiling. No sneering…at him.

Cara didn't know what hit her. One minute—she was sitting reaching for the bedpan and the next, she was pinned to the bed, Roland on top of her.

She fought, legs kicking, arms flailing, hands scratching, yelling, though she could not have said what she yelled, she was that angry. How dare he come in here and do her bodily harm, when he…he was the one that started it. He was to blame!

"Damn it! Cara, stop fighting me! You said I was the one to blame. I think I have the right to know what I did wrong."

Cara snapped her lips shut in a mutinous line, had she really said that out loud? She had to think. She stopped moving about, went limp. She glared at him and ground out, "let go of me!"

"Not just yet. I rather like this position. I think I have said that a time or two before." Roland chuckled.

"Get off!"

"No."

"Roland, damn you, you are hurting me."

A flash of regret shadowed his face, then he must have realized she was lying, at least in part, for physically she was fine; emotionally, well that was another story. He shook his head.

"I am sorry Cara; I don't want to hurt you. But I refuse to let you up so you can throw something else at me or gouge my eyes out. Talk to me. That is the only way I will let you go."

Cara glared.

He smiled.

She fought and bucked beneath him.

He wouldn't move.

"You're too heavy."

Roland took her wrists in one hand, wrapped his legs about hers, and flipped. Now Cara was on top, strapped to him. His body now beneath hers…damn, she was still ensnared.

"Better?" Roland asked smiling.

Cara glared.

"Cat got your tongue?"

Roland bounced with his mid-section, waggling his brows. "Fun?"

Cara glowered at him, pursing her lips together, she turned away. Roland chuckled, taking his free hand, he placed it under her chin, forcing her to turn back and meet his gaze.

"Cara, I'm tired. I don't want to fight. Please. Won't you tell me what I did so I can make it right?"

He brushed her cheek with his thumb, the feel of his soothing was her undoing; she started to cry. Tears rolled down her cheeks in torrents no sound came from her mouth. Her throat had completely closed.

"Oh, Cara. Sweetheart, you don't know what you are doing to me. Please Cara, don't cry. I live for your smiles but your tears, love, they kill me."

"You…you…you deserve to be killed," Cara finally sniffed.

Taking the edge of the blanket, he sopped up her tears as best he could. "Why?"

"You still smell like roses."

"Roses?"

"Yes. Roses!"

"Cara, I don't…oh." Roland's smile grew wider by the second until Cara feared it would swallow his whole face.

"Oh?" Cara couldn't believe he was smiling. Was he thinking of her, his lover, even now? She fought him, he held fast. Smiling.

"I thought you liked roses. Sorry I didn't bathe before coming to bed, I was simply too tired."

"Bathe?" Cara said. "Bathe. You think a bath would hide the fact that for the last three hours, you have been with your whore?"

"Tsk, Tsk, Tsk. Cara, such language, where did you ever learn it?"

"It's a damn good thing I did learn it, otherwise, I wouldn't have known what to call her, now, would I?"

Roland's chuckle shook her.

"Bastard. You think this is f-u-n-n-y…" Her voice broke, "I… was… falling… falling in love with you, and…"

"Cara, don't. Shhh, it's all right love."

"Don't call me that!"

"What? Love? Why not?"

"It's a lie."

"Cara, I love you with all my heart."

Cara looked astonished. "You what?"

"I said I love you; I have since the night of the kidnapping. I knew then I would have you as my wife. You are part me Cara, the best part, how could you not know that?"

Cara bit her lip, hundreds of different emotions warred within her.

"What about the woman."

"What woman?"

"The one you met at Coventry Gardens, the one in the maze?"

"Izzy?"

"Yes, *Izzy*. That's a stupid name, by the by."

"I was always rather fond of it." Roland held up his hand. "The name that is. Izzy was, is, Mrs. Isabelle Dupries. Liberton's mistress."

"Oh? Well, if she was Liberton mistress then what was she doing kissing you?" Cara quipped.

"You do realize we will talk about how you know all this, no, not now, but rest assured, my love, we will talk. Now, for your information, I knew Izzy a long time ago. Seven years ago. And yes, before you ask, she was, for a while, mind, my mistress. That ended five years ago. She means nothing to me now."

"But…"

"Cara, I assume that you snuck out, somehow followed me. You must have been present for the beginning of the meeting, though by all that's holy how I didn't see you or sense you there, I'll never know. However, *you* didn't stick around past the introduction, did you, my love?"

Cara nodded, looking more than a little sheepish, "But…"

"No. I am not finished. Now, had you stayed you would have seen me push Izzy away. More than that, you would have heard me tell her I was married and…" Roland tapped her nose with his finger, "and" *tap*, "that" *tap*, "I", *tap* "was in love with my wife." *Tap. Tap. Tap.*

"Truly?"

"Yes, truly. Now, kiss me and remind me why I love you so much it bloody well hurts."

Cara smiled, bringing with it the sun warming Roland's heart. He released her hands but kept hold on her legs and let her kiss him.

When the kiss ended, Cara was out of breath, her wits scattered; she said the first thing that popped into her head. "You liked that?"

Roland, thinking she was talking about the kiss, replied, "Oh, yes."

"Then I need a diet," she said with soft determination.

"What?" Roland shook his head as if to clear it.

"I'm too curvy," Cara said without a trace of anger, only disappointment.

"You are lovely," Roland replied slowly, catching on to the conversation at hand.

"No. No, I'm not. I'm too short, too rounded. I think I shall dye my hair."

"But I love your hair. Cara, whatever is the matter with you? Love, I fell in love in with all of you, inside and out. Who you are, in here," he pressed his hand to her heart, "and here" touching her temple. "I don't want you to change. In any way… Ever."

"But I am nothing at all like her."

"And I wouldn't want you to be. Izzy was from a time in my life when I cared for nothing, not even myself. My parents had just died, when their boat went down, I couldn't save them. My attitude toward and what happened made me a different person. One I wasn't proud of. I was often too heavily in my cups, and it is fortunate, thinking back that I had enough good sense to realize that my relationship with Izzy would never be more than a bad use of time.

"Beaumont found me," he said, running his hand over her silky hair. "I was a mess. Twenty-three and although I was a Duke, I acted more like a spoiled child than you could ever imagine. I was given a choice. One I hated at the time. Over the years have come to realize I was blessed. I still had people who cared enough about me to want me to be better. 'Beaumont told me Newgate or Home Office'. I didn't think I would fare well in Newgate."

"That sounds vaguely familiar."

Roland grinned. "It should. It is one of his favorite lines."

"That day in the study, before we were married, Beaumont told me Newgate or marriage."

Roland chuckled, "That he did, my love."

Picking up a pillow, Cara smashed Roland over the head. "You knew!"

Feigning innocence, he replied, "Knew what?"

"You knew it was nothing more than an empty threat. And you didn't let on."

"Why would I? I wanted you. Loved you. And you, my dear, can deny it all you like, loved me also. Why not use the Home Office to my advantage for a change."

Cara's heart swelled. He knew she loved him. How could he know something like that when she didn't want to acknowledge it herself? And he loved her? Feeling the tears start, she changed the subject.

"My father?"

"Yes. Your father was my instructor. After Beaumont gave me the ultimatum, which by the way I know my uncle had something to do with, though I will never prove it, he introduced me to your father."

Cara's brow creased. "But how come I have never met you then, I assume that what my father had to impart would take more than a few hours."

Roland nodded, "Yes love, in fact it took two years."

"Two years? Where then... Ah Hah. London."

"Yes. Cara? Cara what's wrong?"

"I...I knew where he went, I had always assumed it was to meet his mistress or gamble, or simply, and probably more truthfully, to get away from me, I mean us. I never in my wildest dreams..."

"Thought your father was a spy?"

"No. I mean yes," Cara said tears drying from relief. "Tell me more."

Roland chuckled, "I will, but first..."

Without another word he was out of bed, arms under Cara he lifted and carried her to his room, stopping in front of the connecting door, he shook his head. "The wardrobe? I should have known."

Cara chuckled into his chest. "I really was quite angry, you know."

"Oh, believe me, after tonight I will never make you angry again. At least not knowingly. And love? Should I do something I am unaware of in the future, please throw something soft first. A pillow perhaps?"

Cara laughed all the way down the hall and into Roland's room. He set her down on the bed, removing her nightgown. Shedding his robe, he slid in naked next to her. Pulling her into his arms, he sighed, "Much better. Now ask away."

"But aren't we going to make love?" Cara asked snuggling in closer.

"We, my dear, have the rest of our lives to make love. For now, let me hold you."

Cara kissed his shoulder. It felt good to have his arms about her. She felt safe, and, more than a little loved. And genuinely happy.

Roland kissed Cara's forehead. No more questions were forth coming. Knowing it was important to share with her all he could so she could never again doubt his love for her, he continued.

He told her of his training, the assignment in America, the landscape, his fears, successes and eventually being recalled. He explained his summons was originally to deal with her father's treason, prove it or disprove it. When he arrived, after the three-month journey, more had changed. Thomas had been killed and information was missing.

He talked while she listened and when the first rays of the morning sun peeped through a crack in the drapes they slept.

Chapter Seventeen

The last couple of days, had gotten them nowhere. Liberton, according to Roland, was a man with no past. How could that be?

Beaumont brought up the fact that the kidnapping had most likely been arranged either by him or someone working for him. Considering this recent development, it could very well mean Cara was still in danger.

Roland had kept her on a very short leash. She knew it was out of fear and love; it still rankled going against her very fiber to be so tightly bound. She was a free spirit. And after two days inside, Cara found the walls closing in on her. She had gone out to the garden and moved all the rose bushes to the back wall, where she would not have to smell roses as soon as she left the back door. Roland explained everything; she'd believed him when he said Izzy meant nothing, but the smell of roses still made her stomach roll. Strict orders of no roses at the front entry, or anywhere else inside Danforth Manor were in effect. Let them think her mad.

Two days. Nothing left to do; she'd finished her novels, spent as much time outside as she could. Still the walls of the garden and her own inactivity were slowly turning the remaining half of her brain to mush.

More times than she cared to admit, her skin pimpled, the little hairs on her arms standing on end because she had the eerie feeling of someone watching her. Surely a product of her overactive imagination. Either that or Beaumont's dire warnings of danger; Cara knew her intuition was wrong, she proved recently it could be and as for Beaumont being a reliable source, well he had lied on more than one occasion to get what he wanted. Was now any different?

Knowing she had to get out, Roland already out conducting research, Cara headed out the front door. Roberts stood between her and the sidewalk, "Excuse me, Your Grace."

"Yes, what is it, Roberts?"

"His Grace left orders that you were not to leave in his absence. I'm dreadfully sorry, Your Grace, won't you allow me to escort you back inside?"

"I will do no such thing. I am going to Hatchard's; if I must be cooped up all day and night, I must have something to read!"

"I could send a footman for you, Madam; surely he could make your purchase."

"No."

"Please, Madam," Roberts pleaded.

"Roberts. I am not a child. If I want to do something, I will do it. Is that clear? Now. Out of my way," Cara said through clenched teeth.

Roberts went in, leaving Cara to her own devices. Now that she was outside, she began to wonder about the wisdom of his decision. She stared back at the closed door. Roberts would be waiting inside. If she returned, he would know she was scared. No. It is the middle of the day. Hardly anyone about; no evil villains lurking in the shadows. Huh, no shadows. Straightening her bonnet strings along with her spine, she stepped out lively basking in the afternoon sun. Freedom.

Progressing down the street, the sunlight, like an ointment to her fears. Her decision to leave the house, her reservations about staying after Roberts shut the door, were gone. Almost. She was on the way to Hatchard's to acquire Mrs. Radcliff's previous novel, as she read the latest only to find out it was a continuation of one in which she had not seen. She really had to know how Algernon came to be. Was he a figment of the dark arts or the master himself? Just the thought of his imagined dark good looks and unleashed power, which could be used for good or evil at will, sent a shiver down her spine.

Or something else entirely?

Cara took a quick glance around. Mrs. Camberley was walking her Bichon, a little white ball of fluff that answered to Mr. Peers. Two girls, about seventeen walked arm-in-arm tittering happily back and forth. Carriages rolled by at sedate paces, well-matched teams pranced; the steady clop of their hooves matched the current pounding of Cara's heart.

All should be perfect, yet the feeling wouldn't pass. A sense that not all was right. She could not dismiss the eerie sensation of danger. Here is the light of a sunny day with the rest of the world going on about her as though nothing was amiss. It was though, it truly was. The weight of some unknown stare surrounded her like an evil shroud.

Forcing herself to draw a deep, calming breath she turned her attention back the pleasant day. *I am perfectly safe. No one is trying to harm me.*

She looked around once more; please God, she prayed, let it be true.

The sickening feeling stayed with her, as she entered Hatchard's. Walking to the Gothic novel location, Cara picked up one book after another; her eyes never left the door. Surely if someone had followed, they would come in, acting as though nothing happened. Oddly, the door remained closed.

Forcing her attention back to the books, she looked for the novel she wanted. It wasn't there. A novel by Caralyn Hutton caught her eye. Deciding it was better than returning home empty-handed, Cara took the novel up to the counter.

The sound of a carriage door closing snapped her out of her revelry with such force Cara jumped. Her heart pounded, she felt like something was stuck in her throat. She glanced around, noted nothing amiss.

Simply a gentleman…

"Oh, I say, Lady Fairhaven, are you quite alright?"

A man… Lord Redding.

"Oh, yes. Thank you, Lord Redding. I'm fine. Just a bit too much sun I fear." Cara wanted to leave as the unease she felt suddenly tripled. She really didn't care for this man, although she had no reason to *not* like him.

"Sun is not good for a lady's constitution; one should possibly carry a parasol," Lord Redding said.

Was he reprimanding her? Surely the man would not be so bold.

"I can guarantee you Lord Redding my constitution is just fine. The best, in fact." She injected hauteur into her voice. Hoping it would replace a little of the backbone that was slowly melting in the face of her fears.

"Sorry if I overstepped. It was simply a recommendation Your Grace. Pray forgive me, I forget myself." Lord Redding bowed, and his words recanted, the look in his eyes, what was that? Anger? Hatred?

"Apology accepted, My Lord, now if you will excuse me His Grace is expecting me. Good day." With that Cara swept away from him not caring one wit if she was rude or not; she just had to get away. She had to get home.

"Lady Fairhaven?" Roberts stated, rather worried as the mistress of the manor flew through the door. She opened and closed it before he even had a chance to reach for the knob. Now she stood leaning against it her hand to her heart, her face as pale as a ghost.

Cara's breath came in quick pants, knowing she couldn't possibly answer Roberts' question; she waved her book in front of her face.

"What is it, Your Grace? Apoplexy? Should I send for the doctor?" Roberts asked frantically, clearly out of his element.

If Cara hadn't been so out of breath she would have laughed, obviously there was one way to tip Roberts' world. Pulling her scattered wits together, she stayed him with her hand when he would have run off through the house looking for anyone to save his Mistress.

"I'm fine. Please, Roberts, all I need is a good strong cup of tea. Please, have Mrs. Leeks bring a pot into the parlor."

Roberts nodded, though he still looked shaken to the quick.

Cara slowly made her way to the divan. Sitting she opened her new book. There, inside was a piece of paper. With a shaking hand she extracted it from the crisp pages, now somewhat crinkled after their adventure.

The young boy had been extremely fast. One minute she was walking down the street, she hadn't even seen him coming. She had left Lord Redding, walking away; she tried to keep her legs from running. He scared her for some reason, but she knew better then to show her fear.

She had reached the corner of Stafford and Dover, his intense angry gaze boring into her back. She didn't turn, knowing he could no longer see her it was but her imagination. Head down she quickly rounded the corner, putting as much distance s possible between her and Hatchard's, and Lord Redding.

The boy ran into her, nearly knocking her back. Her new book fell out of her hand. He retrieved before she did, then with a gaped tooth smile, more like a leer, he handed back the book giving his apologies. Before she could blink, he was gone.

She looked about; the streets seemed usually quiet. Tucking her book under her arm she made for Danforth House most expediently. At first, she thought she had run into him. There was something not right with the whole situation. Her heart was hammering; alarms were ringing in her head, she couldn't think. So, she ran.

Mrs. Leeks came in with refreshments. Cara stuffed the note under her until the housekeeper had departed. Opening the neatly folded paper she read, "Good day Mrs. Black."

Those four simple words scared her to her very core. *Someone knew.* *Someone knew.* If they knew she was Mrs. Black, how much more did they know? Worse how would they use it against her? And why?

She should tell Roland. No. She couldn't in good conscious bother him with something as trivial as this. He had a lot on his mind these days with finding the list for the Home Office. What was, her overactive imagination compared to that?

Cara poured herself a cup of tea, her hands shaking enough to cause the cup to clatter in the saucer. She breathed, a few slow deep breaths, raised the cup to her lips, with a sigh she let the earl grey ease her tension.

That night after dinner, Cara and Roland dressed for an evening at Almacks. Beaumont had deemed it safe enough to go, besides, a newlywed couple was supposed to be out. They had to keep up appearances, after all.

The somewhat plain room glittered with light from hundreds of candles, chandeliers and wall sconces lit the way surrounding the dance floor. People danced; others mingled. Cara tried her best not to appear nervous. She kept a smile plastered on her face, as they spoke to Lord and Lady Bertram. Her cheeks ached.

Roland sneaked a peek at his wife. He had felt the tension resonating from every pore. What the devil was a matter with her? She had been quiet all afternoon. Normally, she would have been thrilled to get out of the house after being stuck inside, no matter how warranted, yet when he told her of Beaumont's suggestion, she had looked like she was about to become ill.

She offered little in the way of conversation throughout dinner, when they had repaired upstairs to ready themselves for the evening, she worked all her wiles on him, not that he was complaining, he rather liked her wiles, just that they would be able to stay home. He regretted leaving the bedroom.

Still his trousers fit a little too snugly. That was the reason for his discomfort, what was hers? When Lord and Lady Bertram moved on, Roland led his wife onto the dance floor for the next set. Mayhap dancing would get her mind of her troubles.

The orchestra struck up a note; Roland swept her into the waltz. Regardless of all Cara's protests, she was indeed a small woman. Her waist fit easily into his hands, and she was as light as a feather in his arms.

They danced well together, very well.

Her head barely reached his chest; he remembered the first time she had run into him, literally, she hadn't seemed overly large then either. She was powerful, though. To him it wasn't the same thing. He had meant what he said, he loved her the way she was her curves, her childlike innocence, and her intellect. All the things that made her his Caralyn.

Roland pulled her close going into a turn and instead of allowing space to come between them when the turn was executed, he held her closer. Damn society and its conventions, he'd hold his wife any way he bloody well pleased.

Redding watched the couple on the floor, his groin tightened. He still wanted her. Was it simply because he could not have her? Or was he starting to be like his father, turned on by a woman's fear. And she feared him; he had seen it in her eyes earlier, and he enjoyed it. Was he to be damned like his father?

Liberton returned, from where he didn't know, to stand beside him.

"You keep drooling at her like that, and people are sure to notice."

Redding turned an icy stare in his father's direction.

"Redding my boy, even as the widow, you would not have been able to keep her alive much less marry the chit."

"Who said anything about marriage?" Redding sneered.

"Well now, that's entirely different."

"I thought you might see it that way." Yes, apparently, he had to be as demented as his father to get any recognition.

"First, we use her to bargain for the information; Fairhaven will surely give it up to get her back. Just look at him. He is so in love with her everyone can see it. It really is a sickening weakness."

Redding looked shocked. "You mean we are going to give her back? Liberton, you said..."

"I know what I said. But Fairhaven doesn't know that now, does he?"

Redding smiled and nodded. Satisfied with the answer, he watched the couple some more, letting his imagination run wild.

"Did you do what I asked?"

Redding nodded.

"Tomorrow will bring about the next step. Are you prepared?"

Again, Redding nodded.

Liberton bid his good night requesting strongly that Redding do the same, then left the hallowed halls of Almacks in search of more gentlemanly pursuits.

Watching Fairhaven and his bride had reminded him he needed to visit an old friend.

"The Times, Your Grace," Roberts said handing Roland the freshly ironed edition.

"Thank you, Roberts. You may go."

Roland sat at the breakfast table with his wife. She still looked a little pale; at least she was eating so her health wasn't in jeopardy. Roland finished his meal opting to stay with Cara for the sole purpose of making sure she finished everything on her plate, uncharacteristically opened the paper scanning the news headline inside.

Cara knew Roland was keeping a careful eye on her. She hadn't succeeded in hiding her feelings of terror last night at Almacks. This morning she was cursing herself for it. He had treated like a precious piece of glass, fearing she would break; it made matters worse. She wasn't breakable and she has hell would not shatter.

At first, she thought seriously about hiding away, limiting her life to Danforth Manor until Liberton could be caught. It was ridiculous really, why would Liberton want her? She didn't even know the man. Roland had pointed him out to her as he was leaving the ballroom in hopes that she might have seen him before in company of her father. She hadn't. Obviously, her father had, if in fact he was the scoundrel forcing her him to do those unspeakable acts against king and country. Of course, she'd recently obtained certain documents that he very well could want...

Still, she was being ridiculous. Wasn't she? Cara's musings were interrupted by a vicious curse from the other end of the table. Cara looked at her husband. "Roland?"

Roland lowered the paper, for the first time Cara could ever remember, his face paled his mouth opened then closed as if he thought better of sharing his news with her.

"Tell me." She hoped there was enough strength of conviction in her voice that he would see she could handle the news.

"It's Liberton's mistress," he said at last.

"Izzy?"

"Yes. Cara, she's dead."

"What?" Cara's now pale face mirrored his own.

"Damn! I shouldn't have said anything."

"Roland, I am not a child! Nor am I a piece of China that will break with unwelcome news. Now either you can tell me now or I will find out on my own later."

"All right." Roland hoped she was right, because if this was how things were going to progress, the violence was escalating. Thankfully, the paper didn't go into much detail, and he could easily skim over the worst of it.

"A woman's body was found floating in the Thames by a dockyard worker. Upon the arrival of Bow Street, the body was retrieved from the murky water and later identified as former actress, Mrs. Isabelle Dupries." Roland set the paper aside.

"Oh, Roland, I am sorry. I know it was a long time ago, still this couldn't be easy for you."

"Cara, I could care less about Izzy. No, that's not completely true, what worries me most..." Roland searched for the best way to secure his wife's compliance in giving up her freedom.

"Yes?"

"Cara, promise you will not leave this house unless you're with me?"

Cara hesitated and Roland was out of his seat, in a flash he had her by her arms painfully pulling her out of her chair and into his arms, *"Please."* He shook her, "Damn it, Cara!"

Cara snapped out of her shock, she looked up into the panic-stricken eyes of her husband. "All right. Roland, I promise."

Roland pulled her closer his arm like steel bands around her back; he said not a word, simply held her as if that alone could keep her safe. He had lost one family; he couldn't bear losing another.

Beaumont beat Roberts to the dining room, he found Roland at the end of the table, his back to him, his wife in a death grip. Cara, who could not see over Roland's shoulder, did see a shadow cast on the table; if she could have, she would have pleaded for Beaumont to help her husband. Thankfully, Beaumont hadn't needed to see her face to know that something was terribly wrong.

He had read the morning news, left his breakfast behind and rushed over. No, it wasn't that he feared Roland would be distraught over the loss of a former mistress, instead he thought to find Roland pretty much as he was, refusing to loosen the hold on his wife. Going to him he placed a hand on his shoulder, he waited for Roland to return to reality before speaking, the process took several minutes.

He turned his head to look at Beaumont, though his vision; his mind was somewhere else entirely. He blinked, one, twice, finally focusing, his arms loosened though not completely.

Cara took a deep breath.

Beaumont, conveying a silent message to Cara, helped escort Roland into the study where, at just after eight in the morning, she poured her husband a stiff shot of the cognac. Pressing it into his hands, he looked at the amber liquid as if determining what to do with it.

"Roland, drink it. Please," Cara said gently. She was still trying to figure out the unspoken message his body exuded. And there was a message. She was sure of it. Someone's death had affected him badly, whose? The mystery would give her something, at least, to spend her time on in the coming days ahead. Nothing could make her step foot outside without Roland now, guilt alone would bind her to her word, for she was no longer simply worried about herself, she was worried about Roland as well.

Beaumont left shortly after he felt Roland was going to be all right. Cara was given instructions to get Roland out of the house, to his aunt and uncles, for a walk in the park, anything that might get his mind cleared and centered on the task that lay ahead.

Loving the outdoors, Cara opted for the park.

Roland found it irritating; every movement had his eyes trained for danger.

Cara didn't know what to do. She thought about the people Roland had lost. Starting with his parents, she quickly dismissed them for as far as she understood it, they died aboard ship. Drowned.

How could that possibly affect the way Roland looked at the loved ones in his life now? No. It had to be something or someone he worked with. Her father was out, though she'd come to realize their relationship was a close one, Roland hadn't been here when he died; therefore, he could not in any way blame himself. She was missing something. What could it be?

A puppy scampered about no sign of his owner, possibly lost or homeless? It seemed affectionate, Cara rubbed behind his ears, and he quickly he dropped to the ground rolling onto his back, tongue lolling and tail wagging. Cara chuckled and began rubbing his belly.

Roland watched the dog's antics, every time Cara tried to shoo him away, he slunk back. He laughed. "Looks like you have a new pet, love. A shame he is such an ugly little mongrel. Couldn't you have possibly chosen a champion? I suppose we could always drop him off at Fairhaven Castle, that way we wouldn't have to look at him."

Cara smacked him playfully on the shoulder. "You could never be that cruel."

A shadow crossed his face, vanishing swiftly.

"What do you say, fella? Would you like a new home?" Roland looked around lest someone was looking for the animal. No one seemed to pay any notice to the dirty reddish-brown matted ball of fur. "All right then, come here." Roland picked the dog up, it wiggled in his arms until finding a position that suited him.

Roland's clothes were a frightful mess. Exactly what the mutt had been into, she was afraid to guess. Cara smiled at the sight of such a big man holding such a small…small what? Cara tilted her head this way and that, the view didn't get any better. Mayhap he would look like something once he was bathed.

Once inside, Roland handed off the parcel to Roberts who looked like he would have objected greatly had it been anyone else. Washing a dog, especially a dog of this animal's breeding, well… it was unthinkable, that is what it was. Nose in the air, arms stretched out as far as possible in front of him, Roberts headed for the kitchen, just shy of a run. Cara and Roland fought hard to contain their laughter.

"I think Roberts is a mite put out," Roland said smiling.

"Do you think he will forgive me anytime soon?" Cara replied in mock horror.

"It is doubtful, I'm afraid."

"Just when I thought he was beginning to like me too," Cara said, deflated before losing her battle to laughter.

Roland quickly ushered her out of the hall so the servants wouldn't hear, most especially the man in question. Halfway to the stairs, there was a knock at the door. Roberts, being otherwise detained, couldn't answer, so Roland took it upon himself to do the task.

There was no one outside.

"Who is it?" Cara asked, coming up behind.

Roland knelt to retrieve a package left on the stoop. Silently, he opened the box, there inside, covered in blood was a black rose. Cara gasped, hand to her throat, she began backing away from the door.

Roland cursed; slamming the door he flung the box, rose and all, down the long hall. Cara watched as it hit the wall and fell to the floor.

"Cara, get your things."

"What? Why?"

"It is no longer safe for you here; I am sending you out of London. Today." Roland was steady in his statement. Knowing better than to argue, Cara went to her rooms. Ringing for Lucy, she stood in front of her wardrobe handing garments to the maid as she prepared herself to once again be sent away. Should she allow it? Could she allow it? More important, could she stop it?

The more clothes Lucy stored away in her trunks. The more determined Cara was to see things through. The quickest way to the end of any problem usually meant giving up something. When it pertained to her lessons Cara had always been unyielding in her method. It was about taking each step slow, one at a time that way she missed nothing. This wasn't a lesson; it was life. Her life, Roland's life…their lives, and therein lay the rub. Their. It meant both of them, together.

Cara found Roland downstairs; Beaumont of course had been summoned. He currently sat watching Roland pace the floor. A quick peek at the wall, before entering the sitting room, told Cara the mess, the splattered trail of blood that led to the floor where the box had fallen, was recently cleaned. Still, she couldn't prevent the shudder that ran through her body.

"Cara," Roland said looking shocked to see her in the doorway, "are you packed then?"

She looked at Beaumont, her determination must have showed for he silently indicated with a small nod that she had his backing, at least that is until he heard what she had to say and then? Who knew?

"Yes and no," Cara said coming to sit in the window seat.

Roland's brows dropped forming a black V. "What do you mean? Either you are packed, or you aren't."

"Yes, I am packed." Cara toyed with the fabric of her mint green day dress. She waited to have their full attention before speaking again. "And no. I will not be sent away."

"Cara, I am not sending you away. I am trying to protect you. Your father, Izzy, I think they were both killed by Liberton. I am not about to just let you stay here and be hurt. I can protect you. It is my vow to protect you. And by God Cara I will!"

"You can. But this is not the way. Roland you are not thinking clearly." They looked like they were going to interject, Cara didn't give them a chance. "No both of you let me speak. Beaumont, you know full well that if Roland was in the field and I was just another agent, things would be handled differently. I said no, Roland. Let me finish." Cara held up her hand to enforce her words.

"Now, as near as I can figure, the only way to put a swift end to the current situation is by giving them what they want. In part at least. It must be done in such a way that they feel they are still in charge. All along they have been one step ahead. If I leave two things could happen, one they come after me and leaving in such haste would have been for not, for they would have me anyway; and two, they kill someone else—that must not happen."

Beaumont's eyes sparkled with consent. "She has the right of it, you know."

Roland gave Beaumont a lethal look, saying not a word, recognizing the truth and not liking it one iota. What of Cara? What of the danger to her? His gut constricted.

"Fairhaven, you know that if Cara was Miss Pebble or any other female agent, you would not be having a problem with this. You are too close to the situation, my friend. Be professional; take a step back and then look. What do you see? I see a very competent young woman willing to do what it takes to save lives. I see a woman who could manage one of my best agents, giving him a run for his money."

"She is not trained, for Christ's sake, Beaumont, she cannot even shoot a gun."

"You could teach me," Cara said quietly.

"With the amount of time we have, you would have to be a very adept pupil. It can't be done, I tell you."

"It can't? Why? Because you think I cannot handle the weapon? Or is it I would not be able to handle the consequences? Is it really, I, Roland, that cannot manage these things? Or is it you?"

"It's me, damn it!"

"Then, you have two choices; get over it and teach me everything you can in the time we have and trust me to learn it, or you can step out of the situation having Beaumont instruct me himself. For I will not, and understand me when I say this Roland, I will not be put away safely while you risk your life to save me."

Cara's chin raised several notches her all too familiar stubbornness radiated from every pore.

Roland fought with his inner demons, running fingers through his hair until it was standing up on end. Seeing him like this, so torn; Cara's resolve almost wavered. No, she had to stand her ground. Remain strong.

After what seemed like an eternity, Roland slouched down in the vacant chair, rubbing his hands over his face, he leaned forward. "What is your plan?"

Cara and Beaumont sighed with relief; he was committed. Now, they would stand a chance. Cara didn't like how her husband looked, but she would sooner have him look ten years older and be alive then play the hero alone. She would not lose him. To anyone.

Chapter Eighteen

"They're moving her. It is just as you thought. Acworth is worried his wife is in danger," Redding said coming into the room.

Liberton nodded, this was good news indeed. "Did Roberts tell you where they were sending her?"

"Not yet. He'll send a note later today. He was sent to walk a dog."

"What? I thought he was the butler."

"He is, though apparently, the Fairhavens are not one to follow tradition."

"Either that or he has been found out," Liberton said in rumination.

"Well, it doesn't matter. Roberts said Lucy was sent up to pack Lady Fairhaven's things yesterday. From what he could dally out of her, Lucy, the maid that is, Lady Fairhaven will be going on a journey for at least a week. Lucy's quite sweet on him; he will be able to get more information before we need it."

"You'd better be right."

Roberts adjusted his clothing. With one last kiss upon Lucy's reddened lips; he slipped quietly into the hall. He was going to miss this place when the time came to move on. Lucy was such a hot little number. Going wild on her enabled him to keep stoic mask in place for the duration of the day. With her he could be himself, that is, if she knew whom he really was. Ah. One of these days he would have enough money set aside, to say good-bye to this life. He'd buy that farmland down by the coast, marry, have children and settle down. No more churning information out of this bloke for that bloke.

"Roberts, I have been looking for you," Cara said.

"Sorry, Your Grace. Is there a problem?"

"No, I'm sorry, Roberts; you are entitled to a break any time you wish. I only sought to find out if His Grace returned. Clearly, since you were not at the door, he could have slipped by you, do not worry, I shall check the study."

"Very well, Madam."

Cara came down the last two stairs, rounded the corner, making her way to the study. Knocking, she waited for the sound of Roland's voice. She was worried he would change his mind.

He was so upset with the situation, even after they had devised a workable plan, Beaumont finally convinced him to go to Gentlemen Jacksons for a few rounds of boxing. He called "enter" and Cara breezed through the doorway coming to a halt at the sight of her sheepishly smiling, battered and bruised husband.

"Your face," she said, waving at the multicolored abrasions that surrounded his eyes, his cheeks, and even his lips.

"I'm fine. Really," Roland said, softly, smiling.

"I can see that." Cara's sarcastic reply made him grin harder; he winced as the corner of his mouth stung. Dabbing it with his finger, he motioned her to come forth.

"A kiss right about now should do the trick I think."

Cara came to him, sitting on his lap, she looked; her nose curled on one side and her eyes mere slits as she contemplated him. "I thought *Gentlemen Jacksons'* was for *gentlemen?* You don't look like you fought with a gentleman; it looks like you were attacked."

"Tibs," Roland answered clearly expecting that one word to explain it all.

"Tibs?"

"Yes, he is back."

"What does that have…? Did Tibs do this to you? Where is he?" Cara was clearly ready to do battle, Roland held her tight to his lap.

"Tibs fared worse than I. I fear we got a little carried away." Roland leaned forward, touching his lips to hers. "Much better. A few more and I will be as good as new."

Cara smiled tenderly, kissing each of his bruises one by one. Ending with a soul-searing kiss that had Roland hard and aching in a totally different way. Moaning into her mouth, he slowly slipped her neckline below her breasts, toying with one nipple then the other until the need to taste was so strong he pulled his mouth from hers, replacing his fingers with his mouth.

Cara arched back over the desk. Roland's hand found the hem of her dress, sliding it upwards until he could cup her feminine mound. She was hot, wet; Cara opened her legs wider. Roland caressed her gently, picking up speed, matching her shortened breaths. He was hard with the need to be inside her.

Standing, he swiped at the desk, things clattered to the floor as he set her down before him, trousers were undone swiftly, he slid his aching member inside with one hard thrust.

Cara bit down on her hand to keep from calling out loud. She met each of his frantic strokes, pushing him deeper and deeper inside. When at last he silently roared, his member stiffening inside her, his muscles strained, Cara let go; she wrapped her legs tightly around his firm buttocks pulling him into her.

When their release came, Roland collapsed on top for a moment while they caught their breath. Disengaging himself, he straightened his clothing; sitting he pulled Cara back down onto his lap and held her close.

Kissing the tip of her nose, he said, "Are you ready for a drive in the country?"

Cara couldn't speak so she inclined her head. Rising slowly, they went to get their things.

Cara awoke with the dawn, her stomach all a flutter, she quickly offered up a prayer that all would go as planned. Her bags were currently being loaded into Beaumont's carriage; she checked her reticule once more making sure the little pistol Roland had purchased was inside. Only a one-shot small, accurate only at close range, but it was only a decoy, patting her leg she felt the second, heavier precise weapon, Roland had strapped to her leg earlier. It would be the one most likely left on her person.

Taking a deep steadying breath, Cara looked about the room once more. It wasn't so much that she was forgetting anything, if all went as planned, she would be back home, by this time tomorrow at the latest, and if it didn't…well, she wasn't about to contemplate failure.

"You sure you want to go through with this?" Roland asked clearly hoping she would abandon this scheme.

Cara nodded steeling her nerve. "It is the only way."

Roland placed his arms about her waist pulling her back into the solid warmth. "I won't be far behind; all you have to do is hold them off until I get there," he whispered, "Just be careful."

Cara sighed. Leaning back, she soaked up his strength and nodded.

Roland helped Cara into the carriage. Beaumont already inside. Saying goodbyes loud enough that those watching, if indeed they were watching and listening, could hear, the carriage pulled out of the drive.

The carriage rattled and groaned as they left the comfortable cobbled London streets traveling westward at a sedate pace through the countryside toward Beaumont's countryseat. They rehashed every detail of the plan, hoping that whoever meant them harm would take the bait. Cara frantically wondered what would happen if they didn't? Would her nerves hold out for another attempt?

Beaumont questioned her on her shooting lessons, and Cara was not a great shot, but she was confident. At close range she should be able to hit anything provided she didn't freeze. Cara unconsciously worried her bottom lip.

Beaumont reached across the expanse of the carriage covering her twisting hands with his own.

"You have an inner talent, Caralyn, good instincts, the same instincts your father possessed, with your own blend of intelligence, use it and all will come out alright."

"My father died," Cara whispered.

Beaumont squeezed her hands. "Your father did something we must never do—he acted alone."

"Only because he didn't know whom he could trust," Cara defended.

"Trust is the chance one must take, I'm afraid. It is the one thing a person cannot live, or work, without. Sometimes, when the lines become murky, we must rely on our instincts to guide us. Help us determine those who those who will help, versus those who would do us harm. I am coming to believe your father's special talent in that area was badly diminished by his fear for his children. If only he had held faith."

Cara didn't bother asking him what he meant. Her recent history with her husband had shown her the value of faith. To place confidence in one is not a task easily performed but when you give over completely, faith multiplies your strength.

"I wonder when they will strike." Cara voiced the one fear out loud.

"It will not be for another couple hours. I know this area; close by there is no place in which they could take you. I am confident they will wait till we reach Southampton. Why don't you rest, or at the very least close your eyes? You'll need it."

Roland mounted Magnus and stayed to the trees as much as possible. He knew the route Beaumont's carriage would take. At various openings, he would check on their progress then duck back into concealment.

He felt like a rookie, only this time the butterflies in stomach were not for him, but for Cara. *Let her be safe.* Forcing impeding thoughts from his mind, Roland nudged Magnus ahead. He needed to get in front of the carriage and familiarize himself with the terrain.

***

The carriage rounded the bend leaving Southampton. They had stopped briefly for a late lunch, to make the trip look as though it were nothing out of the ordinary. The food had tasted like sawdust in Cara's mouth as she dutifully ate the meal set before her.

They conversed offhandedly keeping up pretenses. Beaumont causally glanced around noting faces. Cara could see the wheels turning, as each face came and went from his view; catalogued in his mind, was every criminal known to the Home Office as though he were a book. He checked those faces against the pages of stored information dismissing most and turning back to others that warranted a second glance.

Cara tried not to notice what he was doing, keeping her gaze on her plate; she let him do what he was good at without interruption. She would ask her questions once they were safely on their way. Finishing, Beaumont requested a basket to take with them. Cara wondered exactly how much farther they would be traveling that they would need a basket. Then it hit her; the basket was for Roland and Beaumont. They would need sustenance while giving chase. She didn't know quite how to feel about that, knowing that they would be eating while she…she what? What would they do to her?

The last was like a giant lump in Cara's throat, forcing down the bile, she smiled politely as the basket was placed on the table in front of them.

Beaumont rose; giving Cara his hand to escort her back out to the carriage.

Cara was struck as the sun glinted off his face; he wasn't very old perhaps eight- or ten-years Roland's senior. Forty at the outside?

As they settled in, the coach back underway, Cara with a need to change the subject inquired. Choosing her words carefully, this wasn't exactly a proper topic for her to broach yet since meeting Roland and Beaumont, ceremony wasn't something that came into play all that often.

Beaumont for once was decidedly uneasy, he couldn't remember a time when he had felt a question coming that he couldn't answer. Though one look at Cara you could see she was warring with curiosity and propriety. Curiosity would win out, of this he was quite sure. He only hoped it was something he could answer. With her cloudy eyes, so like Thomas' pinned on him he feared it wasn't or at least something he didn't want to answer for fear of voicing it to himself.

Cara watched shadows gather in Beaumont's eyes; strange, they looked frightened. No, not frightened, haunted. Clearing her throat, the question she tried to hold back surfaced, "Why have you not married? Or are you?"

Beaumont looked at his hands, then out the window. He peered into the trees just beyond the road, just when Cara thought he wouldn't answer, he began to speak, his voice as distant as his gaze.

"There was someone, once." His voice hitched and Beaumont winced, obviously still full of pain. "We were young, too young." As if collecting himself, he finished, "It was a long time ago, but being back here…"

Cara waited for more, when it didn't come, she didn't press. He was still hurting, wounds that like that sometime never healed. Hers hadn't festered near as long as Beaumont's and Roland was able to mend them quickly. She thought of Roland, remembered the torment she had seen on more than one occasion, he was haunted too. With recent events, Cara hadn't been given much of a chance to investigate its source. She would. As Roland's wife, it was her responsibility to try and erase the shadows years had wrought.

One by one, she would do it. She wished Beaumont had someone, to do the same for him. Looking at him again she thought her original assessment of his age wrong. The insecurities and the pain combined to make him appear older than what he was. Cara was sure of it now. He could not be more than thirty-four or thirty-five. Too young, he said. If only Cara could make him realize he was still young.

Too young to give up on happiness, on life and all that went with it.

Roland looked on as the carriage rounded the bend leading out of Southampton. He was waiting for them, knowing they would be safe, to this point. Now as they left the main road, onto less traveled ones leading to Beaumont's estate, they would be at greater risk. He wiped his sweaty brow; the sun beat down unmercifully onto his black-attired body.

Magnus stamped his foot, impatience to be underway. Roland steadied him with a hand on his neck. "Easy boy. Save your strength. You will need it. I will need it. That's right, patience."

Magnus' great black head bounced up and down as if understanding and agreeing with his master. Roland looked on; there was a movement. It was time. It had begun.

The coachman thumped his foot against the front of the coach. Beaumont immediately alert looked to Cara. She nodded. Bracing herself for what was to come.

"Whoa!" Cara heard the coachman yelling for the horses to stop, she could feel him pull back on the reins, everything moved through her mind at a snail's pace. The hollering outside, Beaumont yelling to the driver, the coachman climbing down, the sound of something large being swung and connecting with what she perceived as the driver's head. The grunt of expelled air, the slither of his body down the side of the coach until his unconscious form hit the hard dirt of the road.

Her pulse was racing; there was a ringing in her ears, and her breathing rapid; she forced it to slow. Beaumont yelled again, "Simms, damn it, Simms, why have we stopped?" They both knew Simms would not be able to answer.

The door opened, sun spilled in blinding them to the person now entering; taking a deep breath, Cara forced herself to stay calm.

"Ah, Beaumont," someone said in a gravelly voice. "Still losing the women in your life. And here after twenty years I would have thought you had learned a thing or too. Tsk. Tsk. It appears you haven't. You should have made the right choice years ago, lad."

With that comment, the man smashed Beaumont over the head, and he slumped quickly in his seat. Extending his hand like some great gentleman, he led Cara from the darkened interior.

The sun hit her full force. Blinking, she tried to adjust her sight to the brightness of the afternoon. She yanked out of his grip, turned on her heel and fled. Running blindly, her need to get away real, her reason to cover the truth.

They would expect her to try something.

She hadn't gotten far when she was tackled hard to the earth. Fighting kicking and yelling, Cara was pinned to the road; she cursed herself for not running through the lush green grass. Every time she tried to yell, a mouthful of dirt was all she got for her efforts. When she moved, gravel bit into her skin; soon she ceased her struggles, truly exhausted.

"Ah, my lovely dear Mrs. Black," came the soft caress of a voice…a voice she knew. Redding. Anger bubbled within her. "Or should I say Lady

254

Fairhaven, I know, how about simply Caralyn. How I have longed to have you beneath me. I guess wishes really do come true."

He chuckled wickedly as his hands roamed freely. Cara was repulsed. Finally, after painfully squeezing her breasts, he pulled her up. Cara would have loved to spit in his face; instead, he drew her back tight against his chest, holding her there. Cara tried to distance herself, ineffectively.

"Leave her be." The same gravel-sounding voice commanded.

"I am just having a wee spot of fun, surely you cannot object to that?" Redding said, disgruntled.

"I can and I will. We haven't completed this job, and until we do, the chit is off limits. After I have what I want, she is yours. Not until. Is that clear?"

Redding didn't respond; though Cara could feel the hatred vibrate through his taut muscles. *He didn't like being told what to do. Was it the cause for his ardor toward her? The reason he sought to humiliate her, no, not humiliate…he was using her to get to Liberton, but how and why? And more importantly, could she use that against them?*

Liberton came around front of her. Redding now taking the commanded step back had her arms painfully anchored behind her.

Liberton's hand gripped her face. "I am sorry if you if managed to get yourself a little scratched, *Your Grace*. Running was not a good idea. I am glad you seem to learn quickly. That will help immensely in ensuring your safety."

Cara couldn't stand the feel of his touch on her skin, the way he said 'Your Grace' like she was something disgusting, enraged her. She did the most unladylike thing she could think of. Knowing the consequences would not be good and not caring one whit, Cara took aim, lifted her face to his and spat in his face.

Retribution was swift as the back of his hand connected with her temple. For a few moments Cara could see nothing but stars dancing before her eyes. Her head reeled back with force, hitting Redding's chest. She was still busy trying to right her world when Liberton barked at Redding to get her on the horse.

She was seated in front of Redding who was enjoying feeling her up with one hand in guise of keeping her from falling off. Spurred, the horses headed east across the green grass at full speed.

Roland watched, making his feet stay put, not nudging Magnus on, until the three of them were beyond the trees on the other side of the road. He had wanted nothing more than to kill the bastards without delay; fear of hitting Cara was the only thing that stopped him.

The trio slowed, entering the copse of trees, Roland urged Magnus forward. Loping to the carriage, he jumped from his saddle while the horse was still in motion and peered into the carriage.

Beaumont groaned. Quickly, he helped him up. Bringing him out into the sun for a better look, Roland heard Simms stirring as well.

Beaumont shook off Roland's aiding hand, "I'm fine. I ducked a little when he hit, received nothing but a little tap. I fear Simms encountered the worst."

Kneeling beside Simms, Beaumont checked him over as Roland unhitched the horses from the carriage. Exchanging harness for saddles previously stored under the driver's box, Roland readied the two mounts while Beaumont revived Simms as best, he could. By the time the horses were saddled Beaumont and a somewhat unsteady Simms were ready to mount.

Roland voiced worries about Simms's ability to ride hard were met with deaf ears. Giving up, he mounted speeding eastward towards the trees. Beaumont knew the area, thank God, so the fifteen-minute lead they had would be eaten up shortly. Though the exact destination was unknown, Beaumont seemed to have some idea where they were headed.

Roland wasted no time asking questions; he let Beaumont take the lead. Each to their own mount would be able to move faster than the shared mounts of Redding, *that bastard, I knew he had been up to no good*, and Liberton though he wasn't delusional enough to think they would care enough for their mounts to spare them.

They rode hard, Simms scanning the ground for tracks as they galloped over it. Roland would never understand how someone could read tracks traveling at that speed, apparently Simms could, even with a lump on his head the size of a goose egg.

Coming to a fork in the path, Beaumont pulled his mount to a stop. Simms dismounted, walking the perimeter, he nodded, mounting again he pointed to the trail on the right, silently they continued in pursuit.

Night was falling, soon the tracks or whatever it was that Simms was following, would need closer inspection. It would slow their pace considerably. Roland wondered at the folly of even allowing a plan such as this to take place.

Beaumont sat rigid, his face a pasty white. Of both men, Roland would have thought Simms had the worst of it, though with every mile of ground they ate up, Beaumont looked decidedly more ill.

"There is a crofter's cabin beyond those trees," Beaumont announced in a desiccated voice. "That is where they will be. We must stop. Go the rest of the way on foot. It will be quieter."

"You cannot know that for sure, Beaumont. Simms? What about you? Should we stop or continue?"

"His Lordship is right, Your Grace. The tracks lead in the direction he stated," Simms said with a nod.

"What tracks, damn it, man, I do not even see how you can be sure we are on the right trail," Roland snapped.

"Roland," Beaumont warned. "Simms is the best tracker the agency has. You are overwrought. You need to cool your head, or you will have to stay behind with the horses."

Roland swore. They had his wife for Christ's sakes, how in the hell was he to stay calm. *You must.* His inner voice warned. *Cara is counting on you.* Roland forced himself to calm. Clearing his head of all thoughts of what may come, he focused his energies on what was. Stopping, they concealed the horses as best they could, silently making their way to the appointed cabin.

Thank God. They had finally reached somewhere. Cara could not stand being in the saddle one minute longer. She felt sick and dirty. She feared bathing for weeks would not ease the pains in her body.

They had arrived at a small vacant cabin, old and in need of repair. It looked as though no one had inhabited the place in many years. Cobwebs clung to every corner of the room; broken window shutters hung at awkward angles. No glass remained in the windows if there ever was any.

The cabin was small there was but one room, where Liberton unceremoniously deposited her upon entry; an old musty straw filled mattress lay on the floor. This room was dirty more so than the exterior room. With the sun going down the darkened recesses of this windowless space seem beyond eerie.

There was nothing for Cara to do but wait. At least here in this little room, Redding wasn't around. Though she was angry at Redding and detested his touch, she held no fear of him. No, it was Liberton that induced fear.

She had marked each passing hour, sending up prayers that Roland would be safe. Not once had she thought of her own safety, aside from Liberton's first punch, which she provoked, they hadn't touched her since. Even Redding's roving hands seemed to still when he realized she really didn't appreciate his attentions. Maybe it was the fact Liberton wasn't watching them. Or mayhap it was a case of wishful thinking on her part to hope he wouldn't take her when Liberton no longer had need of her.

Her reticule had been tossed in the carriage, and thankfully, they hadn't searched her person, as Beaumont predicted. A woman agent might have checked further, but Cara had done nothing to link her to the agency. Even if they knew of her brief stint as Rose Black, hopefully they would think her nothing more than a spoiled Duchess…of little or no consequence.

Cara had a lot of time to assess her captors; an unlikely match, something told her Liberton was using Redding, leading him by the nose, as he did everyone else. She sensed something in Redding that she absolutely despised; yet he wasn't evil, not in the way Liberton was. Cara shuddered at the thought.

Liberton, for all his fancy manners, had a temperament of a snake, unpredictable at best and true malevolence at worst. He was an older man, perhaps sixty. Though his stature wasn't all that unpleasing to the eye, there was simply something that radiated from him. Every time he looked at her, she could feel his hatred, but it was nothing compared to the way he had addressed Beaumont back in the carriage.

Such silky-smooth wording, each syllable dripping with venom, almost like Beaumont had hurt him. What could Beaumont have done to earn the wrath of such a man? Whatever it was it would not end without bloodshed. Of that, she was sure.

She listened to ferocious outbursts from beyond her room. Liberton cursing Redding and much more by the sound of the occasional grunt. Her heart went out to him. From what she could make out, Redding was Liberton's son. How? Unless Liberton lied about his name, it was more than possible. Likely even.

Even so how could someone be so cruel to their own flesh and blood? How could they stand there beating and cursing them to hell? Wasn't there an instant bond that formed between a child and its parents? Her thoughts flickered to her own parents. They had their lives, but overall they had loved them as best they could.

She didn't agree with what her father had done; yet it explained the depths of his love. She put her hand to her stomach. If she was with child, she could not do anything save for, love it with her whole being. She would never be capable of hurting him or her intentionally. Never.

She shuddered at the sound of flesh meeting flesh, wood cracked, and Cara could almost envision Redding hitting the floor.

Redding. In truth he was so very young, perhaps, nineteen or twenty. His attitude, his wondering hands could be attributed to the fact that he was trying to live up to his sire's expectations. The evil power his father exuded was astronomical. As much as Cara would have liked to call Redding evil, she could not. Unlike Liberton whom she wished, would meet his maker soon, she could not honestly say the same thing about Redding.

Was she being naïve? Reading more into a human being then he deserved credit for? Pushing unwanted sympathies and unanswerable questions aside Cara used the time to retrieve her gun and place it in a more accessible location in the folds of her skirt. Lucy had done a lovely job of sewing the extra *book* pocket, or so the young maid thought. Although she could not have kept the gun there earlier, she felt it safe to place it there now. Sighing, she lay back to the wall listening, cringing and waiting.

Chapter Nineteen

Roland was rapidly losing his already depleted patience. He would have loved nothing better than to charge into the cabin guns blazing. It was Beaumont and Simms who insisted they wait for the cover of darkness.

Beaumont sat by the trunk of a tree; his thoughts were miles away. Roland knew there was a lot that Beaumont wasn't telling them. Starting with how he knew Liberton's destination. He said nothing when Simms confirmed his directions yet appearing almost hopeful that Simms would find tracks pointing to another direction. Whereas Roland just wanted to get his wife back, and now they were here no more than twenty yards away and still he could not go to her.

Simms waited quietly snacking on food from a small basket. Sure, he could think of his stomach, the man was as big as an ox, and it wasn't his wife held behind the walls of that dilapidated shack. Even the thought of food made Roland queasy, watching Simms devour it was more then he could bear. He turned away.

With the grass and needles crisp beneath his feet too much walking about could result in unwanted detection; gingerly Roland went to sit beside Beaumont.

"I want to know what you're thinking," Roland demanded quietly.

Beaumont looked up startled to see Roland next to him. His eyes haunted.

"What is going on? Damn it, Beaumont my wife is in there. Why are we waiting?"

"You know why we are waiting," Beaumont said with detached calm.

"I know what you said. It is what you didn't say that I want to know. Now."

Beaumont sighed. "I think Liberton will be leaving the cabin if I do not arrive shortly."

"Why you? It's the documents he wants. I have those. Would he not send Redding with his demands?"

"No." Beaumont shook his head.

Roland offered an explicit curse. "The whole plan was devised on the assumption that Liberton wanted that list."

"Most likely he would, I no longer think that is his soul purpose. He wanted, still wants, to make me suffer. He may have a buyer for the information he may not. It's of little consequence."

"Why the hell not?" Roland hissed.

Beaumont ran a shaky hand through his hair. "What better way to revenge me then attacking my credibility. My job is everything." Beaumont saw the questions ready to burst forth from Roland; he stilled him with his hand.

"Liberton is Fredricton Wexter, the Earl of Redding."

"Egads! Redding? You mean to tell me he is that little dandy's father?" Roland said, shocked.

"Yes." Beaumont said. "Why he has targeted me, I do not know for certain. I thought him dead. My association with him was long ago and should have no connection with what is happening now. He said something to me in the carriage, right before he knocked me out. This is personal. Revenge. Though for the life of me I cannot guess what I ever did to the man. If anyone should want revenge it should be me!"

"Well, damn it man, what did he say?"

"It is of no import."

"He has my wife!"

"I realize that. That is why we are waiting. When I do not show after a couple of hours, either Liberton, Redding, or hopefully both, will come in search. Either way we'll have a better chance to get Caralyn out safely."

"If anything happens to her Beaumont, your life is over."

"My life ended over seventeen years ago." Beaumont said completely undone.

Roland made no inquiries as to what that statement meant. Beaumont obviously had his ghosts if they brought harm to his wife he would no longer have to worry over his haunted memories of the past.

They all heard the commotion coming from the cottage. The cursing. The unmistakable sounds of battery. Beaumont stilled Roland with his hand.

"Easy, old chap. It is his son that is getting the beating not Caralyn. Listen."

"I have been listening, the man sounds crazed. I am not about to leave my wife in there." Roland pointed at the cottage now surrounded in darkness. "With him. Who knows when he will turn on her? He has already hit her once."

Beaumont snapped to attention. "He hit her. When?"

"Outside the carriage, damn it! And I could not do anything about it then, for the sake of the bloody Home Office; this is no longer about the Home Office, as you said so yourself, *friend*, it's personal."

Cara couldn't take it anymore. What in the hell was going on out there? She hadn't heard a word from Redding since hearing his chair crash to the floor. Surely Liberton hadn't killed his own son? Gnawing on her bottom lip, she contemplated her options. If she waited, not only could Redding be dead, Liberton could very well come looking for someone else to take his anger out on.

That someone would be her.

She had no doubt that if he was in such a rage, he wouldn't stop at hitting her again. And again... The looks he cast her throughout the journey had shown her he would have no qualms at killing her—but what, did he truly want? Her gun was ready though if she waited, he'd have the upper hand. And if there was one thing she learned, it was getting and maintaining the upper hand.

Surely Roland was close, all she had to do was hold him at bay until he got here, *and not* let him hurt Redding anymore. *What if he is already dead?* Her inner voice yelled. Cara heeding the warning listened intently at the door, please Redding, just move, say something, or moan for God sakes!

Roland heard a woman shout. Cara.

His heart thudding in intense beats, as he stole closer to the ramshackle cottage until he stooped on the ground directly below an open window. Beaumont and Simms followed both taking up position at the one remaining window. Liberton's voice reached his ears. Rising cautiously, he peered over the ledge.

He watched in horrified confusion as Liberton, was holding Redding slumping bleeding form by the scruff of his collar, he raised his hand and struck him across the face. Cara's angry scream filled the air. Redding fell one again into crumpled heap on the floor. Liberton kicked Redding aside as if he were trash and approached Cara.

"Bastard!" she screamed. "How could you do that to your own son?"

Liberton turned toward the windowpane. Roland quickly dropped down. Pressing his back against the cabin he controlled his breathing, forcing himself to bury his vehemence and concentrate.

He had to get them out of there. He hadn't wanted to kill Liberton, at least not until they had had a chance to question him, but he had to be stopped. With Redding now out of the situation, he would turn the brunt force of his anger on Cara. *Damn his beautiful wife and her interfering-caring heart!*

Slipping his knife from his boot, he gave a signal to Beaumont. He had one chance, before Liberton would know he was here, he wished he were close enough he could take care of him without causing more blood. How much more could Cara take? How much was Redding bleeding? How much had she seen?

Beaumont held up two fingers, he would wait for Roland and follow his lead.

About bloody time someone followed his lead. He only wished they would have followed it when they were all safely back at Danforth House before this crazy scheme to use his wife as bait was even hatched.

His best chance would be to come through the door, if he stayed at the window, he would have to throw from his unseen position lest Liberton spot the knife and hurl Cara into its path.

Roland hazarded another peek through the window; Cara had her gun out. It was trained on the center of Liberton's chest. Shaking.

The sound of Liberton's eerily crazed laughter sent chills down his spine as he watched the crazy bastard bear down on his wife. Mentally taking a note of their positions, possible positions at point of entry, he made his way quickly and silently to the door.

"What the hell do you think you are doing? Put down that gun you worthless chit."

"I will not. What have you done to Redding?"

Liberton scoffed, wavy his hand toward his prone son's body, "*My son?*"

"Yes, your son. I heard you. He is your heir therefore he is your son." Cara would have liked to be able to go to Redding. She'd heard him moan before coming out of the room, since the final blow there was no motion, no noise. It was too dark to discern clearly whether the man was even breathing. *Please Roland, come soon.*

Liberton shook his head, chuckling. "To be my heir does not mean that worthless bastard is my son. It matters not. Give me the gun, *Lady* Fairhaven. Now."

For every step he advanced, Cara retreated. How much farther would she be able to go before she ran into the wall? The cabin was small.

"I mean it, Liberton, or Redding, or whatever the hell your name is. Stay where you are. I know how to use this weapon." Cara was surprised to note her voice remained calm even as her insides were trembling.

Roland stood outside the door, battling the panic racing through him. With one last look to Beaumont and a deep breath, he backed up a step, raised his leg, and kicked. Surprise—that would be his only advantage.

Cara and Liberton's heads snapped toward the door. Cara took longer to recover from the sight of her husband standing in the doorway; even as her heart went out to him, Liberton lunged grabbing her, he twisted himself behind her, her gun now pressed against her temple.

Roland's heart stuck in his throat. Cara stood directly in front of Liberton, his beefy arm around her throat, her gun held to her head; Roland didn't have a prayer of throwing without hitting her.

She had to move. He had to get her out of the way…but how?

"Let her go, Liberton, she had nothing to do with this. I have your list," Roland said stalling for time.

A bark of crazed laughter came from Liberton, "The list? Oh yes, the list. Well, I thank you for that, Your Grace." Liberton sneered. "But this is about far more than your precious list. Where is Shelton by the way?"

"I'm here, Wexter; you can have me and the list. Let Lady Fairhaven go," Beaumont said, coming up behind Roland.

"Ah Shelton, your still such a fine-looking man. Too bad we got off to such a wrong start."

Roland peeked at Beaumont; one look told him that he didn't understand what Liberton was talking about either.

"Let my wife go! Liberton," Roland said again controlling the edge in his voice.

"I think not. One less woman in the world… who'd notice, we be a lot better off I'd say. Kind of like taking care of all my loose ends at once," Liberton chuckled, his madness-glazed eyes gleaming in the candlelight.

This was getting them nowhere. Roland needed to disable Liberton and to do that he needed Cara to move.

"Hello, sweetheart. Are you well?"

Cara looked at her husband, was he losing his mind? She was standing in front of him, pistol to her head, and he asked how she was doing. Not very bloody well but thank you for asking. He must be trying to get her to do something. What?

"I am fine, Ro."

Liberton's arm squeezed tighter against her throat. Her eyes widened. She brought her hand up to Liberton's arm, holding it back from crushing her completely. Her toes barely touched the floor.

Roland bit down hard on the inside of his mouth.

"Cara, love? Did you think to load the gun before you left with Beaumont?" Roland tried giving her a sign as to what her answer should be. First, he saw anger flash across her face, he hoped that she would not take this opportunity to brag about how capable she was.

"Of course—"

"Cara, think hard, love. *Did you load the gun?*"

"Oh! Why would I load it? You gave it to me? Doesn't it come ready to shoot? You said, and I quote, aim and pull the trigger!" Cara said, feigning shock, confusion and anger.

"What! What are you two talking about? Stop this at once. This is not how it is going to be. If you cannot keep your minds on the conversation at hand, I will have no choice but to do away with this interfering chit immediately." Liberton waved the gun.

"I'm afraid that won't be possible, at least not with the gun you are currently holding. It seems Her Grace didn't load the weapon."

Liberton roared with laughter. "Isn't that just like a woman, bloody useless if you ask me."

Tossing the gun aside, Liberton continued laughing, his arm like a band of steel about Cara's throat.

Roland acted. He launched himself across the room, landing just behind the laughing madman. Liberton turned. Cara swung, gasping for air.

"I wouldn't, Wexter. My gun, as opposed to Her Grace's, *is* loaded. And I assure you, I am a decent shot."

Liberton's head whipped back toward Beaumont. "You? You would shoot me?" He said clearly offended.

While Liberton seemed distracted at the very thought that Beaumont would do him harm, Roland reached out from behind, grabbing the pronounced cord in his neck, he quickly pinched and turned hard, bringing his other hand up for added pressure. Liberton's eyes rolled then closed before slumping to the floor, taking Cara with him.

"Damn, I wish you'd teach me to do that," Beaumont said in admiration.

"Well, I'll be…" said Simms, peeking over his shoulder into the room was clearly in awe as well.

Roland rushed to her side. She was still wheezing. Helping her to the one remaining chair, he urged her down into it. Kneeling, he checked for any other signs of injury.

"I'm fine," she rasped, her throat raw. "Redding."

Roland touched a hand to her cheek; she grasped it, pressing her lips to it in a silent kiss before she pushed him away. Redding still had a chance, but they would have to hurry. Roland, reluctant to leave Cara's side, shooed Beaumont to Redding.

Beaumont knelt, gingerly turning Redding's injured body. Removing his handkerchief, he tried to remove some blood from the young man's face. He was breathing, albeit labored. "We have to get him out of here. Simms, rig something to carry him. Roland? There's a stream not far from here, fetch some water."

Roland had never seen this side of his friend. It was tender, almost…fatherly. Shaking his head, he quit the small room in search of water.

Cara sat in the chair; she wished she felt well enough to assist. Her air restricted, she looked on trying to sort out all she'd seen and heard. And was still seeing.

Soon, Roland was back with the water; he placed it on the floor in front of Beaumont and made his way back to Cara. Simms was next to arrive; all was set. There was no reason for them to wait in fact it was more important that they head out. Redding would need a doctor.

Leaving Cara, Roland helped Simms and Beaumont lift Redding and take him out to the makeshift bed Simms constructed to pull behind his horse.

Simms mounted slowly, making his way back to Southampton, it was the nearest town, and it would be there they would find a doctor.

"What about Liberton?" Roland asked Beaumont before he mounted.

"Damn. I had forgotten." Beaumont looked back toward the cabin. "Let's throw him over his horse. We will take him with us. He needs to be questioned."

"Bitch!" There was a holler followed by a scream of pain; Roland flew back to the cabin. Cara lay on the floor, clutching her side; Roland heard the commotion by the window. Liberton was getting away.

Let him, he'd deal with that fiend another day; Roland turned his attention to his wife; blood was seeping through her fingers. Where had the bastard cut her? Frantically feeling around in the darkness, Roland looked for the source. Damn darkness! He needed light. Cara moaned as he pressed here and there looking for the wound.

Beyond the cabin, Roland heard a shot. Shouting ensued, though he could not make out whose voice was whose. A short while later Beaumont came rushing through the door.

"How is she?"

"She's in pain. Damn it, Beaumont, I can't see. She's bleeding but I cannot tell where from!"

Beaumont went to the table and retrieved the lamp. He knelt holding the lamp above her pale face, slowly guiding the light downwards. When he reached the spot where her dress was covered in blood, he held firm.

"There, see the hole? It must be staunched. Roland, do you hear me? Snap out of it! Damn it, tear a strip off her petticoat, wad it, and press. Yes! That's it, old man, don't think, just do."

While Roland held tight to the fabric, Beaumont ripped another longer piece, sliding it under and around as Cara moaned once more before going quiet. It was a blessing she had passed out; Roland would be able to concentrate better without her moaning in pain. Or at least Beaumont hoped he would.

"Here, now, move your hand and I'll tie it off. The sooner we get this done, the sooner we can get her back to the inn and to the doctor. She'll be all right, Roland, she's strong."

"She'd better be," Roland growled. "Or dying will be the least of Wexter's worries when I catch up to him."

"Sorry to steal your thunder old man, but my aim was true. I saw the bastard go down just before I came inside. You'll not have to leave your beautiful wife's side to track him down. He is already in hell." Or at least

Beaumont hoped, trying to shake off the fact that there was another time long ago he heard the bastard was dead.

"Looks like we will have to get our answers from Redding. Let's go."

Roland carried Cara to Magnus. Setting her in the saddle, he climbed up behind cradling her between his arms and legs. Giving Magnus his head, he set out to catch up with Simms.

Beaumont watched Roland leave. He had one more thing to do before he could follow. Walking to the trees, in the direction he had seen Wexter drop, he combed the ground looking for his body.

It was dark and Beaumont could see there was no sign of the man. Kneeling, he checked the ground. He found a spot of blood still warm and sticky. He had gotten him—that was something at least. Beaumont took note of the amount of blood soaking the earth and knew Wexter should not last much longer. "Farewell, you crazy bastard." Turning on his heel, Beaumont mounted his horse leaving behind the memories of past and present. All except one.

***

It had taken till dawn to reach Southampton, with Redding and Cara hurt, it was slow going. Beaumont caught them easily enough. Pulling alongside Redding, he appeared to be watching for signs of distress, his eyes never leaving the boy. Roland wondered what the fascination was.

Roland looked down at his unconscious wife as he pulled Magnus to a stop outside of the inn. Gathering her up in his arms, he quickly descended on the side entrance and kicked it open. Calling over his shoulder for a doctor, he strode to his set of rooms. Leaving everyone else to do his bidding or follow.

Cara awoke only once when the doctor began cleaning the wound, a two-inch gash from the blade of Liberton's knife. She tried to speak but didn't succeed.

Dying quickly was too good for that bastard.

"It's better this way," the doctor said, slowly drizzling laudanum into Cara's slack mouth.

Maybe it was, but Roland just wanted her to wake up and speak to him. He had been patient enough and now it was time for her to get up and come to him, hold him, kiss him. Damn it! He couldn't take this waiting!

As Cara's breathing deepened even more and Roland's nerves scratched beneath the surface of his skin the doctor turned back to his work. Painstakingly he stitched, small even spaced stitches, the smaller the stitch the less of a scar it would leave on the Duchess, and he knew without asking that the size of the scar would be the topic of a great many private conversations between the husband and wife. No doubt they would not be good; he could imagine the duke reprimanding her silently as he paced the floor like a caged lion similar to how he was behaving now. The doctor quickly finished, left instructions in case of fever, and let himself out.

Roland knelt beside his wife's bed. Taking her hand, he cursed softly, "Damn you, Caralyn Acworth, you wake up this minute! Do you hear me! If you so much as think you are going to up and leave me to rear those three hellions alone, you have another thing coming! I'll sell Wonderland! Damn you, Cara. Please Love, please just open your eyes and tell me you'll be okay."

But Cara didn't so much as stir and as much as Roland hated leaving her side, he knew he would have to check on the others. If, God forbid, she did develop the fever the doctor spoke of, she would need him; right now, however, she slept. A drug-induced sleep but peaceful, nonetheless.

Simms lay slumped down in a chair in the corner of the room as the doctor was attending Redding. Beaumont sat close by, holding his hand. He hadn't left the young man's side. He was sure to be as tired as Roland, yet Roland had a reason for not sleeping. But Beaumont?

Roland's head was bombarded with events from the previous evening trying to make sense out of them. Liberton clearly hadn't wanted the list… was it because he was mad? Beaumont said it was personal…damn; it was all such a fuddle. Shaking his head, he returned to his wife's room.

Cara moaned. Roland soothed her heated brow with some water from the bowl by the bed, and he listened for signs of labored breathing; thankfully, there were none. Kissing her softly he whispered how much he loved her and needed her, until she settled once again in drowsy laudanum induced sleep.

The sound of a door opening had Roland turning his head. Beaumont waved him over. Roland tucked the blankets around Cara then left, closing the door quietly behind him.

"He should make it as well. We'll know more tomorrow. Your Grace, how is your wife?"

"She still appears in pain, but I hesitate to give her too much laudanum. Her brow is heated, I cooled it. I pray it's not from fever."

"It is a mite early to tell. I'll check in on her before I leave and I'll return later today; if you should need me before that, send your man around to my office."

"Yes, doctor. Thank you," Roland said shaking the man's hand.

Roland heard the other door open and close, an exhausted looking Beaumont now stood in the hall.

"You look beat, old man, why don't you see if the innkeeper has another room available."

Beaumont shook his head. "I can't. I only came out to see how Caralyn was doing. But I should get back in case the boy wakes."

"He's not a boy, Beaumont. He's a young man. Wake Simms to keep watch him if you're afraid he will disappear."

"Disappear? Not much chance of that. He has several broken ribs, his head was bashed in by that maniac, and the doctor had to stitch him. His whole face is bruised and lacerated from Wexter's signet ring." Beaumont ran his fingers through his hair.

"I still don't understand; mad or not, how a man could do that to his own flesh and blood," Roland said.

"I have thought of that too and I don't think he did." Beaumont lowered his head in defeat.

"You really must be out of it, old chap. If you think my wife could have possibly done that to Redding?"

"No. That's not what I meant. Damn. This is so complicated. So surreal, yet there really could not be any other explanation."

"What explanation?" Roland hissed frustrated.

"He's not Wexter's son." Beaumont's eyes pooled with tears. "He's mine."

Roland could not have been more blindsided then if he was hit with a carriage hitch. It made a sort of twisted sense, and still…

"Beaumont, Redding is nineteen or twenty years old. He cannot be your son, for God's sakes, man, you would have had to be his age when you sired him."

Beaumont nodded. "Younger actually. Sixteen." Without another word, he turned and went back into the room.

Roland gaped at the closed door. No. It couldn't be possible. Not that sixteen-year-old boys were celibate. But fatherhood? His eyes drifted to his sleeping wife. He wanted nothing more than to be a father. To watch his child, grow—a beautiful little girl with dark curling locks and laughing opaque eyes shot through with intelligence—the image of her stunning mother, his brave wife.

"Ro…?" Cara's voice croaked.

"I'm here, Love." Roland held her hand to his lips.

"Lay…"

"Cara, you need rest…"

"Hush, I will rest. With you, now quit being such a tyrant and lay with me. I do recall you telling me you would do anything for me, so don't fight me on this." Cara offered him up a small smile.

"All right, Love. You win. But first tell me how you feel. The doctor said to watch for fever. Damn, Cara, you scared the life out of me! I don't know what I would do if I lost you." Roland kissed her still smiling lips then carefully lowered himself down onto the bed. Pulling her back against him, he waited quietly thanking anyone up there who'd listen that he would do anything, anything if they would just see to it that she would be alright from now on.

"I'm sore, but I'll live. And as for that doctor and his talk of fever, well, it's just poppycock. I am strong as an ox. And besides, I'd never in a million years allow you to sell Wonderland. And I am sure, My Lord, that just as soon as I am feeling better, you will pay for that remark…" Her voice trailed off once more and her eyes closed but this time sleep embraced them together.

Epilogue

Wonderland

September 1812

"Your Grace, there is a Mr. Gomersall here to see you. Shall I send him to the study?"

"Yes, thank you Tibs. Please have Mrs. Brown send in refreshments. Oh, and send Ronning to fetch His Grace."

"Yes, Your Grace."

Cara walked the hall to her father's study. Mr. Gomersall, had he finally come with good news. She hated that due to association with her father, his father Mr. Gomersall Sr., a retired lawyer was so badly abused.

"Mr. Gomersall. Please have a seat. Thank you for coming. My husband should return shortly. How is your father?" Cara sat on the chair closest to the window.

"Thank you, Your Grace." Mr. Gomersall sat, crossing his long legs in front of him. "My father, I am happy to announce, is up and about."

Mrs. Brown entered the study, setting the tray on the desk she looked toward Cara, "Shall I pour, Your Grace." She was beaming from ear to ear, since she had seen with her very own eyes Cara's marriage was a love match. She'd changed from the serious dour dragon to a jolly woman with kind words and smiles for everyone. So happy was she to be housekeeper to a Duke and Duchess even if that Duke and Duchess currently resided in a Baronial estate.

Cara's lips wobbled. "That's all right, Mrs. Brown, I will do the honors."

"What honors? Did I miss something?" Roland said coming into the room smiling.

"No. Unless of course, you would like to practice your skill with the teapot?" Cara replied.

Roland shuddered. "Never say, my dear wife, I do not possess skills of every nature."

Cara blushed.

Clearing his throat, uncomfortable with the exchange before him, Mr. Gomersall rose from his chair to shake Roland's hand.

"Mr. Gomersall, Henry, how good to see you again."

"And you, Your Grace."

Roland seated himself behind the desk, and Mr. Gomersall resumed his seat.

"Your father?"

"Is doing wonderfully Your Grace, up and about and complaining as usual."

Cara smothered a chuckle. "Tea?"

There were two nods. Cara poured and gave both men their cups. Taking a sip from her own cup, she set it back down on the saucer. "Did you manage to find the documents my father left?"

"Oh, yes. Father, of course, blamed my filing system for his inability to find the documents. As if I'd bloody, oh beg your pardon, Your Grace. As if I would know where he filed documents when I wasn't even in residence is beyond me. Not to mention the fact his study was buried in a mountain of papers, utter disarray. But you try telling him that." Mr. Gomersall set his cup aside and dug into his coat, a smile on his face. He was clearly relieved that his father was on the mend.

"These." He handed the documents to Roland. "Take a look at them, Your Grace, if you have any questions, I'll be happy to clarify them for you. I am staying in town for the night; I will call back around before my departure to ensure you understand all of it."

With that, Mr. Gomersall bid his farewells, leaving Roland reading the documents and Cara almost bursting with curiosity. After thirty minutes, Cara could not stand it any longer.

"Well?"

Roland looked up, his eyes glimmered with unspent tears. Then before he could utter a word, he burst into laughter; tears poured out of his eyes and down his cheeks.

"Roland! Whatever is the matter with you?"

In answer Roland waved the letter, Cara took it from his shaking hands. It was a letter from her father written to Roland.

30 March 1812

Dear Fairhaven.

I know how you abhor the title. I must say it is time for you to come and face your duties, aside from which, if you are reading this letter, it now means you have my children to consider as well.

Roland, I have left you with far more than my children, I am afraid I have a mess of things. I know if anyone can put my wrongs to right, it would be you. The honor of my family's name lies in your hands.

The Danforth fortune, yes there is a fortune, though the children do not know of it. I had to keep it hidden so investigation by the Home Office would not involve my children.

Let me start by saying I was approached by the Duke of Huntington about obtaining a copy of the list, as the director for the Home Office is no longer capable of managing his duties. His faculties have left him and sometimes the pour man knows naught but his name. I was to get the copies together in one list so that he could pass it on to his successor. How word of this got out, I do not know. It was.

A gentleman by the name of Maxwell Liberton approached me; he wanted a copy of list, or so he said. He made it sound as though he was working with Beaumont, I cannot believe it, but I don't know whom I can trust. I have stalled for as long as I possibly can. I fear my time is running out. Yes, I gave off smaller tidbits, some right, most wrong in hopes of ferreting out the leak or confirming Liberton's accusations. I was unsuccessful.

Liberton is an evil man, had he known of my weakness, my children, Wonderland, he would have destroyed everything I hold dear, to force me to work faster. I could not allow that. Please, when this mess is over, tell them I loved them. With all my being, I will look upon them with love for eternity.

The information you need to solve this case, hopefully, is in a packet accompanying this letter.

Thank you, Roland, please contact these people and get the information they have put together, decoded and in the hands of the Home Office. Then with all due haste get to Danforth Manor before my loveable stubborn daughter does something foolish. I haven't a clue as to what she will do but knowing her as I do, I have put both Tibs and Daniels on standby should she try anything.

I hope you are no longer upset with me for naming you guardian. The children I am sure will run you ragged; I have no doubt they will love you and comfort you as a family should.

Caralyn, as dear and loving as she can be, is also going to be your greatest hurdle. She is as stubborn as she is intelligent. The apple of my eye—she will know how to oversee the Danforth properties if you should find yourself overwhelmed. I don't doubt she will find herself in her fair share of troubles but most of them she will probably instigate, and none should bring her or her siblings to ruin.

If you should find my daughter in such circumstances, please treat her kindly. I fear she suffered most from my actions.

It is my fondest wish that you to find common ground and one day marry. Produce me the grandchild I am unable to see. She is a gem of the greatest proportions. Beauty and astuteness, she may not be the easiest woman to get to know, or perhaps love but I am sure you are up to the task. Like her mother, stubborn as a mule, but she is loyal and will remain true to the man lucky enough to capture her heart.

You were the best I ever trained. Solve the mystery and keep my family safe. Through years, may you find it in your heart to forgive me, for the turmoil I have placed you in, I am sure, you will soon see the blessings far outweigh the downfalls. I shall be watching and praying for your success.

Gratefully Yours,
Thomas Rexley Danforth II

Cara looked up from the letter, written in her father's distinct hand, tears ran down her cheeks, "This is so perfect. He really did love us."

"Yes, my love. As I, with all my heart—now let us put this aside. I have something I want to show you."

Roland stood; taking the letter from her hands he soothed away her tears.

"What about the packet? Is there anyone else we should be leery of?" Cara said hesitantly.

"It will keep. I am sure we have the culprits. There has been no sign of Liberton, and though his body hasn't surfaced, I am sure it is only a matter of time. Beaumont feels he would not have made it through the night. Roberts was a small-time thug for hire doubtless he will not prove future trouble, but we will keep watch for him. And as for Redding, Beaumont had him commissioned to His Majesty's Royal Navy, a few years of discipline and fighting for his country should straighten the boy out. I feel he was a little too soft on the boy; he feels Redding is his son, therefore he owes him."

"You don't sound so sure," Cara said following her husband out of the house.

"I'm not! And it is no longer any of our affair. Wait. Stop right here." Roland stopped her at the start of the drive; placing his fingers in his mouth, he gave a shrill whistle.

Soon Davy appeared leading two, midnight black horses, Magnus, decked out with Roland's saddle and looking more than ready for a good run. Beside him, almost equal in height, sleek lines…

"Oh! Roland. It is Night Dancer!" Cara hopped up and down like an excited child.

"A wedding gift, my love, I purchased him from Redding before he shipped out. I hope you don't mind."

"Mind? Oh, Roland, he's beautiful!" Cara launched herself unceremoniously into Roland's arms giving him, joyous kisses.

"Love? As much as I adore your kisses, do you think we might save it for after the ride, I fear Davy is turning frightfully red."

Cara laughed, walking to Night Dancer, she held out her hand, the same loneliness was in his eyes; soon she would replace it with warmth and love. Davy handed her a carrot he had procured for the horse. Cara placed it in the palm of her hand, feeding him, crooning to him, loving him.

"Mount up," Roland said from behind her.

"Mount up? Roland, I am not in my riding habit. And Night Dancer has a man's saddle on."

"Don't tell me my intelligent Duchess cannot find a way to solve this problem. And as to the man's saddle, I don't want you riding side-saddle until I can make sure of your seat."

"Well!" Cara said, aghast. "You never complained about my seat before."

Roland laughed. "I love your seat," he agreed with a pat.

Cara looked at Night Dancer, her dress then the stirrup. Giving a shrug, she bent over, pulling the back of her muslin day dress through her legs and tucking it into her sash.

Davy's eyes bulged out of his head, as Roland lifted the Duchess into her saddle. The poor boy was still standing rooted in spot as the duo headed slowly down the drive.

"I have a wedding gift for you too," Cara said.

"You do?"

"Yes, however, I cannot give it to you right away."

"That's fine; you can give it to me when we get back," Roland said, looking about at the lush fields of Wonderland.

"I'm afraid that won't be possible either," Cara said, her eyes twinkling with amusement.

"When then?" Roland said cautiously.

"April."

"April?"

Suddenly, Roland's face paled, and a thousand emotions flashed through his eyes. Pulling Magnus to a stop, he turned in his saddle, facing his wife. One look confirmed it. They were having a baby.

Not caring one whit what anyone thought, or indeed if anyone was watching, Roland nudged Magnus closer to Night Dancer. Reaching across, he pulled his wife into his arms.

His mouth came down on hers in a passionate kiss; Cara's arms intertwined about his neck urging him closer. Their blood ignited. At once they were lost. Lost to their surroundings, lost to everything except each other.

For them, it would always be like this; like the picturesque landscape of Wonderland, their love would only grow and flourish, forever.